PENGUIN CLASSICS

KRISTIN LAVRANSDATTER

II: THE WIFE

SIGRID UNDSET (1882–1949) was born in Denmark, the eldest daughter of a Norwegian father and a Danish mother, and moved with her family to Oslo two years later. She published her first novel, *Fru Marta Oulie (Mrs. Marta Oulie)* in 1907 and her second, *Den lykkelige alder (The Happy Age)*, in 1908. The following year she published her first work set in the Middle Ages, *Fortællingen om Viga-Ljot og Vigdis* (later translated into English under the title *Gunnar's Daughter* and now available in Penguin Classics). More novels and stories followed, including *Jenny* (1911, first translated 1920), *Fattige skaebner(Fates of the Poor*, 1912), *Vaaren (Spring*, 1914), *Splinten av troldspeilet* (translated in part as *Images in a Mirror*, 1917), and *De kloge jomfruer (The Wise Virgins*, 1918). In 1920 Undset published the first volume of *Kristin Lavransdatter*, the medieval trilogy that would become her most famous work. *Kransen (The Wreath)* was followed by *Husfrue (The Wife)* in 1921 and *Korset (The Cross)* in 1922. Beginning in 1925 she published the four-volume *Olav Audunssøn i Hestviken* (translated into English under the title *The Master of Hestviken)*, also set in the Middle Ages. In 1928 Sigrid Undset won the Nobel Prize in Literature. During the 1930s she published several more novels, notably the autobiographical *Elleve aar* (translated as *The Longest Years*, 1934). She was also a prolific essayist on subjects ranging from Scandinavian history and literature to the Catholic Church (to which she became a convert in 1924) and politics. During the Nazi occupation of Norway, Undset lived as a refugee in New York City. She returned home in 1945 and lived in Lillehammer until her death in 1949.

TIINA NUNNALLY has translated all three volumes of *Kristin Lavransdatter* for Penguin Classics. She won the PEN/Book-of-the-Month Club Translation Prize for the third volume, *The Cross*. Her translations of the first and second volumes, *The Wreath* and *The Wife*, were finalists for the PEN Center USA West Translation Award, and *The Wife* was also a finalist for the PEN/Book-of-the-Month Club Translation Prize. Her other translations include Hans Christian Andersen's *Fairy Tales*, Undset's *Jenny*, Per Olov Enquist's *The Royal Physician's Visit* (Independent Foreign Fiction Prize); Peter Høeg's *Smilla's Sense of Snow* (Lewis Galantière Prize given by the American Translators Association); Jens Peter Jacobsen's *Niels Lyhne* (PEN Center USA West Translation Award); and Tove Ditlevsen's *Early Spring* (American-Scandinavian Foundation Translation Prize). Also the author of three novels, *Maija, Runemaker,* and *Fate of Ravens,* Nunnally holds an M.A. in Scandinavian Studies from the University of Wisconsin-Madison. She lives in Albuquerque, New Mexico.

SHERRILL HARBISON is a lecturer at the University of Massachusetts, Amherst. She received her B.A. in Art History from Oberlin College and her Ph.D. in English from the University of Massachusetts. Her work on Sigrid Undset has been supported by the Fulbright Association and the Norwegian Marshall Fund, and she has won three times the Aurora Borealis Prize, awarded by the Five Nordic Governments to an American scholar. She has published articles on Undset, Willa Cather, and William Faulkner and has translated some of Undset's shorter works. She is the editor of the Penguin Classics editions of Undset's *Gunnar's Daughter* and Cather's *The Song of the Lark* and wrote the introductions to *The Wife* and *The Cross*.

KRISTIN LAVRANSDATTER II: THE WIFE

SIGRID UNDSET

TRANSLATED WITH NOTES

BY TIINA NUNNALLY

INTRODUCTION

BY SHERRILL HARBISON

PENGUIN BOOKS

PENGUIN BOOKS

Published by the Penguin Group

Penguin Group (USA) Inc., 375 Hudson Street, New York, New York 10014, U.S.A.
Penguin Group (Canada), 90 Eglinton Avenue East, Suite 700, Toronto, Ontario, Canada
M4P 2Y3 (a division of Pearson Penguin Canada Inc.)
Penguin Books Ltd, 80 Strand, London WC2R 0RL, England
Penguin Ireland, 25 St Stephen's Green, Dublin 2, Ireland
(a division of Penguin Books Ltd)
Penguin Group (Australia), 250 Camberwell Road, Camberwell, Victoria 3124, Australia
(a division of Pearson Australia Group Pty Ltd)
Penguin Books India Pvt Ltd, 11 Community Centre, Panchsheel Park, New
Delhi – 110 017, India
Penguin Group (NZ), 67 Apollo Drive, Rosedale, North Shore 0632, New Zealand
(a division of Pearson New Zealand Ltd)
Penguin Books (South Africa) (Pty) Ltd, 24 Sturdee Avenue, Rosebank,
Johannesburg 2196, South Africa

Penguin Books Ltd, Registered Offices: 80 Strand, London WC2R 0RL, England

This translation first published in Penguin Books 1999

17 19 20 18

Translation and notes copyright © Tiina Nunnally, 1999
Introduction copyright © Sherrill Harbison, 1999
All rights reserved

Originally published in Norwegian as *Husfrue*
by H. Aschehoug & Company, Oslo, 1921.

LIBRARY OF CONGRESS CATALOGING-IN-PUBLICATION DATA
Undset, Sigrid, 1882–1949.
[Husfrue. English]
The wife / Sigrid Undset ; translated with notes by Tiina Nunnally;
introduction by Sherrill Harbison.
p.   cm. — (Kristin Lavransdatter : 2)
(Penguin twentieth-century classics)
ISBN 978-0-14-118128-8
I. Nunnally, Tiina.   II. Title.   III. Series: Undset, Sigrid, 1882–1949.
Kristin Lavransdatter (Penguin Books). English   2.
IV. Series: Penguin twentieth-century classics.
PT8950.U5H8313   1999
839.8'2372—dc21   99-23213

Printed in the United States of America
Set in Sabon
Designed by Mia Risberg
Maps by Virginia Norey

CONTENTS

CONTENTS

INTRODUCTION

PEOPLE TODAY STILL take the pilgrimage road Kristin Lavransdatter journeys more than once in this novel, from Gudbrandsdal up through Dovre to Saint Olav's shrine at Nidaros. Most modern travelers are not pilgrims, however, or even medieval historians. Many are retracing the footsteps of Sigrid Undset's heroine, who has become more real to them than the actual historical figures responsible for the sights at their destination. Despite her being a fictional character, Kristin's joys and travails seem to many people more real than Saint Olav himself, the eleventh-century martyr who was once the most popular cult figure in northern Europe, and more real than the visionary Eystein Erlendssøn, the twelfth-century archbishop who recognized the potential of the Olav cult and designed Europe's northernmost Gothic cathedral and shrine to accommodate it. Indeed, in the valley at Sil (today Sel) Kristin herself is enshrined in a greater-than-life-sized statue, to which over 10,000 literary pilgrims pay homage each year.

Kristin Lavransdatter's grandeur of conception, indomitable heroine, and vast gallery of fully realized characters in a Norwegian historical setting have won Undset's trilogy the status of a national epic, and for many people medieval Norway simply *is* the world Sigrid Undset portrayed in her fiction. It is fortunate, therefore, that she was such a meticulous scholar and historian. It is also fascinating to sort out this novel's relation to the actual historical events and people of the period when it is set, and to the historical circumstances in Undset's own time, when it was written.

The historical novel as we know it was invented in the early nineteenth century by Sir Walter Scott. Many of Scott's historical romances were set in the Middle Ages (e.g., *Ivanhoe*, 1819) and his invocation of the colorful age of chivalry touched a nerve in a European century blighted by the defacements and dislocations of industrialism. Scott's immensely popular works set the stage for the nineteenth century's national romantic dreams of bygone mythic heroes, such as Wagner's musical reinterpretations of Germanic myths, Tennyson's *Idylls of the King*, and Ibsen's early historical plays, as well as for nostalgic longings after the craftsmanship of the preindustrial past, including Ruskin's paean to Gothic architecture in *Stones of Venice* and the Pre-Raphaelite William Morris's Arts and Crafts movement.

Undset, who was born in 1882, did not fully belong to this Victorian generation, however, and though she shared many of its concerns, she strongly disagreed with its romantic, idealizing sentiments. She was not a romantic but a realist, and belonged to Norway's group of "epic novelists" (others include Olav Duun, Kristofer Uppdal, Johan Falkberget) whose major works on historical themes appeared in the 1920s. Two factors influenced the flush of historical fiction in Norway at this time: the country had peacefully regained national independence in 1905 after five hundred years of foreign rule, and it had not participated in World War I. Elsewhere in Europe, disaffected Modernists of the post-war period came to disdain the nineteenth-century preoccupation with glorified history as escapist and delusionary, but Norwegian writers of the '20s had a very different project: to establish meaningful ties with a past only recently reclaimed as their own, and to present longer perspectives for a deeply traditional culture now undergoing rapid technological change.

Still, because Undset's trilogy shares certain features with Walter Scott's Romantic prototypes, including a medieval setting, and interest in rural life, readers sometimes come to the book expecting something misty and nostalgic, a latter-day Pre-Raphaelite dream. If so, they are in for a surprise. *Kristin Lavransdatter* is neither dreamy nor sentimental. Like the Icelandic sagas she so much admired, Undset's fiction portrays medieval life with a vigorous, sometimes brutal realism. It paints vivid, highly individualized portraits of women, men, and children—all sympathetic, all flawed, and none of them sweetened. Furthermore, while the Scott prototype uses fictional characters to illustrate the impact of momentous political events (e.g., war, regicide, revolution) on the lives of ordinary people, Undset redefines the genre by telling an epic story about normal occurrences in an ordinary woman's life, set in an unusually quiet historical period. The most dramatic political event in the novel—Erlend Nikulaussøn's attempt to depose the child-king Magnus VII Eirikssøn (which occurs in this volume)—is one Undset invented.

The Norway into which Kristin Lavransdatter was born in 1302 had left the pagan Norse gods behind just three centuries before, and in that compressed period the culture embraced both the missionary fervor of the early Christian era and the intellectual refinements of the high Middle Ages. The last years of the Viking era (780–1030) had been dominated by Norway's two great folk kings, both named Olav: Olav Trygvassøn (reigned 995–1000), who is credited with Christianizing both Norway and Iceland, and Olav Haraldssøn (r. 1016–30), Norway's only native saint. Both Olavs were exposed to Christianity while on Viking adventures abroad, both worked toward the creation of a united Christian nation, and both died in the struggle after making striking progress toward that end. Their personalities were very different, but both have inspired hundreds of legends.

Saint Olav Haraldssøn is mentioned frequently in this novel, and Kristin's pilgrimage to his shrine is one of the most vivid and memorable episodes in this volume. Olav Haraldssøn's reign was marked by dissent and turbulence, but his death in 1030 at Stiklestad (near the royal seat at Nidaros), while attempting to defend his right to the throne, had a spectacular impact on the young country. In the first decade after his death so many miracles collected around his name that in 1041 the English Bishop Grimkell declared Olav a saint, and placed his body over the high altar of the church at Nidaros. His cult spread swiftly abroad, attracting pilgrims from all over Europe, and straining the resources of the town to house and feed them. Because of this unprecedented attention to Norway, Sigrid Undset explains elsewhere, it "became a kingdom conscious of itself, and the kingship was invested with the glamor of the saint who had been Norway's king."

The period between 1030 and 1330 is designated the high Middle Ages in Norway, but unlike southern Europe, which had been Christian for almost a millennium longer, it was distinguished there by a peculiarly intense intellectual activity, as people struggled to accommodate the Christian mentality to old Norse ways.

Saint Olav's faith was widely embraced as more progressive and humane than the arbitrary world of Odin and Thor, yet heathen customs and ideas lingered in popular imagination throughout the Middle Ages. Undset illustrates this in *Kristin Lavransdatter* with many incidents, notably the appearance of the elf-maiden to Kristin in Volume 1, and the frightened people attempting to divert the Black Death with witchcraft in Volume 3.

The eleventh century saw a growth of royal and ecclesiastical power, which eventually had a stabilizing influence on society. Olav had established the Church of Norway in 1024, and with the help of Bishop Grimkell formulated new church laws (known as King Olav's law), the country's first national legal enactments. Nonetheless, Norway remained different from the feudal societies to the south. Though the king had power to enforce the laws through his *hird*, or guardsmen, only freemen assembled in the local or regional *tings* could pass or amend laws, and the king himself was also subject to them.

Trade also increased in importance in this century, and the ancient trading towns of Oslo, Tunsberg, and Bjørgvin (Bergen) grew. Viking raids of monasteries and other European settlements became increasingly unacceptable, and a different hierarchy developed among wealthy landowners, based not on conquest and spoils of war but on skillful husbandry and loyal service to the king. As Christians, landowners were also expected to free their slaves, resulting in a new class of tenants and free laborers.

The twelfth century (1130–1228) was tumultuous, an age of civil wars revolving around an unusual number of vigorous personalities making rival claims to the throne. While royal succession had been established, primogeniture had not, nor was legitimacy a requirement. Many claimants appeared—sometimes arriving from abroad, sometimes offering dubious credentials—to battle it out, and ruthless, pillaging soldiers brought sporadic misery to the countryside. The battles were not always decisive either, and for some periods several kings reigned at once.

In 1152 Nidaros was elevated to an archbishopric due to the efforts of the English Cardinal Nicholas Breakspeare (later Pope Hadrian IV), and the first king to be crowned by an archbishop was fourteen-year-old Magnus V Erlingssøn (r. 1163–77). Magnus took his divine calling seriously and established clearer guidelines for royal succession, but this did not protect him from the challenge of the brilliant and daring Sverre Sigurdssøn, one of the most remarkable persons in the history of Norway. It is with Sverre's reign (1177–1202) that Undset begins to weave the fictional Erlend Nikulaussøn's lineage together with that of real historical families.

Sverre Sigurdssøn was raised in the remote, wind-swept Faroe Islands, and at age twenty-four had already entered the church when his mother informed him that his bloodline gave him a better claim to the crown than Magnus had. Though his royal parentage was never proved, there is no question that Sverre believed he had both a right and responsibility to the kingship, and that he made others believe it. His long campaign against Magnus was waged with the help of an intensely loyal, ragged band of disaffected mountainmen known as Birchlegs, since they were sometimes reduced to using bark for clothing. They were accustomed to extreme conditions and hardship, and for seven years Sverre led them over impassable mountains, through trackless forests, and into outposts so remote that the scattered population had never heard of Christianity or the king. While Magnus was aloof and aristocratic, Sverre was a charismatic champion of the underdog, and before long the ruffian band of Birchlegs was also joined by yeoman farmers of substance.

Sverre defeated and killed Magnus and destroyed most of his fleet in 1184, and for the next eighteen years he held the throne. He established himself at Bjørgvin and made it a new capital of culture, welcoming skalds and scholars to his court. Foreign trade had burgeoned since the middle of the century, and cosmopolitan Bjørgvin was also Norway's most important center for merchants and craftsmen.

Sverre proved not only a commanding leader and tactician but an effective administrator. From the beginning he had been in opposition to the Archbishop of Nidaros, and now he strengthened the royal position through legislation, expanded the *hird* to a large army, and built a new aristocracy of his Birchleg followers—men of humble origin to whom he bequeathed the property of slain aristocrats. In this volume Erlend refers back to Sverre's era—when social mobility was linked to the test of battle, as in Viking times—with longing and nostalgia, reminding the peaceloving

Lavrans and Erling Vidkunssøn that Simon Andressøn was their social equal only because his ancestor, Reidar Darre, was a Birchleg who had come into his fortune this way.

Although Sverre believed in Christian mildness and forgiveness, his reign certainly was not a peaceful one. He was challenged by no fewer than five pretenders to the throne, as well as by tensions with church magnates—part of the then-current European debate over Gregorian church reforms (initiated by Pope Gregory VII, 1073–85) which advanced the idea of a universal church under the Bishop of Rome over that of a national church controlled by the king. After exiling his first archbishop, the brilliant Eystein Erlendssøn, Sverre later made peace with him, and Eystein returned from England inspired by the powerful new cult of Saint Thomas à Becket, begun seven years before when Thomas was martyred in his own church in a similar power play with King Henry II. Eystein recognized the power of legends, that the cult of Saint Olav had potential like that of Saint Thomas, and he wrote *Passio et Miracula Beati Olavi* as its foundation. To give the saint's shrine the impressive setting it deserved, he revised the original Romanesque plans for the Nidaros cathedral to the English Gothic style then under construction at Canterbury.

Sverre, however, ran into trouble again with Eystein's successor Eirik Ivarssøn, who was a strong believer in the superiority of church over state, and who conspired with the pope to put the recalcitrant Sverre under interdict. Eirik's schemes were clandestinely supported by the Bishop of Oslo, Nikulaus Arnessøn (d. 1225), who had been close to the defeated King Magnus—and whom Undset casts as Erlend Nikulaussøn's great-grandfather.

Bishop Nikulaus was crafty, vengeful, and ambitious, at heart more a warrior and politician than a churchman, and his preparation of one of Magnus's sons for the throne—while pretending to support Sverre—caused Norway's bloodiest and most bitter civil war, the *Bagler* (or Crosier) War. Sverre was both a better leader and a better man, however, and when he died in 1202 he was still on the throne. After his son and successor Haakon died two years later—possibly from poison—the Baglers won a brief posthumous victory over Sverre, when the crown passed to Magnus's nephew Ingi Baardsøn (r. 1204–17).

At Ingi's death the most powerful pretender was his half-brother Skule Baardsøn, who had virtually controlled Ingi's government. But Skule's claim was thwarted by Birchlegs faithful to Sverre, who had for years carefully protected and prepared their champion's thirteen-year-old grandson Haakon IV Haakonssøn (r. 1217–63) for the throne. Instead, Skule became a trusted advisor to the young King Haakon, and Haakon rewarded his uncle Skule by making him a duke and by marrying his daughter Margreta. Skule's other daughter, Ragnfrid, married the son of Sverre's old enemy Bishop Nikulaus—which made Duke Skule the fictional Erlend Nikulaussøn's *other* great-grandfather. It was through Erlend's grandmother Ragnrid Skulesdatter, sister to Queen Margreta, therefore, that he was kin to the royal house, a connection that is frequently mentioned in the text. Duke Skule also owned a large estate near Nidaros called Husaby (its foundation can still be seen today), which Erlend would later inherit.

During the early years of Haakon's reign all new attempts at uprisings against the king were quashed by Duke Skule's well-trained army, and by 1228 the last of the civil wars was over. Norway then entered a peaceful century (1228–1319). It had an established royal line and was a more united, better-organized state than most European countries of the era. Its kings were all descendants of Sverre and looked on him as the hero of their dynasty. All were energetic workers, and all were genuinely religious and cultivated men. The king was backed by a consolidated landowning aristocracy, both lay and clerical, which became more powerful as the century progressed.

The Norwegians' devotion to their kings was unusual for the Middle Ages. Unlike other nations, its wars had never been between royalty and aristocracy, but between rival kings. The medieval kings took seriously their coronation oath to serve God and uphold the law, and often fought administrative abuses in their own courts. The country's nobility was also much smaller, less wealthy, and less dominant than in feudalized countries, and its rural population (especially the independent allodial farmers, men of substance and influence in their communities like Lavrans Bjørgulfssøn) was more powerful than in any other country except perhaps Switzerland. Though the church and crown were gradually acquiring greater amounts of land, independent farmers were sensitive to demands of taxes, rents, and tithes, and misuse of power brought resistance. The population's strong sense of justice and personal freedom, held over from the times of pagan chieftains, acted as an internal check on arbitrary use of power. In addition, the *tings* were still in place for ratifying laws and for expressions of popular will, though their importance would diminish by degrees over the century.

The most famous of the thirteenth-century kings was Sverre's above-mentioned grandson Haakon IV Haakonssøn (called the Old). It was for faithful service to Haakon the Old that Lavrans Bjørgulfssøn's family received the manor at Skog—a detail that shows how, even that far back, the interests of Lavrans's and Erlend's families were bound to different parties. For Haakon's support of Erlend's ancestor Duke Skule did not last after the civil wars ended. Skule (like Erlend) was an appealing but flawed character whose misguided pursuit of power finally turned people against him. Also like Erlend, Skule became restless in peacetime, and in 1240 he was killed while attempting to seize the throne for himself (Ibsen used this story for his play *The Pretenders*). It is thus hardly surprising that Erlend wonders, in naming his son after Skule, if the child will inherit his namesake's bad luck.

During Haakon's long reign the country prospered from trade—exports included fish, whale oil, timber, and highly prized luxury items like walrus ivory, falcons, and furs—and wealth brought to court life a splendor not known before in Norway. Haakon was a builder who improved many of the country's castles and fortifications. He kept Icelandic skalds and saga writers at court for entertainment, and for the royal heir's wedding in 1261, he wined and dined 1600 guests in three great halls in Bjørgvin.

Unlike Sverre, Haakon considered himself a partner with, not a rival to, the church, which he strengthened with taxes, gifts, missions, and buildings. Construction of Nidaros cathedral was begun the year after his coronation, and more than a thousand parish churches were built in his century. He also opened the country to the mendicant orders (Franciscan Minorites, like Kristin's mentor Brother Edvin Rikardssøn, and Dominicans like Erlend's brother Gunnulf), who built houses in the major towns and roamed the countryside preaching and teaching. The friars sometimes clashed with the secular clergy (one particularly ugly conflict in Oslo, in which local canons tore down a chapel the Franciscans were building, is referred to in this volume). But they were popular with the people, and did much to spread knowledge of and interest in Christianity, especially in rural areas.

Near the end of Haakon's reign, in 1261, the Norwegian kingdom was peacefully enlarged when Iceland—which for decades had been torn by civil war between rival chieftains—voluntarily submitted itself to Norwegian rule. The political collapse of the proud little republic would reverberate unexpectedly in the finest large body of prose written during the medieval period in any language—the Icelandic family sagas, which made such an indelible impression on the young Sigrid Undset. Already in the 1230s the Icelander Snorri Sturluson had composed his remarkable *Heimskringla*, or *History of the Kings of Norway*, which remains the foundation of Norwegian historiography.

Haakon was succeeded by his son Magnus VI Lawmender (r. 1263–80), a thoughtful and pious man who wore the crown as a burden. With the help of scholars trained in Roman law, he oversaw extensive revision and codification of King Olav's law—one of the most important achievements of the age. Its legal language was modernized and many of the laws and punishments made more humane. The most significant change, however, was in allowing the state to intervene more in daily life: misdeeds were no longer to be considered crimes against the individual or family, as they had been since pagan times, but against the state. This not only promised greater social stability, but also ensured that most of the income from fines would go directly to the royal coffers. The code's wording was adjusted to transfer legislative power from the people to the king. Laws of succession were established to the twelfth degree of consanguinity, and the 1277 Concordat of Tunsberg legally defined the power and position of the church.

Magnus's son Eirik II Magnussøn ("Priesthater," r. 1280–99) was not of age when his father died, and during his mother's regency ruling power was in the hands of squabbling aristocracy. Wrangling between lay and ecclesiastical magnates intensified when the regency interfered with clerical rights, and peace with the church was not restored until 1290. Eirik made an unfortunate war on Denmark, and also allowed the German Hanseatic League to siphon off much of Norway's trade, both of which left the country in weakened economic condition.

In 1299 Eirik was succeeded by his brother Haakon V Magnussøn (r. 1299–1319), who was on the throne when Undset's Kristin Lavransdatter was born in 1302. The remaining fragment of Haakon's stone portrait from the Nidaros Cathedral portrays a serious, intellectual, and worried man. Haakon V was the first king to make his permanent residence in Oslo, elevating the town to the status of capital. In the first volume of this novel, Simon's family takes Kristin to Christmas festivities at Haakon's court in Oslo, and she faints when Erlend Nikulaussøn—who once had served as the king's page—also appears there.

Haakon was learned and literate, and he established a national archive as well as clerical schools at Bergen and Oslo. In deference to his German queen's enthusiasm for chivalric romances, he also sponsored a number of translations, including the stories of Roland, Charlemagne, and Tristan and Isolde, which introduced the flowery continental style to audiences more familiar with the forceful, understated style of sagas and skaldic poetry. At one point in this volume Erlend recalls to his kinsman Erling Vidkunssøn how, when they were young pages together, they were obliged to listen to priests reading aloud the "holy sagas" about bishops' and saints' lives.

Haakon was a strong-willed and gifted leader who sincerely believed that the kingship was established by God for the good of the people, especially those little able to protect themselves—a philosophy that greatly appealed to Lavrans Bjørgulfssøn. He checked the power of the aristocracy, which had taken many liberties in his brother's reign, and abolished the title of baron. He also further strengthened the country's border defenses with modern forts garrisoned by armed soldiers. One was at Vardøy in far northern Finnmark, where Russians competed with Norwegian interests in the fur trade (it was on Erlend's youthful tour of duty at Vardøy that he became involved with Eline Ormsdatter). Others were at Baagahus, on the Swedish border (where Lavrans is wounded and has a vision of Saint Thomas); Tunsberg in the south (where Simon Andressøn travels to petition for Erling Vidkunssøn's help); and Oslo's redoubtable landmark, Akershus (where Erlend is imprisoned).

Haakon's foreign policies were less successful, however, and helped develop the political morass that led to insurgencies under his successor. He failed to check the increasing power of Hanseatic traders in Bergen (one marries Erlend's daughter Margret)—a favoritism that led to broken relations with England and facilitated the monopoly of the Hanseatic League that posed a severe threat to Norwegian shipping. Equally important, he allowed himself to be used by the charismatic, unscrupulous Duke Eirik, brother of the Swedish King Birger, to whom in 1302 (the year of Kristin's birth) Haakon had promised his only child, the one-year-old Ingebjørg, in marriage. Duke Eirik, who was plotting to depose his brother and form a central Scandinavian state under his own rule, led devastating raids on Norway in 1308 and 1310, and Lavrans was among those who fought in the defense. Nonetheless Eirik succeeded in charming his way to asylum at the Norwegian court, where he continued as a central figure in a maze of intrigue and war against Sweden and Denmark. Haakon uneasily supported Eirik's wars after the duke's marriage to the eleven-year-old Ingebjørg in 1312, but in so doing he greatly depleted the country's purse; with the Germans in control of trade, little was coming in.

The year before Haakon's death in 1319, however, Duke Eirik was captured and imprisoned in Sweden, where he died. His brother King Birger was then deposed, leaving Ingebjørg's three-year-old son Magnus Eirikssøn a candidate for the throne in both Norway and Sweden. The complications arising from this vesting of two crowns in one person becomes one of the mainsprings of action in this volume of *Kristin Lavransdatter*.

It was decided that Magnus and his mother, Ingebjørg, acting as regent, would divide time between the two countries, which otherwise would be governed separately. But Ingebjørg continued to nurture Duke Eirik's dream of a united Scandinavian kingdom, and became involved with her Danish lover Knut Porse in a scheme to take over Skaane (the southern part of the Swedish peninsula, then part of Denmark). Together they led a campaign against Denmark largely at Norway's expense, scandalizing the Norwegian public and leaving the treasury so depleted it was impossible to care decently for the child king. Porse's ambition and daring won him some Norwegian admirers even so—among them Erlend Nikulaussøn and Munan Baardssøn, a real grandson of

Duke Skule's whom Undset casts as Erlend's cousin and best friend.

In 1322 the Swedes, at a meeting at Skara, deprived the impressionable Ingebjørg (she was only twenty-one) of all political powers; Norway did the same seven months later. At a large meeting of the *hird* and bishops, the archbishop was authorized to appoint a head of government, whom all promised to support provided he kept the laws and his oath to the king and people. That man was an outstanding young member of the Norwegian nobility, Erling Vidkunssøn, who as viceroy ruled the country with great ability and a high sense of duty until Magnus came of age. As mother of the king, Lady Ingebjørg was treated with respect until she married Porse in 1326; the government then severed all ties with her.

Undset brings Erling Vidkunssøn twice to visit Husaby and Nidaros in this volume, once with the young King Magnus in tow—occasions that serve to introduce these complex political issues both to the unworldly Kristin and to the reader. As viceroy, Erling followed Haakon V's basic policies, but he was more skillful than Haakon in foreign affairs. He concluded a three-year border war with Russia in 1326 (in the wake of this, Erlend is again sent north to Finnmark, to maintain the peace and negotiate with the Sami about trade and taxes), made peace with Denmark, kept the Hanseatic merchants within bounds, and was generally successful at keeping foreign influence and officeholders out of the government. These policies ended, however, in 1331, when fifteen-year-old Magnus Eirikssøn himself took over. By that time Knut Porse had died, leaving Ingebjørg a widow with two small sons, Haakon and Knut.

Several times Undset's characters complain that King Magnus's sympathies were too much with Sweden, where he was educated and continued to spend most of his time. Magnus had also inherited from his parents and stepfather the dream of enlarging the mid-Scandinavian realm under his personal control, and he busied himself with military campaigns to that end. His first Chancellor for Norway was an old antagonist of Erling's, Paal Baardsøn; when in 1333 Magnus made Paal Archbishop, he neglected to appoint another Chancellor. Twice the Norwegian nobles revolted, demanding effective administration; both times the result was a compromise. A 1333 revolt led by Erling Vidkunssøn himself, together with the king's young cousins Jon and Sigurd Haftorssøn, is important in Undset's story because it left Erling and the king estranged, making Simon's mission to seek clemency for Erlend especially difficult.

Several historians have admired Undset's fictional plot, in which Erlend plans to place Ingebjørg's second son on his unpopular half-brother's seat in Norway. Some sympathy returned to Ingebjørg after Knut Porse's death, and Haakon Knutssøn, as a grandson of Haakon V, had a legitimate place in the line of succession. Such a plot very well could have (some even say should have) been conceived. In fact, though, it was 1343 before sovereignty of the two kingdoms was again divided, with one country designated for each of Magnus's sons. And not until 1350—i.e., after the Black Death, and after *Kristin Lavransdatter* ends—was ten-year-old Haakon VI Magnussøn crowned king of Norway at Bjørgvin.

Woven through this intricate story of kings, *tings*, and pretenders is the story of another, equally powerful institution—the medieval church. Religion was so bound up in the medieval mind with the rest of life, however, that it can be misleading to distinguish religious from other activities. For example, the missionary kings were fully convinced that they ruled in God's name, and throughout the Middle Ages clergy and laypeople alike believed that royal blood had holy significance. This was why the man who slew Olav Haraldssøn soon left on a pilgrimage to Jerusalem, never to return—regicide was also a form of deicide.

Thus church and state were both crucial to the foundation of a Christian kingdom, and as royal power grew and consolidated, ecclesiastical power kept step. Their areas of authority were understood to be distinctive and complementary, although talented men with strong personalities were bound to clash when interests overlapped. The different spheres were carefully outlined in *The King's Mirror*, an anonymous didactic work from the thirteenth century cast in the form of a conversation between father and son, which is Norway's most important literary achievement of the medieval period. Written sometime in the reign of Haakon the Old, it concerns good manners and pious conduct, and is designed for the instruction of a royal heir. The king, it explains, represents divine lordship; he is supreme judge of temporal matters and final executor of the law. While both the church and crown are God's houses, the bishop's authority is in "his mouth," while the king's rests in "his hands"—i.e., the bishop represents God's word and can punish by denying access to God's table, whereas the king can punish with the sword—but only in righteousness. To slay out of hatred is not justice but murder, and unlawfully preempts God's judgment. A wise ruler understands that church and crown should support each other and not encroach on each other's realms.

In this period the church was exceptionally well organized, and it produced several great jurists and statesmen. It also inspired and commissioned most of the artistic achievements of the age, including Norway's unique, intricately carved and decorated wooden stave churches; its many Romanesque churches and monasteries; and the splendid example of Gothic architecture at Nidaros, which was at its peak of glory at the time of Kristin's pilgrimage. Increasing numbers of clergy (like Gunnulf Nikulaussøn) studied in universities abroad, and they returned stimulated by books and ideas from Europe and beyond. Such educated men produced the earliest manuscripts extant in Norway—poetry, legends, homilies, and theological writings.

At the mythic level, the king and the church both lived intimately with the population. At the practical level, however, people had far more regular interaction with the church, which offered what we today call social services—education, counseling and health care, and charity. Parish priests like Sira Eirik and Eiliv, as well as wandering friars like Gunnulf and Brother Edvin, instructed people in Christian doctrine and helped them through critical events like birth, illness, and death. It was also left to the clergy to interpret pagan superstitions and sometimes to merge them with Christian ones. Examples of this in the novel include frequent uses of sorcery and witchcraft, and rumors that the devastating fire at Nidaros Cathedral in 1328 was God's punishment for Magnus Eirikssøn's youthful homosexual experiences. Monasteries provided more collective services such as boarding schools (like Oslo's Nonneseter, where Kristin spends a formative year under the tutelage of its real historical abbess, Fru Groa), hospitals (like the one abutting Erlend and Gunnulf's property in Nidaros), and hostels (like Bakke in Nidaros, where Kristin finds refuge on her pilgrimage). They also boarded homeless and elderly laypeople for a fee, a service used in Norway mostly by women (as when Kristin retires to Rein Cloister in Volume 3).

Undset's massive compilation of perfectly rendered historical detail in this novel, framed by her equally precise rendering of Norway's magnificent natural surroundings, is reason enough for the novel's high reputation, but it is not all that makes Kristin's world so "real" to modern readers. Equally compelling is the immediately recognizable psychology of her characters, who seem as though they might easily be our neighbors or ourselves. Some historians have criticized Undset for this, insisting that under other historical circumstances people could not have thought and felt as modern people do. Undset, who had instantly felt kinship with characters in the medieval Icelandic sagas and ballads, disagreed. Historical change affects some things about human life, she argued—ideas, social customs, religious beliefs, and technology, for example—but not others. The elemental passions, such as pride, envy, compassion, greed, and desire, are common to humanity in all eras and places.

If the novel's worldwide popularity is any measure, Undset's conviction of this, and her skill in uniting the historical and human dimensions in her fiction, leads most readers to agree—or at least willingly to suspend disbelief. We can enter her Middle Ages largely because we recognize her characters on an emotional level: Lavrans Bjørgulfssøn's solicitude, upright reticence, and tragically unawakened erotic passion; Ragnfrid's sexual frustration, guilt, and awe of her husband; Simon's earnest goodness and private longings; Kristin's stubborn, unforgiving pride and deep maternal involvement; and Erlend's charm, childishness, and reckless irresponsibility. At the same time, thanks to Undset's scrupulous research and finely honed historical sensibility, we can also learn much about Norway's medieval past in which they lived.

Sherrill Harbison
Amherst, Massachusetts
March 1999

SUGGESTIONS FOR FURTHER READING

The following works have served as a basis for the Introduction.

Bugge, Anders, and Sverre Steen, eds. *Norsk Kulturhistorie: Billeder av folkets dagligliv gjennem årtusener.* Vol. 2, *Fra tunet til bystredet.* Oslo: J. W. Cappelens Forlag, 1939.

The King's Mirror. Translated with Introduction and Notes by Laurence Marcellus Larson. New York: Twayne Publishers with the American Scandinavian Foundation, 1917.

Larsen, Karen. *A History of Norway.* Princeton: Princeton University Press with the American Scandinavian Foundation, 1948.

Moen, Hanne Helliesen. *Opplysninger til Sigrid Undsets middelalderromaner.* Oslo: H. Aschehoug & Co., 1950.

Mørkhagen, Sverre. *Kristins Verden: Om norsk middelalder på Kristin Lavransdatters tid.* Oslo: J. W. Cappelens Forlag, 1995.

Naess, Harald, ed. *A History of Norwegian Literature.* Lincoln, Neb., and London: University of Nebraska Press with the American Scandinavian Foundation, 1993.

Paasche, Fredrik. "Sigrid Undset og norsk middelalder." *Samtiden* (Oslo), 1929.

Sawyer, Birgit, and Peter Sawyer. *Medieval Scandinavia: From Conversion to Reformation, circa 800–1500.* Minneapolis: University of Minnesota Press, 1993.

Snorri Sturluson. *Heimskringla: History of the Kings of Norway.* Translated with Introduction and Notes by Lee M. Hollander. Austin: University of Texas Press with the American Scandinavian Foundation, 1964.

Undset, Sigrid. *Saga of Saints.* Translated by E. C. Ramsden. New York and Toronto: Longmans Green & Co., 1934.

A NOTE ON THE TRANSLATION

Based on the first edition of *Husfrue,* published in Norway in 1921, this is the first unabridged English translation of Volume II of Sigrid Undset's epic work. Certain sections, scattered throughout the novel and totaling approximately eighteen pages, were omitted from the previous English translation. Many are key passages, such as Kristin's lengthy dialogue with Saint Olav in Christ Church, Gunnulf's meditation on the mixture of jealousy and love he has always felt toward Erlend, and Ragnfrid's anguished memory of her betrothal to Lavrans. All of these passages have now been restored, offering the reader crucial insight into the underlying spiritual and psychological turmoil of the story. This translation has been published with the support of a grant from NORLA (Norwegian Literature Abroad).

Tiina Nunnally

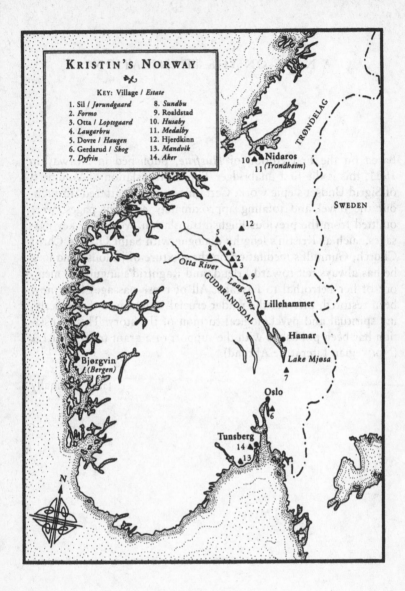

KRISTIN'S NORWAY

KEY: Village / Estate

1. Sil / Jørundgaard
2. Formo
3. Otta / Loptsgaard
4. Laugarbru
5. Dovre / Haugen
6. Gerdarud / Skog
7. Dyfrin
8. Sundbu
9. Roaldstad
10. Husaby
11. Medalby
12. Hjerdkinn
13. Mandvik
14. Aker

TRØNDELAG

SWEDEN

Nidaros
(Trondheim)

Otta River

Laag River

GUDBRANDSDAL

Lillehammer

Hamar

Lake Mjøsa

Bjørgvin
(Bergen)

Oslo

Tunsberg

N

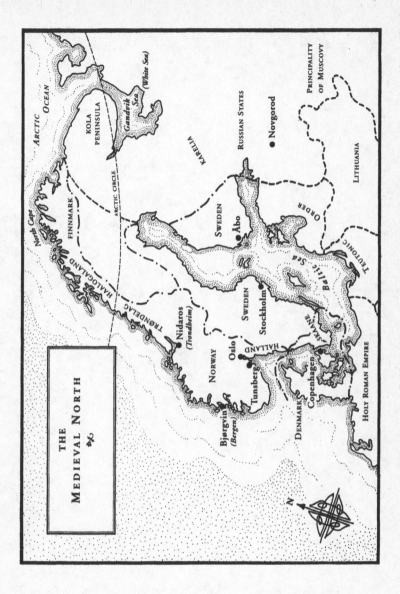

THE
MEDIEVAL NORTH

ARCTIC OCEAN

Arctic Circle

North Cape

KOLA PENINSULA

Gandvik Sea (White Sea)

FINNMARK

HÅLOGALAND

KARELIA

RUSSIAN STATES

PRINCIPALITY OF MUSCOVY

• Novgorod

LITHUANIA

TEUTONIC ORDER

SWEDEN

• Åbo

Baltic Sea

TRØNDELAG

• Nidaros (Trondheim)

SWEDEN

Stockholm

NORWAY

Oslo •

Tunsberg

Bjørgvin (Bergen)

HALLAND

SKÅNE

DENMARK

Copenhagen

HOLY ROMAN EMPIRE

N

KRISTIN
LAVRANSDATTER
II: THE WIFE

IN MEMORY OF MY FATHER

INGVALD UNDSET

PART I

THE FRUIT OF SIN

CHAPTER 1

ON THE EVE of Saint Simon's Day, Baard Petersøn's ship anchored at the spit near Birgsi. Abbot Olav of Nidarholm had ridden down to the shore himself to greet his kinsman Erlend Nikulaussøn and to welcome the young wife he was bringing home. The newly married couple would be the guests of the abbot and spend the night at Vigg.

Erlend led his deathly pale and miserable young wife along the dock. The abbot bantered about the wretchedness of the sea voyage; Erlend laughed and said that his wife was no doubt longing to sleep in a bed that stood firmly next to a wall. And Kristin tried to smile, but she was thinking that she would not go willingly on board a ship again for as long as she lived. She felt ill if Erlend merely came close to her, so strongly did he smell of the ship and the sea—his hair was completely stiff and tacky with salt water. He had been quite giddy with joy the entire time they were on board ship, and Sir Baard had laughed. Out there at Møre, where Erlend had grown up, the boys were constantly out in the boats, sailing and rowing. They had felt some sympathy for her, both Erlend and Sir Baard, but not as much as her misery warranted, thought Kristin. They kept saying that the seasickness would pass after she got used to being on board. But she had continued to feel wretched during the entire voyage.

The next morning she felt as if she were still sailing as she rode up through the outlying villages. Up one hill and down the next, carried over steep moraines of clay, and if she tried to fix her eyes up ahead on the mountain ridge, she felt as if the whole countryside was pitching, rising up like waves, and then tossed up against the pale blue-white of the winter morning sky.

A large group of Erlend's friends and neighbors had arrived at Vigg that morning to accompany the married couple home, so they set off in a great procession. The horses' hooves rang hollowly, for the earth was now as hard as iron from black frost. Steam enveloped the people and the horses; rime covered the animals' bodies as well as everyone's hair and furs. Erlend looked as white-haired as the abbot, his face glowing from the morning drink and the biting wind. Today he was wearing his bridegroom's clothing; he looked so young and happy that he seemed radiant, and joy and wild abandon surged in his beautiful, supple voice as he rode, calling to his guests and laughing with them.

Kristin's heart began quivering so strangely, from sorrow and tenderness and fear. She was still feeling sick after the voyage; she had that terrible burning in her breast that now appeared whenever she ate or drank even the smallest amount. She was bitterly cold; and lodged deep in her soul was that tiny, dull, mute anger toward Erlend, who was so free of sorrow. And yet, now that she saw with what naive pride and sparkling elation he was escorting her home as his wife, a bitter remorse began trickling inside her, and her breast ached with pity for him. Now she wished she hadn't held to her own obstinate decision but had told Erlend when he visited them in the summer that it would not be fitting for their wedding to be celebrated with too much grandeur. And yet she had doubtless wished he might see for himself that they would not be able to escape their actions without humiliation.

But she had also been afraid of her father. And she had thought that after their wedding was celebrated, they would be going far away. She wouldn't see her village again for a long time—not until all talk of her had long since died out.

Now she realized that this would be much worse. Erlend had mentioned the great homecoming celebration that he would hold at Husaby, but she hadn't envisioned that it would be like a second wedding feast. And these guests—they were the people she and Erlend would live among; it was their respect and friendship that they needed to win. These were the people who had witnessed Erlend's foolishness and misfortune all these years. Now he believed that he had redeemed himself in their opinion, that he could take his place among his peers by right of birth and fortune. But he would be ridiculed everywhere, here in the villages, when it became apparent that he had taken advantage of his own lawfully betrothed bride.

The abbot leaned over toward Kristin.

"You look so somber, Kristin Lavransdatter. Haven't you recovered from your seasickness yet? Or are you longing for your mother, perhaps?"

"Oh, yes, Father," said Kristin softly. "I suppose I'm thinking of my mother."

They had reached Skaun. They were riding high up along the mountainside. Beneath them, on the valley floor, the leafless forest stood white and furry with frost; it glittered in the sunlight, and there were glints from a little blue lake down below. Then they emerged from the evergreen grove. Erlend pointed ahead.

"There you can see Husaby, Kristin. May God grant you many happy days there, my wife!" he said warmly.

Spread out before them were vast acres, white with rime. The estate stood on what looked like a wide ledge midway up the mountain slope. Closest to them was a small, light-colored stone church, and directly to the south stood all the buildings; they were both numerous and large. Smoke was swirling up from the smoke vents. The bells began to chime from the church and people came streaming out toward them from the courtyard,[1] shouting and waving. The young men in the bridal procession clanged their weapons against each other—and with much banging and clattering and joyous commotion the group raced toward the manor of the newly married man.

They stopped in front of the church. Erlend lifted his bride down from her horse and led her to the door, where an entire crowd of priests and clerics stood waiting to receive them. It was bitterly cold inside, and the daylight seeped in through the small arched windows in the nave, making the glow of the tapers in the choir pale.

Kristin felt abandoned and afraid when Erlend let go of her hand and went over to the men's side while she joined the group of unfamiliar women, dressed in their holiday finery. The service was very beautiful. But Kristin was freezing, and it seemed as if her prayers were blown back to her when she tried to ease her heart and lift it upwards. She thought it was probably not a good omen that it was Saint Simon's Day—since he was the patron saint of the man whom she had treated so badly.

From the church they walked in procession down toward the
manor; first the priests and then Kristin and Erlend, hand in hand,
followed by the guests, two by two. Kristin was so distracted that
she didn't notice much of the estate. The courtyard was long and
narrow; the buildings stood in two rows along the south and north
sides. They were massive and set close together, but they seemed
old and in disrepair.

The procession stopped at the door to the main house, and the
priests blessed it with holy water. Then Erlend led Kristin inside,
through a dark entryway. On her right a door was thrown open to
brilliant light. She ducked through the doorway and stood next to
Erlend in his hall.

It was the largest room she had ever seen on any man's estate.
There was a hearthplace in the middle of the floor, and it was so
long that fires were burning at both ends. And the room was so
wide that the crossbeams were supported by carved pillars. It
seemed to Kristin more like the interior of a church or a king's
great hall than the hall of a manor. At the east end of the house,
where the high seat[2] stood in the middle of the bench along
the wall, enclosed beds had been built into the walls between
the pillars.

And so many candles were now burning in the room—on the
tables, which groaned with precious vessels and platters, and in
brackets attached to the walls. As was the custom in the old days,
weapons and shields hung between the draped tapestries. The wall
behind the high seat was covered with velvet, and that was where
a man now hung Erlend's gold-chased sword and his white shield
with the leaping red lion.

Serving men and women had taken the guests' outer garments
from them. Erlend took his wife by the hand and led her forward
to the hearthplace; the guests formed a semicircle behind them. A
heavyset woman with a gentle face stepped forward and shook out
Kristin's wimple, which had wrinkled a bit under her cloak. As the
woman stepped back to her place, she bowed to the young couple
and smiled. Erlend bowed and smiled in return and then looked
down at his wife. At that moment his face was so handsome. And
once again Kristin's heart seemed to sink—she felt such pity for
him. She knew what he was now thinking; he saw her standing
there in his hall with the long, snow-white wimple of a married

woman spread out over her scarlet wedding gown. That morning she had been forced to wind a long woven belt tightly around her stomach and waist under her clothing before she could get the gown to fit properly. And she had rubbed her cheeks with a red salve that Fru Aashild had given her. While she was doing this, she had thought with indignation and sadness that Erlend didn't seem to look at her much, now that he had won her—since he hadn't yet noticed her condition. Now she bitterly regretted that she hadn't told him before.

As the couple stood there, hand in hand, the priests walked around the room, blessing the house and the hearth, the bed and the table.

Then a servant woman brought the keys of the house over to Erlend. He hung the heavy key ring on Kristin's belt—and as he did this he looked as if he wanted to kiss her at the same time. A man brought a large drinking horn, ringed in gold, and Erlend put it to his lips and drank to her.

"Health and happiness on your estate, my wife!"

And the guests shouted and laughed as she drank with her husband and then threw the rest of the wine into the hearth fire.

Then the musicians began to play as Erlend Nikulaussøn led his lawful wife to the high seat and the banquet guests sat down at the table.

On the third day the guests began to leave, and by the fifth day, just before mid-afternoon prayers, the last ones had departed. Then Kristin was alone with her husband at Husaby.

The first thing she did was to ask the servants to remove all the bedclothes from the bed, to wash them and the surrounding walls with lye, and to carry out the straw and burn it. Then she had the bed filled with fresh straw and on top she spread the bedclothes that she had brought with her to the estate. It was late at night before the work was done. But Kristin said that this should be done with all the beds on the farm, and all the furs were to be steamed in the bathhouse. The maids would have to start first thing in the morning and do as much as they could before the sabbath. Erlend shook his head and laughed—what a wife she was! But he was quite ashamed.

Kristin had not slept much on the first night, even though the priests had blessed her bed. On top were spread silk-covered pillows, a linen sheet, and the finest blankets and furs, but underneath lay filthy, rotting straw; there were lice in the bedclothes and in the magnificent black bear pelt that lay on top.

Many things she had noticed during those days. Behind the costly tapestries which covered the walls, the soot and the dirt had not been washed from the timbers. There was an abundance of food for the feast, but much of it was spoiled or ill-prepared. And they had lit the fires with raw, wet wood that offered hardly any heat and filled the room with smoke.

Poor management she had seen everywhere when, on the second day, she walked around with Erlend to look at the estate. There would be empty stalls and storerooms after the celebration was over; the flour bins were almost swept clean. And she couldn't understand how Erlend planned to feed all the horses and so much livestock with what was left of the straw and hay; there was not even enough fodder for the sheep.

But there was a loft half-filled with flax, and nothing had been done with it—it seemed to be a large part of several years' harvest. And a storeroom full of ancient, unwashed, and stinking wool, some in sacks and some lying loose all around. When Kristin put her hand into the wool, tiny brown worm eggs spilled out of it—moths and maggots had gotten into the wool.

The cattle were feeble, gaunt, scabrous, and chafed; never had she seen so many old animals in one place. Only the horses were beautiful and well cared for. But none of them was a match for Guldsvein or Ringdrott, the stallion that her father now owned. Sløngvanbauge, the horse that he had given her from home, was the most splendid horse in Husaby's stables. She couldn't resist putting her arm around his neck and pressing her face against his coat when she went over to him. And the gentry of Trøndelag[3] looked at the horse and praised his strong, stout legs, his deep chest and high neck, his small head and broad flanks. The old man from Gimsar swore by both God and the Fiend that it was a great sin that they had gelded the horse—what a battle horse he might have been. Then Kristin had to boast a little about his sire, Ringdrott. He was much bigger and stronger; there wasn't another stallion that could compete with him; her father had even tested him against the most celebrated horses all the way north to this parish. Lavrans had given these horses the unusual names—Ringdrott and

Sløngvanbauge—because they were golden in color and had markings that were like reddish-gold rings. The mother of Ringdrott had strayed from the other mares one summer up near the Boar Range, and they thought that a bear had taken her, but then she came back to the farm late in the fall. And the foal she bore the following year had surely not been bred by a stallion belonging to anyone aboveground. So they burned sulfur and bread over the foal, and Lavrans gave the mare to the church, to be even safer. But the foal had grown so magnificent that he now said he would rather lose half his estate than Ringdrott.

Erlend laughed and said, "You don't talk much, Kristin, but when you talk about your father, you're quite eloquent!"

Kristin abruptly fell silent. She remembered her father's face when she was about to ride off with Erlend and he lifted her onto her horse. Lavrans had put on a happy expression because there were so many people around them, but Kristin saw his eyes. He stroked her arm and took her hand to say farewell. At that time her main thought had been that she was glad to be leaving. Now she thought that for as long as she lived, she would feel a sting in her soul whenever she remembered her father's eyes on that day.

Then Kristin Lavransdatter set about organizing and managing her household. She was up before dawn each morning, even though Erlend protested and pretended that he would keep her in bed by force; no one expected a newly married woman to be running from one building to another long before the light of day.

When she saw into what a sorry state everything had fallen and how much she would have to tend to, then the thought shot through her mind, hard and clear: if she had committed a sin to come to this place, so be it—but it was also a sin to make use of God's gifts as was done here. Shame was deserved by those who had been in charge before, along with all of those who had allowed Erlend's manor to decline so badly. There had not been a proper foreman at Husaby for the past two years; Erlend himself had been away from home much of the time, and besides, he had little knowledge of how to run the estate. So it was only to be expected that his envoys farther out in the countryside cheated him, as Kristin suspected they did, or that the servants at Husaby worked only as much as they pleased and whenever and in whatever manner it suited each of them. It would not be easy now for her to restore order to things.

One day she talked about this with Ulf Haldorssøn, Erlend's personal servant. They should be done with the threshing, at least of the grain on their own land—and there wasn't much of it—before it was time for the slaughtering.

Ulf said, "You know, Kristin, that I'm not a farmer. We were to be Erlend's weapons bearers, Haftor and I—and I am no longer practiced in farming ways."

"I know that," said the mistress. "But as things stand, Ulf, it won't be easy for me to manage this winter, newly arrived as I am in this northern region and unfamiliar with our people. It would be kind of you to help me and advise me."

"I can see, Kristin, that you won't have an easy time this winter," said the man. He looked at her with a little smile—that odd smile he always wore whenever he spoke to her or to Erlend. It was impudent and mocking, and yet there was in his bearing both kindness and a certain esteem for her. And she didn't feel that she had the right to be offended when Ulf assumed a more familiar attitude toward her than might otherwise be fitting. She and Erlend had allowed this man to be a witness to their improper and sinful behavior; now she saw that he also knew in what condition she found herself. That was something she would have to bear. She saw that Erlend too tolerated whatever Ulf said or did, and the man did not show much respect for his master. But they had been friends in their childhood; Ulf was from Møre, the son of a smallholder who lived near Baard Petersøn's estate. He used the familiar form of address when he spoke to Erlend, as he now did with her—but that was more the custom among people up north than back home in her village.

Ulf Haldorssøn was quite a striking man, tall and dark, with handsome eyes, but his speech was ugly and coarse. Kristin had heard terrible things about him from the maids on the farm. When he went into town he would drink ferociously, reveling and carousing in the houses that stood along the alleyways; but when he was home at Husaby, he was the most steadfast of men, the most capable, the hardest worker, and the wisest. Kristin had taken a liking to him.

"It would not be easy for any woman to come to this estate, after all that has gone on here," he said. "And yet, I believe, Mistress Kristin, that you will fare better here than most women might. You're not the kind to sit down and whimper and complain; instead, you think of protecting the inheritance here for your descendants, when no one else gives any thought to that. And you know full well that you can count on me; I'll help you as much as I can. You must remember that I'm unaccustomed to farming ways. But if you will seek my counsel and allow me to advise you, then we should be able to make it through this winter, after a fashion."

Kristin thanked Ulf and went inside the house.

Her heart was heavy with fear and anguish, but she struggled to free herself. Part of her worry was that she didn't understand Erlend—he still didn't seem to notice anything. But the other part, and this was worse, was that she couldn't feel any life in the child she was carrying. She knew that at twenty weeks it should begin to move; now it was more than three weeks past that time. At night she would lie in bed and feel this burden which was growing and becoming heavier but which continued to be as dull and lifeless as ever. And hovering in her thoughts was all that she had heard about children who were born lame, with hardened sinews; about creatures that came to light without limbs, that had almost no human form. Before her closed eyes passed images of tiny infants, hideously deformed; one horrific sight melted into another that was even worse. In the south of Gudbrandsdal, at Lidstad, they had a child—well, it must be full grown by now. Her father had seen it, but he would never speak of it; she noticed that he grew distressed if anyone even mentioned it. She wondered how it looked . . . Oh, no. Holy Olav, pray for me! She must believe firmly in the beneficence of the Holy King. She had given her child into his care, after all. With patience she would suffer for her sins and place her faith, with all her soul, in help and mercy for the child. It must be the Fiend himself who was tempting her with these loathsome sights in order to lure her into despair. But it was worse at night. If a child had no limbs, if it was lame, then the mother would doubtless feel no sign of life. Half-asleep, Erlend noticed that his wife was uneasy. He folded her tighter into his arms and buried his face in the hollow of her neck.

But in the daytime Kristin acted as if nothing was wrong. And each morning she would dress carefully, to hide from the house servants a little while longer that she was not walking alone.

It was the custom at Husaby that after the evening meal the servants would retire to the buildings where they slept. Then she and Erlend would sit alone in the hall. In general the customs here on the manor were more as they had been in the old days, back when people had thralls to do the housework. There was no permanent table in the hall, but each morning and evening a large plank was placed on trestles and then set with dishes, and after the meal it was hung back up on the wall. For the other meals everyone took their food over to the benches and sat there to eat. Kristin knew that this had been the custom in the past. But nowadays, when it was hard to find men to serve at the table and everyone had to be content with maids to do the work indoors, it was no longer practical—the women didn't want to waste their strength by lifting the heavy tables. Kristin remembered her mother telling her that at Sundbu they had a permanent table when she was eight winters old, and the women thought this a great advantage in every way. Then they no longer had to go out to the women's house with their sewing but could sit in the main room and cut and clip, and it looked so fine to have candlesticks and a few lovely vessels always standing there. Kristin thought that in the summer she would ask Erlend to put a table along the north wall.

That's where it stood at home, and her father had his high seat at the head of the table. But at Jørundgaard the beds stood along the wall to the entryway. At home her mother sat at the end of the outer bench so that she could go back and forth and keep an eye on the food being served. Only when there were guests did Ragnfrid sit at her husband's side. But here the high seat was in the middle beneath the east gable, and Erlend always wanted Kristin to sit with him. At home her father always offered God's servants a place in the high seat if they were guests at Jørundgaard, and he and Ragnfrid would serve them while they ate and drank. But Erlend refused to do so unless they were of high rank. He had little love for priests or monks—they were costly friends, he said. Kristin thought about what her father and Sira Eirik always said when people complained about the avarice of clerics: every man forgets the sinful pleasure he has enjoyed when he has to pay for it.

She asked Erlend about life at Husaby in the old days. But he knew very little. Such and such he had heard, if he remembered rightly—but he couldn't recall exactly. King Skule had owned the manor and built it up, presumably intending to make Husaby his home when he donated Rein manor to the convent. Erlend was exceedingly proud that he was descended from the duke, as he always called the king, and from Bishop Nikulaus. The bishop was the father of his grandfather, Munan Biskopssøn. But Kristin thought that he knew less about these men than she did from her own father's stories. At home things were different. Neither her father nor her mother boasted of the power or prestige of their deceased ancestors. But they often spoke of them, holding out the good they knew about them as an example and telling of their faults and the evil that had resulted as a warning. And they knew amusing little tales—about Ivar Gjesling the Elder and his enmity with King Sverre, about Dean Ivar's sharp and witty replies, about Haavard Gjesling's tremendous girth, and about Ivar Gjesling the Younger's wondrous luck in hunting. Lavrans told of his grandfather's brother who abducted the Folkung maiden from Vreta cloister; about his grandfather, the Swedish knight Ketil; and about his grandmother, Ramborg Sunesdatter, who always longed for her home in Västergötaland and who one day drove her sleigh through the ice of Lake Vänern when she was visiting her brother at Solberga. He told of his father's skill with weapons and of his inexpressible sorrow at the death of his young first wife, Kristin Sigurdsdatter, who died in childbed, giving birth to Lavrans. And he read from a book about his ancestor, the Holy Fru Elin of Skøvde, who was blessed to become God's martyr. Lavrans had often said that he and Kristin should make a pilgrimage to the grave of the holy widow. But nothing had ever come of it.

In her fear and need, Kristin tried to pray to this holy woman to whom she was bound by blood. She prayed to Saint Elin for her child and kissed the cross that her father had given her; inside was a scrap of the holy saint's shroud. But Kristin was afraid of Saint Elin, now that she had shamed her lineage so terribly. When she prayed to Saint Olav and Saint Thomas for their intercession, she often felt that her laments reached living ears and sympathetic hearts. Her father loved these two martyrs of righteousness above all the other saints, even more than Saint Lavrans himself, whose name he bore, and whose feast day in late summer he always honored with a great banquet and rich alms. Kristin's father had seen Saint Thomas in his dreams one night when he lay wounded outside of Baagahus. No one could describe how loving and venerable he was in appearance, and Lavrans himself had not been able to utter anything but "Lord, Lord!" But the radiant bishop had tenderly touched the man's wound and promised him life and vigor so that he would once again see his wife and daughter, as he had prayed for. And yet at that time not a soul had believed that Lavrans Bjørgulfsøn would live through the night.

Well, Erlend had said. One heard so many things. Nothing like that had ever happened to him, and it wasn't likely to, either. He had never been a pious man like Lavrans.

Then Kristin asked about the people who had attended their homecoming feast. Erlend had little to say about them either. It occurred to Kristin that her husband did not resemble the people here in the countryside. Many of them were handsome; blond and ruddy-hued, with round, hard heads; strong and stocky in build. Many of the old men were immensely fat. Erlend looked like a strange bird among his guests. He was a head taller than most of the men, thin and lean, with slender limbs and fine joints. And he had black, silken hair and a tan complexion, but pale blue eyes beneath coal black brows and shadowy black lashes. His forehead was high and narrow, his temples hollowed; his nose was a little too big and his mouth a little too small and weak for a man. And yet he was handsome; Kristin had never seen a man who was half as handsome as Erlend. Even his soft, quiet voice was unlike the husky voices of the others.

Erlend laughed and said that his lineage was not from around here, except for his paternal great-grandmother, Ragnrid Skulesdatter. People said that he was much like his mother's father, Gaute Erlendssøn of Skogheim. Kristin asked him what he knew of this man. But he knew almost nothing.

One evening Erlend and Kristin were undressing. Erlend couldn't unfasten the strap on his shoe, so he cut it off, and the knife sliced into his hand. He bled heavily and cursed fiercely. Kristin took a cloth out of her linen chest. She was wearing only her shift. Erlend put his other arm around her waist as she bandaged his hand.

Suddenly he looked down into her face with horror and confusion—and flushed bright red himself. Kristin bowed her head.

Erlend withdrew his arm. He said nothing, and so Kristin walked quietly away and climbed into bed. Her heart thudded hollowly and hard against her ribs. Now and then she cast a glance at her husband. He had turned his back to her, slowly taking off one garment after the other. Then he came over and lay down.

Kristin waited for him to speak. She waited so long that her heart seemed to stop beating and just stood still, quivering in her breast.

But Erlend didn't say a word. And he didn't take her into his arms.

At last he hesitantly placed his hand on her breast and pressed his chin against her shoulder so that the stubble of his beard prickled her skin. When he still said nothing, Kristin turned over to face the wall.

She felt as if she were sinking and sinking. He had not one word to offer her—now that he knew she had been carrying his child these long, difficult days. Kristin clenched her teeth in the dark. She would not beg him. If he remained silent, then she would be silent too, even if it lasted until the day she gave birth. Resentment surged up inside her. But she lay absolutely still next to the wall. Erlend too lay still in the dark. Hour after hour they lay there this way, and each one knew that the other was not asleep. Finally Kristin heard by his regular breathing that Erlend had dozed off. Then she allowed her tears to fall as they would, from sorrow and hurt and shame. This, she felt, she would never be able to forgive him.

For three days Erlend and Kristin went about in this manner—he seemed like a wet dog, thought the young wife. She was burning and stony with anger, becoming wild with bitterness whenever she felt him give her a searching look but then swiftly shift his glance if she turned her eyes toward his.

On the morning of the fourth day Kristin was sitting in the main house when Erlend appeared in the doorway, dressed for riding. He said that he was going west to Medalby and asked whether she wanted to accompany him to visit the manor; it was part of her wedding-morning gift. Kristin assented, and Erlend himself helped her to put on the fur-lined boots and the black cloak with sleeves and silver clasps.

Out in the courtyard stood four saddled horses, but Erlend told Haftor and Egil to stay home and help with the threshing. Then he helped his wife into the saddle. Kristin realized that Erlend was now planning to speak about the matter which lay unspoken between them. Yet he said nothing as they slowly rode off, southward, toward the forest.

It was now nearly the end of the slaughtering month, but still no snow had fallen in the parish. The day was fresh and beautiful; the sun had just come up, and it glittered and sparkled on the white frost everywhere, on the fields and on the trees. They rode across Husaby's land. Kristin saw that there were few cultivated acres or stubble fields, but mostly fallow land and old meadows, tufted with grass, moss-covered, and overgrown with alder saplings. She mentioned this.

Her husband replied merrily, "Don't you know, Kristin—you who know so well how to tend and manage farms—that it does no good to grow grain this close to a trading port? You gain more by trading butter and wool for grain and flour from the foreign merchants."

"Then you should have traded the goods that are lying in your lofts and have rotted long ago," said Kristin. "I also know that the law says that every man who leases land must sow grain on three parts but let the fourth part lie fallow. And surely the estate of the master should not be worse tended than the farms of his leaseholders—that's what my father always said."

Erlend laughed a bit and said, "I have never asked about the law in that regard. As long as I receive what is my due, my tenants can run their farms as they see fit, and I will run Husaby in the manner that seems to me best and most suitable."

"Do you think yourself wiser then," said Kristin, "than our deceased ancestors and Saint Olav and King Magnus, who established these laws?"

Erlend laughed again and said, "I hadn't given any thought to that. What a devilish good grasp you have of our country's laws and regulations, Kristin."

"I have some understanding of these matters," said Kristin, "because Father often asked Sigurd of Loptsgaard to recite laws for us when he came to visit and we sat at home in the evening. Father thought it was beneficial for the servants and the young people to have some knowledge of such things, and so Sigurd would recount one passage or another."

"Sigurd . . ." said Erlend. "Oh, yes, now I remember. I saw him at our wedding. He was the toothless old man with the long drooping nose who slobbered and wept and patted you on the breast. He was still dead drunk in the morning when everyone came up to us and watched as I put the linen wimple of a married woman on your head."

"He has known me for as long as I can remember," said Kristin crossly. "He used to take me on his lap and play with me when I was a little maiden."

Erlend laughed again. "That was an odd kind of amusement—that you had to sit and listen to the old man chanting the law, passage by passage. Lavrans is unlike any other man in every way. Usually it is said that if the tenant knew the full law of the land and the stallion knew his strength, then the Devil would be a knight. . . ."

Kristin gave a shout and struck her horse on the flank. Erlend threw his wife an angry and astonished look as she rode away from him.

Suddenly he spurred his horse. Jesus, the ford in the river—it was impossible to cross there now, the earth had slid away recently. Sløngvanbauge took longer strides when he noticed another horse chasing him. Erlend was deathly afraid—how she was racing down the steep slopes. He bounded past her through the copsewood and doubled back on the road where it flattened out for a short stretch to make her stop. When he came up alongside her, he saw that Kristin herself had grown a little scared.

Erlend leaned over toward his wife and struck her a ringing blow beneath the ear; Sløngvanbauge leaped sideways, startled, and reared up.

"Well, you deserved that," said Erlend, his voice shaking, after the horses had calmed down and they once again rode side by side. "The way you rushed off like that, senseless with fury . . . You frightened me."

Kristin held her hand to her head so that he couldn't see her face. Erlend wished that he hadn't hit her. But he repeated, "Yes, you scared me, Kristin—to dash off like that! And to do so *now* . . . .," he said softly.

Kristin didn't reply, nor did she look at him. But Erlend felt that she was less angry than before, when he had mocked her home. He was greatly surprised by this, but he saw that it was so.

They arrived at Medalby, and Erlend's leaseholder came out and wanted to show them into the main house. But Erlend thought they first ought to inspect the buildings, and Kristin should come along. "She owns the farm now, and she has a better understanding of such things than I do, Stein," he said with a laugh. Several farmers were there too, who were to act as witnesses, and some of them were also Erlend's tenants.

Stein had come to the farm on the last turnover day[4] and since then he had been begging the master to come up and see the condition that the buildings were in when he took over, or to send an envoy in his stead. The farmers testified that not one building had been without leaks, and those that were now in a state of collapse had been that way when Stein arrived. Kristin saw that it was a good farm, but it had been poorly maintained. She saw that this Stein was a capable man, and Erlend was also very amenable and promised him some reductions in his land rent until he was able to repair the buildings.

Then they went into the main house where the table was set with good food and strong ale. The leaseholder's wife asked Kristin's forgiveness for not coming out to greet her. But her husband would not allow her to step out under open sky until she had been to church after giving birth.[5] Kristin greeted the woman kindly, and then she had to go over to the cradle to see the child. It was the couple's first, and it was a son, twelve nights old, big and strong.

Then Erlend and Kristin were led to the high seat, and everyone sat down and ate and drank for a good long time. Kristin was the one who talked most during the meal; Erlend didn't say much, nor did the farmers, and yet Kristin noticed that they seemed to like her.

Then the child woke up, at first whimpering but then shrieking so terribly that the mother had to put him to her breast to calm his cries. Kristin glanced over at the two of them several times, and when the boy had had enough, she took him from the woman and held him in her arms.

"Look, husband," she said, "don't you think he's a handsome and fine young fellow?"

"That he is," said Erlend, not looking in her direction.

Kristin sat and held the child for a while before she gave him back to his mother.

"I will send a gift over here to your son, Arndis," she said. "For he's the first child I've held in my arms since I came up here to the north."

Flushed and defiant, with a little smile Kristin cast a glance at her husband and then at the farmers sitting along the bench. A few of them showed a slight twitch at the corner of the mouth, but then they stared straight ahead, their faces stiff and solemn. After a moment a very old man stood up; he had been drinking heavily. Now he lifted the ladle out of the ale bowl, placed it on the table, and raised the large vessel.

"So let us drink to that, mistress; that the next child you hold in your arms will be the new master of Husaby!"

Kristin stood up and accepted the heavy bowl. First she offered it to her husband. Erlend barely touched it with his lips, but Kristin took a long, deep drink.

"Thank you for that greeting, Jon of Skog," she said with a cheery nod, her eyes twinkling. Then she sent the bowl around.

Kristin could see that Erlend was red-faced and quite angry. She herself merely felt such a foolish urge to laugh and be merry. A short time later Erlend wanted to leave, and so they set off on their way home.

They had been riding for a while without speaking when Erlend suddenly burst out, "Do you think it's necessary to let even our tenants know that you were carrying a child when you were wed? You can wager your soul with the Devil that talk about the two of us will soon be flying through all the villages along the fjord."

Kristin didn't reply at first. She stared into the distance over her horse's head, and she was now so white in the face that Erlend grew frightened.

"I will never forget for as long as I live," she said at last, without looking at him, "that those were the first words you greeted him with, this son of yours that I carry under my belt."

"Kristin!" said Erlend, his voice pleading. "My Kristin," he implored when she said nothing and refused to look at him. "Kristin!"

"Sir?" she replied coldly and courteously, without turning her head.

Erlend cursed so that sparks flew; he spurred his horse and raced ahead along the road. But a few minutes later he came riding back toward her.

"This time I was almost so furious," he said, "that *I* was going to ride away from *you*."

Kristin said calmly, "Then you might have had to wait a good long time before I followed you to Husaby."

"The things you say!" said her husband, resigned.

Once again they rode for some time without talking. In a while they reached a place where a small path led up over a ridge. Erlend said to his wife, "I was thinking that we could ride home this way, over the heights—it will take a little longer, but I've wanted to travel up this way with you for some time."

Kristin nodded indifferently.

After a while Erlend said that now it would be better for them to walk. He tied their horses to a tree.

"Gunnulf and I had a fortress up here on the ridge," he said. "I'd like to see whether there's anything left of our castle."

He took Kristin's hand. She didn't resist, but walked with her eyes downcast, looking at where she set her feet. It wasn't long before they were up on the heights. Beyond the bare, frost-covered forest, in the crook of the little river, Husaby lay on the mountain slope directly across from them, looming big and grand with the stone church and all its massive buildings, surrounded by the broad acres, and the dark forested ridge behind.

"Mother used to come up here with us," said Erlend softly. "Often. But she would always sit and stare off to the south, toward the Dovre Range. I suppose she was always yearning, night and day, to be far away from Husaby. Or she would turn toward the north and gaze out at the gap in the slopes—there where you can see blue in the distance; those are the mountains on the other side of the fjord. Not once did she look at the farm."

Erlend's voice was tender and beseeching. But Kristin neither spoke nor looked at him. Then he went over and kicked at the frozen heath.

"No, there's probably nothing left here of Gunnulf's and my fortress. And it was a long time ago, after all, that we played up here, Gunnulf and I."

He received no answer. Right below where they stood was a small frozen pond. Erlend picked up a stone and threw it. The hollow was frozen solid so that only a tiny white star appeared on the black mirror. Erlend picked up another stone and threw it harder—then another and another. Now he was throwing them in utter fury, and in the end he would have splintered the ice with a vengeance. But then he caught sight of his wife's face—she stood there, her eyes dark with contempt, smiling scornfully at his childishness.

Erlend spun around, but all at once Kristin grew deathly pale and her eyes fell shut. She stood there with her hands stretched out and groping, swaying as if she were about to faint—then she grabbed hold of a tree trunk.

"Kristin—what is it?" Erlend asked in fear.

She didn't answer but stood as if she were listening to something. Her gaze was remote and strange.

Now she felt it again. Deep within her womb it felt as if a fish was flicking its tail. And again the whole world seemed to reel around her, and she felt dizzy and weak, but not as much as the first time.

"What's the matter?" asked Erlend.

She had waited so long for this—she hardly dared to acknowledge the great fear in her soul. She could not speak of it—not now, when they had been fighting all day long. Then *he* said it.

"Was it the child moving inside you?" he asked gently, touching her shoulder.

Then she cast off all her anger toward him, pressed herself against the father of her child, and hid her face on his chest.

Some time later they walked back down to the place where their horses were tied. The short day was almost over; behind them in the southwest the sun was sinking behind the treetops, red and dull in the frosty haze.

Erlend carefully tested the buckles and straps of the saddle before he lifted his wife up onto her horse. Then he went over and untied his own. He reached under his belt for the gloves he had put there, but he found only one. He looked around on the ground.

Then Kristin couldn't resist and said, "It will do you no good to look for your glove here, Erlend."

"You might have said something to me if you saw me lose it—no matter how angry you were with me," he replied. They were the gloves that Kristin had sewn for him and given to him as one of his betrothal presents.

"It fell out of your belt when you hit me," said Kristin very quietly, her eyes downcast.

Erlend stood next to his horse with his hand on the saddlebow. He looked embarrassed and unhappy. But then he burst out laughing.

"Never would I have believed, Kristin—during all the time I was courting you, rushing around and begging my kinsmen to speak on my behalf and making myself so meek and pitiful in order to win you—that you could be such a witch!"

Then Kristin laughed too.

"No, then you probably would have given up long ago—and it certainly would have been in your own best interest."

Erlend took a few steps toward her and placed his hand on her knee.

"Jesus help me, Kristin—have you ever heard it said of me that I did anything that was in my own best interest?"

He pressed his face down in her lap and then looked up with sparkling eyes into his wife's face. Flushed and happy, Kristin bowed her head, trying to hide her smile and her eyes from Erlend.

He grabbed hold of her horse's harness and let his own horse follow behind; and in this manner he escorted her until they reached the bottom of the ridge. Every time they looked at each other he would laugh and she would turn her face away to hide that she was laughing too.

"So," he said merrily as they came out onto the road again, "now we'll ride home to Husaby, my Kristin, and be as happy as two thieves!"

CHAPTER 2

ON CHRISTMAS EVE the rain poured down and the wind blew hard. It was impossible to use sleighs, and so Kristin had to stay home when Erlend and the servants rode off for the evening mass at Birgsi Church.

She stood in the doorway of the main house and watched them go. The pine torches they carried shone red against the dark old buildings, reflected in the icy surface of the courtyard. The wind seized the flames and flattened them out sideways. Kristin stood there as long she could hear the faint sound of their passage in the night.

Inside the hall there were candles burning on the table. The remains of the evening meal were scattered about—lumps of porridge in dishes, half-eaten pieces of bread, and fishbones floating in puddles of spilt ale. The serving maids who were to stay at home had all fallen asleep on the straw spread out on the floor. Kristin was alone with them at the manor, along with an old man named Aan. He had served at Husaby since the time of Erlend's grandfather; now he lived in a little hut down by the lake but he liked to come up to the farm in the daytime to putter around, in the belief that he was working very hard. Aan had fallen asleep at the table that evening, and Erlend and Ulf had laughingly carried him over to a corner and spread a blanket over him.

Back home at Jørundgaard the floor would now be thickly strewn with rushes, for the entire household would sleep together in the main house during the holiday nights. Before they left for church they used to clear away the remains of the meal eaten after their fast, and Kristin's mother and the maids would set the table as beautifully as they could with butter and cheeses, heaps of thin, light bread, chunks of glistening bacon, and the thickest joints of cured mutton. The silver pitchers and horns of mead stood there gleaming. And her father himself would place the ale cask on the bench.

Kristin turned her chair around to face the hearth—she didn't want to look at the loathsome table. One of the maids was snoring so loudly that it was awful to hear.

That was also one of the things that she didn't care for about Erlend. At home on his estate he ate in a manner that was so repugnant and slovenly, pawing through the dishes for good bits of food, hardly bothering to wash his hands before he came to the table. And he let the dogs jump up onto his lap and gulp down food along with him while everyone ate. So it was only to be expected that the servants had no table manners. Back home she had been constrained to eat delicately and slowly. It would not be proper, said her mother, for the master's family to wait while the servants ate, and those who had toiled and labored should have time to eat their fill.

"Here, Gunna," Kristin called softly to the big yellow bitch that lay with a whole cluster of pups against the draft stone by the hearth. She was such an ill-tempered animal, and that's why Erlend had named her after the old mistress of Raasvold.

"You poor wretch," whispered Kristin, petting the dog who had come over and put her head on Kristin's knee. Her backbone was as sharp as a scythe, and her teats almost swept the floor. The pups were literally eating their mother up. "Oh, yes, my poor wretch."

Kristin leaned her head against the back of the chair and looked up at the soot-covered rafters. She was tired.

No, she had not had an easy time of it these past few months that she had spent at Husaby. She had talked with Erlend a little on the evening of the day they had gone to Medalby. Then she realized that he thought she was angry with him because he had brought this upon her.

"I do remember," he said in a low voice, "that day in the spring when we went walking in the woods north of the church. I do remember that you asked me to leave you alone. . . ."

Kristin was pleased that he had told her this. Otherwise she often wondered about all the things that Erlend seemed to have forgotten.

But then he said, "And yet I would not have believed it of you, Kristin, that you could walk around bearing such a secret rancor toward me, and still act so gentle and happy. For you must have known long ago how things stood with you. And I believed that you were as bright and honest as the rays of the sun."

"Oh, Erlend," she said sadly. "You of all people in the world should know best that I have followed forbidden paths and acted falsely toward those who have trusted me most." But she wanted so much for him to understand. "I don't know whether you recall, my dear, but in the past you have behaved toward me in a manner that some might not call proper. And God and the Virgin Mary know that I didn't bear you any grudge, nor did I love you any less."

Erlend's face grew tender.

"So I thought," he said quietly. "But you know too that I have striven all these years to rectify the harm I have done. I consoled myself that in the end I would be able to reward you, for you were so faithful and patient."

Then she said to him, "No doubt you have heard about my grandfather's brother and the maiden Bengta, who fled from Sweden against the wishes of her kinsmen. God punished them by refusing to give the couple a child. Haven't you ever feared, during all these years, that He might punish us in that way too?"

She added, her voice quavering and soft, "You can understand, my Erlend, that I was not very happy this summer when I first became aware of it. And yet I thought . . . I thought that if you should die before we were married, I would rather be left behind with your child than alone. I thought that if I should die in childbirth . . . it was still better than if you had no lawful son who could take your high seat after you, when you must leave this earth."

Erlend replied vehemently, "Then I would think my son was too dearly bought if he should cost you your life. Don't talk like that, Kristin." A little later he said, "Husaby is not so dear to me. Especially since I realized that Orm can never inherit my ancestral property after me."[1]

"Do you care more for *her* son than for mine?" Kristin then asked.

"*Your* son . . . ," Erlend gave a laugh. "Of him I know nothing more than that he will arrive half a year or so before he should. Orm I have loved for twelve years."

Some time later Kristin asked, "Do you ever long for these children of yours?"

"Yes," said her husband. "In the past I often went over to see them in Østerdal, where they are living."

"You could go there now, during Advent," said Kristin quietly.

"You wouldn't be averse to it?" asked Erlend happily.

Kristin said that she would find it reasonable. Then he asked whether she would be against it if he brought the children back home for Christmas. "You will have to see them sometime, after all." And again she had replied that this too seemed reasonable to her.

While Erlend was away, Kristin worked hard to prepare for Christmas. It distressed her greatly to be living among these unfamiliar men and servant women now—she had to take a firm grip on herself whenever she dressed or undressed in the presence of the two maids, whom Erlend had ordered to sleep with her in the hall. She had to remind herself that she would never have dared to sleep alone in the large house—where another had slept with Erlend before her.

The serving women on the estate were no better than could be expected. Those farmers who kept close watch over their daughters did not send them to serve on an estate where the master had lived openly with a concubine and had placed such a woman in charge. The maids were lazy and not in the habit of obeying their mistress. But some of them soon came to like the fact that Kristin was putting the house in good order and personally lent a hand with their work. They grew talkative and joyful when she listened to them and answered them gently and cheerfully. And each day Kristin showed her house servants a kind and calm demeanor. She reprimanded no one, but if a maid refused her orders, then the mistress would act as if the girl did not understand what was asked of her and would quietly show her how the work was to be done. This was how Kristin had seen her father behave toward new servants who grumbled, and no man had tried twice to disobey Lavrans of Jørundgaard.

In this manner they would have to make it through the winter. Later she would see about getting rid of those women she disliked or could not bring around.

There was one type of work that Kristin didn't dare take up unless she was free from the eyes of these strangers. But in the morning, when she was alone in the hall, she would sew the clothing for her child—swaddling clothes of soft homespun, ribbons of red and green fabric from town, and white linen for the christening garments. As she sat there with her sewing, her thoughts would tumble between fear and then faith in the holy friends of humankind, to whom she had prayed for intercession. It was true that the child lived and moved inside her so that she had no peace, night or day. But she had heard about children who were born with a pelt where they should have had a face, with their heads turned around backwards, or their toes where their heels should have been. And she pictured Svein, who was purple over half his face because his mother had inadvertently looked at a fire.[2]

Then Kristin would cast aside her sewing and go over to kneel before the image of the Virgin Mary and say seven *Ave Marias*. Brother Edvin had said that the Mother of God felt an equal joy every time she heard the angel's greeting, even if it came from the lips of the most wretched sinner. And it was the words *Dominus tecum* that most cheered Mary's heart; that was why Kristin always said them three times.

This always helped her for a while. She knew of many people, both men and women, who paid scant honor to God or to His Mother and who kept the commandments poorly—but she hadn't seen that they gave birth to misshapen children because of it. Often God was so merciful that He did not visit the sins of the parents upon their poor children, although every once in a while He had to show people a sign that He could not perpetually tolerate their evil. But surely it would not be *her* child . . .

Then she called in her heart upon Saint Olav.[3] He was the one she had heard so much about that it was as though she had known him while he lived in Norway and had seen him here on this earth. He was not tall, quite stout, but straight-backed and fair, with the gold crown and shining halo on his golden curls, and a curly red beard on his firm, weatherbeaten, and intrepid face. But his deepset and blazing eyes looked straight through everyone; those who had strayed did not dare look into them. Kristin didn't dare either. She lowered her gaze before his eyes, but she was not afraid. It was more as if she were a child and had to lower her eyes before her father's glance when she had done something wrong. Saint Olav looked at her, sternly but not harshly—she had promised to better her life, after all. She longed so fervently to go to Nidaros[4] and kneel down before his shrine; Erlend had promised her this, when they came north—that they would go there very soon. But the journey had been postponed. And now Kristin realized that he was reluctant to travel with her; he was ashamed and afraid of gossip.

One evening when she was sitting at the table with her servants, one of the maids, a young girl who helped in the house, said, "I was wondering, Mistress, whether it wouldn't be better if we started sewing swaddling clothes and infant garments before we set up the loom that you're talking about. . . ."

Kristin pretended not to hear and kept on talking about wool dyeing.

Then the girl continued, "But perhaps you have brought such garments from home?"

Kristin smiled faintly and then turned back to the others. When she glanced at the maid a little while later, she was sitting there bright red in the face and peering anxiously at her mistress. Kristin smiled again and spoke to Ulf across the table. Then the young girl began to weep. Kristin laughed a bit, and the maid cried harder and harder until she was sniffing and snuffling.

"Stop that now, Frida," Kristin finally said calmly. "You hired on here as a grown-up serving maid; you shouldn't behave as if you were a little child."

The maid whimpered. She hadn't meant to be impertinent, and Kristin mustn't be angry.

"No," said Kristin, smiling again. "Eat your food now and stop crying. The rest of us have no more sense, either, than what God has granted us."

Frida jumped up and ran out, sobbing loudly.

Later, when Ulf Haldorssøn stood talking to Kristin about the work that had to be done the next day, he laughed and said, "Erlend should have married you ten years ago, Kristin. Then his affairs would have been in a better state today, in every respect."

"Do you think so?" she asked, smiling as before. "Back then I was nine winters old. Do you think Erlend would have been capable of waiting for a child bride for years on end?"

Ulf laughed and went out.

But at night Kristin would lie in bed and weep with loneliness and humiliation.

Then Erlend came home during the week before Christmas, and Orm, his son, rode at his father's side. Kristin felt a stab in her heart when Erlend led the boy forward and told him to greet his stepmother.

He was the most handsome child. This was how she had thought *he* would look, the son that she carried. Sometimes, when she dared to be happy, to believe that her child would be born healthy and well-formed, and to think ahead about the boy who would grow up at her knee, then it was like this she pictured him—just like his father.

Orm was perhaps a little small for his age, and slight, but handsomely built, with fine limbs and a lovely face, his complexion and hair dark, but with big blue eyes and a soft red mouth. He greeted his stepmother courteously, but his expression was hard and cold. Kristin had not had the chance to talk with the boy further. But she sensed his eyes on her, wherever she walked or stood, and she felt as if her body and gait grew even more heavy and clumsy when she knew the boy was staring at her.

She didn't notice Erlend talking much with his son, but she realized that it was the boy who held back. Kristin told her husband that Orm was handsome and looked intelligent. Erlend had not brought his daughter along; he thought Margret was too young to make the long journey in the winter. She was even more lovely than her brother, he said proudly when Kristin asked about the little maiden—and much more clever; she had her foster parents wrapped around her little finger. She had wavy golden hair and brown eyes.

Then she must look much like her mother, thought Kristin. And she couldn't help the feeling of envy that burned inside her. She wondered whether Erlend loved his daughter the way her father had loved her. His voice had sounded so tender and warm when he spoke of Margret.

Kristin stood up and went over to the main door. It was so dark and heavy with rain outside that there seemed to be no moon or stars. But she thought it must soon be midnight. She picked up a lantern from the entryway, went inside, and lit it. Then she threw on her cloak and went out into the rain.

"In Christ's name," she whispered, crossing herself three times as she stepped out into the night.

At the upper end of the courtyard stood the priest's house. It was empty now. Ever since Erlend had been released from the ban of excommunication, there had not been a private cleric at Husaby; now and then one of the assistant priests from Orkedal would come over to say mass, but the new priest who had been assigned to the church was abroad with Master Gunnulf; they were apparently friends from school. They had been expected home this past summer, but now Erlend thought they wouldn't return until after spring. Gunnulf had had a lung ailment in his youth, so he would be unlikely to travel during the winter.

Kristin let herself into the cold, deserted house and found the key to the church. Then she paused for a moment. It was very slippery, pitch dark, windy, and rainy. It was reckless of her to go out at night, and especially on Christmas Eve, when all the evil spirits were in the air. But she refused to give up—she had to go to the church.

"In the name of God, the Almighty, I here proceed," she whispered aloud. Lighting her way with the lantern, Kristin set her feet down where stones and tufts of grass stuck up from the icy ground. In the darkness the path to the church seemed exceedingly long. But at last she stood on the stone threshold in front of the door.

Inside it was piercingly cold, much colder than out in the rain. Kristin walked forward toward the chancel and knelt down before the crucifix, which she glimpsed in the darkness above her.

After she had said her prayers and stood up, she stopped for a moment. She seemed to expect something to happen to her. But nothing did. She was freezing and scared in the desolate, dark church.

She crept up toward the altar and shone her light on the paintings. They were old, ugly, and stern. The altar was bare stone. She knew that the cloths, books, and vessels lay locked up in a chest.

In the nave a bench stood against the wall. Kristin went over and sat down, placing the lantern on the floor. Her cloak was wet, and her feet were wet and cold. She tried to pull one leg up under-neath her, but the position was uncomfortable. So she wrapped the cloak tightly around her and struggled to focus her thoughts on the fact that now it was once again the holy midnight hour when Christ was born to the Virgin Mary in Bethlehem.

Verbum caro factum est et habitavit in nobis.[5]

Kristin remembered Sira Eirik's deep, pure voice. And Audun, the old deacon, who never attained a higher position. And their church back home where she had stood at her mother's side and listened to the Christmas mass. Every single year she had heard it. She tried to recall more of the holy words, but she could only think about their church and all the familiar faces. In front, on the men's side, stood her father, staring with remote eyes into the daz-zling glow of candles from the choir.

It was so incomprehensible that their church was no more. It had burned to the ground. She burst into tears at the thought. And here she was, sitting alone in the dark on this night when all Chris-tian people were gathered in happiness and joy in God's house. But perhaps that was as it should be, that tonight she was shut out from the celebration of the birth of God's son to a pure and inno-cent maiden.

Her parents were no doubt at Sundbu this Christmas. But there would be no mass in the chapel tonight; she knew that on Christ-mas Eve those who lived at Sundbu always attended the service at the main church in Ladalm.

This was the first time, for as far back as Kristin could remem-ber, that she was not at the Christmas mass. She must have been quite young the first time her parents took her along. She could re-call that she was bundled up in a fur-lined sack, and her father had carried her in his arms. It was a terribly cold night, and they were riding through a forest—the pine torches shone on fir trees heavy with snow. Her father's face was dark red, and the fur border on his hood was chalk-white with frost. Now and then he would bend forward and nip the end of her nose and ask her whether she could feel it. Then, laughing, he would shout over his shoulder to her mother that Kristin's nose hadn't frozen off yet. That must have been while they were still living at Skog; she couldn't have been more than three winters old. Her parents were quite young back then. Now she remembered her mother's voice on that night—clear and happy and full of laughter—when she called out to her husband and asked about the child. Yes, her mother's voice had been young and fresh.

Bethlehem. In Norwegian it means the place of bread. For that was where the bread which will nourish us for eternal life was given to the people.

It was at the mass on Christmas Day that Sira Eirik stepped forward to the pulpit and explained the gospels in the language of his own country.

In between the masses everyone would sit in the banquet hall north of the church. They had brought ale with them and passed it around. The men slipped out to the stables to see to the horses. But on vigil nights, in the summertime before a holy day, the congregation would gather on the church green, and then the young people would dance among the servants.

And the blessed Virgin Mary wrapped her son in swaddling clothes. She placed him in the straw of the manger from which the oxen and asses ate. . . .

Kristin pressed her hands against her sides.

Little son, my own sweet child, my own son. God will have mercy on us for the sake of His own blessed Mother. Blessed Mary, you who are the clear star of the sea,[6] the crimson dawn of eternal life who gave birth to the sun of the whole world—help us! Little child, what is it tonight? You're so restless. Can you feel beneath my heart that I am so bitterly cold?

It was on the Children's Day last year, the fourth day of Christmas, when Sira Eirik preached about the innocent children whom the cruel soldiers had slaughtered in their mothers' arms. But God had chosen these young boys to enter into the hall of heaven before all other blood witnesses. And it would be a sign that such belong to the Kingdom of Heaven. And Jesus picked up a little boy and put him among them. Unless you create yourselves in their image, you cannot enter into the hall of heaven, dear brothers and sisters. So let this be a solace to every man and woman who mourns a young child's death. . . .

Then Kristin had seen her father's eyes meet her mother's across the church, and she withdrew her gaze, because she knew that this was not meant for her.

That was last year. The first Christmas after Ulvhild's death. Oh, but not *my* child! Jesus, Maria. Let me keep my son!

Her father had not wanted to ride in the races on Saint Stefan's Day last year, but the men begged him until he finally agreed. The course extended from the church hill at home, down to the confluence of the two rivers near Loptsgaard; that's where they joined up with the men from Ottadal. She remembered her father racing past on his golden stallion. He stood up in his stirrups and bent low over the horse's neck, shouting and urging the animal on, with the whole group thundering behind.

But last year he had come home early, and he was completely sober. Normally on that day the men would return home late, tremendously drunk, because they had to ride into every farm courtyard and drink from the bowls brought out to them, to honor Christ and Saint Stefan, who first saw the star in the east as he drove King Herod's foals to the River Jordan for water. Even the horses were given ale on that day, for they were supposed to be wild and reckless. On Saint Stefan's Day the farmers were allowed to race their horses until vespers—it was impossible to make the men think or talk of anything but horses.

Kristin could remember one Christmas when they held the great drinking feast at Jørundgaard. And her father had promised a priest who was among the guests that he would be given a young red stallion, son of Guldsvein, if he could manage to swing himself up onto the animal as it ran around unsaddled in the courtyard.

That was a long time ago—before the misfortune with Ulvhild occurred. Her mother was standing in the doorway with the little sister in her arms, and Kristin was holding onto her dress, a bit scared.

The priest ran after the horse and grabbed the halter, leaping so that his ankle-length surcoat swirled around him, and then he let go of the wild, rearing beast.

"Foal, foal—whoa, foal. Whoa, son!" he cried out. He hopped and he danced like a billy goat. Her father and an old farmer stood with their arms around each other's necks, the features of their faces completely dissolved in laughter and drunkenness.

Either the priest must have won Rauden or else Lavrans gave the foal to him all the same, for Kristin remembered that he rode away from Jørundgaard on the horse. By that time they were all sober enough; Lavrans respectfully held the stirrup for him, and the priest blessed them with three fingers in farewell. He was apparently a cleric of high standing.

Oh yes. It was often quite merry at home during the Christmas season. And then there were the Christmas masqueraders. Kristin's father would sling her up onto his back, his tunic icy and his hair wet. To clear their heads before they went to vespers, the men threw ice water over each other down by the well. They laughed when the women voiced their disapproval of this. Kristin's father would take her small, cold hands and press them against his forehead, which was still red and burning hot. This was out in the courtyard, in the evening. A new white crescent moon hung over the mountain ridge in the watery-green air. Once when he stepped into the main house with her, Kristin hit her head on the doorframe so she had a big bump on her forehead. Later she sat on his lap at the table. He lay the blade of his dagger against her bruise, fed her tidbits of food, and let her drink mead from his goblet. Then she wasn't afraid of the masqueraders who stormed into the room.

"Oh Father, oh Father. My dear, kind father!"

Sobbing loudly, Kristin now hid her face in her hands. Oh, if only her father knew how she felt on this Christmas Eve!

When she walked back across the courtyard, she saw that sparks were rising up from the cookhouse roof. The maids had set about preparing food for the churchgoers.

It was gloomy in the hall. The candles on the table had burned out, and the fire in the hearth was barely smoldering. Kristin put more wood on and blew at the embers. Then she noticed that Orm was sitting in her chair. He stood up as soon as his stepmother saw him.

"My dear—" said Kristin. "Didn't you go with your father and the others to mass?"

Orm swallowed hard a couple of times. "I guess he forgot to wake me. Father told me to lie down for a while in the bed on the south wall. He said he would wake me. . . ."

"That's too bad, Orm," said Kristin.

The boy didn't reply. After a moment he said, "I thought you went with them after all. I woke up and was alone here in the hall."

"I went over to the church for a little while," said Kristin.

"Do you dare to go out on Christmas Eve?" asked the boy. "Don't you know that the spirits of the dead could come and seize you?"[7]

"I don't think it's only the evil spirits that are out tonight," she said. "Christmas Eve must be for all spirits. I once knew a monk who is now dead and standing before God, I think, because he was pure goodness. He told me . . . Have you ever heard about the animals in the stable and how they talked to each other on Christmas Eve? They could speak Latin back then. And the rooster crowed: 'Christus natus est!' No, now I can't remember the whole thing. The other animals asked 'Where?' and the goat bleated, 'Betlem, Betlem,' and the sheep said, 'Eamus, eamus.' "

Orm smiled scornfully.

"Do you think I'm such a child that you can comfort me with tales? You should offer to take me on your lap and put me to your breast."

"I told the story mostly to comfort myself, Orm," said Kristin quietly. "I would have liked to go to mass too."

Now she couldn't stand to look at the littered table any longer. She went over, swept all the scraps into a trencher and set it on the floor for the dog. Then she found the whisk made of sedge under the bench and scrubbed off the tabletop.

"Would you come with me over to the western storehouse, Orm? To get bread and salted meat. Then we'll set the table for the holy day," said Kristin.

"Why don't you let your maidservants do that?" asked the boy.

"This is the way I was taught by my father and mother," replied the young mistress. "That at Christmastime no one should ever ask anyone else for anything, but we all should strive to do our utmost. Whoever serves the others most during the holidays is the most blessed."

"But you're asking me," said Orm.

"That's a different matter—you're the son here on the estate."

Orm carried the lantern and they walked across the courtyard together. Inside the storehouse Kristin filled two trenchers with Christmas food. She also took a bundle of large tallow candles.

While they were working, the boy said, "That must be a peasant custom, what you mentioned a moment ago. For I've heard he's nothing more than a homespun farmer, Lavrans Bjørgulfsøn."

"Who did you hear that from?" asked Kristin.

"From Mother," said Orm. "I heard her say it all the time to Father when we were living here at Husaby before. She said he could see that not even a gray-clad farmer would give his daughter's hand in marriage to him."

"It must have been pleasant here at Husaby back then," said Kristin curtly.

The boy didn't reply. His lips quivered.

Kristin and Orm carried the filled trenchers back to the hall, and she set the table. But she had to go back over to the storehouse for food once again.

Orm took the trencher and said, a little awkwardly, "I'll go over there for you, Kristin. It's so slippery in the courtyard."

She stood outside the door and waited until he returned.

Then they sat down near the hearth, Kristin in the armchair and the boy on a three-legged stool nearby. After a moment Orm Erlendssøn said softly, "Tell me another story while we sit here, my stepmother."

"A story?" asked Kristin, her voice equally quiet.

"Yes, a tale or some such—that would be suitable on Christmas Eve," said the boy shyly.

Kristin leaned back in her chair and wrapped her thin hands around the animal heads on the armrests.

"That monk I mentioned—he had also been to England. And he said there is a region where wild rosebushes grow that bloom with white blossoms on Christmas night. Saint Joseph of Arimathea[8] put ashore in that area when he was fleeing from the heathens, and there he stuck his staff into the ground and it took root and flowered. He was the first to bring the Christian faith to Bretland. The name of the region is Glastonbury—now I remember. Brother Edvin had seen the bushes himself. King Arthur, whom you've no doubt heard stories of, was buried there in Glastonbury with his queen. He was one of the seven most noble defenders of Christendom.

"They say in England that Christ's Cross was made of alderwood. But we burned ash during Christmas at home, for it was the ash tree that Saint Joseph, the stepfather of Christ, used when he needed to light a fire for the Virgin Mary and the newborn Son of God. That's something else that Father heard from Brother Edvin."

"But very few ash trees grow up north here," said Orm. "They used them all up for spear poles in the olden days, you know. I don't think there are any ash trees here on Husaby's land other than the one standing east of the manor gate, and Father can't chop that one down, because the spirit of the first owner lives underneath.[9] But you know, Kristin, they have the Holy Cross in Romaborg; so they must be able to find out whether it was made of alderwood."

"Well," said Kristin, "I don't know whether it's true. For you know it's said that the cross was made from a shoot of the tree of life, which Seth was allowed to take from the Garden of Eden and bring home to Adam before he died."

"Yes," said Orm. "But then tell me . . ."

Some time later Kristin said to the boy, "Now you should lie down for a while, kinsman, and sleep. It will be a long time yet before the churchgoers return."

Orm stood up.

"We have not yet toasted each other as kinsmen, Kristin Lavransdatter." He went over and took a drinking horn from the table, drank to his stepmother, and handed her the vessel.

She felt as if ice water were running down her back. She couldn't help remembering that time when Orm's mother wanted to drink with her. And the child inside her womb began to thrash violently. What's going on with him tonight? wondered the mother. It seemed as if her unborn son felt everything that she felt, was cold when she was cold, and shrank in fear when she was frightened. But then I mustn't be so weak, thought Kristin. She took the horn and drank with her stepson.

When she handed it back to Orm, she gently stroked his dark hair. No, I'm certainly not going to be a harsh stepmother to you, she thought. You handsome, handsome son of Erlend.

She had fallen asleep in her chair when Erlend came home and tossed his frozen mittens onto the table.

"Are you back already?" said Kristin, astonished. "I thought you would stay for the daytime mass."

"Oh, two masses will last me for a long time," said Erlend as Kristin picked up his icy cape. "Yes, the sky is clear now, so the frost has set in."

"It was a shame that you forgot to wake Orm," said his wife.

"Was he sad about it?" asked Erlend. "I didn't actually forget," he went on in a low voice. "But he was sleeping so soundly, and I thought . . . You can well believe that people stared enough because I came to church without you. I didn't want to step forward with the boy at my side on top of that."

Kristin said nothing, but she felt distressed. She didn't think Erlend had handled this very well.

CHAPTER 3

THEY DID NOT have many guests at Husaby that Christmas.
Erlend didn't want to travel to any of the places where he was
invited; he stayed home on his manor and was in a bad humor.

As it turned out, he took this act of fate more to heart than his
wife could know. He had boasted so much of his betrothed, ever
since his kinsmen had won Lavrans's assent at Jørundgaard. This
was the last thing Erlend had wanted—for anyone to believe that
he considered her or her kinsmen to be lesser than his own people.
No, everyone must know that he held it to be an honor and a dis-
tinction when Lavrans Bjørgulfsøn betrothed him to his daughter.
Now people would say that Erlend had not considered the maiden
much more than a peasant child, since he had dared to offend her
father in such a manner, by sleeping with the daughter before she
had been given to him in marriage. At his wedding, Erlend had
urged his wife's parents to come to Husaby in the summer to see
how things were on his estate. He wanted to show them that it
was not to paltry circumstances that he had brought their daughter. But he had also looked forward to traveling around and being
seen in the company of these gracious and dignified in-laws; he
realized that Lavrans and Ragnfrid could hold their own among
the most esteemed of people, wherever they might go. And
ever since the time when he was at Jørundgaard and the church
burned down, Erlend had thought that Lavrans was rather fond of
him, in spite of everything. Now it was unlikely that the reunion
between Erlend and his wife's kinsmen would be pleasant for
either party.

It angered Kristin that Erlend so often took his ill temper out on
Orm. The boy had no children of his own age to play with, so he
was frequently peevish and in the way; he also got into a good deal
of mischief. One day he took his father's French crossbow without
permission, and something broke in the lock. Erlend was very an-

gry; he struck Orm on the ear and swore that the boy would not be allowed to touch a bow again at Husaby.

"It wasn't Orm's fault," said Kristin without turning around. She was sitting with her back to the two, sewing. "The spring was bent when he took it, and he tried to straighten it out. You can't be so unreasonable to refuse to allow this big son of yours to use a single bow out of all those you have on the estate. Why don't you give him one of the bows from up in the armory?"

"You can give him a bow yourself, if you feel like it," said Erlend furiously.

"I'll do that," replied Kristin in the same tone as before. "I'll speak to Ulf about it the next time he goes to town."

"You must go over and thank your kind stepmother, Orm," said Erlend, his voice derisive and angry.

Orm obeyed. And then he fled out the door as fast as he could. Erlend stood there for a moment.

"You did that mostly to annoy me, Kristin," he said.

"Yes, I know I'm a witch. You've said that before," replied his wife.

"Do you also remember, my sweet," said Erlend sadly, "that I didn't mean it seriously that time?"

Kristin neither answered nor looked up from her sewing. Then Erlend left, and afterwards she sat there and cried. She was fond of Orm, and she thought Erlend was often unreasonable toward his son. But the fact was that her husband's taciturn and aggrieved demeanor now tormented her so that she would lie in bed and weep half the night. And then she would walk around with an aching head the next day. Her hands had become so gaunt that she had to slip several small silver rings from her childhood days onto her fingers after her betrothal and wedding rings to keep them from falling off while she slept.

On the Sunday before Lent, late in the afternoon, Sir Baard Petersøn arrived unexpectedly at Husaby with his daughter, a widow, and Sir Munan Baardsøn and his wife. Erlend and Kristin went out to the courtyard to bid the guests welcome.

As soon as Sir Munan caught sight of Kristin, he slapped Erlend on the shoulder.

"I see that you've known how to treat your wife, kinsman, so that she is thriving on your estate. You're not so thin and miserable now as you were at your wedding, Kristin. And you have a much healthier color too," he laughed, for Kristin had turned as red as a rosehip.

Erlend did not reply. Sir Baard wore a dark expression, but the two women seemed neither to hear nor see a thing; they greeted their hosts formally and with courtesy.

Kristin had ale and mead brought over to the hearth while they waited for the food. Munan Baardsøn talked without stopping. He had letters for Erlend from the duchess—she was inquiring what had become of him and his bride: whether he was now married to the same maiden that he had wanted to carry off to Sweden. It was hellish traveling now, in midwinter—up through the valleys and by ship to Nidaros. But he was on the king's business, so it would do no good to grumble. He had stopped by to see his mother at Haugen and he brought them greetings from her.

"Were you at Jørundgaard?" Kristin ventured.

No, for he had heard that they had gone to a wake at Blakarsarv. A terrible event had occurred. The mistress, Tora, Ragnfrid's kinswoman, had fallen from the storeroom gallery and had broken her back, and it was her husband who had inadvertently pushed her out. It was one of those old storerooms without a proper gallery; there were merely several floorboards placed on top of the posts at the second-story level. They had been forced to tie up Rolv and keep watch over him night and day ever since the accident occurred. He wanted to lay hands on himself.

Everyone sat in silence, shivering. Kristin didn't know these kinsmen well, but they had come to her wedding. She felt suddenly strange and weak—everything went black before her eyes. Munan was sitting across from her and he leaped to his feet. When he stood over her, his arm around her shoulder, he looked so kind. Kristin realized that it was perhaps not so odd for Erlend to be fond of this cousin of his.

"I knew Rolv when we were young," he said. "People felt sorry for Tora Guttormsdatter—they said he was wild and hard-hearted. But now you can see that he cared for her. Oh yes, many a man may boast and pretend that he'd like to be rid of his spouse, but most men know full well that a wife is the worst thing they can lose—"

Baard Petersøn stood up abruptly and went over to the bench against the wall.

"May God curse my tongue," said Sir Munan in a low voice. "I can never remember to keep my mouth shut either. . . ."

Kristin didn't know what he meant. The dizziness was gone now, but she had such an unpleasant feeling; they all seemed so peculiar. She was glad when the servants brought in the food.

Munan looked at the table and rubbed his hands.

"I didn't think we'd be disappointed if we came to visit you, Kristin, before we have to gnaw on Lenten food. How have you managed to put together such delicious platters in such a short time? One would almost think you had learned to conjure from your mother. But I see that you're quick to set forth everything a wife should offer to please her husband."

They sat down at the table. Velvet cushions had been placed for the guests on the inner benches on either side of the high seat. The servants sat on the outer bench, with Ulf Haldorssøn in the middle, right across from Erlend.

Kristin chatted quietly with the women guests and tried to conceal how ill at ease she felt. Every once in a while Munan Baardsøn would interrupt with words that were meant to tease, and it was always about how Kristin was already moving so slowly. She pretended not to hear.

Munan was an unusually stout man. His small, shapely ears were set deep in the ruddy, fat flesh above his neck, and his belly got in his way when he sat down at the table.

"Yes, I've often wondered about the resurrection of the body," he said. "Whether I'm going to rise up with all this fat that I've put on when that day arrives. You'll be slim-waisted again soon enough, Kristin—but it's much worse for me. You may not believe it, but I was just as slender in the belt as Erlend over there when I was twenty winters old."

"Stop it now, Munan," begged Erlend softly. "You're upsetting Kristin."

"All right then, if that's what you want," replied Munan. "You must be proud now, I can well imagine—presiding over your own table, sitting in the high seat with your wedded wife beside you. And God Almighty knows that it's about time, too—you're plenty old enough, my boy! Of course I'll keep my mouth shut, since that's what you want. But nobody ever told *you* . . . to speak or keep still—back when you were sitting at *my* table. You were often a guest in my house and stayed a long time, and I don't think I ever noticed that you weren't welcome.

"But I wonder whether Kristin dislikes it so much that I tease her a little. What do you say, my fair kinswoman? You weren't as timid in the past. I've known Erlend from the time he was only so high, and I think I can venture to say that I've wished the boy well all his days. Quick and boyish you are, Erlend, with a sword in your hand, whether on horseback or on board ship. But I'll ask Saint Olav to cleave me in half with his axe on the day when I see you stand up on your long legs, look man or woman freely in the eye, and answer for what you have done in your thoughtlessness. No, my dear kinsman, then you will hang your head like a bird in a trap and call on God and your kinsmen to help you out of trouble. And you're such a sensible woman, Kristin, that I imagine you know this. I think you need to laugh a little now; no doubt you've seen enough this winter of shameful memories and sorrows and regrets."

Kristin sat there, her face deep red. Her hands were trembling, and she didn't dare glance at Erlend. Fury was boiling inside her—here sat the women guests and Orm and the servants. So this was the kind of courtesy shown by Erlend's rich kinsmen. . . .

Then Sir Baard said so quietly that only those sitting closest could hear him, "I don't think this is something to banter about—that Erlend has behaved in this way before his marriage. I vouched for you, Erlend, to Lavrans Bjørgulfsøn."

"Yes, and that was devilishly unwise of you, my foster father," said Erlend loudly and fervently. "I can't understand that you could be so foolish. For you know me well."

But Munan was completely intractable.

"Now I'm going to tell you why I think this is so funny. Do you remember what you said to me, Baard, when I came to you and said that we had to help Erlend to achieve this marriage? No, I *am* going to talk about it; Erlend should know what you thought about me. This is the way it stands between them, I said, and if he doesn't win Kristin Lavransdatter, only God and the Virgin Mary know what madness will result. Then you asked me if that was the real reason I wanted him to marry the maiden he had seduced,

because I thought perhaps she was barren since she had managed
to escape for so long. But I think you know me, all of you; you
know that I'm a faithful kinsman to my kin. . . ." And he broke
into tears of emotion.

"As God is my witness along with all holy men: never have I
coveted your property, kinsman—because otherwise there is only
Gunnulf between me and Husaby. But I said to you, Baard, as you
know—to Kristin's firstborn son I would give my gold-encrusted
dagger with its walrus-tusk sheath. Here, take it," he shouted, sobbing, and he tossed the magnificent weapon across the table to her.
"If it's not a son this time, then it'll be one next year."

Tears of shame and anger were pouring down Kristin's hot
cheeks. She struggled fiercely not to break down. But the two
women guests sat and ate as calmly as if they were used to such
commotion. And Erlend whispered that she should take the dagger
"or Munan will just keep on all night."

"Yes, and I'm not going to hide the fact," Munan went on,
"that I wish your father could see, Kristin, that he was too quick
to defend your soul. So arrogant Lavrans was—we weren't good
enough for him, Baard and I, and you were much too delicate and
pure to tolerate a man like Erlend in your bed. He talked as if he
didn't believe that you could stand to do anything in the nighttime
hours except sing in the nuns' choir. I said to him, 'Dear Lavrans,'
I said, 'your daughter is a beautiful and healthy and lively young
maiden, and the winter nights are long and cold here in this
country. . . .' "

Kristin pulled her wimple over her face. She was sobbing loudly
and tried to get up, but Erlend pulled her back down in her seat.

"Try to get hold of yourself," he said vehemently. "Don't pay
any attention to Munan—you can see for yourself that he's dead
drunk."

She sensed that Fru Katrin and Fru Vilborg thought it pitiable
that she didn't have better command of herself. But she couldn't
stop her tears.

Baard Petersøn said furiously to Munan, "Shut your rotten
trap. You've been a swine all your days—but even so, you can
spare an ill woman from that filthy talk of yours."

"Did you say swine? Yes, I do have more bastard children than
you do, be that as it may. But one thing I've never done—and

Erlend hasn't either—we've never paid another man to be the child's father for us."

"Munan!" shouted Erlend, springing to his feet. "Now I demand peace here in my hall!"

"Oh, demand peace in your backside! My children call the man 'father' who sired them—in my swinish life, as you call it!" Munan pounded the table so the cups and small plates danced. "Our sons don't go around as servants in the house of our kinsmen. But here sits your son across the table from you, and he's sitting on the servants' bench. That seems to me the worst of all shame."

Baard leaped up and threw his goblet into the other man's face. The two fell upon each other so the table plank tipped onto its side, and food and vessels slid into the laps of those sitting on the outer bench.

Kristin sat there white-faced, with her mouth agape. Once she stole a glance at Ulf—the man was laughing openly, crudely and maliciously. Then he tipped the table plank back into place and shoved it against the two combatants.

Erlend leaped up onto the table. Kneeling in the middle of the mess, he seized hold of Munan's arms, then grabbed him under the armpits and hauled him up next to him; he turned bright red in the face from the effort. Munan managed to give Baard a kick so that the old man began to bleed from the mouth—then Erlend flung Munan over the table and out onto the floor. He jumped down after him, and stood there huffing like a bellows.

The other man got to his feet and rushed at Erlend, who slipped under his arms a couple of times. Then he fell on Munan and held him entangled in the grip of his long, supple limbs. Erlend was as agile as a cat, but Munan held his ground; strong and bulky, he refused to be forced to the floor. They whirled around and around the room while the serving women shrieked and screamed, and none of the men made a move to separate them.

Then Fru Katrin stood up, heavy and fat and slow; she stepped onto the table as calmly as if she were walking up the storehouse stairs.

"Stop that now," she said in her husky, sated voice. "Let go of him, Erlend! It was wrong, husband—to speak that way to an old man and close kinsman."

The men obeyed her. Munan stood meekly and let his wife wipe

his bloody nose with her wimple. She told him to go to bed, and
he followed docilely when she led him away to the bed on the
south wall. His wife and one of his servants pulled the clothes off
him, toppled him into the bed, and closed the door.

Erlend had walked over to the table. He leaned past Ulf, who
was still sitting as he had before.

"Foster father," said Erlend unhappily. He seemed to have completely forgotten his wife. Sir Baard sat and rocked his head back
and forth, and the tears were dripping down his cheeks.

"He didn't have to become a servant, Ulf didn't," were the
words that came out, but his sobs lodged, gasping, in his chest.
"You could have taken the farm after Haldor, you know that's
what I intended. . . ."

"It wasn't a very good farm that you gave Haldor; you bought
a cheap husband for your wife's serving maid," said Ulf. "He fixed
it up and managed it well, and it seemed to me reasonable that my
brothers should take it over after their father. That's one thing. But
I had no desire to end up as a farmer, either—and least of all up on
the slope, staring down at the Hestnes courtyard. It seemed to me
that I heard every day that Paal and Vilborg were going around
saying vicious things about how you gave much too grand a gift to
your bastard son."

"I offered to help you, Ulf," said Baard, weeping. "When you
wanted to go out traveling with Erlend. I told you everything as
soon as you were old enough to understand. I begged you to return to your father."

"I call the man my father who looked after me when I was
small. That man was Haldor. He was good to Mother and to me.
He taught me to ride a horse and to fight with a sword—the way a
farmer wields his club, I remember Paal once said."

Ulf flung the knife he was holding so that it clattered across the
table. Then he got to his feet, picked up the knife, wiped it on the
back of his thigh, and stuck it in its sheath. He turned to Erlend.
"Put an end to this feast now and send the servants to bed! Can't
you see that your wife is still not used to the banquet customs we
have in our family?"

And with that he left the hall.

Sir Baard stared after him. He seemed so pitifully old and frail
as he sat slumped among the velvet cushions. His daughter, Vil-

borg, and one of his servants helped Baard to his feet and escorted him out.

Kristin sat alone in the high seat, weeping and weeping. When Erlend touched her, she angrily struck his hand aside. She swayed a few times as she walked across the floor, but she replied with a curt "no" when her husband asked if she was ill.

She detested these closed beds. Back home they simply had tapestries hung up facing the room, and thus it was never hot or stuffy. But now it was worse than ever . . . it was so hard for her to breathe. She thought that the hard lump pressing on her all the way up under her ribcage must be the child's head; she imagined him lying with his little black head burrowed in amongst the roots of her heart. He was suffocating her, as Erlend had done before when he pressed his dark-haired head to her breast. But tonight there was no sweetness in the thought.

"Will you never stop your crying?" asked her husband, trying to ease his arm under her shoulder.

He was quite sober. He could tolerate a great deal of liquor, but he usually drank very little. Kristin thought that never in all eternity would this have happened back at her home—never had she heard people fling slanderous words at each other or rip open something that would be better left unsaid. As many times as she had seen her father reeling from intoxication and the hall full of drunken guests, there was *never* a time when he couldn't keep order in his own house. Peace and good will reigned right up until everyone tumbled off the benches and fell asleep in joy and harmony.

"My dearest wife, don't take this so hard," implored Erlend.

"And Sir Baard!" she burst into tears. "Shame on such behavior—this man who spoke to my father as if he were bearing God's message. Yes, Munan told me about it at our betrothal banquet."

Erlend said softly, "I know, Kristin, that I have reason to cast down my eyes before your father. He's a fine man—but my foster father is no worse. Inga, the mother of Paal and Vilborg, lay paralyzed and ill for six years before she died. That was before I came to Hestnes, but I've heard about it. Never has a husband tended to an ailing wife in a more faithful or loving manner. But it was during that time that Ulf was born."

"Then it was an even greater sin—with his sick wife's maid."

"You often act so childish that it's impossible to talk to you," said Erlend in resignation. "God help me, Kristin, you're going to be twenty this spring—and several winters have passed since you had to be considered a grown-up woman."

"Yes, it's true that *you* have the right to scoff at me for that."

Erlend moaned loudly.

"You know yourself that I didn't mean it like that. But you lived all that time at Jørundgaard and listened to Lavrans—so splendid and manly he is, but he often talks as if he were a monk and not a grown man."

"Have you ever heard of any monk who has had six children?" she said, offended.

"I've heard of that man, Skurda-Grim, and he had seven," said Erlend in despair. "The former abbot at Holm . . . No, Kristin, Kristin, don't cry like that. In God's name, I think you've lost your senses."

Munan was quite subdued the next morning. "I didn't think you would take my ale-babble so much to heart, young Kristin," he said somberly, stroking her cheek. "Or I would have kept better watch on my tongue."

He said to Erlend that it must be strange for Kristin with the boy being there. It would be best to send Orm away for the time being. Munan offered to take him in for a while. Erlend approved, and Orm wanted to go with Munan. But Kristin missed the child deeply; she had grown fond of her stepson.

Now she once again sat alone with Erlend in the evenings, and there was not much companionship in him. He would sit over by the hearth, say a few words now and then, take a drink from the ale bowl, and play with his dogs. He would go over to the bench and stretch out—and then he would go to bed, asking a couple of times whether she was coming soon, and then he'd fall asleep.

Kristin sat and sewed. Her breathing was audible, shallow and heavy. But it wouldn't be long now. She couldn't even remember how it felt to be light and slim in the waist—or how to tie her shoes without strain and effort.

Now that Erlend was asleep she no longer tried to hold back her tears. There was not a sound in the hall except the firewood collapsing in the hearth and the dogs stirring. Sometimes she wondered what they had talked about before, she and Erlend. But then they hadn't talked much—they had had other things to do in those brief, stolen hours together.

At this time of year her mother and the maids used to sit in the weaving room in the evenings. Then her father and the men would come to join them and sit down with their work—they would repair leather goods and farm tools and make carvings out of wood. The little room would be crowded with people; conversation flowed quietly and easily among them. Whenever somebody went over to drink from the ale keg, before he hung up the ladle he would always ask whether anyone else would like some—that was the custom.

Then someone would recite a short saga—perhaps about giants in the past who had fought with grave-barrow ghosts and giantesses. Or her father, as he whittled, would recount those tales of knights that he had heard read aloud in Duke Haakon's hall when he was a page in his youth. Strange and beautiful names: King Osantrix, Titurel the knight; Sisibe, Guinevere, Gloriana, and Isolde were the names of the queens. But on other evenings they told bawdy tales and ribald sagas until the men were roaring with laughter and her mother and the maids would shake their heads and giggle.

Ulvhild and Astrid would sing. Ragnfrid had the loveliest voice of all, but they had to plead before they could get her to sing. Lavrans didn't need such persuasion—and he could play his harp so beautifully.

Then Ulvhild would put down her distaff and spindle and press her hands behind her hips.

"Is your back tired now, little Ulvhild?" asked her father, taking her onto his lap. Someone would bring a board game and Ulvhild and her father would move the markers around until it was time for bed. Kristin remembered her little sister's golden locks flowing over her father's brownish-green homespun sleeve. He held the weak little back so tenderly.

Her father's big, slender hands with a heavy gold ring on each little finger . . . They had both belonged to his mother. He had said that the one with the red stone, her wedding ring, Kristin would inherit from him. But the one that he wore on his right hand, with a stone that was half blue and half white, like the emblem on his shield—that one Sir Bjørgulf had ordered made for his wife when she was with child, and it was to be given to her when she had borne him a son. For three nights Kristin Sigurdsdatter had worn the ring; then she tied it around the boy's neck, and Lavrans said that he would wear it to his grave.

Oh, what would her father say when he heard the news about her? When it spread throughout the villages back home, and he had to realize that wherever he went, to church or to the *ting*[1] or to a meeting, every man would be laughing behind his back because he had allowed himself to be fooled? At Jørundgaard they had adorned a wanton woman with the Sundbu crown on her flowing hair.

"People are no doubt saying of me that I can't keep my children in check." She remembered her father's face whenever he said that; he meant to be stern and somber, but his eyes were merry. She had misbehaved in some small way—spoken to him uninvited while guests were present or some such. "And you, Kristin, you don't have much fear of your father, do you?" Then he would laugh, and she laughed along with him. "Yes, but that's not right, Kristin." And neither of them knew *what* was not right—that she didn't have the proper terror of her father, or that it was impossible for him to remain serious when he had to scold her.

It was as if the unbearable fear that something would be wrong with her child diminished and faded away the more trouble and torment Kristin had from her body. She tried to think ahead—to a month from now; by then her son would have already been born. But it didn't seem real to her. She simply yearned more and more for home.

Once Erlend asked Kristin if she wanted him to send for her mother. But she told him no—she didn't think her mother could stand to travel so far in the winter. Now she regretted this. And she regretted that she had said no to Tordis of Laugarbru, who had been so willing to accompany her north and lend a hand during the first winter she was to be mistress. But she felt ashamed before Tordis. Tordis had been Ragnfrid's maid at home at Sundbu and had accompanied her to Skog and then back to the valley. When Tordis married, Lavrans had made her husband a foreman at Jørundgaard because Ragnfrid couldn't bear to be without her beloved maid. Kristin had not wanted to bring along any of the maids from home.

Now it seemed to her terrible that she would have no familiar face above her when her time came to kneel on the floor.[2] She was frightened—she knew so little about what went on at childbirth. Her mother had never spoken to her of it and had never wanted young maidens to be present when she helped a woman give birth. It would only frighten the young, she said. It could certainly be dreadful; Kristin remembered when her mother had Ulvhild. But Ragnfrid said it was because she had inadvertently crawled under a fence—she had given birth to her other children with ease. But Kristin remembered that she herself had been thoughtless and had walked under a rope on board ship.

But that didn't always cause harm—she had heard her mother and other women speak of such things. Ragnfrid had a reputation back home in the village for being the best midwife, and she never refused to go and help, no matter if it was a beggar or the poorest man's seduced daughter, or if the weather was such that three men had to accompany her on skis and take turns carrying her on their backs.

But it was completely unthinkable that an experienced woman like her mother hadn't realized what was wrong with her this past summer, when she was feeling so wretched. It suddenly occurred to Kristin: but then . . . then it was certain that her mother would come, even though they hadn't sent for her! Ragnfrid would never stand for a stranger helping her daughter through the struggle. Her mother was coming—she was probably on her way north right now. Oh, then she could ask for her mother's forgiveness for all the pain she had caused her. Her own mother would support her, she would kneel at her own mother's knees when she gave birth to her child. Mother is coming, Mother is coming. Kristin sobbed with relief, covering her face with her hands. Yes, Mother; forgive me, Mother.

This thought, that her mother was on her way to be with her, became so entrenched in Kristin's mind that one day she thought she could sense that her mother would arrive that very day. In the early morning she put on her cloak and went out to meet her on the road which leads from Gauldal to Skaun. No one noticed her leave the estate.

Erlend had ordered timber to be brought for the improvement of the buildings, so the road was good, but walking was still difficult for her. She was short of breath, her heart pounded, and she had a pain in both sides—it felt as if the taut skin would burst apart after she had walked a short while. And most of the road passed through dense forest. She was afraid, but there had been no word of wolves in the area that winter. And God would protect her, since she was on her way to meet her mother, to fall down before her and beg forgiveness—and she could not stop walking.

She reached a small lake where there were several farms. At the spot where the road led out onto the ice, she sat down on a log. She sat there for a while, walked a little farther when she began to freeze, and waited for many hours. But at last she had to turn back and head for home.

The next day she wandered along the same road. But when she crossed the courtyard of one of the small farms near the lake, the farmer's wife came running after her.

"In God's name, mistress, you mustn't do that!"

When the other woman spoke, Kristin grew so frightened herself that she didn't dare move. Trembling, her eyes wide with fear, she stared at the farmer's wife.

"Through the woods—just think if a wolf caught your scent. Other terrible things could happen to you, too. How can you do something so foolish?"

The farmer's wife put her arm around the young mistress and supported her; she looked into Kristin's gaunt face with the yellowish, brown-flecked skin.

"You must come into our house and rest for a while. Then someone from here will escort you home," said the farmer's wife as she led Kristin indoors.

It was a cramped and impoverished house, and there was great disarray inside; many little children were playing on the floor. Their mother sent them out to the cookhouse, took her guest's cloak, seated her on a bench, and pulled off her snowy shoes. Then she wrapped a fur around Kristin's feet.

No matter how much Kristin begged the woman not to trouble herself, the farmer's wife continued to dish up food and ale from the Christmas cask. All the while the woman thought: So that's how things are at Husaby! She was a poor man's wife; they had little help on the farm, and usually none at all; but Øistein had never allowed her to walk alone outside the courtyard fence when she was with child—yes, even if she was just going out to the cowshed after dark, someone would have to keep watch for her. But the richest mistress in the parish could go out and risk the most hideous death, and not a Christian soul was looking out for her—even though the servants were falling over each other at Husaby and did no work. It must be true then what people said, that Erlend Nikulaussøn was already tired of his marriage and cared nothing for his wife.

But she chatted with Kristin the whole time and urged her to eat and drink. And Kristin was thoroughly ashamed, but she had a craving for food such as she had not felt before—not since the spring. This kind woman's food tasted so good. And the woman laughed and said that the gentry's women probably were created no different from other people. If a woman couldn't stand to look at food at home, someone else's food could often make her almost greedy, even if it was poor and coarse fare.

Her name was Audfinna Andunsdatter, and she was from Updal, she said. When she noticed that it put her guest at ease, she began to talk about her home and her village. And before Kristin knew it, her own tongue was loosened, and she was talking about her own home and her parents and her village. Audfinna could see that the young woman's heart was almost bursting with homesickness, so she stealthily prodded Kristin to keep talking. Hot and giddy from the ale, Kristin talked until she was laughing and crying at the same time. All that she had futilely tried to sob out of her heart during the lonely evening hours at Husaby, now was gradually released as she spoke to this kind farmer's wife.

It was quite dark above the smoke vent, but Audfinna wanted Kristin to wait for Øistein or her sons to return from the woods so they could accompany her. Kristin fell silent and grew drowsy, but she sat there smiling, her eyes shining—she hadn't felt this way since she had to come to Husaby.

Then a man tore open the door, shouting: Had they seen any sign of the mistress? Then he noticed her and went back outside. A moment later Erlend's tall figure ducked through the doorway. He set down the axe he was carrying and leaned back against the wall. He had to put his hands behind him to support himself, and he could not speak.

"You have feared for your wife?" asked Audfinna, going over to him.

"Yes, I'm not ashamed to admit it." Erlend pushed back his hair. "No man has ever been as frightened as I was tonight. When I heard that she had gone through the woods . . ."

Audfinna told him how Kristin had happened to come there. Erlend took the woman's hand.

"I will never forget this—either you or your husband," he said.

Then he went over to where his wife was sitting, stood next to her, and placed his hand on the back of her neck. He didn't say a word to her, but he stood there like that for as long as they remained in the house.

Now they all came inside, the servants from Husaby and men from the nearest farms. Everyone looked as if they could use something fortifying to drink, so Audfinna served ale all around before they left.

The men set off on skis across the fields, but Erlend had given his to a servant; he walked along, holding Kristin under his cape, and headed down the slope. It was quite dark now, but a starry night.

Then they heard it from the forest behind them—a long, drawn-out howl that grew and grew in the night. It was the howl of the wolf—and there were several of them. Shivering, Erlend stopped and let Kristin go. She sensed that he crossed himself while he gripped the axe in his other hand. "If you were now . . . oh, no!" He pulled her to him so hard that she whimpered.

The skiers out in the field turned around and made their way back toward the two as fast as they could. They slung the skis over their shoulders and closed around her in a tight group with spears and axes. The wolves followed them all the way to Husaby—so close that once or twice they caught a glimpse of the beasts in the dark.

When the men entered the hall at home, many of them were gray or white in the face. "That was the most horrifying . . ." said one man, and he at once threw up into the hearth. The frightened maids put their mistress to bed. She could eat nothing. But now that the terrible, sickening fear was over, in an odd way she thought it was good to see that everyone had been so scared on her behalf.

When they were alone in the hall, Erlend came over and sat on the edge of the bed.

"Why did you do that?" he whispered. And when she didn't reply, he said even more softly, "Do you so regret that you came to my manor?"

It took a moment before she realized what he meant.

"Jesus, Maria! How can you think something like that!"

"What did you mean that time when you said—when we were at Medalby, and I was going to ride away from you—that I would have had to wait a good long time before you followed me to Husaby?" he asked in the same tone of voice.

"Oh, I spoke in anger," said Kristin quietly, embarrassed. And now she told him why she had gone out these past few days. Erlend sat quite still and listened to her.

"I wonder when the day will come when you'll think of Husaby here with me as your home," he said, bending toward her in the dark.

"Oh, that time is probably no more than a week away," whispered Kristin, laughing uncertainly. When he lay his face next to hers, she threw her arms around his neck and returned his ardent kisses.

"That's the first time you've ventured to embrace me since I struck you," said Erlend in a low voice. "You hold a grudge for a long time, my Kristin."

It occurred to her that this was the first time, since the night when he realized that she was with child, that she dared to caress him without his asking.

But after that day, Erlend was so kind to her that Kristin regretted every hour that she had spent feeling angry toward him.

CHAPTER 4

Saint Gregor's Day came and went, and Kristin had thought that surely her time would have come by then. But now it would soon be the Feast of the Annunciation, and she was still on her feet.

Erlend had to go to Nidaros for the mid-Lenten *ting*; he said he would certainly be home on Monday evening, but by Wednesday morning he had still not returned. Kristin sat in the hall and didn't know what to do with herself—she felt as if she couldn't bear to start on anything.

Sunlight came flooding down through the smoke vent, and she sensed that outdoors it must be an almost springlike day. Then she stood up and threw a cloak around her shoulders.

One of the maids had mentioned that if a woman carried a child too long, then a good remedy was to let the bridal horse eat grain from her lap. Kristin paused for a moment in the doorway— in the dazzling sunshine the courtyard looked quite brown with glistening rivulets that had washed shiny, icy stripes through the horse manure and dirt. The sky arched bright and silky-blue above the old buildings, and the two dragon figureheads which were carved into the gables of the eastern storehouse glistened against the sky with the remnants of ancient gilding. Water dripped and trickled off the roofs, and smoke whirled and danced in the little, warm gusts of wind.

She walked over to the stable and went inside, filling her skirt with oats from the grain chest. The smell of the stable and the sound of the horses stirring in the dark did her good. But there were people in the stable, so she didn't have the nerve to do what she had come for.

She went out and threw the grain to the chickens that were strutting around in the courtyard, sunning themselves. Absent-mindedly she watched Tore, the stableboy, who was grooming and brushing the gray gelding, which was shedding heavily. Once in a while she would close her eyes and turn her wan, house-pale face up toward the sun.

As Kristin was standing like that, three men rode into the court-yard. The one in front was a young priest she didn't know. As soon as he saw Kristin, he jumped down from his saddle and came straight over to her with his hand outstretched.

"I doubt you had intended to do me this honor, mistress, of standing outside to receive me," he said, smiling. "But I thank you for it all the same. For you must certainly be my brother's wife, Kristin Lavransdatter?"

"Then you must be Master Gunnulf, my brother-in-law," she replied, blushing crimson. "Well met, sir! And welcome home to Husaby!"

"Thank you for your kind greeting," said the priest. He bent down to kiss her cheek in the manner which she knew was the cus-tom abroad, when kinsmen meet. "I hope I find you well, Erlend's wife!"

Ulf Haldorssøn came out and told a servant to take the guests' horses. Gunnulf greeted Ulf heartily.

"Are you here, kinsman? I had expected to find you now a mar-ried and settled man."

"No, I won't be marrying until I have to choose between a wife and the gallows," said Ulf with a laugh, and the priest laughed too. "I've made the Devil as firm a promise to live unwed as you have promised the same to God."

"Well, then you'll be safe, no matter which way you turn, Ulf," replied Master Gunnulf, laughing. "Since you'll do well the day you break the promise that you've given. But then it is also said that a man should keep his word, even if it's to the Devil himself.

"Isn't Erlend home?" he asked, surprised. He offered Kristin his hand as they turned to go into the main house.

To hide her shyness, Kristin busied herself among the servant women and tended to the setting of the table. She invited Erlend's learned brother to sit in the high seat, but since she didn't want to sit there with him, he moved down to the bench next to her.

Now that he was sitting at her side, Kristin saw that Master Gunnulf must be at least half a head shorter than Erlend, but he was much heavier. He was stronger and stockier in build and limbs, and his broad shoulders were perfectly straight. Erlend's shoulders drooped a bit. Gunnulf wore dark clothing, very proper for a priest, but his ankle-length surcoat, which came almost up to the neckband of his linen shirt, was fastened with enameled buttons; from his woven belt hung his eating utensils in a silver sheath.

She glanced up at the priest's face. He had a strong, round head and a lean, round face with a broad, low forehead, somewhat prominent cheekbones, and a finely rounded chin. His nose was straight and his ears small and lovely, but his mouth was wide, and his upper lip protruded slightly, overshadowing the little patch of red made by his lower lip. Only his hair looked like Erlend's—the thick fringe around the priest's shaved crown was black with the luster of dry soot and it looked as silky-soft as Erlend's hair. Otherwise he was not unlike his cousin Munan Baardsøn—now Kristin could see that it might be true after all that Munan had been handsome in his youth. No, it was his Aunt Aashild whom he resembled—now she saw that he had the same eyes as Fru Aashild: amber-colored and bright beneath narrow, straight black eyebrows.

At first Kristin was a little shy of this brother-in-law who had been educated in so many fields of knowledge at the great universities of Paris and Italy. But little by little she lost her embarrassment. It was so easy to talk to Gunnulf. It didn't seem as if he were talking about himself—least of all that he wanted to boast about his learning. But before she knew it, he had told her about so many things that Kristin felt she had never before realized what a vast world there was outside Norway. She forgot about herself and everything around her as she sat and looked up into the priest's round, strong-boned face with the bright and delicate smile. He had crossed one leg over the other under his surcoat, and he sat there with his white, powerful hands clasped around his ankle.

Later in the afternoon, when Gunnulf came into the room to join her, he asked whether they might play a board game. Kristin had to tell him that she didn't think there were any board games in the house.

"Aren't there?" asked the priest in surprise. He went over to Ulf.

"Do you know, Ulf, what Erlend has done with Mother's gold board game? The amusements that she left behind—surely he hasn't let anyone have them?"

"They're in a chest up in the armory," said Ulf. "It's more likely that he didn't want anyone who once lived here on the estate to take them. Shall we go and get the chest, Gunnulf?"

"Yes, Erlend can't have anything against that," said the priest.

A little while later the two men came back with a large, carved chest. The key was in the lock, so Gunnulf opened it. On top lay a zither and another stringed instrument, the like of which Kristin had never seen before. Gunnulf called it a psaltery; he ran his fingers over the strings, but it was badly out of tune. There were also twists of silk, embroidered gloves, silken scarves, and three books with metal clasps. Finally, the priest found the board game; it was checked, with white and gilt tiles, and the markers were made of walrus tusk, white and golden.

Not until then did Kristin realize that in all the time she had been at Husaby, she hadn't seen a single amusement of this type that people might use to pass the time.

Kristin now had to admit to her brother-in-law that she wasn't very clever at board games, nor was she much good at playing the zither. But she was eager to take a look at the books.

"Ah, have you learned to read books, Kristin?" asked the priest, and she could tell him rather proudly that she had already learned to do so as a child. And at the convent she had won praise for her skill in reading and writing.

The priest stood over her, smiling, as she paged through the books. One of them was a courtly tale about Tristan and Isolde,[1] and the other was about holy men—she looked up Saint Martin's story.[2] The third book was in Latin and was particularly beautiful, printed with great, colorful initial letters.

"Our ancestor, Bishop Nikulaus, owned this book," said Gunnulf.

Kristin read half-aloud:

*Averte faciem tuam a peccatis meis
et omnes iniquitates meas dele.
Cor mundum crea in me, Deus
et spiritum rectum innova in visceribus meis.*

*Ne projicias me a facie tua
et Spiritum Sanctum tuum ne auferas a me.*[3]

"Can you understand it?" asked Gunnulf, and Kristin nodded and said that she understood a little. The words were familiar enough that it seemed strange to her that they should appear before her right now. Her face contorted and tears rose up. Then Gunnulf set the stringed instrument on his lap and said he was tempted to try to tune it.

As they sat there they heard horses out in the courtyard, and a moment later Erlend rushed into the hall, beaming with joy. He had heard who had arrived. The brothers stood with their hands on each other's shoulders; Erlend asking questions and not waiting for the replies. Gunnulf had been in Nidaros for two days, so it was a wonder they hadn't met there.

"It's odd," said Erlend. "I thought the whole clergy of Christ Church would have turned out in procession to meet you when you returned home—so wise and exceedingly learned as you now must be."

"How do you know they didn't do just that?" said his brother with a laugh. "I've heard that you never venture too close to Christ Church when you're in town."

"No, my boy—I don't get too close to my Lord the Archbishop if I can avoid it. He once singed my hide," laughed Erlend insolently. "How do you like your brother-in-law, my sweet? I see you've already made friends with Kristin, brother. She thinks very little of our other kinsmen. . . ."

Not until they were about to sit down to eat that evening did Erlend realize he was still wearing his cape and fur cap and his sword at his belt.

That was the merriest evening Kristin had spent at Husaby. Erlend cajoled his brother into sitting in the high seat with her, while he himself sliced off food for him and replenished his goblet. The first time he drank a toast to Gunnulf, he got down on one knee and tried to kiss his brother's hand.

"Health and happiness, sir! We must learn to show the archbishop the proper respect, Kristin—yes, of course, you'll be the archbishop someday, Gunnulf!"

It was late when the house servants left the hall, but the two brothers and Kristin remained behind, sitting over their drink. Erlend was seated atop the table with his face turned toward his brother.

"Yes, I thought about that during my wedding," he said, pointing to his mother's chest, "and that Kristin should have it. And yet I forget things so quickly, while you forget nothing, my brother. But I think Mother's ring has come to grace a fair hand, don't you?" He placed Kristin's hand on his knee and twisted her betrothal ring around.

Gunnulf nodded. He placed the psaltery on Erlend's lap. "Sing now, brother. You used to sing so beautifully and play so well."

"That was many years ago," said Erlend more somberly. Then he ran his fingers over the strings.

> Olav the king, Harald's son,
> rode out in the thick woods,
> found a tiny footprint there—
> and so the news is great.
>
> Then said he, Finn Arnessøn,
> riding before the band:
> Fair must be so small a foot,
> clad in scarlet hose.

Erlend smiled as he sang, and Kristin looked up at the priest a little shyly—to see whether the ballad of Saint Olav and Alvhild might displease him. But Gunnulf sat there smiling too, and yet she suddenly felt certain that it was not because of the ballad but because of Erlend.

"Kristin doesn't have to sing; you must be short of breath now, my dear," Erlend said, caressing her cheek. "But *you* can. . . ." He handed the stringed instrument to his brother.

It could be heard in the priest's playing and in his voice that he had learned well in school.

> North over the mountains rode the king—
> He heard the dove lament bitterly:
> "The hawk took my sweetheart away from me!"

> Then he rode so far and wide
> The hawk flew over the countryside.
>
> Into a garden the hawk then flew,
> Where it blossoms ever anew.
> In that garden there is a hall,
> Draped with purple over all.
>
> There lies a knight, seeping blood,
> He is our Lord so fine and good.
>
> Beneath the blue scarlet he does lie
> And etched atop: *Corpus domini*.

"Where did you learn that ballad?" asked Erlend.

"Oh. Some fellows were singing it outside the hostel where I was staying in Canterbury," said Gunnulf. "And I was tempted to turn it into Norwegian. But it doesn't work so well. . . ." He sat there strumming a few notes on the strings.

"Well, brother, it's long past midnight. Kristin must need to go to bed. Are you tired, my wife?"

Kristin looked up at the men timidly; she was very pale.

"I don't know . . . But I don't think I should sleep in the bed in here."

"Are you ill?" they both asked, bending toward her.

"I don't know," she replied in the same voice. She pressed her hands to her flanks. "It feels so strange in the small of my back."

Erlend leaped up and headed for the door. Gunnulf followed. "It's shameful that you haven't yet brought the women here who will help her," he said. "Is it long before her time?"

Erlend turned bright red.

"Kristin said she didn't need anyone but her maids. They've borne children themselves, some of them." He tried to laugh.

"Have you lost your senses?" Gunnulf stared at him. "Even the poorest wench has servant women and neighbors with her when she takes to childbed. Should your wife crawl into a corner to hide and give birth like a cat? No, brother, so much a man you must be that you bring to Kristin the foremost women of the parish."

Erlend bowed his head, blushing with shame.

"You speak the truth, brother. I will ride down to Raasvold myself, and I'll send men to the other farms. You must stay with Kristin."

"Are you going away?" asked his wife, frightened, when she saw Erlend put on his outer garments.

He went over to Kristin and put his arms around her.

"I'm going to bring back the noblest women for you, my Kristin. Gunnulf will stay with you while the maids get ready for you in the little house," he said, kissing her.

"Couldn't you send word to Audfinna Audunsdatter?" she pleaded. "But not until morning—I don't want her to be wakened from her sleep for my sake—she has so much work to do, I know."

Gunnulf asked his brother who Audfinna was.

"It doesn't seem to me proper," said the priest. "The wife of one of your leaseholders—"

"Kristin must have whatever she wants," said Erlend. And as Gunnulf accompanied him out and Erlend waited for his horse, he told the priest how Kristin had come to meet the farmer's wife. Gunnulf bit his lip and looked pensive.

Now there was noise and commotion on the estate; men rode off and servant women came running in to ask how their mistress was faring. Kristin said there was nothing to worry about yet, but they were to make everything ready in the little house. She would send word when she wanted to be escorted there.

Then she sat alone with the priest. She tried to talk calmly and cheerfully with him as she had before.

"You're not afraid then?" he asked with a little smile.

"Yes, of course, I'm afraid!" She looked up into his eyes—her own were dark and frightened. "Can you tell me, brother-in-law, whether they were born here at Husaby—Erlend's other children?"

"No," replied the priest quickly. "The boy was born at Hune-hals, and the maiden over at Strind, on an estate that he once owned there." A moment later he asked, "Is that it? Has the thought of that other woman here with Erlend tormented you?"

"Yes," said Kristin.

"It would be difficult for you to judge Erlend's behavior in this dealing with Eline," said the priest somberly. "It wasn't easy for Erlend to know what to do. It was never easy for Erlend to know what was right. Ever since we were children, our mother thought whatever Erlend did was right, and our father thought it was wrong. But he has probably told you so much about our mother that you know all about this."

"I can only recall that he has mentioned her two or three times," said Kristin. "But I understood that he did love her. . . ."

Gunnulf said softly, "I doubt there has ever been such a love between a mother and her son. Mother was much younger than my father. But then that whole trouble with Aunt Aashild happened. Our uncle Baard died, and it was said . . . well, you know about this, don't you? Father thought the worst and said to Mother . . . Erlend once flung his knife at Father; he was only a young boy. He rushed at Father more than once in Mother's defense when he was growing up.

"When Mother fell ill, he parted with Eline Ormsdatter. Mother grew sick with sores and scabs on her skin, and Father said it was leprosy.[4] He sent her away—tried to threaten her into taking a corrody[5] with the sisters at the hospice. Then Erlend went to get Mother and took her to Oslo—they stayed with Aashild too; she's a good healer. And the king's French doctor also said that she was not leprous. King Haakon received Erlend kindly then, and bade him seek out the grave of the holy King Erik Valdemarssøn—the king's grandfather. Many people found cures for their skin afflictions there.

"Erlend journeyed to Denmark with Mother, but she died on board his ship, south of Stad. When Erlend brought her home—well, you must remember that Father was very old, and Erlend had been a disobedient son all his days. When Erlend came to Nidaros with Mother's body, Father was staying at our town estate, and he refused to allow Erlend inside until he determined whether the boy had been infected, as he said. Erlend got on his horse and rode off, not resting until he arrived at the manor where Eline was staying with his son. After that he stood by her, in spite of everything, in spite of the fact that he had grown weary of her; and that's how he happened to bring her here to Husaby and put her in charge when he became owner of the estate. She had such a hold on him, and she said that if he deserted her after this, then he deserved to be struck by leprosy himself.

"But it must be time for your women to tend to you, Kristin." He looked down into the young, gray face that was rigid with fear and anguish.

But when he stood up to move toward the door, she cried loudly after him, "No, no, don't leave me!"

"It will soon be over," the priest consoled her, "since you are already so ill."

"That's not it!" She gripped his arm hard. "Gunnulf!"

He thought he had never seen such terror in anyone's face.

"Kristin—you should remember that this is no worse for you than for other women."

"But it is, it is." She pressed her face against the priest's arm. "For now I know that Eline and her children should be sitting here. He had promised her fidelity and marriage before I became his paramour."

"You know about that?" said Gunnulf calmly. "Erlend himself didn't know any better back then. But you must understand that he could not keep that promise; the archbishop would never have given his consent for those two to marry. You mustn't think that your marriage isn't valid. You are Erlend's rightful wife."

"Oh, I gave up all right to walk this earth long before then. And yet it's worse than I imagined. Oh, if only I might die and this child would never be born. I don't think I dare look at what I've been carrying."

"May God forgive you, Kristin—you don't know what you're saying! Would you wish for your child to die stillborn and unbaptized?"

"Yes, for that which I've carried under my heart may already belong to the Devil! It cannot be saved. Oh, if only I had drunk the potion that Eline offered me—that might have been atonement for all the sins we've committed, Erlend and I. Then this child would never have been conceived. Oh, I've thought this whole time, Gunnulf, that when I saw what I had fostered inside me, then I would come to realize that it would have been better for me to drink the leprosy potion that she offered me—rather than drive to her death the woman to whom Erlend had first bound himself."

"Kristin," said the priest, "you've lost your senses. You weren't the one who drove that poor woman to her death. Erlend *couldn't* keep the promise that he'd given her when he was young and knew little of law and justice. He could never have lived with her without sin. And she herself allowed another man to seduce her, and Erlend wanted to marry her to him when he heard of it. The two of you were not to blame for her taking her own life."

"Do you want to know how it happened that she took her life?" Kristin was now so full of despair that she spoke quite calmly. "We were together at Haugen, Erlend and I, when she arrived. She had brought along a drinking horn, and she wanted me to drink with her. I now see that she probably intended it for Erlend, but when she found me there with him, she wanted me to . . . I realized it was treachery—I saw that she didn't drink any herself when she put the horn to her lips. But I wanted to drink and I didn't care whether I lived or died when I found out that she had been with him here at Husaby the whole time. Then Erlend came in—he threatened her with his knife: 'You must drink first.' She begged and begged, and he was about to let her go. Then the Devil took hold of me; I grabbed the horn—'One of us, your two mistresses,' I said—I egged Erlend on—'You can't keep both of us,' I said. And so it was that she killed herself with Erlend's knife. But Bjørn and Aashild found a way to conceal what had happened."

"So Aunt Aashild took part in this concealment," said Gunnulf harshly. "I see . . . she played you into Erlend's hands."

"No," said Kristin vehemently. "Fru Aashild pleaded with us. She begged Erlend and she begged me so that I don't understand how I dared defy her—to step forward in as honorable a manner as was still possible, to fall at my father's feet and implore him to forgive us for what we had done. But I didn't dare. I argued that I was afraid that Father would kill Erlend—but oh, I knew full well that Father would never harm a man who put himself and his case into his hands. I argued that I was afraid he would suffer such sorrow that he would never be able to hold his head high again. But I have since shown that I was not so afraid to cause my father sorrow. You can't know, Gunnulf, what a good man my father is—no one can realize it who doesn't know him, how kind he has been to me all my days. Father has always been so fond of me. I don't want him to find out that I behaved shamelessly while he thought I was living with the sisters in Oslo and learning everything that was right and just. I even wore the clothing of a lay sister as I met with Erlend in cowsheds and lofts in town."

She looked up at Gunnulf. His face was pale and hard as stone.

"Do you see now why I'm frightened? She who took him in when he arrived, infected with leprosy . . ."

"Wouldn't you have done the same?" the priest asked gently.

"Of course, of course, of course." A shadow of that wild, sweet smile of the past flickered across the woman's ravaged face.

"But Erlend wasn't infected," said Gunnulf. "No one except Father ever thought that Mother died of leprosy."

"But I must be like a leper in God's eyes," said Kristin. She rested her face on the priest's arm which she was gripping. "Such as I am, infected with sins."

"My sister," said the priest softly, placing his other hand on her wimple. "I doubt that you are so sinful, young child, that you have forgotten that just as God can cleanse a person's flesh of leprosy, He can also cleanse your soul of sin."

"Oh, I don't know," she sobbed, hiding her face on his arm. "I don't know—and I don't feel any remorse, Gunnulf. I'm afraid, and yet . . . I was afraid when I stood at the church door with Erlend and the priest married us. I was afraid when I went inside for the wedding mass with him, with the golden crown on my flowing hair, for I didn't dare speak of shame to my father, with all my sins unatoned for; I didn't even dare confess fully to my parish priest. But as I went about here this winter and saw myself growing more hideous for each day that passed—then I was even more frightened, for Erlend did not act toward me as he had before. I thought about those days when he would come to me in my chamber at Skog in the evenings. . . ."

"Kristin," the priest tried to lift her face, "you mustn't think about this now! Think about God, who sees your sorrow and your remorse. Turn to the gentle Virgin Mary, who takes pity on every sorrowful—"

"Don't you see? I drove another human being to take her own life!"

"Kristin," the priest said sternly. "Are you so arrogant that you think yourself capable of sinning so badly that God's mercy is not great enough? . . ."

He stroked her wimple over and over.

"Don't you remember, my sister, when the Devil tried to tempt Saint Martin? Then the Fiend asked Saint Martin whether he dared believe it when he promised God's mercy to all the sinners whose confessions he heard. And the bishop answered, 'Even to you I promise God's forgiveness at the very instant you ask for it—if only you will give up your pride and believe that His love is greater than your hatred.' "

Gunnulf continued to stroke the head of the weeping woman. All the while he thought: Was *this* the way that Erlend had behaved toward his young bride? His lips grew pale and grim at the thought.

Audfinna Audunsdatter was the first of the women to arrive. She found Kristin in the little house; Gunnulf was sitting with her, and a couple of maids were bustling about the room.

Audfinna greeted the priest with deference, but Kristin stood up and went toward her with her hand outstretched.

"I must give you thanks for coming, Audfinna. I know it's not easy for your family to be without you at home."

Gunnulf had given the woman a searching look. Now he too stood up and said, "It was good of you to come so quickly. My sister-in-law needs someone she can trust to be with her. She's a stranger here, young and inexperienced."

"Jesus, she's as white as her linen wimple," whispered Audfinna. "Do you think, sir, that I might give her a sleeping potion? She needs to rest a while before it gets much worse."

She set to work, quietly and efficiently, inspecting the bed that the servant women had prepared on the floor, and telling them to bring more cushions and straw. She put small stone vessels of herbs on the fire to heat. Then she proceeded to loosen all the ribbons and ties on Kristin's clothing, and finally she pulled out all the pins from the ill woman's hair.

"I've never seen anything so lovely," she said when the cascading, silky, golden-brown mane tumbled down around the pale face. She had to laugh. "It certainly hasn't lost much of either fullness or sheen, even though you went bareheaded a little longer than was proper."

She settled Kristin comfortably among the cushions on the floor and covered her with a blanket.

"Drink this now, and you won't feel the pains as much—and see if you can sleep a little now and then."

Gunnulf was ready to leave. He went over and bent down toward Kristin.

"You will pray for me, Gunnulf?" she implored him.

"I will pray for you until I see you with your child in your arms—and after that too," he said as he tucked her hand back under the covers.

Kristin lay there, dozing. She felt almost content. The pain in her loins came and went, came and went—but it was unlike anything she had ever felt before, so that each time it was over, she wondered whether she had just imagined it. After the anguish and dread of the early morning hours, she felt as if she were already beyond the worst fear and torment. Audfinna walked about quietly, hanging up the infant clothes, blankets, and furs to warm at the hearth—and stirring her pots a little so the room smelled of spices. Finally Kristin slept between each wave of pain; she thought she was back home in the brewhouse at Jørundgaard and was supposed to help her mother dye a large woven fabric—probably because of the steam from the ash bark and nettles.

Then the neighbor women arrived, one after another—wives from the estates in the parish and in Birgsi. Audfinna withdrew to her place with the maids. Toward evening, Kristin began to suffer terrible pain. The women told her to walk around as long as she could bear it. This tormented her greatly; the house was now crowded with women, and she had to walk around like a mare that was for sale. Now and then she had to let the women squeeze and touch her body all over, and then they would confer with each other. At last Fru Gunna from Raasvold, who was in charge of things, said that now Kristin could lie down on the floor. She divided up the women: some to sleep and some to keep watch. "This isn't going to pass quickly—but go ahead and scream, Kristin, when it hurts, and don't pay any mind to those who are sleeping. We're all here to help you, poor child," she said, gentle and kind, patting the young woman's cheek.

But Kristin lay there biting her lips to shreds and crushing the corners of the blanket in her sweaty hands. It was suffocatingly hot, but they told her that was as it should be. After each wave of pain, the sweat poured off her.

At times she would lie there thinking about food for all these women. She fervently wanted them to see that she kept good order in her house. She had asked Torbjørg, the cook, to put whey in the water for boiling the fresh fish. If only Gunnulf wouldn't regard this as breaking the fast. Sira Eirik had said that it wasn't, for whey was not milk, and the fish broth would be thrown out. They mustn't be allowed to taste the dried fish that Erlend had brought home in the fall, spoiled and full of mites that it was.

Blessed Virgin Mary—will it be long before you help me? Oh, how it hurts, it hurts, it hurts. . . .

She was trying to hold out a little longer, before she gave in and screamed.

Audfinna sat next to the hearth and tended the pots of water. Kristin wished that she dared ask her to come over and hold her hand. There was nothing she wouldn't give to hold on to a familiar and kind hand right now. But she was ashamed to ask for it.

The next morning a bewildered silence hovered over Husaby. It was the day before the Feast of the Annunciation and the farm work was supposed to be finished by mid-afternoon prayers, but the men were distracted and somber, and the frightened maids were careless with their chores. The servants had grown fond of their young mistress, and it was said that things were not going well for her.

Erlend stood outside in the courtyard, talking to his smith. He tried to keep his thoughts on what the man was saying. Then Fru Gunna came rushing over to him.

"There's no progress with your wife, Erlend—we've tried everything we know. You must come. It might help if she sits on your lap. Go in and change into a short tunic. But be quick; she's suffering greatly, your poor young wife!"

Erlend had turned blood-red. He remembered he had heard that if a woman was having trouble delivering a child she had conceived in secrecy, then it might help if she were placed on her husband's knee.

Kristin was lying on the floor under several blankets; two

women were sitting with her. The moment that Erlend came in, he saw her body convulse and she buried her head in the lap of one of the women, rocking it from side to side. But she didn't utter a single whimper.

When the pain had passed, she looked up with wild, frightened eyes, her cracked, brown lips gasping. All trace of youth and beauty had vanished from the swollen, flushed red face. Even her hair was matted together with bits of straw and wool from the fur of a filthy hide. She looked at Erlend as if she didn't immediately recognize him. But when she realized why the women had sent for him, she shook her head vigorously.

"It's not the custom where I come from . . . for men to be present when a woman is giving birth."

"It's sometimes done here in the north," said Erlend quietly. "If it can lessen the pain a little for you, my Kristin, then you must—"

"Oh!" When he knelt beside her she threw her arms around his waist and pressed herself to him. Hunched over and shaking, she fought her way through the pain without a murmur.

"May I have a few words with my husband alone?" she said when it was over, her breathing rapid and harsh. The women withdrew.

"Was it when she was suffering the agony of childbirth that you promised her what she told me—that you would marry her when she was widowed . . . that night when Orm was born?" whispered Kristin.

Erlend gasped for air, as if he had been struck deep in the heart. Then he vehemently shook his head.

"I was at the castle that night; my men and I had guard duty. It was when I came back to our hostel in the morning and they put the boy in my arms. . . . Have you been lying here thinking about this, Kristin?"

"Yes." Again she clung to him as the waves of pain washed over her. Erlend wiped away the sweat that poured down her face.

"Now you know," he said, when she lay quiet once more. "Don't you want me to stay with you, as Fru Gunna says?"

But Kristin shook her head. And finally the women had to let Erlend go.

But then it seemed as if her power to endure was broken. She screamed in wild terror of the pain that she could feel approaching, and begged pitifully for help. And yet when the women talked of bringing her husband back, she screamed "No!" She would rather be tortured to death.

Gunnulf and the cleric who was with him walked over to the church to attend evensong. Everyone on the estate went along who was not tending to the woman giving birth. But Erlend slipped out of the church before the service was over and walked south toward the buildings.

In the west, above the ridges on the other side of the valley, the sky was a yellowish-red. The twilight of the spring evening was about to descend, clear and bright and mild. A few stars appeared, white in the light sky. A little wisp of fog drifted over the bare woods down by the lake, and there were brown patches where the fields lay open to the sun. The smell of earth and thawing snow filled the air.

The little house was at the westernmost edge of the courtyard, facing the hollow of the valley. Erlend went over and stood for a moment behind the wall. The timbers were still warm from the sun as he leaned against them. Oh, how she screamed. . . . He had once heard a heifer shrieking in the grip of a bear —that was up at their mountain pasture, and he was only a half-grown boy. He and Arnbjørn, the shepherd boy, were running south through the forest. He remembered the shaggy creature that stood up and became a bear with a red, fiery maw. The bear broke Arnbjørn's spear in half with its paw. Then the servant threw Erlend's spear, as he stood there paralyzed with terror. The heifer lay there still alive, but its udder and thigh had been gnawed away.

My Kristin, oh, my Kristin. Lord, for the sake of Your blessed Mother, have mercy. He rushed back to the church.

The maids came into the hall with the evening meal. They didn't set up the table, but placed the food near the hearth. The men took bread and fish over to the benches, sat down in their places, not speaking and eating little; no one seemed to have an appetite. No one came to clear away the dishes after the meal, and none of the men got up to go to bed. They stayed sitting there, staring into the hearth fire, without talking.

Erlend had hidden himself in a corner near the bed; he couldn't bear to have anyone see his face.

Master Gunnulf had lit a small oil lamp and set it on the arm of the high seat. He sat on the bench with a book in his hands, his lips moving gently, soundless and unceasing.

At one point Ulf Haldorssøn stood up, walked forward to the hearth, and picked up a piece of soft bread; he rummaged around among the pieces of firewood and selected one. Then he went over to the corner near the doorway where old man Aan was sitting. The two of them fiddled with the bread, hidden behind Ulf's cape. Aan whittled and cut the piece of wood. The men cast a glance in their direction now and then. In a little while Ulf and Aan got up and left the hall.

Gunnulf watched them go, but said nothing. He took up his prayers once more.

Once a young boy toppled off the bench, falling to the floor in his sleep. He got up and looked around in bewilderment. Then he sighed softly and sat down again.

Ulf Haldorssøn and Aan quietly came back in and returned to the places where they had sat before. The men looked at them, but no one said a word.

Suddenly Erlend jumped up. He strode across the floor toward his servants. He was hollow-eyed, and his face was as gray as clay.

"Doesn't anyone know what to do?" he asked. "You, Aan," he whispered.

"It didn't help," replied Ulf, his voice equally quiet.

"It could be that she's not meant to keep this child," said Aan, wiping his nose. "Then neither sacrifices nor runes can help. It's a shame for you, Erlend, that you should lose this good wife so soon."

"Oh, don't talk as if she were already dead," implored Erlend, broken and in despair. He went back to his corner and threw himself down on the enclosed bed with his head near the foot-board.

Later a man went outside and then came back in.

"The moon is up," he said. "It will soon be morning."

A few minutes later Fru Gunna came into the hall. She sank down onto the beggar's bench near the door. Her gray hair was disheveled, her wimple had slid back onto her shoulders.

The men stood up and slowly moved over to her.

"One of you must come and hold her," she said, weeping. "We have no more strength. You must go to her, Gunnulf. There's no telling how this will end."

Gunnulf stood up and tucked his prayer book inside his belt pouch.

"You must come too, Erlend," said the woman.

A raw and broken howl met him in the doorway. Erlend stopped and shivered. He caught a glimpse of Kristin's contorted, unrecognizable face among the sobbing women. She was on her knees, and they were supporting her.

Over by the door several servant women were kneeling at the benches; they were praying loudly and steadily. He threw himself down next to them and hid his head in his arms. She screamed and screamed, and each time he felt himself freeze with incredulous horror. It couldn't possibly be like this.

He ventured a glance in her direction. Now Gunnulf was sitting on a stool in front of her and holding her under the arms. Fru Gunna was kneeling at her side, with her arms around Kristin's waist, but Kristin was fighting her, frightened to death, and trying to push the other woman away.

"Oh no, oh no, let me go—I can't do it—God, God, help me . . ."

"God will help you soon, Kristin," said the priest each time. A woman held a basin of water, and after each wave of pain he would take a wet cloth and wipe the sick woman's face—along the roots of her hair and in between her lips, from which saliva was dripping.

Then she would rest her head in Gunnulf's arms and doze off for a moment, but the torment would instantly tear her out of her sleep again. And the priest continued to say, "Now, Kristin, you will have help soon."

No one had any idea what time of night it was anymore. The dawn was already a gray glare in the smoke vent.

Then, after a long, mad howl of terror, everything fell silent. Erlend heard the women rushing around; he didn't want to look up. Then he heard someone weeping loudly and he cringed again, not wanting to know.

Then Kristin shrieked once more—a piercing, wild cry of lament that didn't sound like the insane, inhuman animal cries of before. Erlend leaped up.

Gunnulf was bending down and holding on to Kristin, who was still on her knees. She was staring with deathly horror at something that Fru Gunna was holding in a sheepskin. The raw and dark red shape looked like nothing more than the entrails from a slaughtered beast.

The priest pulled her close.

"Dear Kristin—you have given birth to as fine and handsome a son as any mother should thank God for—and he's breathing!" said Gunnulf fiercely to the weeping women. "He's breathing—God would not be so harsh as not to hear us."

And as the priest spoke, it happened. Through the exhausted, confused mind of the mother tumbled, hazily recalled, the sight of a bud she had seen in the cloister garden—something from which red, crinkled wisps of silk emerged and spread out to become a flower.

The shapeless lump moved—it whimpered. It stretched out and became a very tiny, wine-red infant in human form. It had arms and legs and hands and feet with fully formed fingers and toes. It flailed and hissed a bit.

"So tiny, so tiny, so tiny he is," she cried in a thin, broken voice and then burst into laughing sobs. The women around her began to laugh and wipe their tears, and Gunnulf gave Kristin into their arms.

"Roll him in a trencher so he can scream better," said the priest as he followed the women carrying the newborn son over to the hearth.

When Kristin awoke from a long faint, she was lying in bed. Someone had removed the dreadful, sweat-soaked garments, and a feeling of warmth and healing was blessedly streaming through her body. They had placed small pouches of warm nettle porridge on her and wrapped her in hot blankets and furs.

Someone hushed her when she tried to speak. It was quite still in the room. But through the silence came a voice that she couldn't quite recognize.

"Nikulaus, in the name of the Father, the Son, and the Holy Ghost . . ."

There was the sound of water trickling.

Kristin propped herself up on her elbow to take a look. Over by the hearth stood a priest in white garb, and Ulf Haldorssøn was lifting a kicking, red, naked child out of the large brass basin; he handed him to the godmother, and then took the lit taper.

She had given birth to a child, and he was screaming so loudly that the priest's words were almost drowned out. But she was so tired. She felt numb and wanted to sleep.

Then she heard Erlend's voice; he spoke quickly and with alarm.

"His head—he has such a strange head."

"He's swollen up," said the woman calmly. "And it's no wonder—he had to fight hard for his life, this boy."

Kristin shouted something. She felt as if she were suddenly awake, to the very depths of her heart. This was her son, and he had fought for his life, just as she had.

Gunnulf turned around at once and laughed; he seized the tiny white bundle from Fru Gunna's lap and carried it over to the bed. He placed the boy in his mother's arms. Weak with tenderness and joy she rubbed her face against the little bit of red, silky-soft face visible among the linen wrappings.

She glanced up at Erlend. Once before she had seen his face look this haggard and gray—she couldn't remember when, her head felt so dizzy and strange, but she knew that it was good she had no memory of it. And it was good to see him standing there with his brother; the priest had his hand on Erlend's shoulder. An immeasurable sense of peace and well-being came over her as she looked at the tall man wearing alb and stole; the round, lean face beneath the black fringe of hair was strong, but his smile was pleasant and kind.

Erlend drove his dagger deep into the wall timber behind the mother and child.

"That's not necessary now," said the priest with a laugh. "The boy has been baptized, after all."

Kristin suddenly remembered something that Brother Edvin

once said. A newly baptized child was just as holy as the holy angels in heaven. The sins of the parents were washed from the child, and he had not yet committed any sins of his own. Fearful and cautious, she kissed the little face.

Fru Gunna came over to them. She was worn out and exhausted and angry at the father, who had not had the sense to offer a single word of thanks to all the women who had helped. And the priest had taken the child from her and carried him over to his mother. She should have done that, both because she had delivered the woman and because she was the godmother of the boy.

"You haven't yet greeted your son, Erlend, or held him in your arms," she said crossly.

Erlend lifted the swaddled infant from the mother's arms—for a moment he lay his face close.

"I don't think I'm going to be properly fond of you, Naakkve, until I forget what terrible suffering you caused your mother," he said, and then gave the boy back to Kristin.

"By all means give him the blame for that," said the old woman, annoyed. Master Gunnulf laughed, and then Fru Gunna laughed with him. She wanted to take the child and put him in his cradle, but Kristin begged to keep him with her for a while. A moment later she fell asleep with her son beside her—vaguely noticing that Erlend touched her, cautiously, as if he were afraid to hurt her, and then she was sound asleep again.

CHAPTER 5

IN THE MORNING of the tenth day after the child's birth, Master Gunnulf said to his brother when they were alone in the hall, "It's about time now, Erlend, for you to send word to your wife's kinsmen about how things are with her."

"I don't think there's any haste with that," replied Erlend. "I doubt they will be overly glad at Jørundgaard when they hear that there's already a son here on the manor."

"Don't you think Kristin's mother would have realized last fall that her daughter was unwell?" Gunnulf asked. "She must be worried by now."

Erlend didn't say a word in reply.

But later in the day, as Gunnulf was sitting in the little house and talking to Kristin, Erlend came in. He was wearing a fur cap on his head, a short, thick homespun coat, long pants, and furry boots. He bent down to his wife and patted her cheek.

"So, dear Kristin—do you have any greetings you wish to send to Jørundgaard? I'm heading there now to bring word of our son."

Kristin blushed bright red. She looked both frightened and happy.

"It's no more than your father would demand of me," said Erlend somberly, "that I bring the news myself."

Kristin lay in silence for a moment.

"Tell them at home," she said softly, "that I have yearned every day since I left home to fall at Father's and Mother's feet to beg their forgiveness."

A few minutes later, Erlend left. Kristin didn't think to ask how he would travel. But Gunnulf went out to the courtyard with his brother. Next to the doorway of the main house stood Erlend's skis and a staff with a spear point.

"You're going to ski there?" asked Gunnulf. "Who's going with you?"

78

"Nobody," replied Erlend, laughing. "You should know best of all, Gunnulf, that it's not easy for anyone to keep up with me on skis."

"This seems reckless to me," said the priest. "There are many wolves in the mountain forests this year, they say."

Erlend merely laughed and began to strap on his skis. "I was thinking of heading up through the Gjeitskar pastures before it gets dark. It will be light for a long time yet. I can make it to Jørundgaard on the evening of the third day."

"The path from Gjeitskar to the road is uncertain, and there are bad patches of fog there too. You know it's unsafe up in the mountain pastures in the wintertime."

"You can lend me your flint," said Erlend in the same tone of voice, "in case I should need to throw mine away—at some elf woman if she demands such courtesies of me as would be unseemly for a married man. Listen, brother, I'm doing now what you said I should do—going to Kristin's father to ask him to demand whatever penances from me that he finds reasonable. Surely you can allow me to decide this much, that I myself choose how I will travel."

And with that Master Gunnulf had to be content. But he sternly commanded the servants to conceal from Kristin that Erlend had set off alone.

To the south the sky arched pale yellow over the blue-tinged snowdrifts of the mountains on the evening when Erlend came racing down past the churchyard, making the snow crust creak and shriek. High overhead hovered the crescent moon, shining white and dewy in the twilight.

At Jørundgaard dark smoke was swirling up from the smoke vents against the pale, clear sky. The sound of an axe rang out cold and rhythmic in the stillness.

At the entrance to the courtyard a pack of dogs started barking loudly at the approaching man. Inside the courtyard a group of shaggy goats ambled around, dark silhouettes in the clear dusk. They were nibbling at a heap of fir boughs in the middle of the courtyard. Three winter-clad youngsters were running among them.

The peace of the place made an oddly deep impression on Erlend. He stood there, irresolute, and waited for Lavrans, who was coming forward to greet the stranger. His father-in-law had been over by the woodshed, talking to a man splitting rails for a fence. Lavrans stopped abruptly when he recognized his son-in-law; he thrust the spear he was holding hard into the snow.

"Is that *you?*" he asked in a low voice. "Alone? Is there . . . is something . . . ?" And a moment later he said, "How is it that you've come here like this?"

"Here's the reason." Erlend pulled himself together and looked his father-in-law in the eye. "I thought I could do no less than to come here myself to bring you the news. Kristin gave birth to a son on the morning of the Feast of the Annunciation.

"And yes, she is doing well now," he added quickly.

Lavrans stood in silence for a moment. He was biting down hard on his lip—his jaw trembled and quivered faintly.

"That was news indeed!" he said then.

Little Ramborg had come over to stand at her father's side. She looked up, her face flaming red.

"Be quiet," said Lavrans harshly, even though the maiden hadn't uttered a word but had merely blushed. "Don't stand here—go away."

He didn't say anything more. Erlend stood leaning forward, with his left hand gripping his staff. His eyes were fixed on the snow. He had stuck his right hand inside his tunic.

Lavrans pointed. "Have you injured yourself?"

"A little," said Erlend. "I slipped down a slope yesterday in the dark."

Lavrans touched his wrist and pressed it cautiously. "I don't think there are any bones broken," he said. "You can tell her mother yourself." He started for the house as Ragnfrid came out into the courtyard. She looked in amazement at her husband; then she recognized Erlend and quickly walked over to him.

She listened without speaking as Erlend, for the second time, presented his message. But her eyes filled with tears when Erlend said at the end, "I thought you might have noticed something before she left here in the fall—and that you might be worried about her now."

"It was kind of you, Erlend," she said uncertainly. "For you to think of that. I think I've been worried every day since you took her away from us."

Lavrans came back.

"Here is some fox fat—I see that you've frozen your cheek, son-in-law. You must stay for a while in the entryway, so Ragnfrid can attend to it and thaw you out. How are your feet? You must take off your boots so we can see."

When the servants came in for the evening meal, Lavrans told them the news and ordered special foreign ale to be brought in so they could celebrate. But there was no real merriment about the occasion—the master himself sat at the table with a cup of water. He asked Erlend to forgive him, but this was a promise he had made during his youth, to drink water during Lent. And so the servants sat there quietly, and the conversation lagged over the good ale. Once in a while the children would go over to Lavrans; he put his arm around them when they stood at his knee, but he gave absentminded answers to their questions. Ramborg replied curtly and sharply when Erlend tried to tease her; she would show that she didn't like this brother-in-law of hers. She was now eight winters old, lively and lovely, but she bore little resemblance to her sisters.

Erlend asked who the other children were. Lavrans told him the boy was Haavard Trondssøn, the youngest child at Sundbu. It was so tedious for him over there among his grown-up siblings; at Christmastime he had decided to go home with his aunt. The maiden was Helga Rolvsdatter. Her kinsmen had been forced to take the children from Blakarsarv home with them after the funeral; it wasn't good for them to see their father the way he was now. And it was nice for Ramborg that she had these foster siblings. "We're getting old now, Ragnfrid and I," said Lavrans. "And she's more wild and playful, this one here, than Kristin was." He stroked his daughter's curly hair.

Erlend sat down next to his mother-in-law, and she asked him about Kristin's childbirth. The son-in-law noticed that Lavrans was listening to them, but then he stood up, went over, and picked up his hat and cape. He would go over to the parsonage, he said, to ask Sira Eirik to come and join them for a drink.

Lavrans walked along the well-trodden path through the fields toward Romundgaard. The moon was about to sink behind the mountains now, but thousands of stars still sparkled above the white slopes. He hoped the priest would be at home—he could no longer stand to sit there with the others.

But when he turned down the lane between the fences near the courtyard, he saw a small candle coming toward him. Old Audun was carrying it, and when he sensed there was someone in the road, he rang his tiny silver bell. Lavrans Bjørgulfsøn threw himself down on his knees in the snowdrift at the side of the road.

Audun walked past with his candle and bell, which rang faintly and gently. Behind him rode Sira Eirik. With his hands he lifted the Host vessel high as he came upon the kneeling man, but he did not turn his head; he rode silently past as Lavrans bowed down and raised his hands in greeting to his Savior.

That was the son of Einar Hnufa with the priest—it must be nearing the end for the old man now. Ah well. Lavrans said his prayers for the dying man before he stood up and walked back home. The meeting with God in the night had nevertheless strengthened and consoled him a great deal.

When they had gone to bed, Lavrans asked his wife, "Did you know anything about this—that things were such with Kristin?"

"Didn't you?" said Ragnfrid.

"No," replied her husband so curtly that she could tell he must have been thinking of it all the same.

"I was indeed fearful for a time this past summer," said the mother hesitantly. "I could see that she took no pleasure in her food. But as the days passed, I thought I must have been mistaken. She seemed so happy during all the time we were preparing for her wedding."

"Well, she certainly had good reason for *that*," said the father with some disdain. "But that she said nothing to you. . . . You, her own mother . . ."

"Yes, you think of that now when she's gone astray," said Ragnfrid bitterly. "But you know quite well that Kristin has never confided in me."

Lavrans said no more. A little later he bade his wife sleep well and then lay down quietly. He realized that sleep would not come to him for some time.

Kristin, Kristin—his poor little maiden.

Not with a single word had he ever referred to what Ragnfrid had confessed to him on the night of Kristin's wedding. And in all fairness she couldn't say he had made her feel it was on his mind. He had been no different in his demeanor toward her—rather, he had striven to show her even more kindness and love. But it was not the first time this winter he had noticed the bitterness in Ragnfrid or seen her searching for some hidden offense in the innocent words he had spoken. He didn't understand it, and he didn't know what to do about it—he would simply have to accept it.

"Our Father who art in Heaven . . ." He prayed for Kristin and her child. Then he prayed for his wife and for himself. Finally, he prayed for the strength to tolerate Erlend Nikulaussøn with a patient spirit for as long as he was forced to have his son-in-law there on his estate.

Lavrans would not allow his daughter's husband to set off for home until they saw how his wrist was healing. And he refused to let Erlend go back alone.

"Kristin would be pleased if you came with me," said Erlend one day.

Lavrans was silent for a moment. Then he voiced many objections. Ragnfrid would undoubtedly not like to be left alone on the farm. And once he had journeyed so far north, it would be difficult to return in time for spring planting. But in the end he set off with Erlend. He took no servant along—he would travel home by ship to Raumsdal. There he could hire horses to carry him south through the valley; he knew people everywhere along the way.

They talked little as they skied, but they got along well together. It was a struggle for Lavrans to keep up with his companion; he didn't want to admit that his son-in-law went too fast for him. But Erlend took note of this and at once adapted his pace to his father-in-law's. He went to great lengths to charm his wife's father—and he had that quiet, gentle manner whenever he wished to win someone's friendship.

On the third evening they sought shelter in a stone hut. They had had bad weather and fog, but Erlend seemed to be able to find his way just as confidently. Lavrans noticed that Erlend had an astoundingly accurate knowledge of all signs and tracks, in the air and on the ground, and of the ways of animals and their habits—

and he always seemed to know where he was. Everything that Lavrans, experienced in the mountains as he was, had learned by observing and paying attention and remembering, the other man seemed to intuit quite blindly. Erlend laughed at this, but it was simply something he knew.

They found the stone hut in the dark, exactly at the moment Erlend had predicted. Lavrans recalled one such night when he had dug himself a shelter in the snow only an arrow's shot away from his own horse shed. Here the snow had drifted up over the hut and they had to break their way in through the smoke vent. Erlend covered the opening with a horsehide that was lying in the hut, fastening it with sticks of firewood, which he stuck in among the roof beams. With a ski he cleared away the snow that had blown inside and managed to build a fire in the hearth from the frozen wood lying about. He pulled out three or four grouse from under the bench—he had put them there on his way south. He packed them in earth from the floor where it had thawed out around the hearth and then threw the bundles into the embers.

Lavrans stretched out on the earthen bench, which Erlend had prepared for him as best he could, spreading out their knapsacks and capes.

"That's what soldiers do with stolen chickens, Erlend," he said with a laugh.

"Yes, I learned a few things when I was in the Earl's service," said Erlend, laughing too.

Now he was alert and lively, not silent and rather sluggish the way his father-in-law had most often seen him. As he sat on the floor in front of Lavrans, he started telling stories about the years when he served Earl Jacob in Halland.[1] He had been head of the castle guard, and he had patrolled the coast with three small ships. Erlend's eyes shone like a child's—he wasn't boasting, he merely let the words spill out. Lavrans lay there looking down at him.

He had prayed to God to grant him patience with this man, his daughter's husband. Now he was almost angry with himself because he was more fond of Erlend than he wanted to be. He thought about that night when their church burned down and he had taken a liking to his son-in-law. It was not that Erlend lacked manhood in his lanky body. Lavrans felt a stab of pain in his heart. It was a pity about Erlend; he could have been fit for better things than seducing women. But nothing much had come of that except boyish pranks. If only times had been such that a chieftain could have taken this man in hand and put him to use . . . but as the world was now, when every man had to depend on his own judgment about so many things . . . and a man in Erlend's circumstances was supposed to make decisions for himself and for the welfare of many other people. And this was Kristin's husband.

Erlend looked up at his father-in-law. He grew somber too. Then he said, "I want to ask one thing, Lavrans. Before we reach my home, I'd like you to tell me what is in your heart."

Lavrans was silent.

"You must know," said Erlend in the same tone of voice, "that I would gladly fall at your feet in whatever manner you wish and make amends in whatever way you deem a fitting punishment for me."

Lavrans looked down into the younger man's face; then he smiled oddly.

"That might be difficult, Erlend—for me to decide and for you to do. But now you must make a proper gift to the church at Sundbu and to the priests, whom you have also deceived," he said adamantly. "I will speak no more of this! And you cannot blame it on your youth. It would have been much more honorable, Erlend, if you had fallen at my feet *before* you held your wedding."

"Yes," said Erlend. "But at the time I didn't know how things stood, or that it would come to light that I had offended you."

Lavrans sat up.

"Didn't you know, when you were wed, that Kristin . . ."

"No," said Erlend, looking crestfallen. "We were married for almost two months before I realized it."

Lavrans gave him a look of surprise but said nothing.

Then Erlend spoke again, his voice low and unsteady, "I'm glad that you came with me, Father-in-law. Kristin has been so melancholy all winter—she has hardly said a word to me. Many times it seemed to me that she was unhappy, both with Husaby and with me."

Lavrans replied somewhat coldly and harshly, "That's no doubt the way things are with most young wives. Now that she's well again, you two will probably be just as good friends as you were before." And he smiled a little mockingly.

But Erlend sat and stared into the glowing embers. He suddenly understood with certainty—but he had realized it from the moment he first saw the tiny red infant face pressed against Kristin's white shoulder. It would never be the same between them, the way it had been before.

When Kristin's father stepped inside the little house, she sat up in bed and held out her hands toward him. She threw her arms around his shoulders and wept and wept, until Lavrans grew quite alarmed.

She had been out of bed for some time, but then she learned that Erlend had set off for Gudbrandsdal alone, and when he failed to return home for days on end, she grew so anxious that she developed a fever. And she had to go back to bed.

It was apparent that she was still weak—she wept at everything. The new manor priest,[2] Sira Eiliv Serkssøn, had arrived while Erlend was away. He had taken it upon himself to visit the mistress now and then to read to her, but she wept over such unreasonable things that soon he didn't know what he dared let her hear.

One day when her father was sitting with her, Kristin wanted to change the child herself so that he could see how handsome and well-formed the boy was. He lay naked on the swaddling clothes, kicking on the wool coverlet in front of his mother.

"What kind of a mark is that on his chest?" asked Lavrans.

Right over his heart the child had several little blood-red flecks; it looked as if a bloody hand had touched the boy there. Kristin had been distressed by it too, the first time she saw this mark. But she had tried to console herself, and she said now, "It's probably just a fire mark—I put my hand to my breast when I saw the church was burning."

Her father gave a start. Well. He hadn't known how long—or how much—she had kept to herself. And he couldn't understand that she had had the strength—his own child, and from him . . .

"I don't think you're truly fond of my son," Kristin said to her father many times, and Lavrans would laugh a bit and say of course he was. He had also placed an abundance of gifts both in the cradle and in the mother's bed. But Kristin didn't think anyone cared enough for her son—least of all Erlend. "Look at him, Father," she would beg. "Did you see he was laughing? Have you ever seen a more beautiful child than Naakkve, Father?"

She asked this same thing over and over. Once Lavrans said, as if in thought, "Haavard, your brother—our second son—was a very handsome child."

After a moment Kristin asked in a timid voice, "Was he the one who lived the longest of my brothers?"

"Yes. He was two winters old. Now you mustn't cry again, my Kristin," he said gently.

Neither Lavrans nor Gunnulf Nikulaussøn liked the fact that the boy was called Naakkve; he had been baptized Nikulaus. Erlend maintained that it was the same name, but Gunnulf disagreed; there were men in the sagas who had been called Naakkve since heathen times. But Erlend still refused to use the name that his father had borne. And Kristin always called the boy by the name Erlend had spoken when he first greeted their son.

In Kristin's view there was only one person at Husaby, aside from herself, who fully realized what a splendid and promising child Naakkve was. That was the new priest, Sira Eiliv. In that way, he was nearly as sensible as she was.

Sira Eiliv was a short, slight man with a little round belly, which gave him a somewhat comical appearance. He was exceedingly nondescript; people who had spoken to him many times had trouble recognizing the priest, so ordinary was his face. His hair and complexion were the same color—like reddish-yellow sand—and his round, watery blue eyes were quite dull. In manner he was subdued and diffident, but Master Gunnulf said that Sira Eiliv was so learned that he could have attained high standing if only he had not been so unassuming. But he was far less marked by his learning than by pure living, humility, and a deep love for Christ and his Church.

He was of low birth, and although he was not much older than Gunnulf Nikulaussøn, he seemed almost like an old man. Gunnulf had known him ever since they went to school together in

Nidaros, and he always spoke of Eiliv Serkssøn with great affection. Erlend didn't think it was much of a priest they had been
given at Husaby, but Kristin immediately felt great trust and affection for him.

Kristin continued to live in the little house with her child, even
after she had made her first visit back to church. That was a bleak
day for Kristin. Sira Eiliv escorted her through the church door,
but he didn't dare give her the body of Christ. She had confessed
to him, but for the sin that she had committed when she became
implicated in another person's ill-fated death, she would have to
seek absolution from the archbishop. That morning when Gunnulf
had sat with Kristin, her spirit in anguish, he had impressed upon
her heart that as soon as she was out of any physical danger, she
must rush to seek redemption for her soul. As soon as she had regained her health, she must keep her promise to Saint Olav. Now
that he, through his intercession, had brought her son, healthy and
alive, into the light and to the baptismal font, she must walk barefoot to his grave and place there her golden crown, the honored
adornment of maidens, which she had guarded so poorly and unjustly worn. And Gunnulf had advised her to prepare for the journey with solitude, prayers, reading, meditation, and even fasting,
although with moderation for the sake of the nursing child.

That evening as she sat in sorrow after going to church, Gunnulf had come to her and given her a *Pater noster* rosary. He told
her that in countries abroad, cloister folk and priests were not the
only ones who used these kinds of beads to help them with their
devotions. This rosary was extremely beautiful; the beads were
made of a type of yellow wood from India that smelled so sweet
and wondrous they might almost serve as a reminder of what a
good prayer ought to be—a sacrifice of the heart and a yearning
for help in order to live a righteous life before God. In between
there were beads of amber and gold, and the cross was painted
with a lovely enamel.

Erlend would give his young wife a look full of longing whenever
he met her out in the courtyard. She had never been as beautiful as
she was now—tall and slender in her simple, earth-brown dress of
undyed homespun. The coarse linen wimple covering her hair,

neck, and shoulders merely showed even more how glowing and pure her complexion had become. When the spring sun fell on her face, it was as if the light were seeping deep into her flesh, so radiant she was—her eyes and lips were almost transparent. When he went into the little house to see the child, she would lower her great pale eyelids if he glanced at her. She seemed so modest and pure that he hardly dared touch her hand with his fingers. If she had Naakkve at her breast, she would pull a corner of her wimple over the tiny glimpse of her white body. It seemed as if they were trying to send his wife away from him to heaven.

Then he would joke, half-angrily, with his brother and father-in-law as they sat in the hall in the evening—just men. Husaby had practically become a collegial church. Here sat Gunnulf and Sira Eiliv; his father-in-law could be considered a half-priest, and now they wanted to turn him into one too. There would be three priests on the estate. But the others laughed at him.

During the spring Erlend Nikulaussøn supervised much of the farming on his manor. That year all the fences were mended and the gates were put up in good time; the plowing and spring farm work were done early and properly, and Erlend purchased excellent livestock. At the new year he had been forced to slaughter a great many animals, but this was not a bad loss, as old and wretched as they were. He set the servants to burning tar and stripping off birch bark, and the farm's buildings were put in order and the roofs repaired. Such things had not been done at Husaby since old Sir Nikulaus had had his full strength. And he also sought advice and support from his wife's father—people knew that. Amidst all this work Erlend would visit friends and kinsmen in the villages along with Lavrans and his brother, the priest. But now he traveled in a suitable manner, with a couple of fit and proper servants. In the past, Erlend had been in the habit of riding around with an entire entourage of undisciplined and rowdy men. The gossip, which had for so long seethed with indignation at Erlend Nikulaussøn's shameless living and the disarray and decline at Husaby, now died down to a good-natured teasing. People smiled and said that Erlend's young wife had achieved a great deal in six months.

Shortly before Saint Botolv's Day, Lavrans Bjørgulfsøn left for

Nidaros, accompanied by Master Gunnulf. Lavrans was to be the priest's guest for several days while he visited Saint Olav's shrine and the other churches in town before starting his journey south to return home. He parted from his daughter and her husband with love and kindness.

CHAPTER 6

KRISTIN WAS TO go to Nidaros three days after the Selje Men's Feast Day. Later in the month the frenzy and tumult in town would have already started as Saint Olav's Day neared, and before that time the archbishop was not in residence.

The evening before, Master Gunnulf came to Husaby, and very early the next morning he went with Sira Eiliv to the church for matins. The dew, gray as a pelt, covered the grass as Kristin walked to church, but the sun was gilding the forest at the top of the ridge, and the cuckoo was singing on the grassy mountainside. It looked as if she would have beautiful weather for her journey.

There was no one in the church except Erlend and his wife and the priests in the illuminated choir. Erlend looked at Kristin's bare feet. It must be ice cold for her to be standing on the stone floor. She would have to walk twenty miles with no escort but her prayers. He tried to lift his heart toward God, which he had not done in many years.

Kristin was wearing an ash-gray robe with a rope around her waist. Underneath he knew that she wore a shift of rough sackcloth. A homespun cloth, tightly bound, hid her hair.

As they came out of the church into the morning sunshine, they were met by a maidservant carrying the child. Kristin sat down on a pile of logs. With her back to her husband she let the boy nurse until he had had his fill before she started off. Erlend stood motionless a short distance away; his cheeks were pale and cold with strain.

The priests came out a little while later; they had taken off their albs in the sacristy. They stopped in front of Kristin. A few minutes later Sira Eiliv headed down toward the manor, but Gunnulf helped her tie the child securely onto her back. Around her neck hung a bag holding the golden crown, some money, and a little bread and salt. She picked up her staff, curtseyed deeply before the

91

priest, and then began walking silently north along the path leading up into the forest.

Erlend stayed behind, his face deathly white. Suddenly he started
running. North of the church there were several small hills with
scraggly grass slopes and shrubs of juniper and alpine birch that
had been grazed over; goats usually roamed there. Erlend raced to
the top. From there he would be able to see her for a little while
longer, until she disappeared into the woods.

Gunnulf slowly followed his brother. The priest looked so tall
and dark in the bright morning light. He too was very pale.

Erlend was standing with his mouth half-open and tears streaming down his white cheeks. Abruptly he bent forward and dropped
to his knees; then he threw himself down full length on the scruffy
grass. He lay there sobbing and sobbing, tugging at the heather
with his long tan fingers.

Gunnulf stood quite still. He stared down at the weeping man
and then gazed out toward the forest where the woman had disappeared.

Erlend raised his head off the ground. "Gunnulf—was it necessary for you to compel her to do this? Was it necessary?" he asked
again. "Couldn't *you* have offered her absolution?"

The other man did not reply.

Then Erlend spoke again. "I made my confession and offered
penance." He sat up. "I bought for *her* thirty masses and an an-
nual mass for her soul and burial in consecrated ground; I confessed my sin to Bishop Helge and I traveled to the Shrine of
the Holy Blood in Schwerin. Couldn't that have helped Kristin a
little?"

"Even though you have done that," said the priest quietly,
"even though you have offered God a contrite heart and been
granted full reconciliation with Him, you must realize that year after year you will still have to strive to erase the traces of your sin
here on earth. The harm you did to the woman who is now your
wife when you dragged her down, first into impure living and then
into blood guilt—you cannot absolve her of that, only God can do
so. Pray that He holds His hand over her during this journey when
you can neither follow her nor protect her. And do not forget,
brother, for as long as you both shall live, that you watched your

wife leave your estate in this manner—for the sake of your sins more than for her own."

A little later Erlend said, "I swore by God and my Christian faith before I stole her virtue that I would never take any other wife, and she promised that she would never take any other husband for as long as we both should live. You said yourself, Gunnulf, that this was then a binding marriage before God; whoever later wed another would be living in sin in His eyes. So it could not have been impure living that Kristin was my . . ."

"It was not a sin that you lived with her," said the priest after a moment, "if it could have been done without breaking other laws. But you drove her into sinful defiance against everyone God had put in charge of this child—and then you brought the shame of blood upon her. I told you this too, back when we talked of this matter. That's why the Church has created laws regarding marriage, why banns must be announced, and why we priests must not marry man and maiden against the will of their kinsmen." He sat down, clasped his hands around one knee, and stared out across the summer-bright landscape, where the little lake glinted blue at the bottom of the valley. "Surely you must realize that, Erlend. You had sown a thicket of brambles around yourself, with nettles and thorns. How could you draw a young maiden to you without her being cut and flayed bloody?"

"You stood by me more than once, brother, during that time when I was with Eline," said Erlend softly. "I have never forgotten that."

"I don't think I would have done so," replied Gunnulf, and his voice quavered, "if I had imagined that you would have the heart to behave in such a manner toward a pure and delicate maiden— and a mere child compared to you."

Erlend said nothing.

Gunnulf asked him gently, "That time in Oslo—didn't you ever think about what would happen to Kristin if she became with child while she was living in the convent? And was betrothed to another man? Her father a proud and honorable man—and all her kinsmen of noble lineage, unaccustomed to bearing shame."

"Of course I thought about it." Erlend had turned his face away. "Munan promised to take care of her—and I told her that too."

"Munan! Would you deign to speak to a man like Munan of Kristin's honor?"

"He's not the sort of man you think," said Erlend curtly.

"But what about our kinswoman Fru Katrin? For surely you didn't intend for him to take Kristin to any of his other estates, where his paramours live. . . ."

Erlend slammed his fist against the ground, making his knuckles bleed.

"The Devil himself must have a hand in it when a man's wife goes to his brother for confession!"

"She hasn't confessed to me," said the priest. "Nor am I her parish priest. She told me her laments during her bitter fear and anguish, and I tried to help her and give her such advice and solace as I thought best."

"I see." Erlend threw back his head and looked up at his brother. "I know that I shouldn't have done it; I shouldn't have allowed her to come to me at Brynhild's inn."

The priest sat speechless for a moment.

"At Brynhild Fluga's?"

"Yes, didn't she tell you that when she told you all the rest?"

"It will be hard enough for Kristin to say such things about her lawful husband in confession," said the priest after a pause. "I think she would rather die than speak of it anywhere else."

He fell silent and then said harshly and vehemently, "If you felt, Erlend, that you were her husband before God and the one who should protect and guard her, then I think your behavior was even worse. You seduced her in groves and in barns, you led her across a harlot's threshold. And finally up to Bjørn Gunnarssøn and Fru Aashild . . ."

"You mustn't speak of Aunt Aashild that way," said Erlend in a low voice.

"You've said yourself that you thought our aunt caused the death of our father's brother—she and that man Bjørn."

"It makes no difference to me," said Erlend forcefully. "I'm fond of Aunt Aashild."

"Yes, so I see," said the priest. A crooked, mocking little smile appeared on his lips. "Since you were ready to leave her to face Lavrans Bjørgulfsøn after you carried off his daughter. It seems as if you think that your affection is worth paying dearly for, Erlend."

"Jesus!" Erlend hid his face in his hands.

But the priest continued quickly, "If only you had seen the torment of your wife's soul as she trembled in horror of her sins, unconfessed and unredeemed—as she sat there, about to give birth to your child, with death standing at the door—so young a child herself, and so unhappy."

"I know, I know!" Erlend was shaking. "I know she lay there thinking about this as she suffered. For Christ's sake, Gunnulf, say no more. I'm your brother, after all!"

But he continued without mercy.

"If I had been a man like you and not a priest, and if I had led astray so young and good a maiden, I would have freed myself from that other woman. God help me, but I would have done as Aunt Aashild did to her husband and then burned in Hell forever after, rather than allow my innocent and dearest beloved to suffer such things as you have done."

Erlend sat in silence for a moment, trembling.

"You say that you're a priest," he said softly. "Are you such a *good* priest that you have never sinned—with a woman?"

Gunnulf did not look at his brother. Blood flushed red across his face.

"You have no right to ask me that, but I will answer you all the same. He who died for us on the cross knows how much I need his mercy. But I tell you, Erlend—if on the whole round disk of this earth he had not one servant who was pure and unmarked by sin, and if in his holy Church there was not a single priest who was more faithful and worthy than I am, miserable betrayer of the Lord that I am, then the Lord's commandments and laws are what we can learn from this. His Word cannot be defiled by the mouth of an impure priest; it can only burn and consume our own lips—although perhaps you can't understand this. But you know as well as I, along with every filthy thrall of the Devil that He has bought with His own blood—God's law cannot be shaken nor His honor diminished. Just as His sun is equally mighty, whether it shines above the barren sea and desolate gray moors or above these fair lands."

Erlend had hidden his face in his hands. He sat still for a long time, but when he spoke his voice was dry and hard.

"Priest or no priest—since you're not such a strict adherent of pure living—don't you see . . . Could you have done that to a woman who had slept in your arms and borne you two children? Could you have done to her what our aunt did to her husband?"

The priest didn't answer at first. Then he said with some scorn, "You don't seem to judge Aunt Aashild too harshly."

"But it can't be the same for a man as for a woman," said Erlend. "I remember the last time they were here at Husaby, and Herr Bjørn was with them. We sat near the hearth, Mother and Aunt Aashild, and Herr Bjørn played the harp and sang for them. I stood at his knee. Then Uncle Baard called to her—he was in bed, and he wanted her to come to bed too. He used words that were vulgar and shameless. Aunt Aashild stood up and Herr Bjørn did too. He left the room, but before he did, they looked at each other. Later, when I was old enough to understand, I thought . . . that it might be true after all. I had begged for permission to light the way for Herr Bjørn over to the loft where he was going to sleep, but I didn't dare, and I didn't dare sleep in the hall, either. I ran outside and went to sleep with the men in the servants' house. By Jesus, Gunnulf—it can't be the same for a man as it was for Aashild that evening. No, Gunnulf—to kill a woman who . . . unless I caught her with another man . . ."

And yet that was exactly what he had done. But Gunnulf wouldn't dare mention *that* to his brother.

Then the priest asked coldly, "Wasn't it true that Eline had been unfaithful to you?"

"Unfaithful!" Erlend abruptly turned to face his brother, furious. "Do you think I should have blamed her for taking up with Gissur, after I had told her so often that it was over between us?"

Gunnulf bowed his head.

"No. No doubt you're right," he said, his voice weary and low.

But having won that small concession, Erlend flared up. He threw back his head and looked at the priest.

"You take so much notice of Kristin, Gunnulf. The way you've been hanging about her all spring—almost more than is decent for a brother and a priest. It's as if you didn't want her to be mine. If things hadn't been the way they were with her when you first met, people might even think . . ."

Gunnulf stared at him. Provoked by his brother's gaze, Erlend jumped to his feet. Gunnulf stood up too. When he continued to stare, Erlend lashed out at him with his fist. The priest grabbed his wrist. He tried to charge at Gunnulf, but his brother stood his ground.

Erlend grew meek at once. "I should have remembered that you're a priest," he said softly.

"Well, you have nothing to repent on that account," said Gunnulf with a little smile. Erlend stood there rubbing his wrist.

"Yes, you always had such devilishly strong hands."

"This is the way it was when we were boys." Gunnulf's voice grew oddly tender and gentle. "I've thought about that often during the years I was away from home—about when we were boys. We often fought, but it never lasted long, Erlend."

"But now," said the other man sorrowfully, "it can never be the same as when we were boys, Gunnulf."

"No," murmured the priest. "I suppose it can't."

They stood in silence for a long time. Finally Gunnulf said, "I'm going away now, Erlend. I'll go down to bid Eiliv farewell, and then I'm leaving. I'm heading over to visit the priest in Orkedal; I won't go to Nidaros while *she* is there." He gave a small smile.

"Gunnulf! I didn't mean . . . Don't leave me this way."

Gunnulf didn't move. He breathed hard several times and then he said, "There's one thing I want to tell you, Erlend—since you now know that I know everything about you. Sit down."

The priest sat down in the same position as before. Erlend stretched out in front of him, lying with one hand propped under his chin and looking up at his brother's strangely tense and rigid face. Then he smiled.

"What is it, Gunnulf? Are you about to confess to me?"

"Yes," said his brother softly. But then he fell silent for a long time. Erlend noticed that his lips moved once, and he clasped his hands tighter around his knee.

"What is it?" He gave him a fleeting smile. "It can't be that you—that some fair woman out there in the southern lands . . ."

"No," said the priest. His voice had a peculiar gruff tone. "This is not about love. Do you know, Erlend, how it happened that I was promised to the priesthood?"

"Yes. When our brothers died and they thought they were going to lose us too . . ."

"No," said Gunnulf. "They thought Munan had regained his health, and Gaute was not ill at all; he didn't die until the next winter. But you lay in bed and were suffocating, and that's when Mother promised that I would serve Saint Olav if he would save your life."

"Who told you that?" asked Erlend after a moment.

"Ingrid, my foster mother."

"Well, I would have been an odd gift to offer to Saint Olav," said Erlend, with a laugh. "He would have been poorly served by me. But you've told me, Gunnulf, that you were pleased even as a boy to be called to the priesthood."

"Yes," said the priest. "But it was not always so. I remember the day you left Husaby along with Munan Baardsøn to journey to our kinsman, the king, to join his service. Your horse danced beneath you, and your new weapons gleamed and shone. I would never bear weapons. You were handsome, my brother. You were only sixteen winters old, and I had already noticed long ago that women and maidens were fond of you."

"All that glory was short-lived," said Erlend. "I learned to cut my nails straight across, to swear on the name of Jesus with every other word, and to resort to my dagger to defend myself when I wielded a sword. Then I was sent north and met *her*—and was banished with shame from the king's retinue, and our father closed his door to me."

"And you left the country with a beautiful woman," said Gunnulf in the same low voice. "We heard at home that you had become a chief of guards at Earl Jacob's castle."

"Well, it wasn't as grand as it seemed back home," said Erlend, laughing.

"You and Father were no longer friends. But he had so little regard for me that he didn't even bother to quarrel with me. Mother loved me, that I know—but she found me less worthy than you. I felt it the most when you left the country. You, brother, were the only one who had any real love for me. And God knows you were my dearest friend on earth. But back when I was young and ignorant, I would sometimes think you had been given so much more than I had. Now I've told you, Erlend."

Erlend lay with his face against the ground.

"Don't go, Gunnulf," he begged.

"I must," said the priest. "Now we've told each other far too much. May God and the Virgin Mary grant that we meet again at a better time. Farewell, Erlend."

"Farewell," said Erlend, but did not look up.

When Gunnulf, wearing traveling clothes, stepped out of the priest's house several hours later, he saw a man riding south across the fields toward the forest. He had a bow slung over his shoulder and three dogs were running alongside his horse. It was Erlend.

In the meantime Kristin was walking briskly along the forest path over the ridge. The sun was now high, and the tops of the fir trees shone against the summer sky, but inside the woods it was still cool and fresh with the morning. A fragrant smell filled the air from spruce boughs, the marshy earth, and the twinflowers that covered the ground everywhere, in bloom with pairs of tiny pink, bell-shaped blossoms. And the path, overgrown with grass, was damp and soft and felt good under her feet. Kristin walked along, saying her prayers; now and then she would look up at the small white, fair-weather clouds swimming in the blue above the treetops.

The whole time she found herself thinking about Brother Edvin. This is how he had walked and walked, year in and year out, from early spring until late in the fall. Over mountain paths, through dark ravines and white snowdrifts. He rested in the mountain pastures, drank from the creeks, and ate from the bread that milkmaids and horse herdsmen brought out to him. Then he would bid them live well and God's peace and bestow blessings on both them and the livestock. Through rustling mountain meadows the monk would hike down into the valley. Tall and stoop-shouldered, with his head bowed, he wandered the main roads past manors and farms—and everywhere he went, he would leave behind his loving prayers of intercession for everyone, like good weather.

Kristin didn't meet a living soul, except for a few cows now and then—there were mountain pastures on the ridge. But it was a clearly marked path, with log bridges across the marshes. Kristin was not afraid; she felt as if the monk were walking invisibly at her side.

Brother Edvin, if it's true that you are a holy man, if you now stand before God, then pray for me!

Lord Jesus Christ, Holy Mary, Saint Olav. She longed to reach the destination of her journey. She longed to cast off the burden of years of concealed sins, the weight of church services and masses which she had stolen, unconfessed and unredeemed. She longed to be absolved and free—just as she had longed to be released from her burden this past spring when she was carrying the child.

He was sleeping soundly, safe on his mother's back. He didn't wake up until she had walked through the woods down to the farms of Snefugl and could look out across Budvik and the arm of the fjord at Saltnes. Kristin sat down in an outlying field, pulled the bundle with the child around into her lap, and loosened her robe at the breast. It felt good to hold him to her breast; it felt good to sit down; and a blessed warmth coursed through her whole body as she felt her stone-hard breasts bursting with milk empty out as he nursed.

The countryside below her lay silent and baking in the sun, with green pastures and bright fields amidst dark forest. A little smoke drifted up from the rooftops here and there. The hay harvesting had begun in a few places.

She traveled by boat from Saltnes Sand over to Steine. Then she was in completely unfamiliar regions. The road through Bynes went past farms for a while; then she reached the woods again, but there was no longer such a great distance between human dwellings. She was very tired. But then she thought about her parents—they had walked barefoot all the way from Jørundgaard at Sil, through Dovre, and on to Nidaros, carrying Ulvhild on a litter between them. She must not think that Naakkve was so heavy on her back.

And yet her head itched terribly from the sweat under her thick homespun wimple. Around her waist, where the rope held her clothing close to her body, her shift had rubbed on her skin so that it felt quite raw.

After a while there were others on the road. Now and then people would ride past her. She caught up with a farmer's cart taking goods to town; the heavy wheels jolted and jounced over roots and stones, screeching and creaking. Two men were driving a beast to slaughter. They glanced at the young woman pilgrim because she was so beautiful; otherwise people were used to such wayfarers in these parts. At one place several men were building a house a short distance from the road; they shouted to her, and an old man came running to offer her some ale. Kristin curtseyed, took a drink, and thanked the man with such words as poor people usually said to her when she gave them alms.

A little while later she had to rest again. She found a small green hill along the road with a trickling creek. Kristin placed the child on the grass; he woke up and cried loudly, so she hurried distractedly through the prayers she had meant to say. Then she picked up Naakkve, held him on her lap, and loosened the swaddling clothes. He had sullied his underclothes, and she had little to change him with; so she rinsed the cloths and spread them out to dry on a bare rock in the sun. She wrapped the outer garments loosely around the boy. He seemed to like this, and lay there kicking as he drank from his mother's breast. Kristin gazed happily at his fine, rosy limbs and pressed one of his hands between her breasts as she nursed him.

Two men rode past at a fast trot. Kristin glanced up briefly—it was a nobleman and his servant. But suddenly the man reined in his horse, leaped from the saddle, and walked back to where she was sitting. It was Simon Andressøn.

"Perhaps you won't be pleased that I stopped to greet you?" he asked. He stood there holding his horse and looking down at her. He was wearing traveling clothes, with a sleeveless leather vest over a light-blue linen tunic; he wore a small silk cap on his head, and his face was rather flushed and sweaty. "It's strange to see you—but perhaps you'd rather not speak to me?"

"Surely you should know . . . How are you, Simon?" Kristin tucked her bare feet under the hem of her skirts and tried to take the child from her breast. But the boy screamed, opening his mouth to suckle, so she had to let him nurse again. She pulled the robe over her breast as best she could and sat with her eyes lowered.

"Is it yours?" asked Simon, pointing to the child. "That was a foolish question," he laughed. "It's a son, isn't it? He's blessed with good fortune, Erlend Nikulaussøn!" He tied his horse to a tree, and now he sat down on a rock not far from Kristin. He placed his sword between his knees and sat with his hands on the hilt, poking at the dirt with the point of the scabbard.

"It was unexpected to meet you here in the north, Simon," said Kristin, just for something to say.

"Yes," said Simon. "I haven't had business in this part of the country before."

Kristin recalled that she had heard something—at the welcome celebration for her at Husaby—about the youngest son of Arne Gjavvaldssøn of Ranheim being betrothed to Andres Darre's youngest daughter. So she asked him whether that's where he had been.

"You know about it?" asked Simon. "Well, I suppose it must have been talked about all through these parts."

"So it's true," said Kristin, "that Gjavvald is to marry Sigrid?"

Simon looked up abruptly, pressing his lips together.

"I see you don't know everything, after all."

"I haven't been beyond the courtyard of Husaby all winter," said Kristin. "And I've seen few people. I heard there was talk of this marriage."

"You might as well hear it from my lips, then—the news will doubtless reach here soon enough." He sat in silence for a moment. "Gjavvald died three days before Winter Night.[1] He fell off his horse and broke his back. Do you remember before you reach Dyfrin how the road heads east of the river and there's a steep drop-off? No, you probably don't. We were on our way to their betrothal celebration; Arne and his sons had come by ship to Oslo." Then Simon fell silent.

"She must have been happy, Sigrid—because she was going to marry Gjavvald," said Kristin, shy and timid.

"Yes," said Simon. "And she had a son by him—on the Feast Day of the Apostles this spring."

"Oh, Simon!"

Sigrid Andresdatter, with the brown curls framing her small round face. Whenever she laughed, deep dimples appeared in her cheeks. The dimples and the small, childish white teeth—Simon had them too. Kristin remembered that when she grew less kindly inclined toward her betrothed, these things seemed to her unmanly, especially after she had met Erlend. They were much alike, Sigrid and Simon; but in her case it seemed charming that she was so plump and quick to laughter. She was fourteen winters old back then. Kristin had never heard such merry laughter as Sigrid's. Simon was always teasing his youngest sister and joking with her; Kristin could see that of all his siblings, he was most fond of her.

"You know that Father loved Sigrid best," said Simon. "That's why he wanted to see whether she and Gjavvald would like each other before he made this agreement with Arne. And they did—in my mind a little more than was proper. They always had to sit close whenever they met, and they would steal looks at each other and laugh. That was last summer at Dyfrin. But they were so young. No one could have imagined this. And our sister Astrid— you know she was betrothed when you and I . . . Well, *she* voiced no objections; Torgrim is very wealthy and kind, and in a certain way . . . but he finds fault with everyone and everything, and he thinks he suffers from all the ailments and troubles that anyone can name. So all of us were happy when Sigrid seemed so pleased with the man chosen for her.

"And then we brought Gjavvald's body to the manor. Halfrid, my wife, arranged things so that Sigrid would come home with us to Mandvik. And then it came out that Sigrid wasn't left alone when Gjavvald died."

They were silent for a while. Then Kristin said softly, "This has not been a joyful journey for you, Simon."

"No, it hasn't." Then he gave a laugh. "But I've gotten used to traveling on unfortunate business, Kristin. And I was the closest one, after all—Father lacked the courage, and they're living with me at Mandvik, Sigrid and her son. But now he'll have a place in his father's lineage, and I could see from all of them there that he won't be unwelcome, the poor little boy, when he goes to live with them."

"But what of your sister?" asked Kristin, breathlessly. "Where is she to live?"

Simon looked down at the ground.

"Father will take her home to Dyfrin now," he said in a low voice.

"Simon! Oh, how can you have the heart to agree to this?"

"You must realize," he replied without looking up, "that it's a great advantage for the boy, that he'll be part of his father's family from the beginning. Halfrid and I, we would have liked to keep both of them with us. No sister could be more loyal and loving toward another than Halfrid is toward Sigrid. None of our kinsmen has been unkind toward her—you mustn't think that. Not even Father, although this has made him a broken man. But can't you see? It wouldn't be right if any of us objected to the innocent boy gaining inheritance and lineage from his father."

Kristin's child let go of her breast. She quickly drew her garments closed over her bosom and, trembling, hugged the infant close. He hiccupped happily a couple of times and then spit up a little over himself and his mother's hands.

Simon glanced at the two of them and said with an odd smile, "You had better luck, Kristin, than my sister did."

"Yes, no doubt it may seem unfair to you," said Kristin softly, "that I'm called wife and my son was lawfully born. I might have deserved to be left with the fatherless child of a paramour."

"That would seem to me the worst thing I could have heard," said Simon. "I wish you only the best, Kristin," he said even more quietly.

A moment later he asked her for directions. He mentioned that he had come north by ship from Tunsberg. "Now I must continue on and see about catching up with my servant."

"Is it Finn who's traveling with you?" asked Kristin.

"No. Finn is married now; he's no longer in my service. Do you still remember him?" asked Simon, and his voice sounded pleased.

"Is Sigrid's son a handsome child?" asked Kristin, looking at Naakkve.

"I hear that he is. I think one infant looks much like another," replied Simon.

"Then you must not have children of your own," said Kristin, giving a little smile.

"No," he said curtly. Then he bid her farewell and rode off.

When Kristin continued on, she didn't put her child on her back. She carried him in her arms, pressing his face against the hollow of her neck. She could think of nothing else but Sigrid Andresdatter.

Her own father would not have been able to do it. Should Lavrans Bjørgulfsøn ride off to beg for a place and rank for his daughter's bastard child among the father's kinsmen? He would never have been able to do that. And never, never would he have had the heart to take her child away from her—to pull a tiny infant out of his mother's arms, tear him away from her breast while he still had mother's milk on his innocent lips. My Naakkve, no he wouldn't do that—even if it were ten times more just to do so, my father would not have done it.

But she couldn't get the image out of her mind: a group of horsemen vanishing north of the gorge, where the valley grows narrow and the mountains crowd together, black with trees. Cold wind comes in gusts from the river, which thunders over the rocks, icy green and frothing, with deep black pools in between. Whoever throws himself into it would be crushed in the rapids at once. Jesus, Maria.

Then she envisioned the fields back home at Jørundgaard on a light summer night. She saw herself running down the path to the green clearing in the alder grove near the river, where they used to wash clothes. The water rushed past with a loud, monotonous roar along the flat riverbed filled with boulders. Lord Jesus, there is nothing else I can do.

Oh, but Father would not have had the heart to do it. No matter how right it was. If I begged and begged him, begged on my knees: Father, you mustn't take my child from me.

Kristin stood on the hill at Feginsbrekka and looked down at the town lying at her feet in the golden evening sun. Beyond the wide, glittering curve of the river lay brown farm buildings with green sod roofs; the crowns of the trees were dark and domelike in the gardens. She saw light-colored stone houses with stepped gables, churches thrusting their black, shingle-covered backs into the air, and churches with dully gleaming roofs of lead. But above the green landscape, above the glorious town, rose Christ Church so magnificently huge and radiantly bright, as if everything lay prone at its feet. With the evening sun on its breast and the sparkling glass of its windows, with its towers and dizzying spires and gilded weather vanes, the cathedral stood pointing up into the bright summer sky.

All around lay the summer-green land, bearing venerable manors on its hills. In the distance the fjord opened out, shining and wide, with drifting shadows from the large summer clouds that billowed up over the glittering blue mountains on the other side. The cloister island looked like a green wreath with flowers of stone-white buildings, softly lapped by the sea. So many ships' masts out among the islands, so many beautiful houses.

Overcome and sobbing, the young woman sank down before the cross at the side of the road, where thousands of pilgrims had lain and thanked God because helping hands were extended to them on their journey through the perilous and beautiful world.

The bells of the churches and cloisters were ringing for vespers as Kristin entered the courtyard of Christ Church. For a moment she ventured to glance up at the west gable—then she lowered her dazzled eyes.

Human beings could not have done this work on their own. God's spirit had been at work in holy Øistein and the men who built the church after him. *Thy kingdom come, Thy will be done, on earth as it is in heaven.* Now she understood those words. A reflection of the splendor of God's kingdom bore witness through the stones that His will was all that was beautiful. Kristin trembled. Yes, God must surely turn away with scorn from all that was vile—from sin and shame and impurity.

Along the galleries of the heavenly palace stood holy men and women, and they were so beautiful that she dared not look at them. The imperishable vines of eternity wound their way upward, calm and lovely, bursting into flower on spires and towers with stone monstrances. Above the center door hung Christ on the cross; Mary and John the Evangelist stood at his side. And they were white, as if molded from snow, and gold glittered on the white.

Three times Kristin walked around the church, praying. The huge, massive walls with their bewildering wealth of pillars and arches and windows, the glimpse of the roof's enormous slanting surface, the tower, the gold of the spire rising high into the heavens—Kristin sank to the ground beneath her sin.

She was shaking as she kissed the hewn stone of the portal. In a flash she saw the dark carved timber around the church door back home, where as a child she had pressed her lips after her father and mother.

She sprinkled holy water over her son and herself, remembering that her father had done the same when she was small. With the child clasped tightly in her arms, she stepped forward into the church.

She walked as if through a forest. The pillars were furrowed like ancient trees, and into the woods the light seeped, colorful and as clear as song, through the stained-glass windows. High overhead animals and people frolicked in the stone foliage, and angels played their instruments. At an even higher, more dizzying height, the vaults of the ceiling arched upward, lifting the church toward God. In a hall off to the side a service was being held at an altar. Kristin fell to her knees next to a pillar. The song cut through her like a blinding light. Now she saw how deep in the dust she lay.

Pater noster. Credo in unum Deum. Ave Maria, gratia plena. She had learned her prayers by repeating them after her father and mother before she could understand a single word, from as far back as she could remember. Lord Jesus Christ. Was there ever a sinner like her?

High beneath the triumphal arch, raised above the people, hung Christ on the cross. The pure virgin, who was his mother, stood looking up in deathly anguish at her innocent son who was suffering the death of a criminal.

And here knelt Kristin with the fruit of her sin in her arms. She hugged the child tight—he was as fresh as an apple, pink and white like a rose. He was awake now, and he lay there looking up at her with his clear, sweet eyes.

Conceived in sin. Carried under her hard, evil heart. Pulled out of her sin-tainted body, so pure, so healthy, so inexpressibly lovely and fresh and innocent. This undeserved beneficence broke her heart in two; crushed with remorse, she lay there with tears welling up out of her soul like blood from a mortal wound.

Naakkve, Naakkve, my child. God visits the sins of the parents upon the children. Didn't I know that? Yes, I did. But I had no mercy for the innocent life that might be awakened in my womb—to be cursed and tormented because of my sin.

Did I regret my sin while I was carrying you inside me, my beloved, beloved son? Oh no, there was no remorse. My heart was hard with anger and evil thoughts at the moment I first felt you move, so small and unprotected. *Magnificat anima mea*

Dominum. Et exultavit spiritus meus in Deo salutari meo.[2] That is
what she sang, the gentle queen of women, when she was chosen
to bear the one who would die for our sins. I didn't think about
the one who was the redeemer of my sin and my child's sin. Oh,
no, there was no remorse. Instead I made myself pitiful and
wretched and begged that the commandments of righteousness be
broken, for I could not bear it if God should keep His promise and
punish me in accordance with the Word that I have known all my
days.

Oh yes, now she knew. She had thought that God was like her
own father, that Holy Olav was like her father. All along she had
expected, deep in her heart, that whenever the punishment became
more than she could bear, then she would encounter not righteousness but mercy.

She wept so hard that she didn't have the strength to rise when
the others stood up during the service; she stayed there, collapsed
in a heap, holding her child. Near her several other people knelt
who did not rise either: two well-dressed farmers' wives with a
young boy between them.

She looked up toward the raised chancel. Beyond the gilded,
grated door, high up behind the altar, Saint Olav's shrine glistened
in the darkness. An ice-cold shiver ran down her back. There
lay his holy body, waiting for Resurrection Day. Then the lid
would spring open, and he would rise up. With his axe in hand, he
would stride through this church. And from the stone floor, from
the earth outside, from every cemetery in all of Norway the dead
yellow skeletons would rise up; they would be clothed in flesh and
would rally around their king. Those who had striven to follow in
his bloodied tracks, and those who had merely turned to him for
help with the burdens of sin and sorrow and illness to which they
had bound themselves and their children, here in this life. They
would crowd around their king and ask him to remind God of
their need.

"Lord, hear my prayer for these people, whom I love so much
that I would rather suffer exile and want and hatred and death
than have a single man or maiden grow up in Norway not knowing that you died to save all sinners. Lord, you who bade us go out
and make everyone your disciple—with my blood I, Olav Har-

aldssøn, wrote your gospel in the Norwegian language for these free men, my poor subjects."

Kristin closed her eyes, feeling sick and dizzy. She saw the king's face before her—his blazing eyes pierced the depths of her soul—now she trembled before Saint Olav's gaze.

"North of your village, Kristin, where I rested when my own countrymen drove me from my ancestral kingdom, because they could not keep God's Commandments—wasn't a church built at that spot? Didn't knowledgeable men come there to teach you of God's Word?

"Thou shalt honor thy father and thy mother. Thou shalt not kill. God visits the sins of the fathers upon the children. I died so that you might learn these teachings. Haven't they been given to you, Kristin Lavransdatter?"

Oh yes, yes, my Lord and King!

Olav's church back home—she saw in her mind the pleasant, brown-timbered room. The ceiling was not so high that it could frighten her. It was unassuming, built in God's honor from dark, tarred wood, in the same way that people constructed their mountain huts and storehouses and cattle sheds. But the timbers had been cut into supple staves, and they were raised and joined to form the walls of God's house. And Sira Eirik taught each year on the church consecration day that in this manner we ought to use the tools of faith to cut and carve from our sinful, natural being a faithful link in the Church of Christ.

"Have you forgotten this, Kristin? Where are the deeds that should bear witness for you on the last day, showing that you were a link in God's church? The good deeds which will bear witness that you belong to God?"

Jesus, her good deeds! She had repeated the prayers that were placed on her lips. She had given out the alms that her father had placed in her hands; she had helped her mother when Ragnfrid clothed the poor, fed the hungry, and tended to the sores of the ill.

But the evil deeds were her own.

She had clung to everyone who offered her protection and support. Brother Edvin's loving admonitions, his sorrow over her sin, his tender intercessionary prayers which she had received—and then she had flung herself into passionate sinful desire as soon as she was beyond the light of his gentle old eyes. She lay down in cowsheds and outbuildings and scarcely felt any shame that she was deceiving the good and honorable Abbess Groa; she had accepted the kind concern of the pious sisters and hadn't even had the wit to blush when they praised her gentle and seemly behavior before her father.

Oh, the worst was thinking about her father. Her father, who had not said a single unkind word when he came to visit this spring.

Simon had concealed the fact that he had caught his betrothed with a man at an inn for wandering soldiers. And she had let him take the blame for her breach of promise, had let him bear the blame before her father.

Oh, but her father, that was the worst. No, her mother, that was even worse. If Naakkve should grow up to show his mother as little love as she had shown her own mother—oh, she couldn't bear it. Her mother, who had given birth to her and nursed her at her breast, kept watch over her when she was sick, washed and combed her hair and rejoiced at its beauty. And the first time that Kristin felt she needed her mother's help and comfort, she had waited for her mother to come, in spite of all her own disdain. "You should know that your mother would have come north to be with you if she had known that it might give you comfort," her father had said. Oh, Mother, Mother, Mother!

She had seen the water from the well back home. It looked so clean and pure when it was in the wooden cups. But her father owned a glass goblet, and when he filled it with water and the sun shone through, the water was muddy and full of impurities.

Yes, my Lord and King, now I see the way I am!

Goodness and love she had accepted from everyone, as if they were her right. There was no end to the goodness and love she had encountered all her days. But the first time someone confronted her, she had risen up like a snake and struck. Her will had been as hard and sharp as a knife when she drove Eline Ormsdatter to her death.

Just as she would have risen up against God Himself if He had placed His righteous hand on the back of her neck. Oh, how could her father and mother bear it? They had lost three young children;

they had watched Ulvhild sicken until she died, after they had striven those long sorrowful years to give the child back her health. But they had borne all these trials with patience, never doubting that God knew what was best for their children. Then she had caused them all this sorrow and shame.

But if there had been anything wrong with her child—if they had taken her child the way they were now taking Sigrid Andresdatter's child from her . . . Oh, *lead us not into temptation, but deliver us from evil.*

She had wandered to the very edge of Hell's abyss. If she should lose her son, after she had thrown herself into the seething rapids, turned away with scorn from any hope of joining the good and dear people who loved her—giving herself into the Devil's power . . .

It was no wonder that Naakkve bore the mark of a bloody hand on his chest.

Oh, Holy Olav, you who heard me when I prayed for you to help my child. I prayed that you would turn the punishment upon me and spare the innocent one. Yes, Lord, I know how I kept my part of the agreement.

Like a wild, heathen animal she had reared up at the first chastisement. Erlend. Not for a moment did she ever believe that he no longer loved her. If she had believed that, then she would not have had the strength to live. Oh no. But she had secretly thought that when she was beautiful again, and healthy and lively—then she would act in such a way that he would have to beg her. It wasn't that he had been unloving during the winter. But she, who had heard ever since she was a girl that the Devil always keeps close to a woman with child and tempts her because she is weak—she had turned a willing ear to the Devil's lies. She had pretended to believe that Erlend didn't care for her because she was ugly and ill, when she noticed that he was distressed because he had made both her and himself the subject of gossip. She had flung his timid and tender words back at him, and when she drove him to say harsh and thoughtless things, she would bring them up later to rebuke him. Jesus, what an evil woman she was—she had been a bad wife.

"Now do you understand, Kristin, that you need help?"

Yes, my Lord and King, now I understand. I am in great need of your support so that I won't turn away from God again. Stay with me, you who are the chieftain of His people, as I step forward with my prayers; pray for mercy for me. Holy Olav, pray for me!

Cor mundum crea in me, Deus, et Spiritum rectum innova in visceribus meis.

Ne projicias me a facie tua.

Libera me de sanguinibus, Deus, Deus salutis meæ.[3]

The service was over. People were leaving the church. The two farmers' wives who were kneeling near Kristin stood up. But the boy between them did not get up. He began moving across the floor by setting his knuckles on the flagstones and hopping along like a fledgling crow. He had tiny legs, bent crooked under his belly. The women walked in such a way as to hide him with their clothes as best they could.

When they were out of sight, Kristin threw herself down and kissed the floor where they had walked past her.

Feeling lost and uncertain, she was standing at the entrance to the chancel when a young priest came out the grated door. He stopped in front of the young woman with the tear-stained face, and Kristin did her best to explain the reason for her journey. At first he didn't understand. Then she pulled out the golden crown and held it out.

"Oh, are you Kristin Lavransdatter, the wife of Erlend of Husaby?" He gave her a rather surprised look; her face was quite swollen from weeping. "Yes, your brother-in-law, Gunnulf, spoke of you, yes he did."

He led her into the sacristy and took the crown; he unwrapped the linen cloth and looked at it. Then he smiled.

"Well, you must realize that there will have to be witnesses and the like. You can't give away such a costly treasure as if it were a piece of buttered *lefse*. But I can keep it for you in the meantime; no doubt you would prefer not to carry it around with you in town.

"Oh, ask Herr Arne if he wouldn't mind coming here," he said to a sexton. "I think that by rights your husband should be present too. But perhaps Gunnulf has a letter from him.

"You wish to speak to the archbishop himself, is that right?

Otherwise there is Hauk Tomassøn, who is the *penitentiarius*. I don't know whether Gunnulf has spoken to Archbishop Eiliv. But you must come here for matins tomorrow, and then you can ask for me after lauds. My name is Paal Aslakssøn. That," and he pointed to the child, "you must leave at the hostel. I seem to remember your brother-in-law saying that you're staying with the sisters at Bakke, is that right?"

Another priest came in, and the two men talked to each other briefly. The first priest then opened a small cupboard in the wall and took out a balance scale and weighed the crown, while the other made a note of it in a ledger. Then they placed the crown in the cupboard and closed the door.

Herr Paal was about to escort Kristin out, but then he asked her whether she would like him to lift her son up to Saint Olav's shrine.

He picked up the boy with the confident, almost indifferent ease of a priest who was used to holding children for baptism. Kristin followed him into the church, and he asked her whether she too would like to kiss the shrine.

I don't dare, thought Kristin, but she accompanied the priest up the stairs to the dais on which the shrine stood. A great, chalk-white light seemed to pass before her eyes as she pressed her lips to the golden chest.

The priest looked at her for a moment, to see whether she might collapse in a faint. But she got to her feet. Then he touched the child's forehead to the sacred shrine.

Herr Paal escorted Kristin to the church door and asked whether she was certain she could find her way to the ferry landing. Then he bade her good night. He spoke the whole time in an even and dry voice, like any other courteous young man in the king's service.

It had started to rain lightly, and a wonderful fragrance wafted blessedly from the gardens and along the street, which, on either side of the worn ruts from the wheel tracks, was as fresh and green as a country courtyard. Kristin sheltered the child from the rain as best she could—he was heavy now, so heavy that her arms were quite numb from carrying him. And he fussed and cried incessantly; he was probably hungry again.

The mother was dead tired from the long journey and from all the weeping and the intense emotions in the church. She was cold, and the rain was coming down harder; the drops splashed on the trees, making the leaves flutter and shake. She made her way down the lanes and came out onto a broad street; from there she could see the rushing river, wide and gray, its surface punctured like a sieve by the falling drops.

There was no ferryboat. Kristin talked to two men who were huddled in a space beneath a warehouse standing on posts at the water's edge. They told her to go out to the sandbanks—there the nuns had a house, and that's where the ferryman was.

Kristin went back up the wide street, wet and tired and with aching feet. She came to a small gray stone church; behind it stood several buildings enclosed by a fence. Naakkve was screaming furiously, so she couldn't go inside the church. But she heard the song from the recessed paneless windows, and she recognized the antiphon: *Lætare, Regina Coeli*—rejoice, thou Queen of Heaven, for he whom you were chosen to bear, has risen, as he promised. Hallelujah!

This was what the Minorites[4] sang after the *completorium*. Brother Edvin had taught her this hymn to the Lord's Mother as Kristin kept vigil over him during those nights when he lay deathly ill in their home at Jørundgaard. She crept out to the churchyard and, standing against the wall with her child in her arms, she repeated his words softly to herself.

"Nothing you do could ever change your father's heart toward you. This is why you must not cause him any more sorrow."

As your pierced hands were stretched out on the cross, O precious Lord of Heaven. No matter how far a soul might stray from the path of righteousness, the pierced hands were stretched out, yearning. Only one thing was needed: that the sinful soul should turn toward the open embrace, freely, like a child who goes to his father and not like a thrall who is chased home to his stern master. Now Kristin realized how hideous sin was. Again she felt the pain in her breast, as if her heart were breaking with remorse and shame at the undeserved mercy.

Next to the church wall there was a little shelter from the rain. She sat down on a gravestone and set about quelling the child's hunger. Now and then she would bend down and kiss his little down-covered head.

She must have fallen asleep. Someone was touching her shoulder. A monk and an old lay brother holding a spade in his hand stood before her. The barefoot brother asked if she was looking for shelter for the night.

The thought raced through her mind that she would much rather stay here tonight with the Minorites, Brother Edvin's brothers. And it was so far to Bakke, and she was nearly collapsing with weariness. Then the monk offered to have the lay servant accompany her to the women's hostel—"and give her a little calamus poultice for her feet; I see that they are sore."

It was stuffy and dark at the women's hostel, which stood outside the fence in the lane. The lay brother brought Kristin water to wash with and a little food, and she sat down near the hearth, trying to soothe her child. Naakkve could no doubt tell from her milk that his mother was worn out and had fasted all day. He fretted and whimpered in between attempts to suckle from her empty breasts. Kristin gulped down the milk that the lay brother brought her. She tried to squirt it from her mouth into the child's, but the boy protested loudly at this new means of being fed, and the old man laughed and shook his head. She would have to drink it herself, and then it would benefit the boy.

Finally the man left. Kristin crept into one of the beds high up beneath the center roof beam. From there she could reach a hatch. There was a foul smell in the hostel—one of the women was in bed with a stomach ailment. Kristin opened the hatch. The summer night was bright and mild, the rain-washed air streamed down on her. She sat in the short bed with her head leaning back against the timbers of the wall; there were few pillows for the beds. The boy was asleep in her lap. She had meant to close the hatch after a moment, but she fell asleep.

In the middle of the night she woke up. The moon, a pale summery honey-gold, was shining down on her and the child and illuminating the opposite wall. At that moment Kristin became aware of a person standing in the midst of the stream of moonlight, hovering between the gable and the floor.

He was wearing an ash-gray monk's cowl; he was tall and stooped. Then he turned his ancient, furrowed face toward her. It was Brother Edvin. His smile was so inexpressibly tender, and a little sly and merry, just as it was when he lived on this earth.

Kristin was not the least bit surprised. Humbly, joyfully, and filled with anticipation, she looked at him and waited for what he would say or do.

The monk laughed and held up a heavy old leather glove toward her; then he hung it on the moonbeam. He smiled even more, nodded to her, and then vanished.

PART II

HUSABY

CHAPTER 1

ONE DAY JUST after New Year's, unexpected guests arrived at Husaby. They were Lavrans Bjørgulfsøn and old Smid Gudleikssøn from Dovre, and they were accompanied by two gentlemen whom Kristin didn't know. But Erlend was very surprised to see his father-in-law in their company—they were Erling Vidkunssøn from Giske and Bjarkøy, and Haftor Graut from Godøy. He hadn't realized that Lavrans knew them. But Sir Erling explained that they had met at Nes; he had served with Lavrans and Smid on the six-man court, which had finally settled the inheritance dispute among Jon Haukssøn's descendants. Then he and Lavrans happened to speak of Erlend; and Erling, who had business in Nidaros, mentioned that he had a mind to pay a visit to Husaby if Lavrans would keep him company and sail north with him.

Smid Gudleikssøn said with a laugh that he had practically invited himself along on the journey. "I wanted to see our Kristin again—the loveliest rose of the north valley. And I also thought that my kinswoman Ragnfrid would thank me if I kept an eye on her husband, to see what kind of decisions he was making with such wise and mighty men. Yes, your father has had other matters on his hands this winter, Kristin, than carousing from farm to farm with us and celebrating the Christmas season until Lent begins. All these years we've been sitting at home on our estates in peace and quiet, with each man tending to his own interests. But now Lavrans wants the men of the valleys who are the king's retainers to ride together to Oslo in the harshest time of the winter—now we're supposed to advise the noblemen of the Council and look after the king's interests. Lavrans says they're handling things so badly for the poor, underaged boy."[1]

Sir Erling looked rather embarrassed. Erlend raised his eyebrows.

"Have you decided to support these efforts, Father-in-law? For the great meeting of the royal retainers?"

"No, no," said Lavrans. "I'm merely going to the meeting, just like the other king's men of the valley, because we have been summoned."

But Smid Gudleikssøn spoke again. It was Lavrans who had persuaded him—and Herstein of Kruke and Trond Gjesling and Guttorm Sneis, as well as others who had not wanted to go.

"Isn't it the custom to invite guests into the house on this estate?" asked Lavrans. "Now we'll see whether Kristin brews ale as good as her mother's." Erlend looked thoughtful, and Kristin was greatly surprised.

"What's this about, Father?" she asked some time later, when he went with her to the little house where she had taken the child in order not to disturb the guests.

Lavrans sat and bounced his grandchild on his knee. Naakkve was now ten months old, big and handsome. He had been allowed to wear a tunic and hose since Christmas.

"I've never heard of you lending your voice to such matters before, Father," she said. "You've always told me that for the country, and for his subjects, it was best for the king to rule, along with those men he called to his side. Erlend says that this attempt is the work of the noblemen in the south; they want to remove Lady Ingebjørg from power, along with those men whom her father appointed to advise her. They want to steal back the power they had when King Haakon and his brother were children. But that brought great harm to the kingdom—you've said so yourself in the past."

Lavrans whispered that she should send the nursemaid away. When they were alone, he asked, "Where did Erlend get this information? Did he hear it from Munan?"

Kristin told him that Orm had brought a letter from Sir Munan when he returned home in the fall. She didn't say that she had read it to Erlend herself—he wasn't very good at deciphering script. But in the letter Munan had complained bitterly that now every man in Norway who bore a coat of arms thought himself better at ruling the kingdom than those men who had stood at King Haakon's side

when he was alive, and they presumed to have a better understanding of the young king's welfare than the highborn woman
who was his own mother. He had warned Erlend that if there were
signs that the Norwegian noblemen had intentions of doing as the
Swedes had done in Skara[2] last summer, of plotting against Lady
Ingebjørg and her old, trusted advisers, then her kinsmen would
stand ready and Erlend should go to meet Munan in Hamar.

"Didn't he mention," asked Lavrans as he tapped his finger under Naakkve's chubby chin, "that I'm one of the men opposed to
the unlawful call to arms that Munan has been carrying through
the valley, in the name of our king?"

"You!" said Kristin. "Did you meet Munan Baardsøn last fall?"

"Yes, I did," replied Lavrans. "And there was not much agreement between us."

"Did you talk about me?" asked Kristin swiftly.

"No, my dear Kristin," said her father, with a laugh. "I can't recall that your name was mentioned by either of us this time. Do
you know whether your husband intends to travel south to meet
with Munan Baardsøn?"

"I think so," said Kristin. "Sira Eiliv drafted a letter for Erlend
not long ago, and he mentioned that he might soon have to go
south."

Lavrans sat in silence for a moment, looking down at the child,
who was fumbling with the hilt of his dagger and trying to bite the
rock crystal embedded in it.

"Is it true that they want to take the regency away from Lady
Ingebjørg?" asked Kristin.

"She's about the same age as you are," replied her father, a
slight smile still on his lips. "No one wants to take from the king's
mother the honor and power that are her birthright. But the archbishop and some of our blessed king's friends and kinsmen have
gathered for a meeting to deliberate how Lady Ingebjørg's power
and honor and the interests of the people should best be protected."

Kristin said quietly, "I can see, Father, that you haven't come to
Husaby this time just to see Naakkve and me."

"No, that was not the only reason," said Lavrans. Then he
laughed. "And I can tell, daughter, that you're not at all pleased!"

He put his hand up to stroke her face, just as he used to do when she was a little girl, any time he had scolded her or teased her.

In the meantime Sir Erling and Erlend were sitting in the armory— that was what the large storehouse was called which stood on the northeast side of the courtyard, right next to the manor gate. It was as tall as a tower, with three stories; on the top floor there was a room with loopholes in the walls for shooting arrows, and that was where all the weapons were stored which were not in daily use on the farm. King Skule had built this structure.

Sir Erling and Erlend were wearing fur capes because it was bitterly cold in the room. The guest walked around looking at the many splendid weapons and suits of armor which Erlend had inherited from his grandfather, Gaute Erlendssøn.

Erling Vidkunssøn was a rather short man, slight in build and yet quite plump, but he carried himself well and with ease. Handsome he was not, although he had well-formed features. But his hair had a reddish tinge, and his eyelashes and brows were white; even his eyes were a very pale blue. That people nevertheless found Sir Erling to be good-looking was perhaps due to the fact that everyone knew he was the wealthiest knight in Norway. But he also had a distinctly winning and modest demeanor. He was exceptionally intelligent, well educated and learned, but because he never tried to boast of his wisdom and always seemed to be willing to listen to others, he had become known as one of the wisest men in the country. He was the same age as Erlend Nikulaussøn, and they were kinsmen, although distant ones, by way of the Stovreim lineage. They had known each other all their lives, but there had never been a close friendship between the two men.

Erlend sat down on a chest and talked about the ship which he had had built in the summer; it was a thirty-two-oar ship, and he deemed it to be a particularly swift sailing ship and easy to steer. He had hired two shipbuilders from the north, and he had personally overseen the work along with them.

"Ships are among the few things I know something about, Erling," he said. "You just wait—it will be a beautiful sight to see *Margygren* cutting through the waves."

"*Margygren*—what a fearfully heathen name you've given your ship, kinsman," said Erling with a little laugh. "Is it your intention to travel south in it?"

"Are you as pious as my wife? She calls it a heathen name, too. She doesn't like the ship much, either, but she's such an inland person—she can't stand the sea."

"Yes, she looks pious and delicate and lovely, your wife," said Sir Erling courteously. "As one might expect from someone of her lineage."

"Yes," said Erlend and laughed. "Not a day passes without her going to mass. And Sira Eiliv, our priest, whom you met, reads to us from the holy books. Reading aloud—that's what he likes best, after ale and sumptuous food. And the poor people come to Kristin for help and advice. I think they would gladly kiss the hem of her skirts; I can scarcely recognize my own servants anymore. She's almost like one of the women described in the holy sagas that King Haakon forced us to sit and listen to as the priest read them aloud—do you remember? Back when we were pages? Things have changed a great deal here at Husaby since you visited us last, Erling."

After a moment he added, "It was odd, by the way, that you were willing to come here that time."

"You mentioned the days when we were pages together," said Erling Vidkunssøn with a smile that became him. "We were friends back then, weren't we? We all expected that you would achieve great things here in Norway, Erlend."

But Erlend merely laughed. "Yes, I expected as much myself."

"Couldn't you sail south with me, Erlend?" asked Sir Erling.

"I was thinking of traveling overland," replied the other man.

"That will be troublesome for you—setting out over the mountains now, in the wintertime," said Sir Erling. "It would be pleasant if you would accompany Haftor and myself."

"I have promised to travel with others," replied Erlend.

"Ah yes, you will join your father-in-law—yes, that seems only fitting."

"Well, no—I don't know these men from the valley who are riding with him." Erlend sat in silence for a moment. "No, I have promised to look in on Munan at Stange," he said quickly.

"You don't need to waste your time looking for Munan there," replied Erling. "He's gone to his estates at Hising, and it might be some time before he comes north again. Has it been a long time since you heard from him?"

"It was around Michaelmas—he wrote to me from Ringabu."

"Well, you know what happened in the valley here last autumn," said Erling. "You don't? Surely you must know that he rode around to the district sheriffs of Lake Mjøsa and all along the valley carrying letters stating that the farmers should pay for provisions and horses for a full campaign[3]—with six farmers for each horse—and that the gentry should send horses but would be allowed to stay at home. Haven't you heard about this? And that the men of the northern valleys refused to pay this war tax when Munan accompanied Eirik Topp to the *ting* in Vaage? And Lavrans Bjørgulfsøn was the one who led the opposition—he demanded that Eirik pursue a lawful course, if anything remained of the lawful taxes, but he called it an injustice against the peasantry to demand war taxes from the farmers to help a Dane in a feud with the Danish king. And yet if our king required the service of his retainers, then he would find them quick enough to respond with good weapons and horses and armed men. But he would not send from Jørundgaard even a goat with a hemp halter unless the king commanded him to ride it himself to the mustering of the army. You truly didn't know about this? Smid Gudleikssøn says that Lavrans had promised his tenants that he would pay the campaign levies for them, if need be."

Erlend sat there stunned.

"Lavrans did that? Never have I heard of my wife's father involving himself in matters other than those concerning his own properties or those of his friends."

"No doubt he seldom does," said Sir Erling. "But this much was clear to me when I was at Nes—when Lavrans Bjørgulfsøn decides to speak about a matter, he receives everyone's full support, for he never speaks without understanding the issue so well that his opinion would be difficult to refute. Now, regarding these events, he has no doubt exchanged letters with his kinsmen in Sweden. Fru Ramborg, his father's mother, and Sir Erngisle's grandfather were the children of two brothers, so Lavrans has strong family ties over there. No matter how quiet his manner, your father-in-law commands power of some consequence in those parishes where people know him—although he doesn't often make use of it."

"Well, now I can understand why you have taken up with him, Erling," said Erlend, laughing. "I was rather surprised that you had become such good friends."

"Why should that surprise you?" replied Erling soberly. "It would be an odd man who would not want to call Lavrans of Jørundgaard his friend. You would be better served, kinsman, to listen to him than to Munan."

"Munan has been like an older brother to me, ever since the day when I left home for the first time," said Erlend, a little heatedly. "He has never failed me whenever I was in trouble. So if he's in trouble now . . ."

"Munan will manage well enough," said Erling Vidkunssøn, his voice still calm. "The letters he carried were written and sealed with the royal seal of Norway—unlawful, but that's not his problem. Oh yes, there's more. That to which he testified and attached his seal when he was a witness to the maiden Eufemia's betrothal[4]—but this cannot be easily revealed without mentioning someone whom we cannot . . . If truth be told, Erlend, I think Munan will save himself without your support—but you may harm yourself if you—"

"It's Lady Ingebjørg that all of you want to depose, I see," said Erlend. "But I've promised our kinswoman to serve her both here and abroad."

"I have too," replied Erling. "And I intend to keep that promise—as does every Norwegian man who has served and loved our lord and kinsman, King Haakon. And she is now best served by being separated from those advisers who counsel so young a woman to the detriment of her son and herself."

"Do you think you're capable of *that?*" asked Erlend, his voice subdued.

"Yes," said Erling Vidkunssøn firmly. "I think we are. And everyone else thinks so too, if they refuse to listen to malicious and slanderous talk." He shrugged his shoulders. "And those of us who are kinsmen of Lady Ingebjørg should be the last to do that."

A servant woman raised the hatch in the floor and said that if it suited them, the mistress would now have the food carried into the hall.

While everyone was sitting at the table, the conversation, such as it was, constantly touched on the great news that was circulating. Kristin noticed that both her father and Sir Erling refused to join in; they brought up news of bride purchases and deaths, inheritance disputes and property trades among family and acquaintances. She grew uneasy but didn't know why. They had business with Erlend—this much she understood. And yet she didn't want to admit this to herself. She now knew her husband so well that she realized Erlend, with all his stubborn-mindedness, was easily influenced by anyone who had a firm hand in a soft glove, as the saying goes.

After the meal, the gentlemen moved over to the hearth, where they sat and drank. Kristin settled herself on a bench, put her needlework frame in her lap, and began twining the threads. A moment later Haftor Graut came over, placed a cushion on the floor, and sat down at Kristin's feet. He had found Erlend's psaltery; he set it on his knee and sat there strumming it as he chatted. Haftor was quite a young man with curly blond hair and the fairest features, but his face was covered with freckles. Kristin quickly noticed that he was exceedingly talkative. He had recently made a rich marriage, but he was bored back home on his estates; that was why he wanted to travel to the gathering of the king's retainers.

"But it's understandable that Erlend Nikulaussøn would want to stay home," he said, laying his head in her lap. Kristin moved away a bit, laughed, and said with an innocent expression that she knew only that her husband was intending to travel south, "for whatever reason that might be. There's so much unrest in the country right now; it's difficult for a simple woman to understand such things."

"And yet it's the simplicity of a woman that's the main cause of it all," replied Haftor, laughing and moving closer. "At least that's what Erling and Lavrans Bjørgulfsøn say—I'd like to know what they mean by that. What do you think, Mistress Kristin? Lady Ingebjørg is a good and simple woman. Perhaps right now she is sitting as you are, twining silk threads with her snow-white fingers and thinking: It would be hard-hearted to refuse the loyal chieftain of her deceased husband some small assistance to improve his lot."

Erlend came and sat down next to his wife so that Haftor had to move over a bit.

"The women chatter about such nonsense in the hostels when their husbands are foolish enough to take them along to the meeting."

"Where I come from, it's said that there's no smoke unless there's fire," said Haftor.

"Yes, we have that saying too," said Lavrans; he and Erling had come over to join them. "And yet I was duped, Haftor, this past winter, when I tried to light my torch with fresh horse droppings." He perched on the edge of the table. Sir Erling at once brought his goblet and offered it to Lavrans with a word of greeting. Then the knight sat down on a bench nearby.

"It's not likely, Haftor," said Erlend, "that up north in Haalogaland you would know what Lady Ingebjørg and her advisers know about the undertakings and enterprises of the Danes. I suspect you might have been short-sighted when you opposed the king's demand for help. Sir Knut[5]—yes, we might as well mention his name since he's the one that we're all thinking about—he seems to me a man who wouldn't be caught unawares. You sit too far away from the cookpots to be able to smell what's simmering inside them. And better to prepare now than regret later, I say."

"Yes," said Sir Erling. "You might almost say that they're cooking for us on the neighboring farm—we Norwegians will soon be nothing more than their wards. They send over the porridge they've made in Sweden and say: Eat this, if you want food! I think our lord, King Haakon, made a mistake when he moved the cookhouse to the outskirts of the farm and made Oslo the foremost royal seat in the land. Before then it was in the middle of the courtyard, if we stay with this image—Bjørgvin[6] or Nidaros—but now the archbishop and chapter[7] rule here alone. What do you think, Erlend? You who are from Trøndelag and have all your property and all your power in this region?"

"Well, God's blood, Erling—if that's what you want: to carry home the cookpot and hang it over the proper hearth, then—"

"Yes," said Haftor. "For far too long we up here in the north have had to settle for smelling the soup cooking while we spoon up cold cabbage."

Lavrans joined in.

"As things stand, Erlend, I would not have presumed to be spokesman for the people of the district back home unless I had letters in my possession from my kinsman, Sir Erngisle. Then I knew that none of the lawful rulers plans to break the peace or the alliance between the countries, neither in the realm of the Danish king nor in that of our own king."

"If you know who now rules in Denmark, Father-in-law, then you know more than most men," said Erlend.

"One thing I do know. There is one man that nobody wants to see rule, not here nor in Sweden nor in Denmark. That was the purpose of the Swedes' actions in Skara last summer, and that is the purpose of the meeting we will now hold in Oslo—to make clear to everyone who has not yet realized it, that on this matter all sober-minded men are agreed."

By this time they had all drunk so much that they had grown boisterous, except for old Smid Gudleikssøn; he was slumped in his chair next to the hearth.

Erlend shouted, "Yes, you're all so sober-minded that the Devil himself can't trick you. It makes sense that you'd be afraid of Knut Porse. You don't understand, all you good gentlemen, that he's not the kind who can be satisfied with sitting quietly, watching the days drift past and the grass grow as God wills. I'd like to meet that knight again; I knew him when I was in Halland. And I'd have no objections to being in Knut Porse's place."

"That's not something *I* would dare say if my wife could hear me," said Haftor Graut.

But Erling Vidkunssøn had also drunk a good deal. He was still trying to maintain his chivalrous manner, but he finally gave up. "You!" he said, laughing uproariously. "You, kinsman? No, Erlend!" He slapped the other man on the shoulder and laughed and laughed.

"No, Erlend," said Lavrans bluntly, "more is needed for that than a man who is capable of seducing women. If there was no more to Knut Porse than his ability to play the fox in the goose pen, then all of us Norwegian noblemen would be much too lazy to make the effort to leave our manors to chase him off—even if the goose was our own king's mother. But no matter who Sir Knut may lure into committing foolish acts in his behalf, he never commits follies without having some reason for doing so. He has his purpose, and you can be certain that he won't take his eyes off it."

There was a pause in the conversation. Then Erlend spoke, and his eyes glittered.

"Then I would wish that Sir Knut were a Norwegian man!"

The others were silent. Sir Erling drank from his goblet and said, "God forbid. If we had such a man among us here in Norway, then I fear there would be a sudden end to peace in the land."

"Peace in the land!" said Erlend scornfully.

"Yes, peace in the land," replied Erling Vidkunssøn. "You must remember, Erlend, that we knights are not the only ones who live in this country. To you it might seem amusing if an adventurous and ambitious man like Knut Porse should rise up here. In the past, things were such in the world that if a man stirred up a group of rebels, it was always easy for him to win a following among the noblemen. Either they won and acquired titles and land, or their kinsmen won and they were granted a reprieve for both their lives and their estates. Yes, those who lost their lives have been entered in the records, but the majority survived, no matter whether things went one way or the other—that's how it was for *our* fathers. But the farmers and the townspeople, Erlend—the workers who often had to make payments to two masters many times in a single year, but who still had to rejoice each time a band of rebels raced through their villages without burning their farms or slaughtering their cattle—the peasants, who had to endure such intolerable burdens and attacks—I think *they* must thank God and Saint Olav for old King Haakon and King Magnus and his sons, who fortified the laws and secured the peace."

"Yes, I can believe you would think that way." Erlend threw back his head. Lavrans sat and stared at the young man—Erlend was now fully alert. A flush had spread over his dark, fierce face, the sinews of his throat were arched taut in his slender, tan neck. Then Lavrans glanced at his daughter. Kristin had let her needlework sink to her lap, and she was intently following the men's conversation.

"Are you so sure that the farmers and common men think this way and are rejoicing over the new sovereign?" said Erlend. "It's true that they often had difficult times—back when kings and their rivals waged war throughout the land. I know they still remember the time when they had to flee to the mountains with their livestock and wives and children while their farms stood in flames down below in the valley. I've heard them talking about it. But I know they remember something else—that their own fathers were part of the hordes. We weren't alone in the battle for power, Erling. The sons of farmers were part of it too—and sometimes they even won our ancestral estates. When law rules the land, a bastard son from Skidan who doesn't know his own father's name cannot win a baron's widow and her estate, such as Reidar Darre did. His descendant was good enough to be betrothed to your daughter, Lavrans; and now he's married to your wife's niece, Erling! Now law and order rule—and I don't understand how it happens, but I do know that farmers' lands have fallen into our hands, and lawfully so. The more entrenched the law, the more quickly they lose their power and authority to take part in their own affairs or those of the realm. And that, Erling, is something that the farmers know too! Oh, no, don't be too certain, any of you, that the peasants aren't longing for the past when they might lose their farms by fire and force—but they could also win with weapons more than they can win with law."

Lavrans nodded. "There may be some truth in what Erlend says," he murmured.

But Erling Vidkunssøn stood up. "I believe you're right; the peasants remember better the few men who rose up from meager circumstances to become lords—in the time of the sword—than the unspeakable numbers who perished in filthy poverty and wretchedness. And yet none was a sterner master to the commoners than they were. I think it was of them that the saying was first spoken: kinsmen behave worst toward their own. A man must be born to be a master, or he will turn out to be a harsh one. But if he has spent his childhood among servant men and women, then he will have an easier time understanding that without the commoners, we are in many ways helpless children all our days, and that for God's sake as well as our own, we ought to serve them in turn with our knowledge and protect them with our chivalry. Never has it been possible to sustain a kingdom without noblemen who had the ability and the will to secure with their power the rights of those poorer than themselves."

"You could compete in sermonizing with my brother, Erling," said Erlend with a laugh. "But I think the people of Outer Trøndelag liked the gentry better back when we led their sons on military incursions, let our blood run and mingle with theirs across the planks, and split apart rings and divided up the booty with our serving men. Yes, as you can hear, Kristin, sometimes I sleep with one ear open when Sira Eiliv reads aloud from the great books."

"Property that is unlawfully won shall not be handed down to the third heir," said Lavrans Bjørgulfsøn. "Haven't you ever heard that before, Erlend?"

"Of course I've heard that!" Erlend laughed loudly. "But I've never seen it happen."

Erling Vidkunssøn said, "Things are such, Erlend, that few are born to rule, but everyone is born to serve; the proper way to rule is to be your servants' servant."

Erlend clasped his hands behind his neck and stretched, smiling. "I've never thought about that. And I don't think my leaseholders have any favors to thank me for. And yet, strange as it may seem, I think they're fond of me." He rubbed his cheek against Kristin's black kitten, which had jumped up onto his shoulder and was now walking around his neck, purring and with its back arched. "But my wife here—she is the most eager to serve of all women, although you wouldn't have reason to believe me, since the pitchers and mugs are now empty, my Kristin!"

Orm, who had been sitting quietly and listening to the men's conversation, stood up at once and left the room.

"Your wife grew so bored that she fell asleep," said Haftor, smiling. "And the blame is yours—you could have let me talk to her in peace—a man who knows how to speak to women."

"All this talk has no doubt gone on much too long for you, mistress," began Sir Erling contritely, but Kristin answered with a smile.

"It's true, sir, that I haven't understood everything that's been said here this evening, but I will remember it well, and I will have plenty of time to think about it later."

Orm came back with several maids who brought in more ale. The boy walked around, pouring for the men. Lavrans looked sorrowfully at the handsome child. He had tried to start up a conversation with Orm Erlendssøn, but he was a taciturn boy, although he had a striking and noble bearing.

One of the maids whispered to Kristin that Naakkve was awake over in the little house and crying terribly. Kristin then bid the men good night and followed the maids out when they left.

The men started drinking again. Sir Erling and Lavrans exchanged occasional glances, and then the former said, "There is something, Erlend, that I meant to discuss with you. A campaign force will certainly be summoned from the countryside here around the fjord and from Møre. People to the north are afraid that the Russians will return this summer, stronger than before, and they won't be able to handle their defense alone. This is the first benefit for which we can thank the royal union with Sweden—but it wouldn't be right for the people of Haalogaland[8] to profit from it alone. Now, things are such that Arne Gjavvaldssøn is too old and sickly—so there has been talk of making you chieftain of the farmers' ships from this side of the fjord. What would you think of that?"

Erlend pounded one fist into the palm of his other hand. His whole face glowed. "What I would think of it!"

"It's unlikely that a large contingent could be mustered," said Erling, admonishingly. "But perhaps you should find out what the sheriffs think. You're well known in this area—there has been talk among the men on the council that you were perhaps the man who could do something about this matter. There are those who still remember that you won more than a little honor when you were a guardsman for Earl Jacob. I myself recall hearing him say to King Haakon that he had acted unwisely when he dealt so harshly with a capable young man. He said you were destined to be a support to your king."

Erlend snapped his fingers. "You're not thinking of becoming our king, Erling Vidkunssøn! Is that what all of you are plotting?" he asked, laughing boisterously. "To make Erling king?"

Erling said impatiently, "No, Erlend. Can't you tell that now I was speaking in earnest?"

"God help me—were you joking before? I thought you were

speaking in earnest all evening. All right then, let's speak seriously. Tell me about this matter, kinsman."

Kristin was asleep with the child at her breast when Erlend came into the little house. He stuck a pine branch into the embers of the hearth and then let it shine on the two of them for a long time.

How beautiful she was. And he was a handsome child, their son. Kristin was always so sleepy in the evening now. As soon as she lay down and placed the boy close to her, they would both fall asleep. Erlend laughed a bit and tossed the twig back into the hearth. Slowly he undressed.

Northward in the spring with *Margygren* and three or four warships. Haftor Graut with three ships from Haalogaland. But Haftor had no experience; Erlend would be able to command him as he liked. Yes, he realized that he would have to take charge himself because this Haftor did not look either fearful or indecisive. Erlend stretched and smiled in the dark. He was thinking of finding a crew for *Margygren* outside of Møre. But there were plenty of bold and hearty boys both here in the parish and in Birgsi—he would be able to choose from the finest of men.

He had been married little more than a year. Childbirth, penance, and fasting. And now the boy, always the boy, night and day. And yet . . . she was still the same sweet, young Kristin, whenever he could make her forget the priest's words and the greedy suckling child for a brief time.

He kissed her shoulder, but she didn't notice. Poor thing—he would let her sleep. He had so much to think about tonight. Erlend turned away from her and lay staring across the room at the tiny glowing dot in the hearth. He ought to get up and cover the ashes, but he didn't feel like it.

In bits and pieces, memories from his youth came back to him. A quivering ship's prow that paused a scant moment, waiting for the approaching swell; then the sea washing over it. The mighty sound of the storm and the sea. The whole vessel shuddered under the press of the waves, the top of the mast cut a wild arc through the scudding clouds. It was somewhere off the coast of Halland. Overwhelmed, Erlend felt tears fill his eyes. He hadn't realized himself how much these years of idleness had tormented him.

* * *

The next morning Lavrans Bjørgulfsøn and Sir Erling Vidkunssøn were standing at the end of the courtyard, watching some of Erlend's horses that were running loose outside the fence.

"I think," said Lavrans, "that if Erlend is to come to this meeting, then he is of such high position and birth, being the kinsman of the king and his mother, that he must step forward to join the ranks of the foremost men. But I don't know, Sir Erling, whether you feel you can trust that his judgment in these matters won't lead him to the opposing side. If Ivar Ogmundssøn attempts to make a countermove . . . Erlend is also strongly tied to the men who will follow Sir Ivar."

"I think it unlikely that Sir Ivar will do anything," said Erling Vidkunssøn. "And Munan . . ." He gave a slight smile. "He's wise enough to stay away. He knows that otherwise it might become clear to everyone how much or how little influence Munan Baardsøn wields." They both laughed. "The truth is . . . Yes, no doubt you know better than I, Lavrans Lagmanssøn,[9] you who have your ancestors and kinsmen over there, that the Swedish nobles are reluctant to consider our knighthood equal to their own. For that reason it's important that we exclude no man who is among the richest and most highborn. We cannot afford to let a man like Erlend win permission to stay at home, jesting with his wife and tending to his estates—in whatever manner he tends to them," he said when he saw Lavrans's expression.

A smile flickered across Lavrans's face.

"But if you think it unwise to pressure Erlend in order to make him join us, then I will not do so."

"I think, dear sir," said Lavrans, "that Erlend would do more good here in the villages. As you said yourself—we can expect that this war levy will be met with opposition in the districts south of Namdalseid, where the people feel they have nothing to fear from the Russians. It's possible that Erlend might be the man who could change people's minds about these matters in some way."

"He has such a cursed loose tongue," Sir Erling exclaimed.

Lavrans replied with a small smile. "Perhaps that's the language that will appeal more to people than . . . the speech of more insightful men." Again they looked at each other and laughed. "However that may be, he could do more harm if he went to the meeting and spoke too loudly."

"Well, if you cannot restrain him, then . . ."

"No, I can do so only until he meets up with the kind of birds he's used to flying around with; my son-in-law and I are too unlike each other."

Erlend came over to them. "Have you benefited so much from the mass that you need no breakfast?"

"I haven't heard mention of breakfast—I'm as hungry as a wolf, and thirsty." Lavrans stroked a dirty-white horse that he had been examining. "Whoever the man is who tends to your horses, son-in-law, I would drive him off my estate before I sat down to eat, if he was *my* servant."

"I don't dare, because of Kristin," said Erlend. "He has gotten one of her maids with child."

"And do you deem it such a great achievement here in these parts," said Lavrans, raising his eyebrows, "that you now find him irreplaceable?"

"No, but you see," said Erlend, laughing, "Kristin and the priest want them to be married—and they want me to place the man in such a position that he'll be able to support the two of them. The girl refuses and her guardian refuses, and Tore himself is reluctant. But I'm not allowed to drive him off; she's afraid that then he would flee the village. But Ulf Haldorssøn is his overseer, when he's home."

Erling Vidkunssøn walked over toward Smid Gudleikssøn. Lavrans said to his son-in-law, "It seems to me that Kristin is looking a little pale these days."

"I know. Can't you talk to her, Father-in-law?" Erlend said eagerly. "That boy is sucking the marrow out of her. I think she wants to keep him at her breast until the third fast, like some kind of pauper's wife."

"Yes, she is certainly fond of her son," said Lavrans with a slight smile.

"I know." Erlend shook his head. "They can sit there for three hours—Kristin and Sira Eiliv—talking about a rash he has here or there; and for every tooth he gets, they seem to think a great miracle has occurred. I've never heard otherwise but that all children get teeth. And it would be more wondrous if our Naakkve should have none."

CHAPTER 2

ONE EVENING A year later, toward the end of the Christmas holidays, Kristin Lavransdatter and Orm Erlendssøn arrived quite unexpectedly to visit Master Gunnulf at his residence in Nidaros.

The wind had raged and sleet had fallen all day long, since before noon, but now, late in the evening, the weather had grown worse until it was an actual snowstorm. The two visitors were completely covered in snow when they stepped into the room where the priest was sitting at the supper table with the rest of his household.

Gunnulf asked fearfully whether something was wrong back at the manor. But Kristin shook her head. Erlend was away on a visit in Gelmin, she said in reply to her brother-in-law's queries, but she was so weary that she hadn't felt like going with him.

The priest thought about how she had come all the way into town. The horses that she and Orm had ridden were exhausted; during the last part of the journey they had barely been able to struggle their way through the snowdrifts. Gunnulf sent his two servant women off with Kristin to find dry clothing for her. They were his foster mother and her sister—there were no other women at the priest's house. He attended to his nephew himself. And all the while, Orm talked steadily.

"I think Kristin is ill. I told Father, but he got angry."

She had been so unlike herself lately, said the boy. He didn't know what was wrong. He couldn't remember whether it was her idea or his for them to come here—oh yes, she had mentioned first that she had a great longing to go to Christ Church, and he had said that he would accompany her. So this morning, just as soon as his father had ridden off, Kristin told him she wanted to go today. Orm had agreed, even though the weather was threatening—but he didn't like the look in her eyes.

Gunnulf thought to himself that he didn't like it either, when

Kristin returned to the room. She looked terribly thin in Ingrid's black dress; her face was as pale as bast and her eyes were sunken, with dark blue circles underneath. Her gaze was strange and dark.

It had been three months since he had last seen her, when he attended the christening at Husaby. She had looked good then as she lay in bed in her finery, and she said she felt well—the birth had been an easy one. So he had protested when Ragnfrid Ivarsdatter and Erlend wanted to give the child to a foster mother; Kristin cried and begged to be allowed to nurse Bjørgulf herself. The second son had been named after Lavrans's father.

Now the priest asked first about Bjørgulf; he knew that Kristin was not pleased with the wet nurse to whom they had given the child. But she said he was doing well and that Frida was fond of him and took better care of him than anyone had expected. And what about Nikulaus? asked her brother-in-law. Was he still so handsome? A little smile flitted across the mother's face. Naakkve grew more and more handsome every day. No, he didn't talk much, but otherwise he was ahead of his years in every way, and so big. No one would believe he was only in his second winter; even Fru Gunna said as much.

Then Kristin fell silent again. Master Gunnulf glanced at the two of them—his brother's wife and his brother's son—who were sitting on either side of him. They looked weary and sorrowful, and his heart felt uneasy as he gazed at them.

Orm had always seemed melancholy. The boy was now fifteen years old, and he would have been the most handsome of fellows if he hadn't looked so delicate and weak. He was almost as tall as his father, but his body was much too slender and narrow-shouldered. His face resembled Erlend's too, but his eyes were much darker blue, and his mouth, beneath the first downy black mustache, was even smaller and weaker, and it was always pressed tight with a sad little furrow at each corner. Even the back of Orm's thin, tan neck under his curly black hair looked oddly unhappy as he sat there eating, slightly hunched forward.

Kristin had never sat at table with her brother-in-law in his own house. Last year she had come to town with Erlend for the springtime *ting*, and they had stayed at this residence, which Gunnulf had inherited from his father; but at that time the priest was living on the estate of the Brothers of the Cross, substituting for one of the canons. Master Gunnulf was now the parish priest for Steine, but he had a chaplain to assist him while he oversaw the work of copying manuscripts for the churches of the archbishopric while the cantor,[1] Herr Eirik Finssøn, was ill. And during this time he lived in his own house.

The main hall was unlike any of the rooms Kristin was used to. It was a timbered building, but in the middle of the end wall, facing east, Gunnulf had had masons construct a large fireplace, like those he had seen in the countries of the south; a log fire burned between cast andirons. The table stood along one wall, and opposite were benches with writing desks. In front of a painting of the Virgin Mary burned a brass lamp, and nearby stood shelves of books.

This room seemed strange to her, and her brother-in-law seemed strange too, now that she saw him sitting at the table with members of his household—clerics and servant men who looked oddly priestlike. There were also several poor people: old men and a young boy with thin, reddish eyelids clinging like membranes to his empty eye sockets. On the women's bench next to the old housekeepers sat a young woman with a two-year-old child on her lap; she was hungrily gulping down the stew and stuffing her child's mouth so that his cheeks were about to burst.

It was the custom for all priests at Christ Church to give supper to the poor. But Kristin had heard that fewer beggars came to Gunnulf Nikulaussøn than to any of the other priests, and yet—or perhaps this was the very reason—he seated them on the benches next to him in the main hall and received every wanderer like an honored guest. They were served food from his own platter and ale from the priest's own barrels. The poor would come whenever they felt in need of a supper of stew, but otherwise they preferred to go to the other priests, where they were given porridge and weak ale in the cookhouse.

As soon as the scribe had finished the prayers after the meal, the poor guests wanted to leave. Gunnulf spoke gently to each of them, asking whether they would like to spend the night or whether they needed anything else; but only the blind boy remained. The priest implored in particular the young woman with the child to stay and not take the little one out into the night, but she murmured an excuse and hurried off. Then Gunnulf asked a servant to make sure that Blind Arnstein was given ale and a good bed in the guest room. He put on a hooded cape.

"You must be tired, Orm and Kristin, and want to go to bed. Audhild will take care of you. You'll probably be asleep when I return from the church."

Then Kristin asked to go with him. "That's why I've come here," she said, fixing her despairing eyes on Gunnulf. Ingrid lent her a dry cloak, and she and Orm joined the small procession departing from the parsonage.

The bells were ringing as if they were right overhead in the black night sky—it wasn't far to the church. They trudged through deep, wet, new snow. The weather was calm now, with a few snowflakes still drifting down here and there, shimmering faintly in the dark.

Dead tired, Kristin tried to lean against the pillar she was standing next to, but the stone was icy cold. She stood in the dark church and stared up at the candles in the choir. She couldn't see Gunnulf up there, but he was sitting among the priests, with a candle beside his book. No, she would not be able to speak to him, after all.

Tonight it seemed to her that there was no help to be found anywhere. Back home Sira Eiliv admonished her because she brooded so much over her everyday sins—he said this was the temptation of pride. She should simply be diligent with her prayers and good deeds, and then she wouldn't have time to dwell on such matters. "The Devil is no fool; he'll realize that he will lose your soul in the end, and he won't feel like tempting you as much."

She listened to the antiphony and remembered the nuns' church in Oslo. There she had raised her poor little voice with others in the hymn of praise—and down in the nave stood Erlend, wrapped in a cape up to his chin, and the two of them thought only of finding a chance to speak to each other in secret.

And she had thought that this heathen and burning love was not so terrible a sin. They couldn't help themselves—and they were both unmarried. It was at most a transgression against the laws of men. Erlend wanted to escape from a terrible life of sin, and she imagined that he would have greater strength to free himself from the old burden if she put her life and her honor and her happiness into his hands.

The last time she knelt here in this church she had fully realized that when she said such things in her heart she had been trying to deceive God with tricks and lies. It was not because of their virtue but because of their good fortune that there were still commandments they had not broken, sins they had not committed. If she had been another man's wife when she met Erlend . . . she would not have been any more sparing of his salvation or his honor than she was of the man she had so mercilessly spurned. It seemed to her now that there was nothing that wouldn't have tempted her back then, in her ardor and despair. She had felt her passion temper her will until it was sharp and hard like a knife, ready to cut through all bonds—those of kinship, Christianity, and honor. There was nothing inside her except the burning hunger to see him, to be near him, to open her lips to his hot mouth and her arms to the deadly sweet desire which he had taught her.

Oh, no. The Devil was probably not so convinced that he was going to lose her soul. But when she lay here before, crushed with sorrow over her sins, over the hardness of her heart, her impure life, and the blindness of her soul . . . then she had felt the saintly king take her in under his protective cloak. She had gripped his strong, warm hand; he had pointed out to her the light that is the source of all strength and holiness. Saint Olav turned her eyes toward Christ on the cross—see, Kristin: God's love. Yes, she had begun to understand God's love and patience. But she had turned away from the light again and closed her heart to it, and now there was nothing in her mind but impatience and anger and fear.

How wretched, wretched she was. Even she had realized that a woman like herself would need harsh trials before she could be cured of her lack of love. And yet she was so impatient that she felt her heart would break with the sorrows that had been imposed on her. They were small sorrows, but there were many of them, and she had so little patience. She glanced at her stepson's tall, slender figure over on the men's side of the church.

She couldn't help it. She loved Orm as if he were her own child; but it was impossible for her to be fond of Margret. She had tried and tried and even commanded herself to like the child, ever since that day last winter when Ulf Haldorssøn brought her home to Husaby. She thought it was dreadful; how could she feel such ill will and anger toward a little maiden only nine years old? And she knew full well that part of it was because the child looked so fearfully like her mother Eline. She couldn't understand Erlend; he was simply proud that his little golden-haired daughter with the brown eyes was so pretty. The child never seemed to arouse any bad memories in the father. It was as if Erlend had completely forgotten the mother of these children. But it wasn't *only* because Margret resembled the other woman that Kristin lacked affection for her stepdaughter. Margret would not tolerate anyone instructing her; she was arrogant and treated the servants badly. She was dishonest too, and she fawned over her father. She didn't love him the way Orm did; she would snuggle up to Erlend with affection and caresses only because she wanted something. And Erlend showered her with gifts and gave in to the maiden's every whim. Orm wasn't fond of his sister, either—that much Kristin had noticed.

Kristin suffered because she felt so harsh and mean since she couldn't watch Margret's behavior without feeling indignant and censorious. But she suffered even more from observing and listening to the constant discord between Erlend and his eldest son. She suffered most of all because she realized that Erlend, deep in his heart, felt a boundless love for the boy—and he treated Orm unjustly and with severity because he had no idea what to do with his son or how he might secure his future. He had given his bastard children property and livestock, but it seemed unthinkable that Orm would ever be fit to be a farmer. And Erlend grew desperate when he saw how frail and weak Orm was; then he would call his son rotten and rage at him to harden himself. He would spend hours with his son, training him in the use of heavy weapons that the boy couldn't possibly handle, urging him to drink himself sick in the evenings, and practically breaking the boy on dangerous and exhausting hunting expeditions. In spite of all this, Kristin saw the fear in Erlend's soul; she realized that he was often wild with sorrow because this fine and handsome son of his was suited for only one position in life—and there his birth stood in the way. And Kristin had come to understand how little patience Erlend possessed whenever he felt concern or compassion for someone he loved.

She saw that Orm realized this too. And she saw that the young boy's soul was split: Orm felt love and pride for his father, but also contempt for Erlend's unfairness when he allowed his child to suffer because he was faced with worries which he himself, and not the boy, had caused. But Orm had grown close to his young stepmother; with her he seemed to breathe easier and feel freer. When he was alone with her, he was able to banter and laugh, in his own quiet way. But Erlend was not pleased by this; he seemed to suspect that the two of them were sitting in judgment of his conduct.

Oh, no, it wasn't easy for Erlend; and it wasn't so strange that he was sensitive when it came to those two children. And yet . . .

She still trembled with pain whenever she thought about it.

The manor had been filled with guests the week before. When Margret came home, Erlend had furnished the loft which was at the far end of the hall, above the next room and the entry hall—it was to be her bower, he said. And there she slept with the servant girl whom Erlend had ordered to keep watch over and serve the maiden. Frida also slept there along with Bjørgulf. But since they had so many Christmas guests, Kristin had made up beds for the young men in this loft room; the two maids and the infant were to sleep in the servant women's house. But because she thought Erlend might not like it if she sent Margret off to sleep with the servants, she had made up a bed for her on one of the benches in the hall, where the women and maidens were sleeping. It was always difficult to get Margret up in the morning. On that morning Kristin had woken her many times, but she had lain back down, and she was still asleep after everyone else was up. Kristin wanted to clean the hall and put things in order; the guests must be given breakfast—and so she lost all patience. She yanked the pillows from under Margret's head and tore off the covers. But when she saw the child lying there naked on the sheet made of hides, she took her own cloak from her shoulders and placed it over Margret. It was a garment made from plain, undyed homespun; she only wore it when she went back and forth to the cookhouse and the storerooms, tending to the food preparation.

At that moment Erlend came into the room. He had been sleeping in a chamber above a storeroom with several other men, since Fru Gunna was sharing Kristin's bed. And he flew into a rage. He grabbed Kristin by the arm so hard that the marks from his fingers were still on her skin.

"Do you think my daughter should be lying on straw and homespun cloth? Margit is mine, even though she may not be yours. What's not good enough for your own children is good enough for her. But since you've mocked the innocent little maiden in the sight of these women, then you must rectify matters before their eyes. Put back the covers that you took from Margit."

It so happened that Erlend had been drunk the night before, and he was always bad-tempered the following day. And no doubt he thought the women must have been gossiping among themselves when they saw Eline's children. And he grew sensitive and testy about their reputation. And yet . . .

Kristin had tried to talk to Sira Eiliv about it. But he couldn't help her with this matter. Gunnulf had told her that she need not mention the sins to which she had confessed and repented before Eiliv Serkssøn became her parish priest unless she thought that he should know about them in order to judge and advise her. So there were many things she had never told him, even though she felt that by not doing so she would seem, in Sira Eiliv's eyes, to be a better person than she was. But it was so good for her to have the friendship of this kind and pure-hearted man. Erlend made fun of her, but she gained such comfort from Sira Eiliv. With him she could talk as much as she liked about her children; the priest was willing to discuss with her all the small bits of news that bored Erlend and drove him from the room. The priest got on well with children, and he understood their small troubles and illnesses. Erlend laughed at Kristin when she went to the cookhouse herself to prepare special dishes, which she would send over to the parsonage. Sira Eiliv was fond of good food and drink, and it amused Kristin to spend time on such matters and to try out what she had learned from her mother or seen at the convent. Erlend didn't care what he ate as long as he was always served meat if it wasn't a time for fasting. But Sira Eiliv would come over to talk and thank her, praising her skill after she had sent him grouse on a spit, wrapped in the best bacon, or a platter of reindeer tongues in French wine and honey. And he gave her advice about her garden, obtaining cuttings for her from Tautra, where his brother was a monk, and from the Olav monastery, whose prior was a good friend of his. And he also read to her and could recount so many wonderful things about life out in the world.

But because he was such a good and pious man, it was often difficult to speak to him about the evil she saw in her own heart. When she confessed to him how embittered she felt at Erlend's behavior that day with Margret, he had impressed upon her that she must bear with her husband. But he seemed to think that Erlend alone had committed an offense when he spoke so unjustly to his wife—and in the presence of strangers. Kristin doubtless agreed with him. And yet deep in her heart she felt a complicity which she could not explain and which caused her great pain.

Kristin looked up at the holy shrine, which glittered a dull gold in the dim light behind the high altar. She had been so certain that if she stood here again, something would happen—a redemption of her soul. Once more a living fount would surge up into her heart and wash away all the anguish and fear and bitterness and confusion that filled her.

But no one had any patience for her tonight. Haven't you learned yet, Kristin—to lift your self-righteousness to the light of God's righteousness, your heathen and selfish passion to the light of love? Perhaps you do not *want* to learn it, Kristin.

But the last time she knelt here she had held Naakkve in her arms. His little mouth at her breast warmed her heart so well that it was like soft wax, easy for the heavenly love to shape. And she *did* have Naakkve; he was playing back home in the hall, so lovely and sweet that her breast ached at the mere thought of him. His soft, curly hair was now turning dark—he was going to have black hair like his father. And he was so full of life and mischief. She made animals for him out of old furs, and he would throw them into the air and then chase after them, racing with the young dogs. And it usually ended with the fur bear falling into the hearth fire and burning up, with smoke and a foul smell. Naakkve would howl, hopping up and down and stomping, and then he would bury his head in his mother's lap—that's where all of his adventures still ended. The maids fought for his favor; the men would pick him up and toss him up to the ceiling whenever they came into the room. If the boy saw Ulf Haldorssøn, he would run over and cling to the man's leg. Ulf sometimes took him along out to the farmyard. Erlend would snap his fingers at his son and set him on his shoulder for a moment, but he was the one person at Husaby who paid the least attention to the boy. And yet he *was* fond of Naakkve. Erlend *was* glad that he now had two lawfully born sons.

Kristin's heart clenched tight.

They had taken Bjørgulf away from her. He whimpered whenever she tried to hold him, and Frida would put him to her own breast at once. His foster mother kept a jealous watch over the boy. But Kristin would refuse to let the new child go. Her mother and Erlend had said that she should be spared, and so they took her newborn son away and gave him to another woman. She felt an almost vengeful joy when she thought that their only accomplishment was that she would now be having a third child before Bjørgulf was even eleven months old.

She didn't dare speak of this to Sira Eiliv. He would merely think that she was resentful because now she would have to go through all of that again so soon. But that wasn't it.

She had come home from her pilgrimage with a deep dread in her soul—never would that wild desire have power over her again. Until the end of summer she lived alone with her child in the old house, weighing in her mind the words of the archbishop and Gunnulf's speech, vigilantly praying and repenting, diligently working to put the neglected farm in order, to win over her servants with kindness and concern for their welfare, eager to help and serve all those around her as far as her hands and her power might reach. A cool and wondrous peace descended upon her. She sustained herself with thoughts of her father, she sustained herself with prayers to the holy men and women Sira Eiliv read to her about, and she pondered their steadfastness and courage. And tender with joy and gratitude, she remembered Brother Edvin, who had appeared before her in the moonlight on that night. She had understood his message when he smiled so gently and hung his glove on the moonbeam. If only she had enough faith, she would become a good woman.

When their first year of marriage came to an end, she had to move back in with her husband. Whenever she felt doubtful, she would console herself that the archbishop himself had impressed upon her that in her life with her husband she should show her new change of heart. And she strove zealously to tend to his welfare and his honor. Erlend himself had said: "And so it has happened after all, Kristin—you have brought honor back to Husaby." People showed her great kindness and respect; everyone seemed willing to forget that she had begun her marriage a little impetuously. Whenever the women gathered, they would seek out her advice; people praised her housekeeping at the manor, she was summoned to assist with weddings and with births on the great estates, and no one made her feel that she was too young or inexperienced or a newcomer to the region. The servants would remain sitting in the hall until late into the evening, just as they did back home at Jørundgaard—they all had something to ask their mistress about. She felt a rush of exhilaration that people were so kind to her and that Erlend was proud of her.

Then Erlend took charge of the men called up for duty on the ships south of the fjord. He dashed around, riding or sailing, and he was busy with people who came to see him and letters that had to be sent. He was so young and handsome, and so happy—the listless, dejected look that she had often seen come over him in the past seemed to have been swept away. He sparkled with alertness, like the morning. He had little time left over for her now; but she grew dizzy and wild whenever he came near her with his smiling face and those adventure-loving eyes.

She had laughed with him at the letter that had come from Munan Baardsøn. The knight had not attended the gathering of the king's retainers himself, but he ridiculed the entire meeting and especially the fact that Erling Vidkunssøn had been appointed leader of the realm. But first Erling had probably given himself new titles—no doubt he would want to be called regent now. Munan also wrote about her father:

The mountain wolf from Sil crept under a rock and sat there mutely. I mean that your father-in-law took lodgings with the priests at Saint Laurentius Church and did not let his fair voice be heard at the discussions. He had in his possession letters bearing the seals of Sir Erngisle and Sir Karl Turessön; if they haven't yet been worn out it's because the parchment was tougher than the soles of Satan's shoes. You should also know that Lavrans gave eight marks of pure silver to Nonneseter. Apparently the man realized that Kristin was not as docile when she was there as she should have been.

Kristin felt a stab of pain and shame at this, but she had to laugh along with Erlend. For her the winter and spring had passed in exhilarating merriment and happiness, with now and then a squall for Orm's sake—Erlend couldn't decide whether he should take the boy north with him. It ended with an outburst during Easter. One night Erlend wept in her arms: he didn't dare take his son on board for fear that Orm wouldn't be able to hold his own during a war. She had comforted him and herself—and the youth. Perhaps the boy would grow stronger over the years.

On the day she rode with Erlend to the anchorage at Birgsi, she couldn't feel either fearful or sad. She was almost intoxicated with him and with his joy and high spirits.

At that time she didn't know she was already carrying another child. When she felt unwell she had thought . . . Erlend was so exuberant, there had been so much commotion and drinking at home, and Naakkve was sucking the strength out of her. When she felt the new life stir inside her, she was . . . She had been looking forward to the winter, to traveling to town and around the valley with her bold and handsome husband; she was young and beautiful herself. She had planned to wean the boy by autumn; it was troublesome always having to take him and the nursemaid along wherever she went. She was certain that in this Russian campaign Erlend would prove fit for something other than ruining his name and his property. No, she had not been glad, and she told this to Sira Eiliv. Then the priest had reprimanded her quite sternly for her unloving and worldly disposition. And all summer long she had tried to be happy and to thank God for the new child she was to have, and for the good reports she heard about Erlend's courageous actions in the north.

Then he returned home just before Michaelmas. And she saw that he was not pleased when he realized what was to come. He said as much that evening.

"I thought that when I finally had you, it would be like celebrating Christmas every day. But now it seems that there will be mostly long periods of fasting."

Every time she thought about this, the blood would rush to her face, just as hot as on that evening when she turned away from him, flushing deep red and shedding no tears. Erlend had tried to make amends with love and kindness. But she couldn't forget it. The fire inside her, which all her tears of remorse had been unable to extinguish and all her fear of sin could not smother—it was as if Erlend had stomped it out with his foot when he said those words.

Late that night they sat in front of the fireplace in Gunnulf's house—the priest and Kristin and Orm. A jug of wine and a few small goblets stood at the edge of the hearth. Master Gunnulf had suggested several times that his guests ought to seek rest. But Kristin begged to stay sitting there a little longer.

"Do you remember, brother-in-law," she said, "that I once told you that the priest back home at Jørundgaard counseled me to enter a cloister if Father would not give his consent for Erlend to marry me?"

Gunnulf glanced involuntarily at Orm. But Kristin said with a wry little smile, "Do you think this grown-up boy doesn't know that I'm a weak and sinful woman?"

Master Gunnulf replied softly, "Did you feel a yearning for the life of a nun back then, Kristin?"

"No doubt God would have opened my eyes once I had decided to serve Him."

"Perhaps He thought that your eyes needed to be opened so you would learn that you ought to serve Him wherever you are. Your husband, children, and the servants at Husaby need to have a faithful and patient servant woman of God living among them and tending to their welfare.

"Of course the maiden who makes the best marriage is the one who chooses Christ as her bridegroom and refuses to give herself to a sinful man. But the child who has already done wrong . . ."

" 'I wish that you could have come to God with your wreath,' " whispered Kristin. "That's what he said to me, Brother Edvin Rikardssøn, the monk I've often told you about. Do you feel the same way?"

Gunnulf Nikulaussøn nodded. "And yet many a woman has

pulled herself up from a life of sin with such strength that we dare pray for her intercession. But this happened more often in the past, when she was threatened with torture and fire and glowing tongs if she called herself a Christian. I have often thought, Kristin, that back then it was easier to tear oneself away from the bonds of sin, when it could be done forcefully and all at once. And yet we humans are so corrupt—but courage is by nature present in the heart of many, and courage is what often drives a soul to seek God. The torments have incited just as many people to faithfulness as they have frightened others into apostasy. But a young, lost child who is torn from sinful desire even before she has learned to understand what it has brought upon her soul—a child placed in an order of nuns among pure maidens who have given themselves up to watch over and pray for those who are asleep out in the world . . .

"I wish it would soon be summer," he said suddenly and stood up.

The other two looked at him in amazement.

"Oh, I happened to think about when the cuckoo was singing on the slopes in the morning back home at Husaby. First we would hear the one on the ridge to the east, behind the buildings, and then the other would reply from far off, in the woods close to By. It sounded so lovely out across the lake in the stillness of the morning. Don't you think it's beautiful at Husaby, Kristin?"

"The cuckoo in the east is the cuckoo of sorrow," said Orm Erlendssøn quietly. "Husaby seems to me the fairest manor in the world."

The priest placed his hands on his nephew's narrow shoulders for a moment.

"I thought so too, kinsman. It was my father's estate for me too. The youngest son stands no closer to inheriting the ancestral farm than you do, dear Orm!"

"When Father was living with my mother, you were the closest heir," said the young boy in the same quiet voice.

"We're not to blame, Orm—my children and I," said Kristin sorrowfully.

"You must have noticed that I bear you no rancor," he replied softly.

"It's such an open, wide landscape," said Kristin after a moment. "You can see so far from Husaby, and the sky is so . . . so vast. Where I come from, the sky is like a roof above the mountain slopes. The valley lies sheltered, round and green and fresh. The world seems just the right size—neither too big nor too small." She sighed and her hands began fidgeting in her lap.

"Was his home there—the man your father wanted you to marry?" asked the priest, and Kristin nodded.

"Do you ever regret that you refused to have him?" he then asked, and she shook her head.

Gunnulf went over and pulled a book from the shelf. He sat down near the fire again, opened the clasps, and began turning the pages. But he didn't read; he sat with the open book on his lap.

"When Adam and his wife had defied God's will, then they felt in their own flesh a power that defied *their* will. God had created them, man and woman, young and beautiful, so that they would live together in marriage and give birth to other heirs who would receive the gifts of His goodness: the beauty of the Garden of Eden, the fruit of the tree of life, and eternal happiness. They didn't need to be ashamed of their bodies because as long as they were obedient to God, their whole body and all of their limbs were under the command of their will, just as a hand or a foot is."

Blushing blood-red, Kristin folded her hands under her breast. The priest bent toward her slightly; she felt his strong amber eyes on her lowered face.

"Eve stole what belonged to God, and her husband accepted it when she gave him what rightfully was the property of their Father and Creator. They wanted to be His equal—and they noticed that the first way in which they became His equal was this: Just as they had betrayed His dominion over the great world, so too was their dominion betrayed over the small world, the soul's house of flesh. Just as they had forsaken their Lord God, the body would now forsake its master, the soul.

"Then these bodies seemed to them so hideous and hateful that they made clothes to cover them. First a short apron of fig leaves. But as they became more and more familiar with their own carnal nature, they drew the clothes up over their heart and their back, which is unwilling to bend. Until today, when men dress themselves in steel all the way to their fingertips and toes and hide their faces behind the grids of their helmets. In this way unrest and deceit have grown in the world."

"Help me, Gunnulf," begged Kristin. She was white to the very edge of her lips. "I don't know my own will."

"Then say: Thy will be done," replied the priest softly. "You know you must open your heart to His love. Then you must love Him once more with all the power of your soul."

Kristin abruptly turned to face her brother-in-law.

"You can't know how much I loved Erlend. And my children!"

"Dear sister—all other love is merely a reflection of the heavens in the puddles of a muddy road. You will become sullied too if you allow yourself to sink into it. But if you always remember that it's a reflection of the light from that other home, then you will rejoice at its beauty and take good care that you do not destroy it by churning up the mire at the bottom."

"Yes, but as a priest, Gunnulf, you have promised God that you would shun these . . . difficulties."

"As you have too, Kristin—when you promised to forsake the Devil and his work. The Devil's work is what begins in sweet desire and ends with two people becoming like the snake and the toad, snapping at each other. That's what Eve learned, when she tried to give her husband and her descendants what belonged to God. She brought them nothing but banishment and the shame of blood and death, which entered the world when brother killed brother in that first small field, where thorns and thistles grew among the heaps of stones around the patches of land."

"Yes, but you're a priest," she said in the same tone of voice. "You're not subjected to the daily trial of trying to agree patiently with the will of another." And she broke into tears.

The priest said with a little smile, "About that matter there is disagreement between body and soul in every mother's child. That's why marriage and the wedding mass were created—so that man and woman would be given help in their lives: married folk and parents and children and house servants as loyal and helpful companions on the journey toward the house of peace."

Kristin said quietly, "It seems to me that it would be easier to watch over and pray for those who are asleep out in the world than to struggle with one's own sins."

"That may be," said the priest sharply. "But you mustn't believe, Kristin, that there has ever been a priest who has not had to guard himself against the Fiend at the same time as he tried to protect the lambs from the wolf."

Kristin said in a quiet and timid voice, "I thought that those who live among the holy shrines and possess all the prayers and powerful words . . ."

Gunnulf leaned forward, tended to the fire, and then sat with his elbows on his knees.

"It was almost exactly six years ago that we arrived in Rome, Eiliv and I, along with two Scottish priests whom we had met in Avignon. We journeyed the whole way on foot.

"We arrived in the city just before Lent. That's when people in the southern countries hold great celebrations and feasts—they call it *carnevale*. The wine, both red and white, flows in rivers from the taverns, and people dance late into the night, and there are torches and bonfires in the open marketplaces. It is springtime in Italy then, and the flowers are blooming in the meadows and gardens. The women adorn themselves with blossoms and toss roses and violets down to the people strolling along the streets. They sit up in the windows, with silk and satin tapestries hanging from the ledge over the stone walls. All buildings are made from stone down there, and the knights have their castles and strongholds in the middle of town. There are apparently no town statutes or laws about keeping the peace in the city—the knights and their men fight in the streets, making the blood run.

"There was such a castle on the street where we were staying, and the knight who ruled it was named Ermes Malavolti. Its shadow stretched over the entire narrow lane where our hostel stood, and our room was as dark and cold as the dungeon in a stone fortress. When we went out we often had to press ourselves up against the wall as he rode past with silver bells on his clothing and a whole troop of armed men. Muck and filth would splash up from the horses' hooves, because in that country people simply throw all their slops and offal outdoors. The streets are cold and dark and narrow like clefts in a mountain—quite unlike the green lanes of our towns. In the streets during *carnevale* they hold races—they let the wild Arabian horses race against each other."

The priest sat in silence for a moment, then he continued.

"This Sir Ermes had a kinswoman living at his house. Isota was her name, and she might have been Isolde the Fair One herself.

Her complexion and hair were as light as honey, but her eyes were no doubt black. I saw her several times at a window. . . .

"But outside the city the land is more desolate than the most desolate heaths in this country, and nothing lives there but deer and wolves; and the eagles scream. And yet there are towns and castles in the mountains all around, and out on the green plains you can see traces everywhere that people once lived in this world. Great flocks of sheep graze there now, along with herds of white oxen. Herdsmen with long spears follow them on horseback; they are dangerous folk for wayfarers to meet, for they will kill and rob them and throw their bodies into pits in the ground.

"But out on these green plains are the pilgrim churches."

Master Gunnulf paused for a moment.

"Perhaps this land seems so inexpressibly desolate because the city is nearby—the one that was the queen of the entire heathen world and then became Christ's betrothed. The guards have abandoned the city, which in the teeming din of the feasting seems like an abandoned woman. The revelers have settled into the castle where the husband is absent, and they have lured the mistress into joining their carousing, with their merriment and spilling of blood and strife.

"But underground there are splendors that are more precious than all the splendors on which the sun shines. That's where the graves of the holy martyrs are, dug into the very rock, and there are so many that the thought of them can make you dizzy. When you remember how numerous they are—the tortured witnesses who have suffered death for the sake of Christ—then it seems as if every speck of dust that is whirled up by the hooves of the revelers' horses must be holy and worthy of worship."

The priest pulled out a thin chain from under his robe and opened the little silver cross hanging from it. Inside was something black that looked like tinder-moss, and a tiny green bone.

"One day we were down in those catacombs all day long, and we said our prayers in caves and oratories where the first disciples of Saint Peter and Saint Paul once gathered for mass. Then the monks who owned the church into which we had descended gave us these sacred relics. This is a piece of the sponge which the pious maidens used to wipe up the martyr blood so that it would not be lost, and this is a knuckle from the finger of a holy man—but only

God knows his name. Then all four of us vowed that every day we would invoke this holy man, whose honor is unknown to any human. And we chose this nameless martyr as a witness so that we might never forget how completely unworthy we are of God's reward or the honors of men, and always remember that nothing in this world is worthy of desire except His mercy."

Kristin kissed the cross with deference and handed it to Orm, who did the same.

Then Gunnulf said suddenly, "I want to give you this relic, kinsman."

Orm sank down on one knee and kissed his uncle's hand. Gunnulf hung the cross around the boy's neck.

"Wouldn't you have a mind to see these places, Orm?"

The boy's face lit up with a smile. "Yes, I now know that someday I will go there."

"Have you ever had a mind to become a priest?" asked his uncle.

"Yes," replied the boy. "Whenever Father curses these weak arms of mine. But I don't know whether he would like me to be a priest. And then there's that other matter, as you know," he murmured.

"Dispensation can be sought for your birth," said the priest calmly. "Perhaps we might journey south together sometime, Orm, you and I."

"Tell me more, Uncle," Orm implored.

"That I will." Gunnulf put his hands on the armrests of his chair and stared into the fire.

"As I wandered there, seeing nothing but reminders of the tortured witnesses and thinking of the intolerable torments they had borne in the name of Jesus, a terrible temptation came over me. I thought about the way the Savior had hung nailed to the cross all those hours. But his disciples had suffered inexpressible torments for many days. Women watched their children tortured to death before their very eyes; delicate young maidens had their flesh raked from their bones with iron combs; young boys were forced to confront beasts of prey and enraged oxen. Then it occurred to me that many of these people had suffered more than Christ himself.

"I pondered this until I felt that my heart and mind would burst. But finally I received the light that I had prayed and begged for. And I realized that just as they had suffered, so should we all have the courage to suffer. Who would be so foolish not to accept pain and torment if this was the way to a faithful and steadfast bridegroom who waits with open arms, his breast bloody and burning with love.

"But he loved humankind. And that's why he died as the bridegroom who has gone off to rescue his bride from the robbers' hands. And they bind him and torture him to death, but he sees his sweetest friend sitting at the table with his executioners, bantering with them and mocking his pain and his loyal love."

Gunnulf Nikulaussøn hid his face in his hands.

"Then I realized that this mighty love sustains everything in the world—even the fire in Hell. For if God wanted to, He could take our souls by force; then we would be completely powerless in His grasp. But since He loves us the way the bridegroom loves the bride, He will not force her; if she won't embrace Him willingly, then He must allow her to flee and to shun Him. I have also thought that perhaps no soul is lost for all eternity. For I think every soul must desire this love, but it seems too dearly bought to let go of every other precious possession for the sake of this love alone. When the fire has consumed all other will that is rebellious and hostile to God, then at last the will toward God, even if it was no bigger in a person than one nail in a whole house, shall remain inside the soul, just as the iron remains in a burned-out ruin."

"Gunnulf—" Kristin rose halfway to her feet. "I'm afraid."

Gunnulf looked up, pale, with blazing eyes.

"I was also afraid. For I understood that the torment of God's love will never end as long as men and maidens are born on this earth, and that He must be afraid of losing their souls—as long as He daily and hourly surrenders his body and his blood on thousands of altars and there are those who reject the sacrifice.

"And I was afraid of myself because I, an impure man, had served at his altar, said mass with impure lips, and held up the Host with impure hands. And I felt that I was like the man who led his beloved to a place of shame and betrayed her."

He caught Kristin in his arms when she fainted, and he and Orm carried the unconscious woman over to the bed.

After a while she opened her eyes; she sat up and covered her face with her hands. She burst into tears and uttered a wild and plaintive cry, "I can't, Gunnulf, I can't—when you talk like that, then I realize that I can never . . ."

Gunnulf took her hand. But she turned away from the man's pale and agitated face.

"Kristin. You cannot settle for anything less than the love that is between God and the soul.

"Kristin, look around at what the world is like. You who have given birth to two children—have you never thought about the fact that every child who is born is baptized in blood, and the first thing a person breathes on this earth is the smell of blood? Don't you think that as their mother you should put all your effort into one thing? To ensure that your sons do not fall back on that first baptismal pact with the world but instead hold on to the other pact, which they affirmed with God at the baptismal font."

She sobbed and sobbed.

"I'm afraid of you," she said again. "Gunnulf, when you talk like that, then I realize I'll never be able to find my way to peace."

"God will find you," said the priest quietly. "Stay calm and do not flee from Him who has been seeking you before you even existed in your mother's womb."

He sat in silence for a moment near the edge of the bed. Then he asked calmly and evenly whether he should wake Ingrid and ask the woman to come and help her undress. Kristin shook her head.

He made the sign of the cross over her three times. He bade Orm good night and went into the alcove where he slept.

Orm and Kristin undressed. The boy seemed deeply absorbed in his own thoughts. After Kristin was in bed, he came over to her. He looked at her tear-stained face and asked whether he should sit with her until she fell asleep.

"Oh, yes . . . oh, no, Orm, you must be tired, you who are so young. It must be very late."

Orm stood there a little longer.

"Don't you think it's strange," he said suddenly. "Father and Uncle Gunnulf—they're so unlike each other—and yet they're alike in a certain way."

Kristin lay there, thinking to herself, Yes, perhaps. They're unlike any other men.

A moment later she was asleep, and Orm went over to the other bed. He took off the rest of his clothes and crept under the covers. There was a linen sheet underneath and linen cases on the pillows. With pleasure the boy stretched out on the smooth, cool bed. His heart was pounding with excitement at these new adventures which his uncle's words had pointed out to him. Prayers, fasts, everything he had practiced because he had been taught to do so, suddenly seemed new to him—weapons in a glorious war for which he longed. Perhaps he would become a monk—or a priest— if he could obtain dispensation because he had been born of adultery.

Gunnulf's bed was a wooden bench with a sheet made from a hide spread over a little straw and a single, small pillow; he had to stretch himself out full length to sleep. The priest took off his surcoat, lay down wearing his undergarments, and pulled the thin homespun blanket over himself.

He left the little candlewick burning that was twined around an iron stake.

His own words had oppressed him with fear and uneasiness.

He felt faint with longing for that time—would he ever again find that nuptial joy in his heart that had filled him all spring long in Rome? Together with his three brothers he had wandered in the sunshine across the green, flower-starred meadows. He grew weak and trembled when he saw how beautiful the world was—and then to know that all of this was nothing compared to the riches of that other life. And yet this world greeted them with a thousand small joys and sweet reminders of the bridegroom. The lilies in the field and the birds in the sky reminded them of his words; he had spoken of donkeys like the ones they saw and of wells like the stone-lined cisterns they passed. They received food from the monks at the churches they visited, and when they drank the blood-red wine and broke off the golden crust from the bread made of wheat, all four priests from the barley lands understood why Christ had honored wine and wheat, which were purer than all other foodstuffs that God had given humankind, by manifesting himself in their likeness during the holy communion.

During that spring he had not felt any uneasiness or fear. He had felt himself released from the temptations of the world to such an extent that when he sensed the warm sun on his skin, then everything he had pondered before with such anguish seemed so easy to comprehend. How this body of his could be cleansed by fire to become the transfigured form . . . Feeling light and released from the demands of the earth, he needed no more sleep than the cuckoo, dozing in the spring nights. His heart sang in his breast; his soul felt like a bride in the arms of the bridegroom.

He realized full well that this would not last. No man could live on earth in this manner for long. And he had received each hour of that bright springtime like a pledge—a merciful promise that would strengthen his endurance when the skies darkened over him and the road led down into a dark ravine, through roaring rivers and cold snowdrifts.

But it wasn't until he returned to Norway that the uneasiness seized hold of his mind.

There were so many things. There was his wealth. The great inheritance from his father—and the richly endowed benefice.[2] There was the path he envisioned before him. His place in the cathedral chapter; he knew it was intended for him—provided he didn't renounce everything he owned, enter the friars' order, take the vows of a monk, and submit to their rules. That was the life he desired—with half his heart.

And then when he grew old enough and hardened enough in the battle . . . In the kingdom of Norway there were people who lived like utter heathens or were led astray by the false teachings which the Russians put forward in the name of Christianity—the Finns and the other half-wild peoples,[3] who were constantly on his mind. Wasn't it God who had awakened in him this desire to journey to their villages, bringing the Word and the Light?

But he pushed aside these thoughts with the excuse that he had to obey the archbishop. And Lord Eiliv counseled him against it. Lord Eiliv had talked to him and listened to him and shown him clearly that he was speaking to the son of his old friend, Sir Nikulaus of Husaby. "But you are not capable of moderation, you who are descended from the daughters of Skogheims-Gaute, whether it be good or bad, whatever you have set your mind to." The salvation of the Finns weighed heavily on the archbishop's heart as well—but they had no need of a spiritual teacher who wrote and spoke Latin as well as his own language, who was no less knowledgeable about the law than about *Aritmetica* and *Algorismus*. Gunnulf had acquired his learning in order to use it, hadn't he? "But it is unclear to me whether you have the gift to talk with the poor and simple people up there in the north."

Oh, that sweet spring when his learning seemed to him no more venerable than the learning that every little maiden acquires from her mother—how to spin and brew and bake and milk—the training that every child needs to tend to his place in the world.

He had complained to the archbishop about the uneasiness and fear that came over him whenever he thought about his riches and how much he enjoyed being wealthy. For the needs of his own body he required little; he himself lived like a poor monk. But he liked to see many people sitting at his table; he liked to forestall the needs of the poor with his gifts. And he loved his horses and his books.

Lord Eiliv spoke somberly about the honors of the Church. Some were called to honor it with a stately and dignified demeanor, while others were called to show the world a voluntary poverty; wealth was nothing in itself. He reminded Gunnulf of those archbishops and prelates and priests who had been forced to suffer attacks, banishment, and offenses by kings in the past because they asserted the right of the Church. Time after time they had shown that if it was required of Norwegian clergymen, they would renounce everything to follow God. And God Himself would give the sign if it should be required—if only they all kept this firmly in sight, then they need not be afraid that wealth might become an enemy of the soul.

All this time Gunnulf noticed that the archbishop was not pleased that he thought and pondered so much on his own. It seemed to Gunnulf that Lord Eiliv Kortin and his priests were like men who were adding more and more bricks to their house. The honor of the Church and the power of the Church and the right of the Church. God knew that Gunnulf could be just as zealous as any other priest about matters of the Church; he was not one to avoid the work of hauling stones or carrying mortar for the building. But they seemed to be afraid of entering the house and resting inside. They seemed to be afraid of going astray if they thought too much.

That was not what *he* feared. It was impossible for a man to succumb to heresy if he kept his eye steadfastly fixed on the cross and unceasingly surrendered himself to the protection of the Holy Virgin. That was not the danger for him.

The danger was the unquenchable longing in his soul to win the favor and friendship of others.

He who had felt in the depths of his being that God loved him; to God his soul was as dear and precious as all other souls on earth.

But here at home it rose up in him again: the memory of everything that had tormented him during his childhood and youth. That his mother had not been as fond of him as she was of Erlend. That his father hadn't wanted to pay any attention to him, the way he had constantly paid attention to Erlend. Later, when they lived with Baard at Hestnes, it was Erlend who was praised and Erlend who did wrong—Gunnulf was merely the brother. Erlend, Erlend was the chieftain for all the young boys, Erlend was the one the serving maids cursed at and then laughed at just the same. And Erlend was the one he himself loved above all others on earth. If only Erlend would be fond of him; but he could never be satisfied with the love Erlend gave him. Erlend was the only one who cared for him—but Erlend cared for so many.

And now he saw the way his brother handled everything that had fallen to his lot. God alone must know how it would end with the riches of Husaby; there was gossip enough in Nidaros about Erlend's imprudent management. To think he took so little notice, when God had given him four handsome children; and they *were* handsome, even the children he had begotten in his dissolute days. Erlend perceived this not as a gift of grace but as something that was simply as it should be.

And finally he had won the love of a pure, delicate young maiden of good family. Gunnulf thought about the way Erlend had dealt with her; he could no longer respect his brother after he found that out. He grew impatient with himself when he noticed traits he had in common with his brother. Erlend, as old as he was, would turn pale or blush crimson as easily as a half-grown maiden, and Gunnulf would rage because he felt the blood coming and going just as easily in his own face. They had inherited this from their mother; a single word could make her change color.

Now Erlend assumed it was no more than reasonable that his

wife was a good woman, a mirror for all wives—in spite of the fact that year after year he had tried to corrupt this young child and lead her astray. But Erlend didn't even seem to imagine that things might be otherwise; he was now married to the woman whom he had trained in sensual pleasures, betrayal, and dishonesty. He didn't seem to think it was something he should honor his wife for—that in spite of her fall, she was still truthful and faithful, modest and good.

And yet, when the news arrived this past summer and autumn about Erlend's actions in the north . . . Then he had yearned for only *one* thing: to be with his brother. Erlend, the king's military protector in Haalogaland; and he, the preacher of God's words in the desolate, half-heathen districts near the Gandvik Sea[4] . . .

Gunnulf stood up. On one wall of the alcove hung a large crucifix, and in front of it, on the floor, lay a big slab of stone.

He knelt down on the stone and stretched out his arms to either side. He had hardened his body to tolerate this position, and he could remain like this for hours, as motionless as stone. With his eyes fastened on the crucifix, he waited for the solace that would come when he was able to focus all his attention on his contemplation of the cross.

But the first thought that now came to him was this: Should he part with this image? Saint Francis and his friars had crosses which they carved themselves from a couple of tree branches. He ought to give away this beautiful rood—he could give it to the church at Husaby. Peasants, children, and women who went there for mass might gain strength from such a visible display of the Savior's loving gentleness during his suffering. Simple souls like Kristin. For him it shouldn't be necessary.

Night after night he had knelt here with his senses closed off and his limbs numb, until he saw the vision. The hill with the three crosses against the sky. The cross in the middle, which was meant to bear the king of heaven and earth, shook and trembled; it bent like a tree in a storm, in fear of bearing the much too precious burden, the sacrifice for all the sins of the world. The lord of the storm tents forced it, the way a knight forces his defiant stallion; the chieftain of heaven carried it into battle. Then that miracle occurred which was the key to ever deeper miracles. The blood that ran down from the cross in redemption for all sins and penance for all sorrows—that was the visible sign. With this first miracle the eye of the soul could be opened to contemplate those still hidden— God, who came down to earth and became the son of a virgin and brother to the human kin, who lay waste to Hell and who, with the released souls that were his spoils of war, stormed toward the dazzling sea of light from which the world was born and which sustains the earth. It was toward that unfathomable and eternal depth of light that his thoughts were drawn, and there they perished in the light, vanishing like a flock of birds into the radiance of an evening sky.

Not until the bells of the church rang for matins did Gunnulf get up. There was not a sound as he walked through the main hall— they were both asleep, Kristin and Orm.

Out in the dark courtyard the priest paused for a moment. But none of the servants appeared to accompany him to church. He didn't require them to attend more than two services a day. But Ingrid, his foster mother, almost always went with him to matins. This morning she was evidently still asleep too. Well, she had been up late the night before.

All that day the three kinsmen spoke little to each other, and then only about unimportant things. Gunnulf looked tired, but he kept up his bantering just the same. "How foolish we were last night. We sat here so mournfully, like three fatherless children," he said once. Many funny little things went on in Nidaros, with the pilgrims and such, which the priests often jested about among themselves. An old man from Herjedal had come to offer prayers on behalf of his fellow villagers, but he managed to mix them all up— and he later realized that things would have looked bad in his village if Saint Olav had taken him at his word.

Late that evening Erlend arrived, soaking wet. He had come to Nidaros by ship, and now the wind was blowing hard again. He was furious and fell upon Orm at once with angry words.

Gunnulf listened for a while and said, "When you speak to Orm in that manner, Erlend, you sound like our father—the way he used to speak to you."

Erlend abruptly fell silent. Then he shouted, "But I know I

never acted so senselessly when I was a boy—running off from the manor in a snowstorm, a woman who is ill and a whelp of a boy! There's not much else to boast of about Orm's manhood, but you can see that he's not afraid of his father!"

"You weren't afraid of Father either," replied his brother with a smile.

Orm stood before his father without saying a word and tried to look indifferent.

"Well, you can go now," said Erlend. "I'm tired of the whole lot at Husaby. But one thing I know—this summer Orm will go north with me, then I'll make something of this pampered lamb of Kristin's. He's no bumbler, either," he said eagerly to his brother. "He has a sure aim, I can tell you that. And he's not afraid; but he's always surly and morose, and it seems as if he has no marrow in his bones."

"If you often rage at your son the way you did just now, then it's not so strange that he would be morose," said the priest.

Erlend's mood shifted; he laughed and said, "I often had to suffer much worse from Father—and God knows I didn't grow morose from that. It could very well be . . . but now that I've come here, we should celebrate Christmas, since it's Christmastime, after all. Where's Kristin? What was it she had to talk to you about again that she would . . ."

"I don't think there was anything she wanted to talk to me about," said the priest. "She had a mind to attend mass here during Christmas."

"It seems to me that she could have made do with what we have at home," said Erlend. "But it's hard for her—all her youth is being stripped from her in this way." He rammed one fist against the other. "I don't understand why our Lord should think we need a new son every year."

Gunnulf looked up at his brother.

"Well . . . I have no idea what our Lord thinks you may need. But what Kristin no doubt needs most is for you to be kind to her."

"Yes, I suppose she does," murmured Erlend.

The next day Erlend went to morning mass with his wife. They set off for Saint Gregor's Church; Erlend always attended mass there when he was in Nidaros. The two of them went alone, and in the lane where the snow lay piled up in drifts, heavy and wet, Erlend led his wife by the hand, in a refined and courtly fashion. He hadn't said a word to her about her flight, and he had been kind toward Orm after his first outburst.

Kristin walked along, pale and silent, with her head bowed slightly; the ankle-length, black fur cloak with the silver clasps seemed to weigh heavily on her frail, thin body.

"Would you like me to ride back home with you? Then Orm can travel home by ship," her husband said. "I suppose you would prefer not to travel across the fjord."

"No, you know I'm reluctant to journey by ship."

The weather was calm and mild now—every once in a while mounds of heavy wet snow would slide down off the trees. The sky hung low and dark-gray over the white town. There was a watery, greenish-gray sheen to the snow; the timbered walls of the houses, the fences, and the tree trunks looked black in the damp air. Never, thought Kristin, had she seen the world look so cold and faded and pale.

KRISTIN SAT WITH Gaute on her lap and stared into the distance from the hill north of the manor. It was such a lovely evening. Below, the lake lay glistening and still, reflecting the mountain ridges, the buildings of By, and the golden clouds in the sky. The strong smell of leaves and earth rose up after the rainfall earlier in the day. The grass in the meadows must be knee-deep by now, and the fields were covered with spears of grain.

Sounds traveled a long way on such an evening. Now the pipes and drums and fiddles began playing down on the green near Vinjar; they sounded so splendid up on the hill.

The cuckoo fell silent for long periods, but then it would cry out a few notes, far away in the woods to the south. And birds whistled and warbled in all the groves around the farm—but sporadic and quiet, because the sun was still high.

The livestock were bellowing and their bells were ringing as they returned home from the pasture across from the farmyard gate.

"Now Gaute will soon have his milk," she cooed to the infant, lifting him up. The boy lay as he usually did, with his heavy head resting on his mother's shoulder. Now and then he would press closer, and Kristin took this as a sign that he understood her endearing words and chatter.

She walked down toward the buildings. Outside the main hall Naakkve and Bjørgulf were leaping around, trying to entice a cat down from the roof where it had taken refuge. Then the boys took up the broken dagger which belonged to both of them and went back to digging a hole in the earthen floor of the entryway.

Dagrun came into the hall carrying a basin of goat milk, and Kristin let Gaute drink ladle after ladle of the warm liquid. The boy grunted crossly when the servant woman spoke to him; when she tried to take him away, he struck out at her and hid his face on his mother's breast.

"But it seems to me that he's getting better," said the milkmaid.

Kristin cupped the little face in her hand; it was yellowish-white, like tallow, and his eyes were always tired. Gaute had a big, heavy head and thin, frail limbs. He had turned two years old on the eighth day after Saint Lavrans's Day, but he still couldn't stand on his own, he had only five teeth, and he couldn't speak a word.

Sira Eiliv said that it wasn't rickets; and neither the alb nor the altar books had helped. Everywhere the priest went he would ask advice about this illness that had overtaken Gaute. Kristin knew that he mentioned the child in all his prayers. But to her he could only say that she must patiently submit to God's will. And she should let him have warm goat milk.

Her poor little boy. Kristin hugged him and kissed him after the woman had left. How handsome, how handsome he was. She thought she could see that he took after her father's family—his eyes were dark gray and his hair as pale as flax, thick and silky soft.

Now he began to whimper again. Kristin stood up and paced the floor as she held him. Small and weak though he was, he still grew heavy after a while. But Gaute refused to leave his mother's arms. So she walked back and forth in the dim hall, carrying the boy and lulling him to sleep.

Someone rode into the courtyard. Ulf Haldorssøn's voice echoed between the buildings. Kristin went over to the entryway door with the child in her arms.

"You'll have to unsaddle your own horse tonight, Ulf. All the men have gone off to the dance. It's a shame you should have to be troubled with this, but I'm afraid it can't be helped."

Ulf muttered with annoyance, but he unsaddled the horse. Naakkve and Bjørgulf swarmed around him and wanted to ride the horse over in the pasture.

"No, Naakkve, you must stay with Gaute—play with your brother so he doesn't cry while I'm in the cookhouse," said Kristin.

The boy frowned unhappily. But then he got down on all fours, roaring and butting at his little brother whom Kristin had put down on a cushion near the entryway door. She bent down and stroked Naakkve's hair. He was so good to his younger brothers.

When Kristin came back to the hall holding the big trencher in her hands, Ulf Haldorssøn was sitting on the bench, playing with the children. Gaute liked to be with Ulf as long as he didn't see his mother—but now he began crying at once and reached out for her. Kristin put down the trencher and picked Gaute up.

Ulf blew on the foam of the newly tapped ale, took a swallow, and then began taking food from the small bowls on the trencher.

"Are all of your maidservants out tonight?"

Kristin said, "There are fiddles and drums and pipes—a group of musicians arrived from Orkedal after the wedding. And you know that as soon as they heard about them . . . They're young girls, after all."

"You let them run around too freely, Kristin. I think you're most afraid that it'll be hard to find a wet nurse this autumn."

Kristin involuntarily smoothed down her gown over her slender waist. She had blushed dark red at the man's words.

Ulf laughed harshly. "But if you keep carrying around Gaute this way, then things may go as they did last year. Come here to your foster father, my boy, and I'll give you some food from my plate."

Kristin didn't reply. She set her three small sons in a row on the bench along the opposite wall, brought the basin of milk porridge, and pulled over a little stool close by. There she sat, feeding the boys, although Naakkve and Bjørgulf grumbled—they wanted spoons so they could feed themselves. The oldest was now four, and the other would soon be three years old.

"Where's Erlend?" asked Ulf.

"Margret wanted to go to the dance, and so he went with her."

"It's good he understands he should keep a watchful eye on that maiden of his," said Ulf.

Again Kristin did not reply. She undressed the children and put them to bed—Gaute in the cradle and the other two in her own bed. Erlend had resigned himself to having them there after she recovered from her long illness the year before.

When Ulf had eaten his fill, he stretched out on the bench. Kristin pushed the chair carved from a tree stump over to the cradle, got her basket of wool, and began to wind up balls of yarn for her loom as she gently and quietly rocked the cradle.

"Shouldn't you go to bed?" she asked once without turning her head. "Aren't you tired, Ulf?"

The man got up, poked at the fire a bit, and came over to Kristin. He sat down on the bench across from her. Kristin saw that he was not as spent from carousing as he usually was whenever he had been in Nidaros for a few days.

"You don't even ask about news from town, Kristin," he said, looking at her as he leaned forward with his elbows on his knees.

Her heart began pounding with fear. She could see from the man's expression and manner that again there was news that wasn't good. But she said with a gentle and calm smile, "You must tell me, Ulf—have you heard anything?"

"Yes, well . . ." But first he took out his traveling bag and unpacked the things he had brought from town for her. Kristin thanked him.

"I understand that you've heard some news in Nidaros," she said after a while.

Ulf looked at the young mistress; then he turned his gaze to the pale, sleeping child in the cradle.

"Does he always sweat like this?" he asked softly, gently pushing back the boy's damp, dark hair. "Kristin—when you were betrothed to Erlend . . . the document that was drawn up regarding the ownership of both your possessions—didn't it state that you should manage with full authority those properties which he gave you as betrothal and wedding gifts?"

Kristin's heart pounded harder, but she said calmly, "It's also true, Ulf, that Erlend has always asked my advice and sought my consent in all dealings with those properties. Is this about the sections of the estate in Verdal that he has sold to Vigleik of Lyng?"

"Yes," said Ulf. "He has bought a ship called *Hugrekken* from Vigleik. So now he's going to maintain two ships. And what do you gain in return, Kristin?"

"Erlend's share of Skjervastad and two plots of land in Ulfkelstad—each taxed by one month's worth of food—and what he owns of Aarhammar," she said. "Surely you didn't think Erlend would sell that estate without my permission or without repaying me?"

"Hmm . . ." Ulf sat in silence for a moment. "And yet your income will be reduced, Kristin. Skjervastad—that was where Erlend obtained hay this past winter and in return he released the farmer from the land tax for the next three years."

"Erlend was not to blame because we had no dry hay last year. I know, Ulf, you did everything you could, but with all the misery we had here last summer—"

"He sold more than half of Aarhammar to the sisters at Rein back when he was preparing to flee the country with you." Ulf laughed. "Or pledged it as security, which amounts to the same thing, in Erlend's case. Free of war levies—the entire burden rests on Audun, who oversees the farm which you will now call your own."

"Can't he lease the land from the convent?" asked Kristin.

"The nuns' tenant farmer on the neighboring estate has leased it," said Ulf. "It's difficult and risky for leaseholders to manage when lands are split up the way Erlend is bent on doing."

Kristin was silent. She knew he was right.

"Erlend is working quickly," said Ulf, "to increase his lineage and to destroy his property."

When she didn't reply, Ulf went on, "You will soon have *many* children, Kristin Lavransdatter."

"But none I would give up," she said, with a slight quaver in her voice.

"Don't be so fearful for Gaute—I'm sure he'll grow strong over time," said Ulf softly.

"It must be as God wills, but it's difficult to wait."

He could hear the concealed suffering in the mother's voice; a strange sense of helplessness came over the ponderous, gloomy man.

"It's of such little avail, Kristin. You have accomplished much here at Husaby, but if Erlend is now going to set off with two ships . . . I have no faith that there will be peace in the north, and your husband has so little cunning; he doesn't know how to turn to his advantage what he has gained in the past two years. Bad years they have been, and you have been constantly ill. If things should continue in this way, you'll be brought to your knees in the end, and as such a young woman. I've helped you as best I could here on the estate, but this other matter, Erlend's lack of prudence—"

"Yes, God knows you have," she interrupted him. "You've been the best of kinsmen toward us, Ulf my friend, and I can never fully thank you or repay you."

Ulf stood up, lit a candle at the hearth, and set it in the candlestick on the table; he stood there with his back turned to Kristin. She had let her hands sink into her lap as they talked, but now she began winding up the yarn and rocking the cradle with her foot again.

"Can't you send word to your parents back home?" he asked. "So that Lavrans might journey north in the fall along with your mother when she comes to help you?"

"I hadn't thought of troubling my mother this fall. She's getting older, and it happens much too often now that I must lie down in the straw to give birth. I can't ask her to come every time." Her smile looked a bit strained.

"Do it this time," said Ulf. "And ask your father to come along, so you can seek his advice on these matters."

"I will not ask my father's advice about this," she said quietly but firmly.

"What about Gunnulf then?" asked Ulf after a moment. "Can't you speak to him?"

"It's not proper to disturb him with such things now," said Kristin in the same tone of voice.

"Do you mean because he has entered a monastery?" Ulf laughed scornfully. "I've never noticed that monks had less understanding about managing estates than other people."

When she didn't answer, he said, "But if you won't seek advice from anyone, Kristin, then you must speak to Erlend. Think of your sons, Kristin!"

She sat in silence for a long time.

"You who are so good toward our children, Ulf," she said at last. "It would seem to me more reasonable if you married and had your own worries to tend to—than that you should stay here, tormenting yourself . . . with Erlend's and my troubles."

Ulf turned to face her. He stood with his hands gripping the edge of the table behind him and looked at Kristin Lavransdatter. She was still straight-backed and slender and beautiful as she sat there. Her gown was made of dark, hand-dyed woolen cloth, but she wore a fine, soft linen wimple around her calm, pale face. The belt from which her ring of keys hung was adorned with small silver roses. On her breast glittered two chains with crosses, the larger one on gilded links which hung almost to her waist; that one had been given to her by her father. On top lay the thin silver chain with the little cross which Orm had given to his stepmother, asking her to wear it always.

So far she had recovered from each childbirth looking just as lovely as ever—only a little quieter, with heavier responsibilities on her young shoulders. Her cheeks were thinner, her eyes a little darker and more somber beneath the wide, white forehead, and her lips were a little less red and full. But her beauty would soon be worn away before many more years had passed if things continued in this fashion.

"Don't you think, Ulf, that you would be happier if you settled down on your own farm?" she continued. "Erlend told me that you've bought three more plots of land at Skjoldvirkstad—you will soon own half the estate. And Isak has only the one child—Aase is both beautiful and kind, a capable woman, and she seems to like you—"

"And yet I don't want her if I have to marry her," sneered the man crudely and laughed. "Besides, Aase Isaksdatter is too good for . . ." His voice changed. "I've never known any other father but my foster father, Kristin, and I think it's my fate not to have any other children but foster children."

"I'll pray to the Virgin Mary that you'll have better fortune, kinsman."

"I'm not so young, either. Thirty-five winters, Kristin," he laughed. "It wouldn't take many more than that and I could be your father."

"Then you must have begun your sinful ways early," replied Kristin. She tried to make her voice sound merry and light-hearted.

"Shouldn't you go to sleep now?" Ulf asked.

"Yes, soon—but you must be tired too, Ulf. You should go to bed."

The man quietly bade her good night and left the room.

Kristin took the candlestick from the table and shone the light on the two sleeping boys in the enclosed bed. Bjørgulf's eyelashes were not festering—thank God for that. The weather would stay

fine for a while yet. As soon as the wind blew hard or the weather
forced the children to stay inside near the hearth, his eyes would
grow inflamed. She stood there a long time, gazing at the two
boys. Then she went over and bent down to look at Gaute in his
cradle.

They had been as healthy as little fledglings, all three of her
sons—until the sickness had come to the region last summer. A
fever had carried off children in homes all around the fjord; it was
a terrible thing to see and to hear about. She had been allowed to
keep hers—all her own children.

For five days she had sat near the bed on the south wall where
they lay, all three of them, with red spots covering their faces and
with feverish eyes that shunned the light. Their small bodies were
burning hot. She sat with her hand under the coverlet and patted
the soles of Bjørgulf's feet while she sang and sang until her poor
voice was no more than a whisper.

> Shoe, shoe the knight's great horse.
> How are we to shoe it best?
> Iron shoes will pass the test.
>
> Shoe, shoe the earl's great horse.
> How are we to shoe it best?
> Silver shoes will pass the test.
>
> Shoe, shoe the king's great horse.
> How are we to shoe it best?
> Golden shoes will pass the test.

Bjørgulf was less sick than the others, and more restless. If she
stopped singing for even a minute, he would throw off the coverlets at once. Gaute was then only ten months old; he was so ill that
she didn't think he would survive. He lay at her breast, wrapped in
blankets and furs, and had no strength to nurse. She held him with
one arm as she patted the soles of Bjørgulf's feet with her other
hand.

Now and then, if all three of them happened to fall asleep for a
while, she would stretch out on the bed beside them, fully dressed.

Erlend came and went, looking helplessly at his three small sons. He tried to sing to them, but they didn't care for their father's fine voice—they wanted their mother to sing, even though she didn't have the voice for it.

The servant women would come in, wanting their mistress to rest; the men would come in to inquire about the boys; and Orm tried to play with his young brothers. At Kristin's advice, Erlend had sent Margret over to Østerdal, but Orm wanted to stay—he was grown up now, after all. Sira Eiliv sat at the children's bedside whenever he wasn't out tending to the sick. Through work and worry the priest had shed all the corpulence he had acquired at Husaby; it grieved him greatly to see so many fair young children perish. And some grownups had died too.

By the evening of the sixth day, all the children were so much better that Kristin promised her husband to undress and go to bed that night. Erlend offered to keep watch along with the maids and to call Kristin if need be. But at the supper table she noticed that Orm's face was bright red and his eyes were shiny with fever. He said it was nothing, but he jumped up abruptly and rushed out. When Erlend and Kristin went out to him, they found him vomiting in the courtyard.

Erlend threw his arms around the youth.

"Orm, my son. Are you ill?"

"My head aches," complained the boy, and he let his head sink heavily onto his father's shoulder.

That night they kept vigil over Orm. Most of the time he lay there muttering in delirium—then screaming loudly and flailing his long arms about, seeming to see hideous things. What he said they could not understand.

In the morning Kristin collapsed. It turned out that she must have been with child again; now it went very badly for her, and afterwards she lay as if immersed in a deathlike sleep; later she was seized by a terrible fever. Orm had been in the grave for more than two weeks before she learned of her stepson's death.

At the time she was so weak that she couldn't properly grieve. She felt so bloodless and faint that nothing seemed to reach her— she was content to lie in bed, only half-alive. There had been a dreadful time when the women hardly dared touch her or tend to her cleanliness, but that had all merged with the confusion of the fever. Now it felt good to submit to the care of others. Around her bed hung many fragrant wreaths of mountain flowers which were meant to keep the flies away—the people from the mountain pastures had sent them, and they smelled especially sweet whenever there was rain in the air. One day Erlend brought the children to her. She saw that they were haggard from their illness, and that Gaute didn't recognize her, but even that didn't trouble her. She merely sensed that Erlend seemed always to be at her side.

He went to mass every day, and he knelt at Orm's grave to pray. The cemetery was next to the parish church at Vinjar, but some of the infants in the family had been given a resting place inside the manor church at Husaby—Erlend's two brothers and one of Munan Biskopssøn's little daughters. Kristin had often felt sorry for these little ones who lay so alone under the flagstones. Now Orm Erlendssøn had his final resting place among these children.

While the others feared for Kristin's life, processions of beggars on their way to Nidaros just before Saint Olav's Day began to pass through the region. They were mostly the same wandering men and women who had made the journey the year before; the pilgrims in Nidaros were always generous to the poor, since intercessions of this kind were considered particularly powerful. And they had learned to travel by way of Skaun during the years since Kristin had settled at Husaby. They knew that there on the estate they would be given shelter, alms, and an abundance of food before they continued on. This time the servants wanted to send them away because the mistress was ill. But when Erlend, who had been up north the last two summers, heard that his wife was accustomed to receiving the beggars so kindly, he ordered that they should be given food and lodging, just as they had before. And in the morning he himself tended to the wanderers, helping the servants to pour the ale and bring in food for them; he gave them alms as he quietly asked for their prayers of intercession for his wife. Many of the beggars wept when they heard that the gentle young woman lay close to death.

All of this Sira Eiliv had told Kristin when she began to regain her health. Not until Christmastime was she strong enough to take up her keys again.

Erlend had sent word to her parents as soon as she fell ill, but at the time they were in the south, attending a wedding at Skog. Later they came to Husaby; she was better by then, but so tired that she had little energy to talk to them. What she wanted most was simply to have Erlend at her bedside.

Weak and pale and always cold, she would cling to his healthy body. The old fire in her blood had gone. It had disappeared so completely that she could no longer remember how it felt to love in that way, but with it had also vanished the worry and bitterness from the past few years. She felt that things were better now, even though the sorrow over Orm's death lay heavily on both of them, and even though Erlend didn't realize how frightened she was for little Gaute. But things were so good between them. She saw that he had feared terribly that he might lose her.

And so it was difficult and painful for her to speak to him, to touch on matters that might destroy the peace and joy they now shared.

She was standing outside in the bright summer night, in front of the entrance to the main house, when the servants returned from the dance. Margret was clinging to her father's arm. She was dressed and adorned in a fashion that would have been more suited to a wedding feast than to a dance out on the green, where all manner of folk came together. But her stepmother had stopped interfering in the maiden's upbringing. Erlend could do as he pleased in raising his own daughter.

Erlend and Margret were both thirsty, so Kristin brought ale for them. The girl sat and talked with them for a while; she and her stepmother were good friends now that Kristin no longer attempted to instruct her. Erlend laughed at everything his daughter said about the dance. But finally Margret and her maid went up to the loft to sleep.

Erlend continued roaming around the hall; he stretched, yawned, but claimed he wasn't tired. He ran his fingers through his long black hair.

"There wasn't time for it after we were in the bathhouse. Because of the dance. I think you'll have to cut my hair, Kristin; I can't walk around like this during the holy days."

Kristin protested that it was too dark, but Erlend laughed and pointed to the vent hole in the ceiling; it was already daylight again. Then she relit the candle, told him to sit down, and draped a cloth around his shoulders. As she worked, he squirmed from the tickling, and laughed when the scissors came too close to his neck.

Kristin carefully gathered up the hair clippings and burned them in the hearth; she shook out the cloth over the fire as well. Then she combed Erlend's hair straight down from his scalp and snipped here and there, wherever the ends weren't quite even.

Erlend grabbed her hands tightly as she stood behind him, placed them at his throat, and smiled as he tilted his head back to look up at her.

But then he let her go, saying, "You're tired." And he stood up with a little sigh.

Erlend sailed to Bjørgvin right after Midsummer. He was disconsolate because his wife was again unable to travel with him. She smiled wearily; all the same, she wouldn't have been able to leave Gaute.

And so Kristin was once again alone at Husaby in the summer. But she was glad that this year she wouldn't give birth until Saint Matthew's Day; it would be difficult both for her and for the women who would attend her if it occurred during the harvest season.

She wondered whether it would always be this way. Times were different now than when she was growing up. She had heard her father speak of the Danish war, and she remembered when he was away from home during the campaign against Duke Eirik. That was how he got the terrible scars on his body. But back home in the valleys, war had still seemed so far away, and no doubt most people thought it would never return. It was mostly peaceful, and her father was home, managing his estates, and thinking about and caring for all of them.

Nowadays there was always unrest—everyone talked about wars and campaigns and the ruling of the kingdom. In Kristin's mind it all merged with her image of the sea and the coast, which she had seen only once since she had moved north. From the coast they sailed and to the coast they came—men whose heads were full of ideas and plans and counterplots and deliberations; clergymen and laymen. To these men belonged Erlend, by virtue of his high birth and his wealth. But she felt that he stood partially outside their circles.

She pondered and thought about this. What was it that caused her husband to have such a position? How did his peers truly regard him?

When he was simply the man she loved, she had never asked about such things. She could see that he was short-tempered and impetuous and rash, that he had a particular penchant for acting unwisely. But back then she had found excuses for everything, never troubling to think about what his temperament might bring upon them both. When they had won her father's consent to marry, everything would be different—that was how she had consoled herself. Gradually it dawned on her that it was from the moment a child was born to them that she began to think about things. What kind of man was Erlend, whom people called irresponsible and imprudent, a man whom no one could trust?

But she had trusted him. She remembered Brynhild's loft, she remembered how the bond between him and that other woman had finally been severed. She remembered his conduct after she had become his lawful bride. But he had stood by her in spite of all the humiliations and rejections; and she had seen that he did not want to lose her for all the gold on earth.

She thought about Haftor of Godøy. He was always following her around, speaking words of nonsense and affection whenever they met, but she had never cared for his attentions. That must be his way of jesting. She didn't think it was more than that; she had been fond of the handsome and boisterous man, and she was still fond of him. But to think that anyone would act that way in mere jest—no, she didn't understand it.

She had met Haftor Graut again at the royal banquets in Nidaros, and he sought out her company there too, just as he usually did. One evening he convinced her to go into a loft room, and she lay down with him on a bed that stood there. Back home in Gudbrandsdal she would never have thought of doing such a thing—there it was not a banquet custom for men and women to slip away, two by two. But here everyone did it; no one seemed to find it improper—it was apparently common practice among knights in other countries. When they first entered the room, Fru Elin, the wife of Sir Erling, was lying on the other bed with a

Swedish knight; Kristin could hear that they were talking about the king's earache. The Swede looked pleased when Fru Elin wanted to get up and go back to the hall.

When Kristin realized that Haftor was quite serious about the intentions behind his request as they lay there and talked, she was so astonished that she failed to be either frightened or suitably indignant. They were both married, after all, and they both had children with their spouses. She had never truly believed that such things actually went on. In spite of all she herself had done and experienced—no, she hadn't believed that such things happened. Haftor had always been merry and affectionate and full of laughter. She couldn't say that what he wanted was to try to seduce her; he hadn't been serious enough for that. And yet he wanted her to commit the worst of sins.

He got off the bed the minute she told him to go. He had turned submissive, but he seemed more surprised than ashamed. And he asked in utter disbelief: Did she truly think that married people were never unfaithful? But she must know that few men could admit to never having a paramour. Women were perhaps a little better than the men, and yet . . .

"Did you believe everything the priests preach about sin and the like even back when you were a young maiden?" he asked. "Then I don't understand, Kristin Lavransdatter, how Erlend ever managed to have his way with you."

Then he had looked into her eyes—and her eyes must have spoken, although she wouldn't have discussed this matter with Haftor for any amount of gold. But his voice rang with amazement as he said, "I thought that was only something they wrote about—in ballads."

Kristin had not mentioned this episode to anyone, not even Erlend. He was fond of Haftor. And of course it was dreadful that some people could behave as recklessly as Haftor Graut, but she couldn't see that it was any concern of hers. And he hadn't attempted to be overly familiar toward her since then. Now whenever they met, he would simply sit and stare at her with obvious astonishment in his sea-blue eyes.

No, if Erlend behaved rashly, it was not in that fashion, at any rate. And was he truly so imprudent? she wondered. She saw that people were startled by things he said, and afterwards they would put their heads together to talk. There was often much that was truthful and just in the opinions that Erlend Nikulaussøn expressed. The problem was that he never saw what the other men never allowed to slip from view: the cautious hindsight with which they kept an eye on each other. Intrigue, Erlend called it, and then he would laugh insolently, which seemed to provoke people at first but eventually won them over. They would laugh too, slap him on the shoulder, and say that he could be sharp-witted enough, but short-sighted.

Then he would undo his own words with raucous and impudent banter. And people tolerated a great deal of this sort of behavior from Erlend. His wife was dimly aware of why everyone put up with his reckless talk, and it made her feel humiliated. For Erlend would yield as soon as he encountered any man who held firm to his own opinion; even if he understood no more than that this opinion was foolish, Erlend would nevertheless relinquish his own view on the matter. But he covered his retreat with disrespectful gossip about the man. And people were satisfied that Erlend had this cowardice of spirit—reckless as he was with his own welfare, adventurous, and boldly enamored of any danger that could be faced with armed force. All the same, they had no need to worry about Erlend Nikulaussøn.

The year before, toward the end of winter, the regent had come to Nidaros, and he had brought the young king along with him. Kristin attended the grand feast at the king's palace. With quiet dignity, wearing a silk wimple and with all her best jewelry adorning her red bridal gown, she had sat there among the most highborn women at the banquet. With alert eyes she studied her husband's conduct among the men, watching and listening and pondering—just as she watched and listened and pondered wherever she went with Erlend, and wherever she noticed that people were talking about him.

And she had learned several things. Sir Erling Vidkunssøn was willing to risk every effort to assert the right of the Norwegian Crown north to the Gandvik Sea, to defend and protect Haalogaland. But the Council and the knights opposed him and were reluctant to support any endeavor that might help. The archbishop himself and the clergy of the archdiocese were not unwilling to offer financial support—this she knew from Gunnulf—but otherwise the men of the Church all over the country were opposed to the war, even though it was against the enemies of God: heretics and heathens. And the noblemen were working against the regent, at least here in Trøndelag. They had grown accustomed to disregarding the words of the law books and the rights of the Crown, and they were not pleased that Sir Erling so sternly invoked the spirit of his blessed kinsman King Haakon in these matters. But it was not for these reasons that Erlend refused to allow himself to be used, as Kristin now understood that the regent had intended to use her husband. For Erlend it was simply because the other man's somber and dignified demeanor bored him, so he took revenge by lightly ridiculing his powerful kinsman.

Kristin now thought she understood Sir Erling's attitude toward Erlend. On the one hand, he had felt a certain affection for Erlend ever since their youth; no doubt he thought that if he could win the support of the noble and fearless master of Husaby, who also had some experience in the art of war from the days when he served Earl Jacob—at any rate more than most of the other men who had stayed at home—then it would be of benefit to both Erling Vidkunssøn's plans and to Erlend's welfare. But that's not how things had turned out.

For two summers Erlend had stayed out at sea until late autumn, patrolling the waters off the long northern coast and chasing off pirate vessels with the four small ships that bore his banner. One day he had arrived in search of fresh provisions at a new Norwegian settlement far north in Tana just as the Karelians[1] were in the process of plundering it. With the handful of men he had brought ashore, he captured eighteen of the pirates and hanged them from the roof beam in the half-burned barn. He cut down a troop of Russians attempting to flee into the mountains; he vanquished and burned several enemy ships somewhere out among the distant skerries. Rumors of his speed and boldness spread through the north; his men from Outer Trøndelag and Møre loved their chieftain for his toughness and his willingness to share in all the toil and travails of his crew. He had won friends among the peasants and the young sons on the estates of the chieftains up north in Haalogaland, where people had almost grown accustomed to having to defend their own coasts alone.

But even so, Erlend was of no help to the regent and his plans for a great crusade north. In Trøndelag people boasted of Erlend's exploits in the Russian campaign—if talk turned to this subject, they would point out that he was one of their own. Yes, it had turned out that the young boys from the fjord possessed a fair share of good old-fashioned valor. But no matter what Erlend of Husaby said or did, it was not enough to impress grown-up and sensible men.

Kristin saw that Erlend continued to be counted among the young, even though he was a year older than the regent. She realized that this suited many, because then his words and actions could be disparaged as those of a young and reckless man. People liked him, humored him, and boasted of him—but he was never considered a fully entitled man. And she saw how willingly he accepted the role that his peers wanted him to play.

He spoke in favor of the Russian war; he talked about the Swedes who shared the Norwegian king. But they refused to acknowledge the Norwegian lords and knights as noblemen, equal with their own. In other countries, for as long as the world had existed, had anyone ever heard of demanding payment of war levies from noblemen in any other form than having them ride their own horses and bear their own shields into battle? Kristin knew this was much the same thing her father had said that time at the *ting* in Vaage, and Lavrans had also mentioned it to Erlend when his son-in-law had not wanted to oppose Munan Baardsøn's plans. No, Erlend now said—and he would allude to his father-in-law's powerful kinsmen in Sweden—he knew full well how the Swedish noblemen regarded the Norwegians. "And if we don't show them what we're capable of, we'll soon be considered nothing more than wards of the Swedes."

And people agreed that there was some truth to this. But then they would go back to talking about the regent. Sir Erling had his own reasons for lamenting what went on in the north. One year the Karelians had burned down Bjarkøy in defiance of his overseer and persecuted his leaseholders. But Erlend would change his tone and jest—Erling Vidkunssøn wasn't thinking of his own affairs, he was sure of that. Sir Erling was such a noble and refined and distinguished knight; they couldn't have found a better man to serve as leader for all of them. By God, Erling was as honorable and venerable as the most beautiful golden initial capital at the beginning of the book of law. People laughed, less impressed with Erlend's praise of the regent's integrity than with Erlend's comparing him to a gilded letter.

No, they didn't take Erlend seriously—not now, when he was in some ways respected. But back in the days when he was young and stubborn and desperate, when he lived with his concubine and refused to send her away in spite of the king's command and excommunication from the Church—back then they did take him seriously, turning away from him in bitter fury at his ungodly and disgraceful life. Now it was all forgiven and forgotten, and Kristin realized that it was partly out of gratitude for this that her husband so willingly acquiesced and behaved in the way people wanted him to behave. He must have suffered bitterly during that time when he was banished from the company of his peers in Norway. But the problem was, it made her think of her father, when he released incompetent men from their obligations or debts with a mere shrug of his shoulders. It was a Christian duty to bear with those who could not conduct themselves properly. Was it in this manner that Erlend had been forgiven the sins of his youth?

But Erlend *had* paid the consequences for his actions when he was living with Eline. He had answered for his sins right up until the moment when he met Kristin and she eagerly followed him into new sin. Was she then the one who . . .

No. Now she was afraid of her own thoughts.

And she tried to block out of her mind all the worries about things she could not change. She wanted only to think about matters in which she could do something with her compassion. Everything else she would have to place in God's hands. God had helped her in every instance when her own hard work could do some good. Husaby had now been transformed into a prosperous farm, as it had been in the past—in spite of the bad years. Three healthy and handsome sons He had given her, and each year He had granted her new life whenever she was faced with death in childbirth. He had allowed her to recover her full health after each convalescence. She had been permitted to keep all three of her small sons the year before, when illness took the lives of so many fair children in the region. And Gaute—Gaute *would* regain his health, that she firmly believed.

It must be as Erlend had said: It was necessary for him to lead his life and maintain his estates in as costly a fashion as he did. Otherwise he wouldn't be able to assert himself among his peers and win the rights and revenues that were his birthright under the Crown. She would have to believe that he understood this better than she did.

It was senseless to think that things might have been better in some ways for him—and even for her—back when he was living tangled up in sin with that other woman. In glimpses of memory she saw his face from that time, ravaged with sorrow, contorted with passion. No, no, things were fine as they were now. He was merely a little too carefree and thoughtless.

Erlend returned home just before Michaelmas. He had hoped to find Kristin confined to bed, but she was still on her feet. She came to meet him out on the road. Her gait was terribly cumbersome this time—but she had Gaute in her arms, as usual; the two older sons came running ahead of her.

Erlend jumped down from his horse and lifted the boys onto the saddle. Then he took his youngest son from his wife so he could carry him. Kristin's pale, worn face lit up when Gaute wasn't frightened by his father; he must have recognized him, after all. She asked nothing about her husband's travels, but talked only about Gaute's four new teeth which had made him so sick.

Then the boy started to scream; he had scraped his cheek bloody on the filigree brooch on his father's chest. He wanted to go back to his mother, and she wanted to take him, no matter how much Erlend protested.

Not until evening, when they were sitting alone in the hall and the children were asleep, did Kristin ask her husband about his journey to Bjørgvin—as if she only then happened to think about it.

Erlend glanced furtively at Kristin. His poor wife—she looked so miserable. He began to tell her all kinds of news. Erling had asked him to send his greetings and give her this—it was a bronze dagger, corroded with verdigris. They had found it in a heap of stones out at Giske; it was supposed to be beneficial to place such a thing in the cradle in case it was rickets that had stricken Gaute.

Kristin wrapped up the dagger again, awkwardly rose from her chair, and went over to the cradle. She put the bundle under the bedclothes with everything else that lay there: a stone axe found buried in the ground, the musk gland of a beaver, a cross made from daphne twigs, old silver, flint, roots of a Mariahand orchid, and an Olav's Beard fern.

"Lie down now, dear Kristin," Erlend said tenderly. He came over and pulled off her shoes and stockings. All the while he talked.

Haakon Ogmundssøn had come back, and peace with the Russians and Karelians had been concluded and sealed. Erlend himself would have to travel north this fall. For it was certain that calm would not be restored at once, and a man was needed at Vargøy who knew the region. He would be given full authority as the king's officer in command at the fortress up there, which had to be better secured so that peace could be defended at the new border markers.

Erlend looked up into his wife's face with excitement. She seemed a bit alarmed—but she didn't ask many questions, and it was clear that she had little understanding of what his news meant. He saw how tired she was, so he spoke no more about this matter but remained sitting on the edge of her bed for a while.

He understood the gravity of what he had taken on. Erlend laughed quietly to himself as he took his time undressing. There would be no sitting back with his silver belt around his belly, holding feasts for friends and kinsmen, and filing his nails straight and clean as he dispatched his vassals and lieutenants here and there—the way the king's commanders of the castles did here in the south of Norway. And the castle at Vargøy was quite a different sort of fortress.

Finns, Russians, Karelians, and mixed breeds of all kinds—troll rabble, conjurers, heathen dogs, the Devil's own precious lambs who had to be taught to pay taxes to the Norwegian emissaries and to leave the Norwegian settlements in peace, which were spread out with as much distance between each other as from Husaby all the way to Møre. Peace—perhaps the king's peace would be possible up there someday, but in his lifetime there would be peace only when the Devil attended mass. And he would have his own roughnecks to keep in check too. Especially toward the spring, when they began to grow despondent from the darkness and the cold and the hellish roar of the sea—when the flour and butter and liquor were in short supply, and they began fighting over their women, and life on the island grew unbearable. Erlend had witnessed some of this when he was there as a young boy with Gissur Galle. No, he wouldn't be lying about idle!

Ingolf Peit, who was now in charge, was able enough. But Erling was right: A man from the knighthood should take control of things up there—not until then would anyone realize that it was the Norwegian king's firm intention to assert his power over the land. Ha, ha—in that territory he would be like a needle in a coverlet. Not a single Norwegian settlement until as far south as Malang.

Ingolf was a capable fellow, but only as long as he had someone in command over him. He would put Ingolf in charge of his ship *Hugrekken. Margygren* was the most splendid of ships; that much he had now learned. Erlend laughed softly and happily. He had told Kristin so often before, this was one mistress she would have to put up with.

He was awakened by one of the children crying in the dark. Over by the bed on the opposite wall, he could hear Kristin stirring and speaking gently—it was Bjørgulf who was complaining. Sometimes the boy woke up in the night and couldn't open his festering eyes; then his mother would moisten them with her tongue. Erlend had always been repelled by the sight of this.

Kristin was softly humming. The thin, weak sound of her voice annoyed him.

Erlend remembered what he had been dreaming. He was walking along a shore somewhere; it was low tide, and he was leaping from stone to stone. In the distance the sea was glistening and pale, lapping at the seaweed; it was like a silent, cloudy summer evening, with no sun. At the mouth of the silvery fjord he saw the ship anchored, black and sleek, rocking gently on the waves. There was an ungodly, delicious smell of sea and kelp.

His heart grew sick with longing. Now in the darkness of the night, as he lay here in the guest bed and listened to the monotonous sound of the lullaby gnawing at his ear, he felt how strong his longing was. To be away from this house and the swarms of children who filled it, away from talk of farming matters and servants and tenants and children—and from his anguished concern for her, who was always ill and whom he always had to pity.

Erlend clasped his hands over his heart. It felt as if it had stopped; it merely lay there, shivering with fright inside his breast. He longed to be away from her. When he thought about what she would have to endure, as weak and frail as she now was—and he knew that it could happen at any hour—he felt as if he would suffocate from fear. But if he should lose Kristin . . . He didn't know how he would be able to live without her. But he didn't feel able to live *with* her, either, not now. He wanted to flee from everything and breathe freely—as if it were a matter of life itself for him.

Jesus, my Savior—oh, what kind of man was he! He realized it now, tonight. Kristin, my sweet, my dearest wife—the only time he had known deep, heartfelt joy with her was when he was leading her astray.

He who had been so convinced on that day when he was given Kristin to have and to hold before God and man that everything bad would be driven from his life so completely that he would forget it had ever existed.

He must be the kind of man who couldn't tolerate anything truly good or pure to be near him. Because Kristin . . . Ever since she had emerged from the sin and impurity into which he had led her, she had been like an angel from God's heaven. Kind and faithful, gentle, capable, deserving of respect. She had returned honor to Husaby. She had become once again the person she had been on that summer night, when the pure young maiden had crept under his cape there in the convent garden; and he had thought when he felt that slender young body against his side: The Devil himself wouldn't dare harm this child or cause her sorrow.

Tears streamed down Erlend's face.

It must be true, what the priests had told him, that sin ate up a man's soul like rust—for he could find no rest or peace here with his sweet beloved. He longed to be away from her and everything that was hers.

He had wept himself almost to sleep when he sensed that she was up and pacing the floor, quietly humming and singing.

Erlend sprang out of bed, stumbled in the dark over a child's shoes on the floor, and went right over to his wife and took Gaute from her. The boy started screaming, and Kristin said crossly, "I had almost lulled him to sleep!"

The father shook the crying child, gave him a few slaps on the bottom—and when the boy shrieked even louder, he hushed him so harshly that Gaute fell silent with fear. Nothing like that had ever happened to him before.

"It's time for you to use what good sense you have, Kristin." His fury robbed him of all power as he stood there, startled and naked and freezing in the pitch-dark room with a sobbing child in his arms. "There has to be an end to this, I tell you—what do you have nursemaids for? The children will sleep with them; you can't keep on this way."

"Won't you allow me to have my children with me during the time I have left?" replied his wife, her voice low and plaintive.

Erlend refused to acknowledge what she meant.

"During the time you have left, you need *rest*. Go to bed now, Kristin," he implored her more calmly.

He took Gaute with him to bed. He hummed to him for a while, and in the dark he found his belt lying on the step of the bed. The little silver medallions adorning it clinked and clattered as the boy played with the belt.

"The dagger isn't in it, is it?" asked Kristin anxiously from her bed, and Gaute began howling again when he heard his mother's voice. Erlend hushed him and made the belt clink—at last the child stopped crying and grew calm.

Perhaps it would be unwise to wish for this poor little boy to grow to adulthood—it was not certain that Gaute possessed all his wits.

Oh no, oh no. Blessed Virgin Mary, he didn't mean that. He didn't wish death for his own little son. No, no. Erlend held the child close in his arms and pressed his face to the soft, fine hair.

Their handsome sons. But he grew so weary of listening to them all day long; of stumbling over them whenever he came home. He couldn't understand how three small children could be everywhere at once on such a large estate. But he remembered how furious he had been with Eline because she showed no interest in their children. He must be an unreasonable man, for he was also resentful that he no longer saw Kristin without children clinging to her.

When he held his lawfully born sons in his arms he never felt the same way he had when they gave him Orm to hold for the first time. Oh Orm, Orm, my son. He had been so tired of Eline by then—sick and tired of her stubbornness and her vehemence and her uncontrollable ardor. He had seen that she was too old for him. And he had begun to realize what this madness would eventually cost him. But he hadn't felt that he could send her away—not after she had given up everything for his sake. The boy's birth had given him a reason to tolerate the mother, it seemed to him. He had been so young when he became Orm's father, and he hadn't fully understood the child's position, since the mother was another man's lawful wife.

Sobs overcame him once more, and he held Gaute tighter. Orm—he had never loved any of his children the way he loved that boy; he missed him terribly, and he bitterly regretted every harsh and impatient word he had ever said to him. Orm couldn't have known how much his father loved him. Bitterness and despair had gradually seized Erlend as it became abundantly clear that Orm would never be considered his lawful son, that he would never be able to inherit his father's coat of arms. And Erlend felt jealousy too because he saw his son draw closer to his stepmother than to him, and it seemed to him that Kristin's calm, gentle kindness toward the boy was a form of reproach.

Then came those days and nights that Erlend could not bear to remember. Orm lay on his bier in the loft, and the women came to tell him that they didn't think Kristin would live. They dug a grave for Orm over in the church, and they asked whether Kristin should be buried there too. Or should she be taken instead to Saint Gregor's Church to be laid to rest beside his parents?

Oh . . . He held his breath in fear. Behind him lay an entire lifetime of memories from which he had fled, and he couldn't bear to think of it. Now, tonight, he understood. He could forget about it to some extent from day to day. But he couldn't protect himself from the memories turning up at some moment such as this—and then it felt as if all courage had been conjured out of him.

Those days at Haugen—he had almost succeeded in forgetting about them entirely. He hadn't been back to Haugen since that night when he drove off, and he hadn't seen Bjørn or Aashild again after his wedding. And now . . . He thought about what Munan had told him—it was said that their spirits had come back. Haugen was so haunted that the buildings stood deserted; no one wanted to live there, even if they were given the farm free.

Bjørn Gunnarssøn had possessed a type of courage that Erlend knew he himself would never have. His hand had been steady when he stabbed his wife—right through the heart, said Munan.

It would be two years this winter since Bjørn and Fru Aashild died. People had not seen smoke coming from the buildings at Haugen for nearly a week; finally several men gathered their courage and went over there. Herr Bjørn was lying in bed with his throat cut; he was holding his wife's body in his arms. On the floor next to the bed lay his bloody dagger.

Everyone knew what had happened, and yet Munan Baardsøn and his brother managed to have the two buried in consecrated ground. Perhaps they had fallen victim to robbers, people said, although the chest containing Bjørn's and Aashild's valuables had not been touched. And the bodies were untouched by mice or rats—in fact, those kinds of vermin never came to Haugen, and people took this as a sign of the woman's sorcery skills.

Munan Baardsøn had been terribly distressed by his mother's death. He had set off on a pilgrimage to Santiago de Compostela[2] at once.

Erlend remembered the morning following his own mother's death. They were anchored in Moldøy Sound, but the fog was so white and thick that only occasionally could they catch a glimpse of the mountain ridge towering above them. But there was a muffled echo from the hollow sound of the boat being rowed to shore with the priest. Erlend stood in the bow and watched them rowing away from the ship. Everything he came near was wet with fog; beads of moisture covered his hair and clothing. And the priest and his acolyte, who were strangers to Erlend, sat in the bow of the boat, their shoulders hunched as they bent over the holy vessels they held on their laps. They looked like hawks in the rain. The slap of the oars and the scrape of the oarlocks and the echo from the mountain continued to resound long after the boat had been spirited away by the fog.

On that day Erlend had also vowed to make a pilgrimage. He had only had one thought back then: that he be allowed to see his mother's lovely, sweet face again, the way it had been before, with

its soft, smooth, light tan complexion. Now she lay dead be-
lowdecks, with her face ravaged by the terrible sores that ruptured
and seeped little drops of clear fluid whenever she had tried to
smile at him.

He was not to blame for the way his father had received him.
Nor for the fact that he had turned to someone who was outcast,
like himself. But then Erlend had pushed the pilgrimage from his
mind, and he had refused to think any more about his mother. As
painful as her life had been here on earth, she must now be in that
place of peace—and there was not much peace for him, after he
took up with Eline again.

Peace—he had known it only once in his life; on that night
when he sat behind the stone wall near the woods of Hofvin and
held Kristin as she slept on his lap—the safe, tender, undisturbed
sleep of a child. He hadn't been able to hold out for long before he
shattered her tranquillity. And it wasn't peace that he found with
her later on, and he had no peace with her now. And yet he saw
that everyone else in his home did find peace in the presence of his
young wife.

Now he longed only to go away to that strife-torn place. He
yearned madly and wildly for that remote promontory and for the
thundering sea surrounding the forelands of the north, for the endless coastline and the enormous fjords which could conceal all
manner of traps and deceptions, for the people whose language he
understood only slightly, for their sorcery and inconstancy and
cunning, for war and the sea, and for the singing of weapons, both
his own and his men's.

At last Erlend fell asleep, and then woke up again—what was it
he had dreamed? Oh yes. That he was lying in a bed with a black-
haired Finnish girl on either side of him. Something half-forgotten
that had happened to him back when he was up north with Gissur. A wild night when they had all been drunk and reeling. He
couldn't recall much more of the whole night than the rank, wild-
beast smell of the women.

And now here he lay with his sick little son in his arms and
dreamed of such things. He was so shocked at himself that he
didn't dare try to sleep anymore. And he couldn't bear to lie awake
in bed. He must truly be fated to unhappiness. Rigid with anguish

he lay motionless and felt the clench of his heart in his breast, while he longed for the redemption of dawn.

He persuaded Kristin to stay in bed the next day. He didn't think he could stand to see her so miserable, dragging herself around the house. He sat with her and played with her hand. She had had the loveliest arms—slim and yet so plump that the small, delicate bones were hardly visible in the slender joints. Now they stood out like knots on her gaunt forearm, and the skin underneath was bluish-white.

Outside it stormed and rained so hard that water gushed down the slopes. Erlend came out of the armory later in the day and heard Gaute screaming and crying from somewhere in the court-yard. He found his small sons in the narrow passageway between two of the buildings, sitting directly under the dripping eaves. Naakkve was clutching the youngest boy while Bjørgulf was trying to force-feed him a worm—he had a whole fistful of pink worms, twisting and squirming.

The boys looked crestfallen as their father scolded them. It was Old Aan, they said, who had mentioned that Gaute's teeth would come in with no trouble if they could get him to take a bite of a live worm.

They were soaked through from head to toe, all three of them. Erlend bellowed for the nursemaids, who came rushing out—one from the workroom and the other from the stable. Their master cursed them roundly, stuffed Gaute under his arm like a piglet, and then chased the other two ahead of him into the hall.

A little while later, dry and content in their best blue tunics, the boys sat in a row on the step of their mother's bed. Erlend had brought a stool over, and he chattered nonsense and fussed over his sons, hugging them close and laughing in order to drive out the remnants of the nighttime terror from his mind. But Kristin smiled happily because Erlend was playing with their children. Erlend told them that he had a Finnish witch; she was two hundred win-ters old, and so wizened that she was no bigger than this. He kept her in a leather pouch in the big chest that stood in his boathouse. Oh yes, he gave her food, all right; every Christmas he gave her the thigh of a Christian man—that was enough to last her the whole year. And if they weren't nice and quiet and didn't stop plaguing their mother, who was ill, then he would put them in the pouch too.

"Mother is sick because she's carrying our sister," said Naakkve, proud that he knew about such matters.

Erlend pulled the boy by the ears down onto his knee.

"Yes, and after she's born, this sister of yours, I'm going to let my old Finnish woman work her magic on all three of you and turn you into polar bears so you can go padding around in the wild forest, but my daughter will inherit all that I own."

The children shrieked and tumbled into their mother's bed. Gaute didn't understand, but he yelled and scrambled up there too, after his brothers. Kristin complained—Erlend shouldn't tease them so horribly. But Naakkve toppled off the bed again; in an ecstasy of laughter and fright he rushed at his father, hung on to his belt, and bit at Erlend's hands, while he shouted and cheered.

Erlend didn't get the daughter he had wished for this time, either. His wife gave birth to two big, handsome sons, but they almost cost Kristin her life.

Erlend had them baptized; one of them was named after Ivar Gjesling and the other after King Skule. His name had otherwise not been continued in their family; Fru Ragnrid had said that her father was a man fated to misfortune, and no one should be named for him. But Erlend swore that none of his sons bore a prouder name than the youngest.

It was now so late in the autumn that Erlend had to journey north as soon as Kristin was out of the worst danger. And he felt in his heart that it was just as well that he left before she was out of bed again. Five sons in five years—that should be enough, and he didn't want to have to worry that she would die in childbirth while he sat up north at Vargøy.

He could see that Kristin had thought much the same. She no longer complained that he was going to leave her behind. She had accepted each child that came as a precious gift from God, and the suffering as something to which she had to submit. But this time the experience had been so appallingly difficult that Erlend could tell that all courage seemed to have been stripped from her. She lay in bed listlessly, her face yellow as clay, staring at the two little bundles at her side; and her eyes were not as happy as they had been with the others.

Erlend sat beside her and went over the entire trip north in his mind. It would doubtless be a hard sea voyage so late in the fall—and strange to arrive there for the long nights. But he felt such an unspeakable yearning. This last bout of fear for his wife had completely broken all resistance in his soul—helplessly he surrendered to his own longing to flee from home.

CHAPTER 4

ERLEND NIKULAUSSØN SERVED as the king's military commander and chieftain at the fortress of Vargøy for almost two years. In all that time he never ventured farther south than to Bjarkøy, when he and Sir Erling Vidkunssøn once arranged a meeting there. During the second summer Erlend was away, Heming Alfssøn finally died, and Erlend was appointed sheriff of Orkdøla county in his place. Haftor Graut traveled north to succeed him at Vargøy.

Erlend was a happy man when he sailed south in the autumn, several days after the Feast of the Birth of Mary. This was the redress he had been seeking all these years—to become sheriff of the region as his father had once been. Not that this had been a goal which he had ever worked to achieve. But it had always seemed to him that this was what he needed in order to assume the standing which he rightfully deserved—both in his own eyes and those of his peers. Now it no longer mattered that he was considered somewhat different from the men who were bench sitters—there was no longer anything awkward about his special position.

And he longed for home. It had been more peaceful in Finnmark than he had expected. Even the first winter took its toll on him; he sat idle in the castle and could do nothing about repairing the fortress. It had been well restored seventeen years before, but now it had fallen into terrible disrepair.

Then came spring and summer with great activity and commotion—meetings at various places along the fjords with the Norwegian and half-Norwegian tax collectors and with spokesmen for the peoples of the inland plains. Erlend sailed here and there with his two ships and enjoyed himself immensely. On the island the buildings were repaired and the castle fortified. But the following year, peace still prevailed.

Haftor would no doubt see to it that troubles commenced soon

enough. Erlend laughed. They had sailed together almost as far as
Trjanema, and there Haftor had found himself a Sami woman
from Kola[1] whom he had taken with him. Erlend had spoken to
him sternly. He had to remember that it was important for the heathens to realize that the Norwegians were the masters. And he
would have to conduct himself so as not to provoke anyone un-
necessarily, considering the small group of men he had with him.
He shouldn't intervene if the Finns fought and killed each other;
they were to be granted that pleasure without interference. But act
like a hawk over the Russians and the Kola people, or whatever
that rabble was called. And leave the women alone—for one thing,
they were all witches; and for another, there were plenty who
would offer themselves willingly. But the Godøy youth would just
have to take care of himself, until he learned.

Haftor wanted to get away from his estates and his wife. Erlend
now wanted to go back home to his. He felt a blissful longing for
Kristin and Husaby and his home district and all his children—for
everything that was back home with Kristin.

At Lyngsfjord he got word of a ship with several monks on
board; they were supposedly Dominican friars from Nidaros who
were heading north to try to plant the true faith among heathens
and heretics in the border territories.

Erlend felt certain that Gunnulf was among them. And three
nights later he was indeed sitting alone with his brother in a sod
hut that belonged to a little Norwegian farm near the shore where
they had found each other.

Erlend felt strangely moved. He had attended mass and had taken
communion with his crew for the first time since he had come
north, except when he was at Bjarkøy. The church at Vargøy was
without a priest; a deacon lived at the castle, and he had made an
effort to observe the holy days for them, but otherwise the Norwegians in the north had found little help for their souls. They had to
console themselves with the thought that they were part of a kind
of crusade, and surely their sins would not be judged so severely.

Erlend sat talking to Gunnulf about this, and his brother listened with an odd, remote smile on his thin, compressed lips. It
looked as if he were constantly sucking on his lower lip, the way a

person often does when he is thinking hard about something and is on the verge of understanding but has not yet achieved full clarity in his mind.

It was late at night. All the other people on the farm were asleep in the shed; the brothers knew that they were now the only ones awake. And they were both struck by the strange circumstance that the two of them should be sitting there alone.

The muffled and muted sound of the storm and the roaring sea reached them through the sod walls. Now and then gusts of wind would blow in, breathe on the embers of the hearth, and make the flame of the oil lamp flicker. There was no furniture in the hut; the brothers were sitting on the low earthen bench which ran along three sides of the room, and between them lay Gunnulf's writing board with ink horn, his quill pen, and a rolled-up parchment. Gunnulf had been writing down a few notes as his brother told him about meetings and Norwegian settlements, about navigation markers and weather indications and words in the Sami language—everything Erlend happened to think of. Gunnulf was piloting the ship himself; it was named *Sunnivasuden*,[2] for the friars had chosen Saint Sunniva[2] as the patron saint for their endeavor.

"As long as you don't suffer the same fate as the martyred Selje men," said Erlend, and Gunnulf again gave him a little smile.

"You call me restless, Gunnulf," Erlend continued. "Then what should we call you? First you wander around in the southern lands for all those years, and then you've barely returned home before you give up your benefice and prebends[3] to go off to preach to the Devil and his offspring up north in Velliaa. You don't know their language and they don't know yours. It seems to me that you're even more inconstant than I am."

"I own neither manors nor kinsmen to answer for," said the monk. "I have now freed myself from all bonds, but you have bound yourself, brother."

"Yes, well . . . I suppose the man who owns nothing is free."

Gunnulf replied, "A man's possessions own him more than he owns them."

"Hmm. No, by God, I might concede that Kristin owns me. But I won't agree that the manor and the children own me too."

"Don't think that way, brother," said Gunnulf softly. "For then you might easily lose them."

"No, I refuse to be like those other old men, up to their chins in the muck of their land," said Erlend, laughing, and his brother smiled with him.

"I've never seen fairer children than Ivar and Skule," he said. "I think you must have looked like them at that age—it's no wonder our mother loved you so much."

Both brothers rested a hand on the writing board, which lay between them. Even in the faint light of the oil lamp it was possible to see how unlike the hands of these two men were. The monk's fingers bore no rings; they were white and sinewy, shorter and stubbier than the other man's fingers, and yet they looked much stronger—even though the palm of Erlend's fist was now as hard as horn and a blue-white scar from an arrow wound furrowed the dark skin from his wrist all the way up his sleeve. But the fingers of Erlend's slender, tanned hand were dry and knotty-jointed like tree branches, and they were completely covered with rings of gold and precious stones.

Erlend had an urge to take his brother's hand, but he was too embarrassed to do so; instead, he drank a toast to him, grimacing at the bad ale.

"And you think that Kristin has now regained her full health?" Erlend continued.

"Yes, she had blossomed like a rose when I was at Husaby in the summer," said the monk with a smile. He paused for a moment and then said somberly, "I ask this of you, brother—think more about the welfare of Kristin and your children than you have done in the past. Abide by her advice and agree to the decisions she and Eiliv have made; they're only waiting for your consent to conclude them."

"I'm not greatly in favor of these plans you speak of," said Erlend with some reluctance. "And now my position will be quite different."

"Your lands will gain in value if you consolidate your property more," replied the monk. "Kristin's plans seemed sensible when she explained them to me."

"And there isn't another woman in all of Norway who offers advice more freely than she does," said Erlend.

"But in the end you're the one who commands. And you now command Kristin too, and can do as you please," Gunnulf said, his voice strangely weak.

Erlend laughed softly from deep in his throat, then stretched and yawned. Suddenly somber, he said, "You have also counseled her, my brother. And at times your advice may well have come between our friendship."

"Do you mean the friendship between you and your wife, or the friendship between the two of us?" the monk asked hesitantly.

"Both," replied Erlend, as if the thought had just now occurred to him.

"It isn't usually necessary for a laywoman to be so pious," he continued in a lighter tone of voice.

"I have counseled her as I thought best. As it *was* best," Gunnulf corrected himself.

Erlend looked at the monk dressed in the rough, grayish-white friar's robes, with the black cowl thrown back so that it lay in thick folds around his neck and over his shoulders. The crown of his head was shaved so that only a narrow fringe of hair now remained, encircling his round, gaunt, pallid face; but his hair was no longer thick and black as it had been in Gunnulf's younger days.

"Well, you aren't as much my brother anymore as you are the brother of all men," said Erlend, surprising himself by the great bitterness in his own voice.

"That's not true—although it ought to be."

"So help me God, I think that's the real reason that you want to go up there to the Finns!"

Gunnulf bowed his head. His amber eyes smoldered.

"To some extent that's true," he said swiftly.

They spread out the furs and coverlets they had brought with them. It was too cold and raw in the room for them to undress, so they bade each other good night and lay down on the earthen bench, which was quite low to the floor to escape the smoke from the hearth.

Erlend lay there thinking about the news he had received from home. He hadn't heard much during the past years—two letters from his wife had reached him, but they had been outdated by the time they arrived. Sira Eiliv had written them for her. Kristin could write, and she had a beautiful hand, but she was never eager to do so, because she didn't think it quite proper for an uneducated woman.

She would no doubt become even more pious now that they had acquired a holy relic in the neighboring village, and it was from a man whom she had known while he was alive. And Gaute had now won release from his illness there, and Kristin herself had recovered her full health after having been weak ever since giving birth to the twins. Gunnulf said that the friars of Hamar had finally been forced to give Edvin Rikardssøn's body back to his brothers in Oslo, and they had now written down everything about Brother Edvin's life and about the miracles he was said to have performed, both during his lifetime and after death. It was their intention to send these writings to the Pope in an attempt to have the monk proclaimed a saint. Several brothers from Gauldal and Medaldal had journeyed south to bear witness to the wonders that Brother Edvin had achieved with his prayers of intercession in the parishes and with a crucifix he had carved; it was now at Medalhus. They had vowed to build a small church on Vatsfjeld, the mountain where he had spent several summers, living a hermit's existence, and where a mountain spring had become endowed with healing powers. And the brothers were given a hand from his body to enshrine in the church.

Kristin had contributed two silver bowls and the large cloak clasp with blue stones which she had inherited from her grandmother, Ulvhild Haavardsdatter, so that Tiedeken Paus in Nidaros could fashion a silver hand for Brother Edvin's bones. And she had been to Vatsfjeld with Sira Eiliv and her children and a great entourage when the archbishop consecrated the church at Midsummer the year after Erlend had departed for the north.

Afterwards, Gaute's health quickly improved; he had learned to walk and talk, and he was now like any other child his age. Erlend stretched out his limbs. That was the greatest joy they had been granted—that Gaute was now well. He would donate some land to the church. Gunnulf had told him that Gaute was blond, with a fair complexion, like his mother. If only he had been a little maiden, then he would have been named Magnhild. Yes, he was also longing for his handsome sons now.

Gunnulf Nikulaussøn lay there thinking about the spring day three years ago when he rode toward Husaby. On the way he met a man from the manor. The mistress was not at home, he had said; she was tending to a woman who was ill.

He was riding along a narrow, grass-covered road between old split-rail fences. Young, leafy trees covered the slopes, from the top all the way down to the swollen river rushing through the ravine below. He rode into the sun, and the tender green leaves glittered like golden flames on the branches, but inside the forest the shadows were already spreading, cool and deep, across the grassy floor.

Gunnulf reached a place where he could catch a glimpse of the lake, with a reflection of the dark opposite shore and the blue of the sky, and an image of the great summer clouds constantly merging and dispersed by the ripples. Far below the road was a small farm on green, flower-strewn slopes. A group of women wearing white wimples stood outside in the courtyard, but Kristin was not among them.

A little farther away he saw her horse; it was walking around in the pasture with several others. The road dipped down into a hollow of green shadows ahead of him, and where it curved up over the next rise in the hills, he saw her standing next to the fence beneath the foliage, listening to the birds singing. He looked at her slim, dark figure, leaning over the fence, facing the woods; there was a gleam of white from her wimple and her arm. He reined in his horse and rode toward her slowly, step by step. But when he drew closer, he saw that it was the slender stump of an old birch tree standing there.

The next evening, when his servants sailed his ship into Nidaros, the priest himself was at the helm. He felt his heart beating in his chest, steadfast and newborn. Now nothing could deter his purpose.

He now knew that what had held him back in life was the unquenchable longing he had carried with him ever since childhood. He wanted to win the love of others. To do so he had been kind-hearted, gentle, and good-natured toward the poor; he had let his wisdom shine, but with moderation and humility, among the priests of the town so that they would like him; he had been submissive toward Lord Eiliv Kortin because the archbishop was friends with his father, and he knew how Lord Eiliv wanted people to behave. He had been loving and gentle toward Orm, in order to win the boy's affection away from his moody father. And Gunnulf had been stern and demanding toward Kristin because he saw what she needed: to encounter something that would not give way when she reached for help, something that would not lead her astray when she came, ready to follow.

But now he realized that he had sought to win her trust for himself more than he had tried to strengthen her faith in God.

Erlend had found expression for it this evening: Not as much my brother anymore as the brother of all men. This was the detour he would have to take before his brotherly love could benefit anyone at all.

Two weeks later he had divided up his possessions among his kinsmen and the Church and donned the robes of a friar. And now, this spring, when everyone was profoundly troubled by the terrible misfortune that had befallen the country—lightning had struck Christ Church in Nidaros and partially destroyed Saint Olav's shrine—Gunnulf had won the support of the archbishop for his old plan. Together with Brother Olav Jonssøn, who was an ordained priest like himself, and three younger monks—one from Nidaros and two from the order in Bjørgvin—he was now headed north to bring the light of the Word to the lost heathens who lived and died in darkness within the boundaries of a Christian land.

Christ, you who were crucified! Now I have given up everything that could bind me. And I have placed myself in your hands, if you would find my life worthy enough to be freed from its servitude to Satan. Take me so that I may feel that I am your slave, for then I will possess you in return.

Then someday, once again, his heart would crow and sing in his chest, as it did when he walked across the green plains at Romaborg, from pilgrim church to pilgrim church: "I am my Beloved's, and to Him belongs my desire."

The two brothers lay there, each on his own bench in the little hut, and let their thoughts lull them to sleep. A tiny ember smoldered in the hearth between them. Their thoughts took them farther and farther away from each other. And the following day one of them headed north, and the other south.

Erlend had promised Haftor Graut to go out to Godøy and take his sister south with him. She was married to Baard Aasulfssøn of Lensvik, who was also one of Erlend's kinsmen, but distantly related.

On the first morning, as *Margygren* cut through the waters of

Godøy Sound with its sails billowing against the blue mountains in the fine breeze, Erlend was standing on the raised afterdeck of the ship. Ulf Haldorssøn had the helm. Then Fru Sunniva came up to them. The hood of her cloak was draped over her shoulders, and the wind was blowing her wimple back from her curly, sun-yellow hair. She had the same sea-blue, gleaming eyes as her brother, and like him she had a fair complexion, but with many freckles, which also covered her small, plump hands.

From the first evening Erlend saw her at Godøy—their eyes met, and then they looked away, both of them smiling secretively—he was convinced that she knew him, and he knew her. Sunniva Olavsdatter—he could take her with his bare hands, and she was waiting for him to do so.

Now, as he stood with her hand in his—he had helped her up onto the deck—he happened to look into Ulf's coarse, dark face. No doubt Ulf knew it too. Erlend felt oddly ashamed under the other man's gaze. He suddenly remembered everything that this kinsman and weaponsbearer had witnessed—every mad prank that Erlend had gotten caught up in, ever since his youth. Ulf didn't need to look at him so scornfully. Erlend consoled himself that he hadn't intended to come any closer to this woman than honor and virtue permitted. He was old enough by now, and wise from his mistakes; he could be allowed north to Haalogaland without getting himself tangled up in some foolishness with another man's wife. He had a wife himself now. He had been faithful to Kristin from the very first time he saw her and to this day. No reasonable man would count those few incidents that had occurred up north. But otherwise he hadn't even looked at another woman—in that way. He knew . . . with a Norwegian woman, and even worse, with one of their peers . . . no, he would never have a moment's peace in his heart if he betrayed Kristin in that way. But this voyage south with her on board—it might easily prove risky.

It helped somewhat that they had stormy weather along the way, so he had other things to do than banter with the woman. They had to seek harbor in Dynøy and wait a few days. While they were anchored there, something happened that made Fru Sunniva seem less enticing to him.

Erlend and Ulf and a couple of the servants slept in the same cabin where she and her maids slept. One morning he was there alone, and Fru Sunniva had not yet gotten up. Then she called to him, saying that she had lost a gold ring in her bed. He had to agree to come and help her look for it. She was crawling around in bed on her knees, wearing only her shift. Now and then they would bump into each other, and every time they would both get a devilish glint in their eyes. Then she grabbed hold of him. And it's true that his behavior had not been overly proper, either; time and place were both against him. But she was so bold and disgracefully willing that he grew suddenly cold. Blushing with shame, he turned away from that face, which had dissolved with laughter and wantonness. He tore himself away without further explanation and left; then he sent in Fru Sunniva's maidservants to her.

No, by Satan, he was not some young pup who allowed himself to be caught in the bedstraw. It was one thing to seduce—but to be seduced was something else entirely. But he had to laugh; here he stood, having fled from a beautiful woman like Joseph the Hebrew. Yes, strange things happened both at sea and on land.

No, Fru Sunniva. No, he had to think of one woman—a woman that he knew. She had come to meet him in a hostel for wandering soldiers—and she came with as much chasteness and dignity as a royal maiden going to mass. In groves and in barns she had been his. God forgive him—he had forgotten her birthright and her honor; and she had forgotten them for his sake, but she hadn't been able to fling them away. Her lineage was evident in her, even when she did not think of it.

God bless you, dear Kristin. So help me, God—I will keep the promise that I made to you in secret and at the church door, or I will never be a man. So be it.

Then Erlend had Fru Sunniva put ashore at Yrjar where she had kinsmen. And best of all, she didn't seem overly angry when they parted. There had been no need for him to bow his head with a somber expression, like a monk; they had chased each other out over the oarlocks, as the saying goes. In parting, Erlend gave her several costly furs for a cloak, and she promised that one day he would see her wearing that cloak. They would surely meet again. Poor thing, her husband was sickly and no longer young.

But Erlend was glad to come home to his wife with nothing on his conscience that he would have to conceal from her, and he was proud of his own newly tested steadfastness. He was quite giddy

and wild with longing for Kristin. She was the sweetest and loveliest rose and lily—and she was his!

Kristin came out to the skerries to meet him when Erlend anchored
at Birgsi. Fishermen had brought word to Vigg that *Margygren*
had been seen near Yrjar. She had brought along her two eldest
sons and Margret, and back home at Husaby a feast was being
prepared for friends and kinsmen to celebrate Erlend's homecoming.

She had grown so beautiful that it took Erlend's breath away
when he saw her. But she had changed. The girlish demeanor
which had returned each time she had recovered from a childbirth—the frail and delicate nunlike face beneath the wimple of a
married woman—was now gone. She was a blossoming young
woman and mother. Her cheeks were round and a healthy pink,
framed by the white wimple; her breasts were high and firm, covered with glittering chains and brooches. Her hips were rounder
and wider, soft beneath the belt bearing her ring of keys and the
gilded sheath holding her scissors and knife. Oh yes, she had
grown even more lovely. She didn't look as if she might be easily
carried off to heaven as she had before. Even her large, slender
hands had grown fuller and whiter.

They stayed at Vigg that night, in the abbot's house. And this
time it was a young, flushed, and happy Kristin, gentle and glowing with joy, who rode with Erlend to the celebration at Husaby
when they set off for home the next day.

There were so many important matters that she had to speak with
her husband about when he came home. There were hundreds of
things about the children, about her worries for Margret, and
about her plans to set the estates back on their feet. But all this
was swallowed up in the festivities.

They went from one banquet to another, and she accompanied
the new sheriff on his rounds. Erlend now had more men serving
at Husaby. Messages and letters flew between him and his subordi-
nates and envoys. Erlend was full of high spirits and merriment.
Why shouldn't he be a capable sheriff? He who had beat his head
against nearly every barrier of Norwegian law and Christian com-

mandment. Such things were well learned and not easily forgotten. The man was quick-witted and he had been taught well in his youth. Now all this became apparent in him again. He grew accustomed to reading letters himself, and he had acquired an Icelander as his scribe. In the past, Erlend had put his seal on everything that was read aloud to him, barely casting a glance at even a single line—this is what Kristin had discovered during the two years in which she had become familiar with all the papers she found in his chests of letters.

Now a certain recklessness came over her, which she had never felt before. She grew livelier and more talkative when she was among other people—for she sensed that she was beautiful now, and she felt completely healthy and well for the first time since she had been married. And in the evening, when she and Erlend lay together in a strange bed in the loft of one of the great estates or in a farmer's house, they would laugh and whisper and jest about the people they had met and the news they had heard. Erlend was more rash in his speech than ever, and people seemed to like him even better than before.

Kristin could see it in their own children. They would grow flustered with delight whenever their father occasionally took notice of them. Naakkve and Bjørgulf now spent all their time with such things as bows and spears and axes. Every once in a while their father would stop on his way across the courtyard, glance at them, and then correct whatever they were doing. "Not like that, my son—you should hold it like this." And then he would shift the grip of the boy's small fist and place his fingers in the proper position. Then they would be filled with zeal.

The two eldest sons were inseparable. Bjørgulf was the biggest and strongest of the children, as tall as Naakkve, who was a year and a half older, but stouter. Bjørgulf had tightly curled, raven black hair; his small face was broad but handsome, his eyes dark blue. One day Erlend asked Kristin anxiously whether she knew that Bjørgulf saw poorly out of one eye—he also had a slight squint. Kristin said she didn't think there was anything wrong and that he'd probably grow out of it. As things had turned out, this child was the one she had given the least attention; he had been born when she was worn out from caring for Naakkve, and Gaute had followed soon afterwards. He was the hardiest of the children, no doubt also the smartest, but taciturn. Erlend was more fond of this son than the others.

Although he wouldn't admit it to himself, Erlend bore some ill will toward Naakkve because the boy had arrived so inopportunely and because he was named for his grandfather. And Gaute was not as he'd expected. The boy had a large head, which was understandable, since for two years it seemed as if only his head had grown—and now his limbs had to catch up. His wits were good enough, but he spoke very slowly because if he talked fast he would slur his words or stutter, and then Margret would make fun of him. Kristin had a great weakness for the boy, even though Erlend could see that in some ways the eldest son was her favorite child. But Gaute had been so frail, and he looked a bit like Kristin's father, with his flaxen hair and dark gray eyes. And he was always clinging to his mother. He was a rather solitary child, between the two oldest ones, who always stuck together, and the twins, who were still so little that they kept close to their foster mothers.

Kristin had less time for her children now, and she had to do as the other women did and let the serving maids look after them; but the two oldest sons preferred to follow the men around on the farm. She no longer brooded over them with that old, sickly tenderness, but she played and laughed with them more, whenever she had time to gather them around her.

At the beginning of the New Year, they received a letter at Husaby under the seal of Lavrans Bjørgulfsøn. It had been written in his own hand and sent with the priest of Orkedal, who had been traveling in the south, so it was two months old. The biggest news in the letter was that Lavrans had betrothed Ramborg to Simon Andressøn of Formo. The wedding would take place on Holy Cross Day in the spring.

Kristin was surprised beyond words. But Erlend said he had thought this might happen—ever since he had heard that Simon Darre had become a widower and had settled on his estate at Sil after old Sir Andres Gudmundssøn had died.

CHAPTER 5

SIMON DARRE HAD accepted it as only proper when his father had arranged the marriage with Lavrans Bjørgulfsøn's daughter for him. It had always been the custom in his family for the parents to make these decisions. He was pleased when he saw that his betrothed was so beautiful and charming. And he had always thought that he would be good friends with the woman his father had chosen for him. He and Kristin were well-suited in age and wealth and birth. Lavrans may have come from a somewhat better lineage, but Simon's father was a knight and had been close to King Haakon, while Lavrans had always lived quietly on his estates. And Simon had never seen married couples not get on well together, as long as they were equals.

Then came that evening in the loft at Finsbrekken, when the people tried to torment the innocent young child. From that moment he knew that he felt greater affection for his betrothed than was merely expected of him. He didn't dwell on this—he was happy. He could see that the maiden was modest and shy, but he didn't give this much thought either. Then came that time in Oslo, when he was forced to think about these things—and then the night in Fluga's loft.

He had been faced with something he had never imagined could happen in this world—not between honorable people of good family, and not in these times. Blinded and confused, he had staggered his way out of the betrothal, although his demeanor had been cool and calm and steady as he talked over these matters with his father and hers.

Then he had found himself outside the traditions of his family, and so he did what was also unheard of in his lineage: Without even consulting his father, he had courted the rich young widow of Mandvik. It dazzled him when he realized that Fru Halfrid was fond of him. She was much wealthier and more highborn than

Kristin; she was the niece of Baron Tore Haakonssøn of Tunsberg and the widow of Sir Finn Aslakssøn. And she was beautiful, with such a gracious and noble bearing that compared to her, the women in his circle were little more than peasant women, he thought. The Devil take him if he wouldn't show everyone that he could win the noblest wife; she was even more resplendent with wealth and other possessions than that man from Trønder who had lured Kristin into shame. And a widow—that was good and proper; then he knew where he stood. By Satan, he would never trust a maiden again.

He had learned that it was not as simple to live in this world as he had thought back home at Dyfrin. There his father ruled over everything, and his views were always right. Simon had been one of the king's retainers, and he had served as a page for a while; he had also been taught by his father's resident priest at home. At times he would find what his father said a bit old-fashioned. Occasionally he would voice his opposition, but it was only meant in jest, and it was taken as such. "What a quick wit Simon has," laughed his father and mother and siblings, who never spoke against Sir Andres. But everything was done as his father commanded, and Simon himself thought this reasonable.

During the years he was married to Halfrid Erlingsdatter and lived at Mandvik, he learned a little more each day that life could be more complicated and difficult than Sir Andres Gudmundssøn had ever dreamed.

Simon could never have imagined that he would not be happy with such a wife as he had now won. Deep in his soul he felt a painful sense of amazement whenever he looked at his wife, as she moved about the house all day long, so lovely, with her gentle eyes, and her mouth so sweet as long as it was closed. He had never seen any other woman wear gowns and jewelry with such grace. But in the dark gloom of the night his aversion to her stripped him of all youth and vigor. She was sickly, her breath was tainted, and her caresses plagued him. And yet she was so kind that he felt a desperate sense of shame, but he still could not overcome his dislike of her.

They hadn't been married long before he realized that she would never give him a healthy, living child. He could see that she herself grieved over this even more than he did. The pain he felt was like knives in his heart whenever he thought of *her* fate in this matter. One way or another he had heard that she was this way because Sir Finn had kicked and struck her so badly that she had miscarried many times while she was married to him. He had been insanely jealous of his beautiful young wife. Her kinsmen wanted to take her away from him, but Halfrid felt that it was a Christian wife's duty to stay with her lawful husband, no matter how he behaved.

But as long as Simon had no children with her, he would feel all his days that it was *her* land they lived on and *her* riches that he managed. He managed sensibly and carefully, but during those years there rose up in his soul a longing for Formo, his grandmother's ancestral estate, which he had always been destined to inherit after his father. He began to feel that he belonged north in Gudbrandsdal even more than at Romerike.

People continued to call Halfrid "the knight's wife," as they had during the time of her first husband. And this made Simon feel even more as if he were merely her advisor at Mandvik.

Then one day, Simon and his wife were sitting alone in the hall. One of the maids had just come in on some errand. Halfrid stared after her as she left.

"I'm not sure," she said, "but I'm afraid that Jorunn is with child this summer."

Simon was holding a crossbow on his lap, adjusting the locking device. He adjusted the crank, sighted down the spring assembly, and said without looking up, "Yes, and it's mine."

His wife didn't reply. When he finally looked up at her, she was sitting there sewing, going about her work just as steadily as he had been doing his.

Simon was truly sorry. Sorry he had offended his wife in this manner, and sorry he had taken up with this girl, regretting that he had now assumed the burden of fatherhood. He was far from certain that it was actually his—Jorunn had loose ways. And he had never really liked her; she was ugly, but she was quick-witted and amusing to talk to. And she was the one who had always sat up to wait for him whenever he came home late the winter before. He had spoken rashly because he expected his wife to berate and denounce him. That was foolish of him; he should have known that

Halfrid would consider herself above such conduct. But now it was done, and he wouldn't retreat from his own words. He would have to put up with being called father of his maid's child, whether he was or not.

Halfrid didn't mention the matter until a year later; then she asked Simon one day whether he knew that Jorunn was to be married over at Borg. Simon knew this quite well, since he himself had given her a dowry. Where was the child to live? his wife wanted to know. With the mother's parents, where she now was, replied Simon.

Then Halfrid said, "It seems to me that it would be more proper for your daughter to grow up here on your manor."

"On *your* manor, you mean?" asked Simon.

A slight tremor flickered across his wife's face.

"You know full well, dear husband, that as long as we both live, you are the one who rules here at Mandvik," she said.

Simon went over and placed his hands on his wife's shoulders.

"If it's true, Halfrid, that you think you can stand to see that child here with us, then I owe you great thanks for your generosity."

But he didn't like it. Simon had seen the girl several times—she was a rather unattractive child, and he couldn't see that she looked like him or anyone else in his family. He was even less inclined to believe that he was the father. And he had resented it deeply when he heard that Jorunn had the child baptized Arngjerd, after his mother, without asking his permission. But he would have to let Halfrid do as she wished. She brought the child to Mandvik, found a foster mother for her, and saw to it that the girl lacked for nothing. If she caught sight of the child, she would often take her onto her lap and chat with her, kindly and lovingly. And gradually, as Simon saw more of the child, he grew fond of the little maiden—he had great affection for children. Now he also thought he could see some resemblance between Arngjerd and his father. It was possible that Jorunn had been wise enough to restrain herself after the master had come too close to her. If so, then Arngjerd was indeed his daughter, and what Halfrid had persuaded him to do was honorable and right.

After they had been married for five years, Halfrid bore her husband a fully formed son. She was radiant with joy, but soon after the birth she fell ill, and it quickly became clear to everyone that she would die. And yet she was without fear, the last time that she had her full wits about her for a moment. "Now you will sit here, Simon, master of Mandvik, and rule over the estate for your lineage and mine," she told her husband.

After that her fever rose so sharply that she was no longer aware of anything, and so she did not have to suffer the grief, while she was still in this world, of hearing that the boy had died one day before his mother. And no doubt in that other home she would not feel sorrow over such things, but would be glad that she had their Erling with her, thought Simon.

Later, Simon remembered that on the night when the two bodies were laid out in the loft, he had stood leaning over the fence next to a field down by the sea. It was just before Midsummer, and the night was so bright that the glow of the full moon was barely visible. The water was gleaming and pale, rippling and lapping along the shore. Simon had slept no more than an hour at a time, off and on, since the night the boy was born. That seemed to him very long ago now, and he was so tired that he scarcely felt able to grieve.

He was then twenty-seven years old.

In the middle of the summer, after the inheritance had been settled,[1] Simon turned over Mandvik to Stig Haakonssøn, Halfrid's cousin. He left for Dyfrin and stayed there all winter.

Old Sir Andres lay in bed, suffering from dropsy and numerous ailments and pains; he was approaching the end now, and he complained a great deal. Life had not been so easy for him in the long run, either. Things had not gone as he had wished and expected for his handsome and promising children. Simon sat with his father and tried hard to adopt the calm and lighthearted tone from the past, but the old man moaned incessantly. Helga Saksesdatter, whom Gyrd had married, was so refined that there was no end to the unreasonable demands she could dream up—Gyrd didn't even dare belch in his own manor without asking his wife for permission. And then there was Torgrim, who was always whining about his stomach. Sir Andres would never have given his daughter to Torgrim if he had known the man was so loathsome that he was incapable of either living or dying. Astrid would have no joy from her youth or her wealth as long as her husband was alive. Sigrid wandered around the estate, broken and grieving—all smiles and merriment had deserted her, that good daughter of his. And she had borne that child, while Simon had none. Sir Andres wept, miserable and old and ill. Gudmund had refused all of the marriages suggested by his father, who had grown so old and frail that he had let the boy wear him down.

But the misfortunes had begun when Simon and that foolish maiden had defied their parents. And Lavrans was to blame—as bold a man as he was among men, his knees buckled before his womenfolk. No doubt the girl had sobbed and screamed, and he at once relented and sent word to that gilded whoremaster from Trøndelag who couldn't even wait until he and his bride were married. But if Lavrans had been master of his house, then he, Andres Darre, would have shown that he could teach a beardless whelp sensible behavior. Kristin Lavransdatter—she certainly had children enough. A healthy, squirming son every eleventh month, he had heard.

"It's going to be costly, Father," said Simon, laughing. "Their inheritance will be divided up many times." He picked up Arngjerd and set her on his lap. She had just come toddling into the room.

"Well, that one there won't cause your inheritance to be divided up into too many parts after you—whoever does inherit it," said Sir Andres crossly. He was fond of his son's daughter in his own way, but it infuriated him that Simon had a bastard child. "Have you thought of marrying anew, Simon?"

"You must let Halfrid grow cold in her grave first, Father," said Simon, stroking the child's pale hair. "I'll probably marry again, but there's no reason to make haste."

Then he picked up his crossbow and skis and set off for the forest to find some respite. With his dogs at his side he tracked elk through the mountain pass and shot wood grouse in the treetops. At night he slept in the forest hut belonging to Dyfrin, thinking that it felt good to be alone.

There was the sound of skis scraping outside in the pass; the dogs leaped up, and other dogs responded from outdoors. Simon threw open the door to the moon-blue night, and Gyrd came in, slender and tall, handsome and silent. He now looked younger than Simon, who had always been rather stout and had grown a good deal heavier during those years at Mandvik.

The brothers sat with the sack of provisions between them, eating and drinking and staring into the hearth.

"I suppose you know," said Gyrd, "that Torgrim will make a great deal of noise and ruckus when Father is gone. And he has won Gudmund's support. And Helga's. They will not grant Sigrid the full rights of a sister with us."

"I realize that. But she must be given her share as a sister; you and I should be able to force them to agree, brother."

"It would be best if Father himself saw to this matter before he dies," said Gyrd.

"No, let Father die in peace," replied Simon. "You and I will manage to protect our sister, so they don't rob her because she has suffered such misfortune."

So the heirs of Sir Andres Darre parted in bitter enmity after his death. Gyrd was the only one Simon said farewell to when he left home, and now he knew that Gyrd wouldn't have many pleasant days with that wife of his. Sigrid moved to Formo with Simon; she would keep house for him, and he in turn would manage her properties.

He rode into his own estate on a grayish-blue day as the snow was melting, when the alder trees along the Laag River were brown with buds. As he was about to cross the threshold of the main house with Arngjerd in his arms, Sigrid Andresdatter asked, "Why are you smiling like that, Simon?"

"Was I smiling?"

He had been thinking that this was a different kind of homecoming than what he had once dreamed of—when he would one day settle down here on his grandmother's estate. A seduced sister and a paramour's child—these were now his companions.

During that first summer he saw little of the people at Jørundgaard; he diligently avoided them.

But on the Sunday after the Feast of the Birth of Mary in the fall, he happened to be standing next to Lavrans Bjørgulfsøn in church, and so the two of them had to give each other the traditional kiss after Sira Eirik had prayed for the peace of the Holy

Church to be bountiful among them. And when Simon felt the older man's thin, dry lips on his cheek and heard him whisper the prayer of peace, he was strangely moved. He realized that Lavrans meant more by this than if he were simply obeying the ritual of the Church.

He hastened outside after the mass was done, but over by the horses he again ran into Lavrans, who invited him to come to Jørundgaard for dinner. Simon replied that his daughter was sick and that his sister was sitting with her. Lavrans then prayed that God might heal the child and shook his hand in farewell.

Several days later they had been working hard at Formo to bring in the harvest because the weather looked threatening. Most of the grain had been brought in by evening, when the first showers opened up. Simon ran across the courtyard in the downpour; great bands of bright sunshine broke through the clouds and lit up the main building and the mountain wall beyond. Then he caught sight of a little maiden standing in front of the door in the rain and the sunlight. She had his favorite dog with her. The dog pulled loose and leaped at Simon, dragging along a woven woman's belt, which was tied to his collar.

He saw that the girl came from highborn family. She was bareheaded and wore no cloak, but her wine-red dress was made from foreign cloth, and it was embroidered across the breast and fastened with a gilded brooch. A silken cord held her rain-dark hair back from her brow. The girl had a lively little face with a broad forehead, a sharp chin, and big, shining eyes. Her cheeks were flaming red, as if she had been running hard.

Simon knew who the maiden must be and greeted her by name: Ramborg.

"What might be the reason for you honoring us with this visit?"

It was the dog, she told Simon, as she followed him into the house and out of the rain. The dog had gotten into the habit of running off to Jørundgaard; now she was bringing him back. Oh yes, she knew it was his dog; she had seen the animal running alongside when he rode.

Simon scolded her a bit because she had come alone. He said he would have horses saddled and escort her home himself. But first she must have some food. Ramborg ran at once over to the bed where little Arngjerd lay ill; both the child and Sigrid were pleased with their guest, for Ramborg was both lively and merry. She wasn't like her sisters, thought Simon.

He rode with Ramborg as far as the manor gate and was then about to turn around when he met Lavrans, who had just learned that the child was not with her foster sisters at Laugarbru. He was on his way out with his servants to look for her—he was quite worried. Now Simon had to come inside, and as soon as he sat down in the hall of the main house, his shyness left him and he soon felt at home with Ragnfrid and Lavrans. They sat up late over their ale, and since the weather had grown quite fierce, he accepted their invitation to stay the night.

There were two beds in the hall. Ragnfrid made up one of them nicely for the guest, and then she asked where Ramborg should sleep—with her parents or in the other building?

"No, I want to sleep in my own bed," said the child. "Can't I sleep with you, Simon?" she begged.

Her father said that their guest should not be bothered with children in his bed, but Ramborg continued to insist that she wanted to sleep with Simon. Finally Lavrans said sternly that she was too big to share a bed with a strange man.

"No, I'm not, Father," she protested. "I'm not too big, am I, Simon?"

"You're too little," said Simon, laughing. "Offer to sleep with me five years from now and I certainly won't say no. But by then you'll no doubt want a different sort of man than a hideous, fat old widower, little Ramborg!"

Lavrans didn't seem pleased by the jest; he told her sharply to keep quiet now and go lie down in her parents' bed.

But Ramborg shouted, "Now you have asked for me, Simon Darre, so my father could hear you!"

"So be it," replied Simon with a laugh. "But I'm afraid he would refuse me, Ramborg."

After that day the people of Formo and Jørundgaard were constantly together. Ramborg went over to the neighboring estate as often as she had the chance, tending to Arngjerd as if the child were one of her dolls, following Sigrid around and helping with household chores, sitting on Simon's lap when they were in the main house. He fell into the habit of teasing and chattering with the maiden as he had in the old days when she and Ulvhild were like sisters to him.

Simon had lived in the valley for two years when Geirmund Hersteinssøn of Kruke asked for the hand of Sigrid Andresdatter. The family of Kruke was an old lineage, but even though some of the men had served in the retinues of kings, they had never won fame outside their own district. Yet it was the best marriage Sigrid could expect to make, and she was quite willing to marry Geirmund. Her brothers made the arrangements, and Simon was to hold his sister's wedding on his estate.

One evening just before the wedding, when they were rushing about making preparations for the feast, Simon said in jest that he didn't know how things would go with his household after Sigrid left. Then Ramborg said, "You'll have to manage as best you can for two more years, Simon. At fourteen a maiden reaches a marriageable age, and then you can bring me home."

"No, *you* I wouldn't want," said Simon with a laugh. "I don't trust my ability to harness a wild maiden like you."

"It's the ponds with still water that have deceptive bottoms, my father says," replied Ramborg. "I may be wild, but my sister was meek and quiet. Have you forgotten Kristin, Simon Andressøn?"

Simon jumped up from the bench, took the maiden in his arms, and raised her to his chest. He kissed her throat so hard that he left a little red mark. Horrified and astounded by his own actions, he let her go; then he grabbed Arngjerd, tossed her in the air, and hugged her in the same way so as to hide his feelings. He ran about, chasing the girls, the half-grown maiden and the little one, so that they fled up onto the tables and along the benches, until finally he lifted them up onto the crossbeam nearest the door and then ran outside.

They almost never mentioned Kristin at Jørundgaard when he was within earshot.

Ramborg Lavransdatter grew up to be a lovely maiden. The local gossips were busy marrying her off. One time it was Eindride Haakonssøn of the Valders-Gjeslings. They were third cousins but Lavrans and Haakon were both so wealthy that they should be able to send a letter to the Pope in Italy and obtain dispensation.[2] That would finally put an end to some of the old legal disputes that had continued ever since the old Gjeslings had sided with Duke Skule, and King Haakon had taken the Vaage estate away from them and given it to Sigurd Eldjar. Ivar Gjesling the Younger had, in turn, acquired Sundbu through marriage and the exchange of properties, but these matters had caused an endless number of quarrels and disagreements. Lavrans himself laughed at the whole thing; whatever compensation he might be able to claim for his wife wasn't worth the parchment and wax he had used up on this matter—not to mention the toil and traveling. But he had been embroiled in the dispute ever since he had become a married man, so he couldn't give it up.

But Eindride Gjesling celebrated his marriage to another maiden, and the people at Jørundgaard didn't seem overly troubled by this. They were invited to the banquet, and Ramborg told everyone proudly when she came home that four men had spoken to Lavrans about her, either on their own behalf or for kinsmen. Lavrans had told them he wouldn't agree to any betrothal for his daughter until she was old enough to have some say in the matter herself.

And that's how things stood until the spring of the year when Ramborg was fourteen winters old. One evening she was out in the cowshed at Formo with Simon, looking at a new calf. It was white with a brown patch, and Ramborg thought the patch looked very much like a church. Simon was sitting on the edge of the grain bin, the maiden was leaning on his knees, and he was tugging at her braids.

"It looks as if you will soon be riding in a bridal procession to church, Ramborg!"

"You know quite well that my father wouldn't refuse you if you asked for my hand," she said. "I'm old enough now that I could be married this year."

Simon gave a little start, but he tried to laugh.

"Are you talking about that foolishness again?"

"You know it's not foolishness," said the girl, looking up at him with her big eyes. "I've known for a long time that what I want is to move over here to Formo with you. Why have you kissed me and held me on your lap so often for all these years if you didn't want to marry me?"

"Certainly I would like to marry you, dear Ramborg. But I've never thought that such a young, beautiful maiden would be intended for me. I'm seventeen years older than you; no doubt you haven't thought about how you would end up with an old, bleary-eyed, big-bellied husband while you were a woman in the best of her years."

"These *are* my best years," she said, her face radiant. "And besides, you're not so decrepit, Simon!"

"But I'm ugly too. You'd soon grow tired of kissing me!"

"You have no reason to think that," she replied, laughing again as she tilted her face up toward him for a kiss. But he didn't kiss her.

"I won't take advantage of your imprudence, my sweet. Lavrans wants to take you with him to the south this summer. If you haven't changed your mind when you return, then I will thank God and Our Lady for better fortune than I had ever expected—but I will not bind you to this, fair Ramborg."

He took his dogs, his spear, and his bow and went up into the mountains that same evening. There was still a great deal of snow on the high plateau. He went to his hut to get a pair of skis and then stayed out by the lake south of the Boar Range and hunted reindeer for a week. But on the night he headed back toward the village, he grew uneasy and afraid again. It would be just like Ramborg to have said something to her father all the same. As he crossed the meadow near Jørundgaard's mountain hut, he saw smoke and sparks coming from the roof. He thought Lavrans himself might be there, so he went over to the hut.

From the other man's demeanor Simon thought he had guessed right. But they sat and talked about the bad summer the year before and about when might be a good time to move the livestock up to the mountain pastures; about the hunting and about Lavrans's new falcon, which was sitting on the floor, flapping its wings over the entrails of the birds roasting on a spit over the fire. Lavrans had come up to see to his horse shed in Ilmandsdal; it was reported to have collapsed, according to several people from Alvdal who had passed through earlier that day. The two men spent most of the evening in this fashion.

Then Simon finally said, "I don't know whether Ramborg has

said anything to you about a matter which we discussed one evening?"

Lavrans said slowly, "I think you should have spoken to me first, Simon. You might imagine what kind of answer you would have received. Yes, well—I can understand how it happened that you mentioned it first to the maiden—and it will make no difference. I'm happy to give my child into the hands of a good man."

Then there's not much more to say, thought Simon. And yet it was strange—here he sat, a man who had never intended to come too close to any virtuous maiden or woman, and now he was bound on his honor to marry a girl he did not truly want. But he made an attempt.

"It's not true, Lavrans, that I've been courting your daughter behind your back. I thought I was so old that she wouldn't consider it anything but brotherly affection from the past if I talked with her so often. And if you think I'm too old for her, I wouldn't be surprised nor would I allow it to end the friendship between us."

"I've met few men I would rather see take a son's place than you, Simon," replied Lavrans. "And I would rather give Ramborg away myself. You know who would be the man to arrange her marriage after I'm gone." That was the first time any mention was made between them of Erlend Nikulaussøn. "In many ways my son-in-law is a better man than I took him for when I first met him. But I don't know whether he's the right person to make a wise decision about a young maiden's marriage. And I can tell that this is what Ramborg wants herself."

"She thinks so now," said Simon. "But she's hardly more than a child, and I don't intend to press you, if you think we should wait a little longer."

"And I," said Lavrans with a slight frown, "do not intend to force my daughter upon you—you mustn't believe that."

"You should know," said Simon quickly, "that there is not another maiden in all of Norway I would rather have than Ramborg. If truth be told, Lavrans, my good fortune seems much too great if I'm to have such a fair, young, and good bride, who is rich and descended from the best lineage. And you as my father-in-law," he added, a little self-consciously.

Lavrans chuckled with embarrassment. "You know how I feel about you. And you will deal with my child and her inheritance in such a way that her mother and I will never have cause to regret this arrangement."

"That I promise you, with the help of God and all the saints," said Simon.

Then they shook hands. Simon remembered the first time he had secured such an arrangement by clasping Lavrans's hand. His heart felt small and pained in his breast.

But Ramborg *was* a better match than he could have expected. There were only the two daughters to divide up the inheritance after Lavrans's death. He would step into the role of son with the man whom he had always respected and loved above all others he knew. And Ramborg was indeed young and sweet and lively.

Surely he must have acquired the wisdom of a grown man by now. Had he actually thought he could win Kristin as a widow even though he couldn't have her as a maiden? After the other man had enjoyed her youth—and with a dozen stepsons of his lineage? No, then he deserved to have his brothers declare him incapable and refuse to let him handle his own affairs. Erlend would live to be as old as the stone of the mountain—that type of fellow always did.

So now they would be called brothers-in-law. They hadn't seen each other since that night in the house in Oslo. Well, no doubt it would be even more uncomfortable for Erlend than for him to be reminded of that.

He would be a good husband to Ramborg, with no deceptions. And yet it was possible that the child had lured him into a trap.

"You're sitting there laughing?" said Lavrans.

"Was I laughing? It was just something that struck me . . ."

"You must tell me what it is, Simon, so I can laugh too."

Simon Andressøn fixed his small, sharp eyes on the other man's face.

"I was thinking about . . . women. I wonder whether any woman respects the laws and beliefs of men as we do among ourselves—when she or her own kind can win something by stepping over them. Halfrid, my first wife . . . Well, I haven't spoken of this to a single Christian soul before you, Lavrans Bjørgulfsøn, and I will never speak of it again. She was such a good and pious and

virtuous woman that I don't think she has ever had an equal.
I've told you about what she did when Arngjerd was born. But
back when we realized how things stood with Sigrid—well, Halfrid wanted us to hide my sister and she would pretend that she
herself was with child and then present Sigrid's child as her own.
In that way we would have an heir and the child would be cared
for, and Sigrid could live with us and wouldn't have to be separated from her son. I don't think Halfrid realized that this would
have been a betrayal of her own kinsmen."

After a moment Lavrans said, "Then you could have stayed at
Mandvik, Simon."

"Yes." Simon Darre laughed harshly. "And perhaps with just as
much right as many other men occupy lands they call their ancestral estates. Since we have nothing more to rely on in such matters
except the honor of women."

Lavrans pulled the hood over the falcon's head and lifted the
bird onto his wrist.

"This is a strange topic of conversation for a man who is thinking of marriage," he said quietly. There was a hint of displeasure in
his voice.

"Of course no one would think such things of *your* daughters,"
replied Simon.

Lavrans looked down at his falcon, scratching it with a twig.

"Not even about Kristin?" he whispered.

"No," said Simon firmly. "She didn't deal with me kindly, but I
never found that she was untruthful. She told me honestly and
openly that she had met another man whom she cared for more
than me."

"When you so willingly let her go," said Lavrans softly, "that
was not because you had heard . . . any rumors about her?"

"No," said Simon in the same firm voice. "I never heard rumors
about Kristin."

It was agreed that the betrothal would be celebrated that very
summer and the wedding would take place during Easter of the
following year, after Ramborg had turned fifteen.

Kristin had not seen Jørundgaard since the day she rode away as a
bride, and that was eight winters ago. Now she returned with a

great entourage: her husband, Margret, five sons, nursemaids, serving men and women, and horses carrying their traveling goods. Lavrans had ridden out to meet them and found them at Dovre. Kristin no longer cried as easily as she had in her youth, but when she saw her father riding toward them, her eyes filled with tears. She reined in her horse, slipped down from the saddle, and ran to greet her father; when she reached him, she grabbed his hand and kissed it humbly. Lavrans at once jumped down from his horse and took his daughter in his arms. Then he shook hands with Erlend, who had done as the others had and came to meet his father-in-law on foot, with respectful words of greeting.

The next day Simon came over to Jørundgaard to see his new kinsmen. Gyrd Darre and Geirmund of Kruke were with him, but their wives had stayed behind at Formo. Simon was going to hold the wedding at his own estate, so there was much work for the women to do.

It turned out that when they met, Simon and Erlend greeted each other openly and without restraint. Simon kept his feelings in check, and Erlend was so unabashed and merry that the other man thought he must have forgotten where they had last met. Then Simon gave Kristin his hand. The two of them were more uncertain, and their eyes barely met for more than a moment.

Kristin thought his looks had faded a good deal. In his youth, Simon had been quite handsome, even though he was much too stout and his neck was too thick. His steel-gray eyes had seemed small under his full eyelids, his mouth was too little, and his dimples were too big in his round, childish face. But he had had a healthy complexion and a broad, milky-white forehead under his beautiful, curly, light-brown hair. His hair was still curly, and just as thick and nut-brown, but his whole face was now reddish-brown; he had lines under his eyes, heavy jowls, and a double chin. He had become heavyset, and he had a noticeable belly. He didn't look like a man who would take time to lie down on the edge of the bed in the evening to whisper to his betrothed. Kristin felt sorry for her young sister; she was so lively and lovely and childishly happy about her marriage. On the very first day she showed Kristin all the chests containing her dowry and Simon's betrothal gifts. And she said she had heard from Sigrid Andresdatter about a gilded chest that was up in the bridal loft at Formo; there were twelve costly wimples inside, and this was what her husband was going to give her on their first morning. Poor little thing, she had no idea what marriage was like. It was too bad that Kristin hardly knew her little sister; Ramborg had been to Husaby twice, but there she was always sullen and unfriendly. She didn't care for Erlend or for Margret, who was the same age.

Simon thought to himself that he had expected—perhaps even hoped—that Kristin would look more careworn than she did, after having so many children. But she was glowing with youth and health, her posture was still erect, and her bearing just as lovely, although her step was a little firmer than before. She was the most beautiful mother with her five handsome small sons.

She was wearing a homemade gown of rust-brown wool with dark-blue birds woven into the cloth; Simon remembered standing next to her loom while she sat and worked on that cloth.

There was some commotion when they were about to sit down at the table in the loft of the main house. Skule and Ivar began screaming; they wanted to sit between their mother and foster mother, as they usually did. Lavrans didn't think it proper for Ramborg to sit farther down than her sister's servant woman and children, so he invited his daughter to sit in the high seat next to him, since she would soon be leaving home.

The small sons from Husaby were unruly and seemed to have no table manners. They had barely started eating before the little blond boy ducked under the table and popped up on the cushion next to Simon's knee.

"Can I look at that odd sheath you have on your belt, kinsman Simon?" he asked. The boy spoke slowly and solemnly. It was the large silver-studded sheath holding a spoon and two knives that he had caught sight of.

"Yes, you may, kinsman. And what is your name, cousin?"

"My name is Gaute Erlendssøn, cousin." He put the scrap of bacon he was holding onto the lap of Simon's silver-gray Flemish surcoat, pulled a knife out of the sheath, and examined it carefully. Then he took the knife that Simon was eating with, and the spoon, and put them all back in place so he could see how the sheath looked when everything was inside. He was quite earnest, and his fingers and face were very greasy. Simon smiled at the eager expression on the small, handsome face.

A few minutes later the two oldest boys came over to the men's bench too. The twins toppled under the table and began rolling around between everyone's feet; then they went over to the dogs near the fire. There was little peace for the adults as they ate their supper. Their mother and father reprimanded the boys and told them to sit quietly, but the children paid them no mind. And their parents kept laughing at them and seemed not to take their mischievous behavior too seriously—not even when Lavrans, in a rather sharp voice, told one of his men to take the whelps down to the room below so people in the hall could hear themselves speak.

Everyone from Husaby was to sleep in the loft of the main house, and after the meal, while more ale was being brought in for the men, Kristin and her maids took the children over to a corner of the hall to undress them. They had gotten so dirty while eating that their mother wanted to wash them up a bit. But the youngest boys refused to be washed, and the older ones splashed the water, and then all of them started rushing around the hall as the maids pulled one piece of clothing after another off them. Finally they were all put into one bed, but they continued to yell and play and shove each other, laughing and shrieking. Pillows and coverlets and sheets were hurled this way and that, making dust fly, and the smell of chaff filled the whole room. Kristin laughed and explained calmly that they were so high-spirited from being in a strange place.

Ramborg accompanied her betrothed outside and walked with him for a short distance between the fences in the spring night. Gyrd and Geirmund had ridden on ahead while Simon stopped to say good night. He had already put his foot in the stirrup when he turned back to the maiden, took her in his arms, and held the delicate child so close that she whimpered happily.

"God bless you, dear Ramborg—you're so fine and so fair—much too fine and fair for me," he murmured into her mass of curls.

Ramborg stood watching Simon as he rode off into the misty moonlight. She rubbed her arm—he had gripped her so hard that it hurt. Dizzy with joy, she thought: Now there were only three days left until she would be married to him.

Lavrans stood next to Kristin at the children's bedside and watched her tucking in her small sons. The eldest were already big boys with lanky bodies and slender, lean limbs; but the two smallest ones were chubby and rosy, with folds in their skin and dimples at their joints. Lavrans thought it a lovely sight to see them lying there, pink and warm, their thick hair damp with sweat, breathing quietly as they slept. They were healthy, beautiful boys—but never had he seen such poorly behaved children as his grandsons. Luckily Simon's sister and sister-in-law hadn't been present tonight. But he wasn't the one to speak to Kristin about discipline. Lavrans gave a small sigh and then made the sign of the cross over the small boys' heads.

Then Simon Andressøn celebrated his wedding to Ramborg Lavransdatter, and it was magnificent and grand in every way. The bride and bridegroom looked happy, and it seemed to many that Ramborg was more lovely on her wedding day than her sister had been—perhaps not as striking as Kristin, but much happier and gentler. Everyone could see in the bride's clear, innocent eyes that she wore the golden crown of her Gjesling ancestors with full honor on that day.

And full of joy and pride, with her hair pinned up, she sat in the armchair in front of the bridal bed as the guests came upstairs to greet the young couple on the first morning. With laughter and bold teasing, they watched as Simon placed the wimple of a married woman over his young wife's head. Cheers and the clanging of weapons filled the room as Ramborg stood up, straight-backed and flushed beneath the white wimple, and gave her husband her hand.

It was not often that two noble children from the same district were married—when all the branches of the lineage were studied, it was often found that the kinship was too close. So everyone considered this wedding to be a great and joyous occasion.

ONE OF THE first things Kristin noticed at home was that all the carvings of old men's heads which sat carved above the crossbeams on the building gables were now gone. They had been replaced by spires with foliage and birds, and there was a gilded weather vane atop the new house. The old posts on the high seat in the hearth room had also been replaced with new ones. The old ones had been carved to look like two men—rather hideous, but they had apparently been there since the house was built, and the servants used to polish them with fat and wash them with ale before the holy days. On the new posts her father had carved two men with crosses on their helmets and shields. They weren't meant to be Saint Olav himself, Lavrans said, for he didn't think it would be proper for a sinful man to have images of the saint in his house, except those he knelt in front of to say his prayers. But they could very well be two of Olav's men. Lavrans had chopped up and burned all the old carvings himself. The servants didn't dare. It was with some reluctance that he still allowed them to take food out to the great stone at Jørund's grave on the evening before holy days; Lavrans conceded that it would be a shame to take away from the original owner of the estate something he had grown accustomed to receiving for as long as anyone had lived on the land. He died long before Christianity came to Norway, so it wasn't his fault that he was a heathen.

People didn't like these changes that Lavrans Bjørgulfsøn had made. That was fine for him, since he could afford to buy his security elsewhere. And it seemed to be equally powerful, because he continued to have the same good fortune with his farming as before. But there was some talk that the spirits might take their revenge when the estate was taken over by a master who was less pious and not as generous about everything that belonged to the Church. And it was easier for poor folk to give the ancestors what they were used to receiving instead of stirring up strife with them by siding too much with the priests.

Otherwise it was rather uncertain how things would go with the friendship between Jørundgaard and the parsonage after Sira Eirik was gone. The priest was old now and in poor health, and he had been forced to bring in a curate to assist him. At first he had talked to the bishop about his grandson Bentein Jonssøn; but Lavrans had also had a word with the bishop, who had been his friend in the past. People thought this unfair. No doubt the young priest had been overly importunate toward Kristin Lavransdatter on that evening, and he may have even frightened the girl; but it was also possible that she herself might have been to blame for the young man's boldness. It had later turned out that she was not as shy as she seemed to be. But Lavrans had always believed his daughter to be good, and he treated her as if she were a holy shrine.

After that there was a coldness between Sira Eirik and Lavrans for some time. But then Sira Solmund arrived, and he was immediately embroiled in a dispute with the parish priest over a piece of land and whether it belonged to the parsonage or to Eirik himself. Lavrans had the best grasp of any man in the district about land purchases and such matters back to ancient times, and it was his testimony that determined the outcome. Since then, he and Sira Solmund had not been friends. But it might be said that Sira Eirik and Audun, the old deacon, practically lived at Jørundgaard now, for they went over there every day to sit with Lavrans and complain of all the injustices and troubles they had to endure from the new priest; and they were waited on as if they were bishops.

Kristin had heard a little about this from Borgar Trondssøn of Sundbu; his wife came from Trøndelag, and he had been a guest at Husaby several times. Trond Gjesling had been dead for a few years now. But this was not considered a great loss, since he had been like an intruder in the ancient lineage—surly, avaricious, and sickly. Lavrans was the only one who had any patience with Trond, for he pitied his brother-in-law and even more Gudrid, his wife. Now they were both gone, and all four of their sons lived together on the estate. They were intrepid, promising, and handsome men; people thought them a good replacement for the father. There was great friendship between these men and the master of Jørundgaard. Lavrans rode to Sundbu a couple of times each year to join them in hunting on the slopes of Vestfjeld. But Borgar said that it seemed completely unreasonable the way Lavrans and Ragnfrid were now worrying themselves with penances and devotions.

"He gulps down water during fasts just as eagerly as always, but your father doesn't speak to the ale bowls with the same heartiness he used to show in the past," said Borgar. No one could understand the man—it was unthinkable that Lavrans might have some secret sin to repent. As far as people could tell, he had lived as Christian a life as any child of Adam, apart from the saints.

Deep inside Kristin's heart, a foreboding began to stir about why her father was always striving so hard to come closer to God. But she didn't dare think about it too much.

She didn't want to acknowledge how changed her father was. It wasn't that he had aged excessively: he was still slim, with an erect and noble bearing. His hair was quite gray now, but it wasn't overly noticeable, since he had always been so fair. And yet . . . Kristin's memory was haunted by the image of the young and radiantly handsome man—the fresh roundness of his cheeks in the narrow face, the pure blush of his skin under the sheen of tan, and the crimson fullness of his lips with the deep corners. Now his muscular body had withered to bone and sinew, his face was brown and sharp, as if carved out of wood, and his cheeks were flat and gaunt, with a knot of muscle at the corners of his mouth. Well, he was no longer a young man—and yet he wasn't very old, either.

He had always been quiet, sober-minded, and pensive, and Kristin knew that even in childhood he had obeyed the Christian commandments with particular zeal. He loved the holy mass and prayers spoken in Latin, and he regarded the church as the place where he felt the most joy. But everyone had sensed a daring courage and zest for life flowing calmly in this quiet man's soul. Now it seemed as if something had ebbed out of him.

Since she had come home, she hadn't seen him drunk except on one occasion—an evening during the wedding celebration at Formo. Then he had staggered a bit and slurred his words, but he hadn't been especially merry. She thought back to her childhood, to the banquets and great ale drinking on feast days, when her father would roar with laughter and slap his thighs at every jest—offering to fight or wrestle with any man renowned for his physical strength, trying out horses, and leaping into dance, but laughing most at himself when he was unsteady on his feet, and lavishly handing out gifts, brimming over with good will and kindness toward everyone. She understood that her father needed this sort of exhilaration from time to time, amidst the constant work, the strict fasts he kept, and the sedate home life with his own people, who saw him as their best friend and supporter.

She also saw that her husband never had this need to get drunk because he put so few restrictions on himself, no matter how sober he might be. He regularly gave in to his impulses, without brooding over right or wrong or what was considered good and proper behavior for sensible people. Erlend was the most moderate man she had ever met when it came to strong liquor. He drank in order to quench his thirst and for the sake of camaraderie, but otherwise he didn't particularly care for it.

Lavrans Bjørgulfsøn had now lost his old sense of enjoyment for the ale bowls. He no longer had that craving inside him that needed to be released through revelry. It had never occurred to him before to drown his sorrows in drunkenness, and it didn't occur to him now—he had always thought that a man ought to bring his joy to the drinking table.

He had turned elsewhere with his sorrows. There was an image that had always hovered dimly in his daughter's memory: Lavrans on the night when the church burned down. He stood beside the crucifix he had rescued, holding on to the cross and supporting himself with it. And without thinking it through, Kristin had the feeling that what had changed Lavrans was partly his fear for the future of herself and her children with the husband she had chosen, along with the awareness of his own powerlessness.

This knowledge secretly gnawed at her heart. And she had returned home to Jørundgaard, worn out by the tumult of the previous winter and by her own rashness in accepting Erlend's nonchalance. She knew he was wasteful and always would be, and he had no idea how to manage his properties, which were slowly but constantly diminishing under his control. She had been able to get him to agree to a few things which she and Sira Eiliv had advised, but she didn't have the heart to speak to him about such matters time and again. And it was tempting simply to be happy with him now. She was tired of arguing and fighting with everything both outside and inside her own soul. But she was also the kind of person who was made anxious and weary by such heedless behavior.

Here at home she had expected to rediscover the peace from her childhood, under the protection of her father.

No, she felt so uneasy. Erlend now had a good income from his position as sheriff, but he also lived with greater ostentation, with more servants and an entourage befitting a chieftain. And he had begun to shut her out of everything that didn't concern their domestic life together. She realized that he didn't want to have her watchful eyes on what he was doing. With other men he would talk willingly about all he had seen and experienced up north—to her he never said a word. And there were other things as well. He had met with Lady Ingebjørg, the king's mother, and Sir Knut Porse several times over the past few years. But it had never been opportune for Kristin to accompany him. Now Sir Knut was a duke in Denmark, and King Haakon's daughter had bound herself to him in marriage. This had aroused bitter indignation in the souls of many Norwegian men; measures had been taken against the king's mother which Kristin did not understand. And the bishop in Bjørgvin had secretly sent several chests to Husaby. They were now on board *Margygren,* and the ship was anchored at Nes. Erlend had been given boxes of letters and was to sail to Denmark later in the summer. He wanted Kristin to go along with him, but she refused. She could see that Erlend moved among these noble people as an equal and a dear kinsman, and this worried her—it wasn't safe with such an impetuous man as Erlend. But she didn't dare travel with him; she wouldn't be able to advise him in these matters, and she didn't want to run the risk of consorting with people among whom she, a simple wife, could not assert herself. And she was also afraid of the sea. For her, seasickness was worse than the most difficult childbirth.

So she spent the days at Jørundgaard with her soul shivering and uneasy.

One day she went with her father to Skjenne. There she saw again the strange treasure which they kept on the estate. It was a spur of

he purest gold, shaped in a bulky and old-fashioned style, with
peculiar ornamentation. She, like every other child in the area,
knew where it had come from.

It was soon after Saint Olav had brought Christianity to the valley that Audhild the Fair of Skjenne was lured into the mountain.
The villagers carried the church bell up onto the slopes and rang it
for the maiden. On the third evening she came walking across the
meadow, adorned with so much gold that she glittered like a star.
Then the rope broke, the bell tumbled down the scree, and Audhild had to return to the mountain.

But many years later, twelve warriors came to the priest—this
was the first priest here at Sil. They wore golden helmets and silver
coats of mail, and they rode dark-brown stallions. They were the
sons of Audhild and the mountain king, and they asked that their
mother might be given a Christian funeral and be buried in consecrated ground. She had tried to maintain her faith and observe the
holy days of the Church inside the mountain, and this was her
earnest prayer. But the priest refused. And people said that because
of this, he himself had no peace in the grave. On autumn nights he
could be heard walking through the grove north of the church,
weeping with remorse at his own cruelty. That same night Audhild's sons had gone to Skjenne to bring greetings from their
mother to her old parents who still lived there. The next morning
the golden spur was found in the courtyard. And the sons doubtless continued to regard the Skjenne men as their kin, for they always had exceptional good fortune in the mountains.

Lavrans said to his daughter as they rode home in the summer
night, "The sons of Audhild repeated Christian prayers that their
mother had taught them. They couldn't mention the name of God
or Jesus, but they said the Lord's Prayer and credo like this: 'I believe in the Almighty, I believe in the only begotten Son, I believe in
the mightiest Spirit.' And then they said: 'Hail to the Lady, you
who are the most blessed of women—and blessed is the fruit of
your womb, the solace of all the earth.' "

Kristin timidly glanced up at her father's gaunt, weatherbeaten
face. In the bright summer night it seemed more ravaged with sorrows and worries than she had ever seen it.

"You've never told me that before," she said softly.

"Haven't I? Well, I may have thought it would give you more melancholy thoughts than your years could bear. Sira Eirik says that it is written according to Saint Paul the Apostle that humankind is not alone in sighing with agony."

One day Kristin was sitting and sewing at the top of the stairs leading up to the high loft when Simon came riding into the courtyard and stopped just below where she sat, although he didn't see her. Her parents both came out of the house. No, Simon wouldn't dismount; Ramborg had merely asked him to find out, when he was passing this way, whether they had sent the sheep that had been her pet lamb up to the mountain pastures. She wanted to bring it to Formo.

Kristin saw her father scratching his head. Ramborg's sheep. Yes, well . . . He gave an exasperated laugh. It was a shame, but he had hoped she would have forgotten about it. He had given each of his two eldest grandsons a little axe, and the first thing they had used them for was to kill Ramborg's sheep.

Simon laughed. "Yes, those Husaby boys, they're rascals all right."

Kristin ran down the loft stairs and unfastened the silver scissors from her belt.

"You can give these to Ramborg, as compensation for my sons killing her sheep. I know she's wanted to have these scissors ever since she was a child. No one must say that my sons . . ." She had spoken in anger, but now she fell silent. She had noticed her parents' faces—they were giving her a look of dismay and astonishment.

Simon didn't take the scissors; he felt embarrassed. Then he caught sight of Bjørgulf and rode over to him, leaning down to lift the boy up into the saddle in front of him.

"I hear you've been making raids around the countryside—now you're my prisoner, and tomorrow your parents can come over to see me and we'll negotiate the ransom."

And with that he gave a laugh and a wave and rode off with the boy wriggling and laughing in his arms. Simon had become great friends with Erlend's sons. Kristin remembered that he had always had a way with children; her younger sisters had loved him dearly.

Oddly enough it made her cross that he should be so fond of children and take pleasure in playing with them when her own husband had little interest in listening to children's prattle.

The next day, when they were at Formo, Kristin realized that Simon had not won any favors with his wife by bringing this guest home with him.

"No one should expect Ramborg to care much for children yet," said Ragnfrid. "She's hardly more than a child herself. Things will be different when she's older."

"No doubt you're right." Simon and his mother-in-law exchanged a look and a little smile.

Ah, thought Kristin. Well, it had already been two months since the wedding.

Distressed and agitated as Kristin now was, she took her feelings out on Erlend. He had accepted this stay at his wife's ancestral estate with the satisfaction and pleasure of a righteous man. He was good friends with Ragnfrid and made it known that he had a deep fondness for his wife's father. And Lavrans, in turn, seemed to have affection for his son-in-law. But Kristin had now become so sensitive and wary that she saw in her father's kindness toward Erlend much of the same tolerant tenderness that Lavrans had always shown toward every living creature he felt was less able to take care of itself. His love for his other son-in-law was different; he treated Simon as a friend and equal. And even though Erlend was much closer in age to his father-in-law than Simon was, it was Lavrans and Simon who addressed each other in the informal manner. Ever since Erlend had become betrothed to Kristin, Lavrans had addressed Erlend informally, while Erlend had continued to use the more formal mode. It was up to Lavrans to change this, but he had never offered to do so.

Simon and Erlend got along well whenever they were together, but they didn't seek out each other's company. Kristin still felt a secret shyness toward Simon Darre—because of what he knew about her, and even more because she knew that he was the one whose conduct had been honorable, while Erlend had acted with shame. It made her furious when she realized that Erlend could forget even this. And so she wasn't always amenable toward her husband. If Erlend was in a mood to bear her irritability with good humor and gentleness, it would annoy her that he wasn't taking her words seriously. On some other day he might have little patience, and then his temper would flare, but she would respond with bitterness and coldness.

One evening they were sitting in the hearth room at Jørundgaard. Lavrans always felt most comfortable in this building, especially in weather that was rainy and oppressive, as it was on that day. In the main building, up in the hall, the ceiling was flat and the smoke from the fireplace could be bothersome. But in the hearth room the smoke would rise up to the central beam in the pitched roof, even when they had to close the smoke vent because of the weather.

Kristin sat near the hearth, sewing. She was feeling out of sorts and bored. Right across from her was Margret, dozing over her needlework and yawning now and then. The children were noisily running about the room. Ragnfrid was at Formo, and most of the servants were elsewhere. Lavrans sat in the high seat, with Erlend at his elbow, at the end of the outer bench. They had a chessboard between them and they were moving the pieces in silence, after much reflection. Once, when Ivar and Skule were tugging on a puppy, trying to tear it in half, Lavrans stood up and took the poor howling animal away from them. He didn't say a word, but simply sat down to his game again with the dog on his lap.

Kristin went over to them and stood with one hand on her husband's shoulder, watching the game. Erlend was a much less skilled chess player than his father-in-law, so he was most often the loser when they took out the board in the evening, but he bore this with gentle equanimity. This evening he was playing especially badly. Kristin stood there castigating him, and not in a particularly kind or sweet way.

Finally Lavrans said rather harshly, "Erlend can't keep his thoughts on the game when you're standing here bothering him. What do you want, anyway, Kristin? You've never understood board games!"

"No, you don't seem to think I understand much at all."

"There's one thing I see that you don't understand," said her father sharply, "and that's the proper way for a wife to speak to her husband. It would be better if you went and reined in your sons—they're behaving worse than a pack of Christmas trolls."

Kristin went over and set her children in a row on a bench and then sat down next to them.

"Be quiet now, my sons," she said. "Your grandfather doesn't want you to play in here."

Lavrans glanced at his daughter but didn't speak. A little later the foster mothers came in, and Kristin left with her maids and Margret to put the children to bed.

Erlend said after a moment, when he and Lavrans were alone, "I would have wished, Father-in-law, that you hadn't reprimanded Kristin in that way. If it gives her some comfort to carp at me when she's in a bad temper, then . . . It does no good to talk to her, and she won't stand for anyone saying a word against her children."

"And what about you?" said Lavrans. "Do you intend to allow your sons to grow up so ill-behaved? Where were the maids who are supposed to watch and tend to the children?"

"In the servants' house with your men, I would think," said Erlend, laughing and stretching. "But I don't dare say a word to Kristin about her serving maids. Then she flies into a fury and tells me that she and I have never been examples for anyone."

The following day Kristin was picking strawberries in the meadow south of the farm when her father called to her from the smithy door and asked her to come over to him.

Kristin went, though rather reluctantly. It was probably Naakkve again—that morning he had left a gate open, and the cows had wandered into a barley field.

Lavrans pulled a glowing iron from the forge and set it on the anvil. His daughter sat down to wait, and for a long time there was no sound other than the pounding of the hammer against the glowing piece of iron and the ringing reply of the anvil. Finally Kristin asked her father what he wanted to say to her.

The iron was now cold. Lavrans put down his tongs and hammer and came over to Kristin. With soot on his face and hair, his clothing and hands blackened, and garbed as he was in the big leather apron, Lavrans looked much sterner than usual.

"I called you over here, my daughter, because I want to tell you this. Here on my estate you will show your husband the respect that is proper for a wife. I refuse to hear my daughter speaking the way you did to Erlend last night."

"This is something new, Father, for you to think Erlend is a man worthy of people's respect."

"He's *your* husband," said Lavrans. "I didn't force you to arrange this marriage. You should remember that."

"You're such warm friends," replied Kristin. "If you had known him back then the way you know him now, then you might well have done so."

Lavrans looked down at her, his face somber and sad.

"Now you're speaking rashly, Kristin, and saying things that are untrue. I didn't try to force you when you wanted to cast off the man to whom you were lawfully betrothed, even though you know I was very fond of Simon."

"No, but Simon didn't want me either."

"Oh, he was much too high-minded to demand his rights when you were unwilling. But I don't know whether he would have been so against it in his heart if I had done as Andres Darre wanted. He said we should pay no attention to the whims of you two young people. And I wonder whether the knight might have been right—now that I see you can't live in a seemly fashion with the husband you insisted on winning."

Kristin gave a loud and ugly laugh.

"Simon! You would never have been able to threaten Simon into marrying the woman he had found with another man in such a house."

Lavrans gasped for air. "House?" he repeated involuntarily.

"Yes, what you men call a house of sin. The woman who owned it was Munan's paramour. She warned me herself not to go there. I told her I was going to meet a kinsman—I didn't know he was *her* kinsman." She gave another laugh, wild and harsh.

"Silence!" said her father.

He stood there for a moment. A tremor flickered across his countenance—a smile that made his face blanch. She thought suddenly of the foliage on the mountain slope which turns white when gusts of wind twist each leaf around—patches of pale and glittering light.

"A man can learn a great deal without asking."

Kristin broke down as she sat there on the bench, supporting herself on one elbow, with her other hand covering her eyes. For the first time in her life she was afraid of her father—deathly afraid.

He turned away from her, picked up the hammer, and put it back in its place next to the others. Then he gathered up the files and small tools and went about putting them back on the cross-beam between the walls. He stood with his back to his daughter; his hands were shaking violently.

"Have you never thought about the fact, Kristin, that Erlend kept silent about this?" Now he was standing in front of her, looking down into her pale, frightened face. "I told him no, quite firmly, when he came to me in Tunsberg with his rich kinsmen and asked for your hand. I didn't know then that *I* was the one who should have thanked *him* for wanting to redeem my daughter's honor. Many a man would have told me so.

"Then he came again and courted you with full honor. Not all men would have been so persistent in winning a wife who was . . . who was . . . what you were back then."

"I don't think any man would have dared say such a thing to you."

"Erlend has never been afraid of cold steel." A great weariness suddenly came over Lavrans's face, and his voice lost all vigor and resonance. But then he spoke again, quietly and deliberately.

"As bad as this is, Kristin—it seems to me even worse that you speak of it now that he's your husband and the father of your sons.

"If things were as you say, then you knew the worst about him before you insisted on entering into marriage with him. And yet he was willing to pay as dearly for you, as if you had been an honest maiden. He has granted you much freedom to manage and rule; you must do penance for your sin by ruling sensibly and make up for Erlend's lack of caution—that much you owe to God and your children.

"I myself have said, and others have said the same, that Erlend doesn't seem to be capable of much else than seducing women. You are also to blame for this being said, according to your own testimony. But since then he has shown he is capable of other

things—your husband has won a good name for himself through
courage and swiftness in battle. It's no small benefit for your sons
that their father has acquired a reputation for his boldness and
skill with weapons. That he is . . . incautious . . . you must realize
this better than anyone. It would be best for you to redeem your
shame by honoring and helping the husband whom you yourself
have chosen."

Kristin was bending forward, with her head in her hands. Now
she looked up, her face pale and despairing. "It was cruel of me
to tell you this. Oh . . . Simon begged me . . . It was the only thing
he asked of me—that I should spare you from knowing the
worst."

"Simon asked you to spare me?" Kristin heard the pain in her
father's voice. And she realized it was also cruel of her to tell him
that a stranger saw fit to remind her to spare her own father.

Then Lavrans sat down beside her, took her hand in both of his,
and placed it on his knee.

"Yes, it was cruel, my Kristin," he said gently and sadly. "You
are good to everyone, my dear child, but I have also realized that
you can be cruel to those you love too dearly. For the sake of Jesus,
Kristin, spare me the need to be so worried for you—that your impetuous spirit might bring more sorrow upon you and yours. You
struggle like a colt that has been tied up in the stable for the first
time, whenever your heartstrings are bound."

Sobbing, she sank against her father, and he held her tight in his
arms. They sat there for a long time in that manner, but Lavrans
said no more. Finally he lifted her face.

"You're covered in soot," he said with a little smile. "There's a
cloth over in the corner, but it will probably just make you blacker.
You must go home and wash; everyone can see that you've been
sitting on the blacksmith's lap."

Gently he pushed her out the door, closed it behind her, and
stood there for a moment. Then he staggered a few steps over to
the bench, sank down onto it, and leaned his head back against the
timbers of the wall with his contorted face tilted upward. With all
his might he pressed a fist against his heart.

It never lasted long. The shortness of breath, the black dizziness, the pain that radiated out into his limbs from his heart,
which shuddered and struggled, giving a few fierce thuds and then

quivering quietly again. His blood hammered in the veins of his neck.

It would pass in a few minutes. It always did after he sat still for a while. But it was happening more and more often.

Erlend had called his crews to a meeting at Veøy on the eve of Saint Jacob's Day, but then he stayed on at Jørundgaard a while longer to accompany Simon on a hunt for a vicious bear that had killed some of the livestock in the mountain pastures. When Erlend returned from the hunting expedition, there was a message for him. Some of his men had gotten into trouble with the towns-people, and he had to hurry north to win their release. Lavrans had business up there too, and so he decided to ride along with his son-in-law.

It was already nearing the end of Saint Olav's Day by the time they reached the island. Erling Vidkunssøn's ship was anchored offshore, and they met the regent at vespers in Saint Peter's Church. He went back to the monastery with them, where Lavrans had taken lodgings. There he dined with them, sending his men down to the ship for some particularly good French wine, which he had brought along from Nidaros.

But the conversation waned as they sat drinking. Erlend was lost in his own thoughts; his eyes sparkled as they always did when he was out on some new adventure, but he seemed distracted as the others talked. Lavrans merely sipped at his wine, and Sir Erling had fallen silent.

"You look tired, kinsman," Erlend said to him.

Yes, they had encountered stormy weather near Husastadvik the night before; he hadn't gotten any sleep.

"And now you'll have to ride swiftly if you're going to reach Tunsberg by Saint Lavrans's Day. I doubt you'll have much peace or comfort there either. Is Master Paal with the king now?"

"Yes. Are you thinking of coming to Tunsberg?"

"If I did, it would have to be to ask the king whether he'd like to send filial greetings to his mother." Erlend laughed. "Or whether Bishop Audfinn wants to send word to Lady Ingebjørg."

"Many are surprised that you're heading for Denmark, just as the chieftains are gathering for a meeting in Tunsberg," said Sir Erling.

"Yes, isn't it odd how people are always surprised by me? Maybe I have a mind to see some of the folk customs I haven't seen since I was last in Denmark—maybe even participate in a tournament. And our kinswoman has invited me, after all. No one else in her lineage here in Norway wants anything to do with her now, except Munan and myself."

"Munan . . ." Erling frowned. Then he laughed and said, "Is there so much life left in the old boar? I'd almost thought he wouldn't have the energy to move his bulk about anymore. So Duke Knut is organizing a tournament, is he? And is Munan going to join in the jousting?"

"Yes—it's too bad, Erling, you can't come along to see it." And Erlend laughed as well. "I can see you fear that Lady Ingebjørg has invited us to this christening-ale so that we might brew a different kind of ale and invite her in. But you know very well that I'm too heavy-footed and too lighthearted to be used in making secret plans. And from Munan you've yanked out every tooth."

"Oh no, we're not afraid of secret plans from those quarters, either. Ingebjørg Haakonsdatter must have realized by now that she squandered all rights in her own country when she married Knut Porse. It would be unwise for her to set foot inside the door here after giving her hand to that man, when we don't want to see even his little finger within our boundaries."

"Yes, it was clever of you to separate the boy from his mother," said Erlend gloomily. "He's still only a child—and now all of us Norwegian men have reason to hold our heads up high when we think about the king whom we have sworn to protect."

"Be quiet!" said Erling Vidkunssøn in a low, dejected voice. "That's . . . surely that's not true."

But the other two could see from his face that he knew it was true. Although King Magnus Eirikssøn might still be a child, he had already been infected by a sin which was unseemly to mention among Christian men. A Swedish cleric, who had been assigned to guide his book learning while he was in Sweden, had led him astray in an unmentionable manner.

Erlend said, "People are whispering on every estate and in every house around us in the north that Christ Church burned because our king is unworthy to sit in Saint Olav's seat."

"In God's name, Erlend—I tell you it's not certain this is true!

And we must believe that the child, King Magnus, is innocent in God's eyes. He can surely redeem himself. And you say that *we* have separated him from his mother? I say that God punishes the mother who deserts her child the way Ingebjørg has deserted her son—and do not put your trust in such a woman, Erlend. Keep in mind that these are treacherous people you're now setting off to meet!"

"I think they've been admirably loyal toward each other. But you speak as if letters from Christ himself were floating down into the lap of your robe every day—that must be why you've decided that you dare to be so bold as to provoke a fight with the highest authorities of the Church."

"Now you must stop, Erlend. Talk about things that you understand, my boy, but otherwise keep quiet." Sir Erling got to his feet; they were both standing up now, angry and red in the face.

Erlend grimaced with disgust.

"If an animal has been mistreated, we kill it and toss the corpse into a waterfall."

"Erlend!" The regent gripped the edge of the table with both hands. "You have sons yourself . . ." he said softly. "How can you say such a thing? And you'd better watch your tongue, Erlend. Think before you speak in that place where you're now going. And think about it twenty times over before you do anything."

"If that's how you act, you who rule over the affairs of the kingdom, then it doesn't surprise me that everything has gone awry. But I don't think you need to be afraid," Erlend sneered. "I doubt that I'll do anything. But what a splendid thing it has become to live in this country. . . .

"Well, you have to set out early in the morning. And my father-in-law is tired."

The other two men remained sitting there, without speaking, after Erlend had bid them good night. He was going to sleep aboard his ship. Erling Vidkunssøn sat and turned his goblet around and around in his hand.

"Are you coughing?" he asked, just for something to say.

"Old men catch cold easily. We have so many ailments, dear sir, which you young men know nothing about," said Lavrans with a smile.

They sat in silence again. Until Erling Vidkunssøn said, as if to himself, "Yes, everyone thinks the same—that it doesn't bode well for this kingdom. Six years ago in Oslo, I thought it was clear that there was a firm desire to support the Crown—among the men who are born to this task by virtue of their lineage. I . . . was counting on that."

"I think back then your perception was correct, sir. But you yourself said that we're accustomed to rallying around our king. This time he's merely a child—and he spends half his time in another country."

"Yes. Sometimes I think . . . nothing is so bad that it's not good for something. In the past, when our kings frolicked around like stallions—then there were enough fine colts to choose from; our countrymen simply had to select the one who was the best fighter."

Lavrans gave a laugh. "Yes, well . . ."

"We spoke three years ago, Lavrans Lagmanssøn, when you returned from your pilgrimage to Skøvde and had paid a visit to your kinsmen in Götaland."

"I remember, sir, that you honored me by seeking me out."

"No, no, Lavrans, you need not be so formal." A little impatiently, Erling threw out his hands. "It was as I said," he continued gloomily. "There's no one here who can unite the nobles of this country. Whoever has the greatest hunger forces his way forward—there's still some food in the trough. But those who might attempt to win power and wealth in an honorable manner, as was done in the time of our fathers, are not the ones who come forward now."

"That seems to be true. But honor follows the banner of the chieftains."

"Then men must think that my banner carries with it little honor," said Erling dryly. "You have avoided everything that might have won you renown, Lavrans Lagmanssøn."

"I've done so ever since I became a married man, sir. And that was at a young age; my wife was sickly and had little tolerance for the company of others. And it looks as if our lineage will not continue to thrive here in Norway. My sons died young, and only one of my brother's sons has lived to be a man."

Lavrans regretted that he had come to speak of this matter. Erling Vidkunssøn had endured great sorrow of his own. His daughters were healthy children and had grown to adulthood, but he too

had only been allowed to keep a single son, and the boy was said
to be in poor health.

But Sir Erling merely said, "And you have no close kinsmen
from your mother's lineage, either, as I recall."

"No, no closer than the children of my grandfather's sister. Sigurd Lodinssøn had only two daughters, and they both died giving
birth to their first child—and my aunt took hers to the grave
with her."

They sat in silence again for a while.

"Men like Erlend," said the regent in a low voice. "They're the
most dangerous kind. Men who think a little farther than their
own interests, but not far enough. Don't you think Erlend is just
like an indolent youth?" He slid his wine goblet around on the
table with annoyance. "But he's intelligent, isn't he? And of good
family, and courageous? But he never wants to listen to any matter
long enough to understand it fully. And if he bothers to hear a
man out, he forgets the first part before the discussion comes to
an end."

Lavrans glanced over at the other man. Sir Erling had aged a
great deal since he had last seen him. He looked careworn and
weary; he seemed to have shrunk in his chair. He had fine, clear
features, but they were a little too small, and he had a pallid complexion, as he always had. Lavrans felt that this man—even
though he was a knight with integrity, who was wise and willing to
serve without deceit, never sparing himself—fell somewhat short
in every way as a leader. If he had been a head taller, he might have
won full support more easily.

Lavrans said quietly, "Sir Knut is also clever enough that he
would realize—if they're contemplating any kind of incursion
down there—that he wouldn't have much use for Erlend in any secret council."

"You're rather fond of this son-in-law of yours, aren't you,
Lavrans?" said the other man, almost crossly. "If truth be told,
you have no reason to love him."

Lavrans sat running his finger through a puddle of spilled wine
on the table. Sir Erling noticed that his rings were quite loose on
his fingers now.

"Do *you*?" Lavrans looked up with a little smile. "And yet I
think that you too are fond of him!"

"Well . . . God knows . . . But I swear to you, Lavrans, Sir Knut has plenty of things going through his mind right now. He's the father of a son who is the grandson of King Haakon."

"Even Erlend must realize that the child's father has much too broad a back for that poor young nobleman ever to get around it. And his mother has all the people of Norway against her because of this marriage."

A little while later Erling Vidkunssøn stood up and strapped on his sword. Lavrans had politely taken his guest's cape from the hook and was holding it in his hands, when he suddenly swayed and was about to collapse, but Sir Erling caught him in his arms. With difficulty he carried the man, who was heavy and tall, over to the bed. It wasn't a stroke, but Lavrans lay there with his lips pale blue, his limbs weak and limp. Sir Erling raced across the court-yard to wake up the hostel priest.

Lavrans felt quite embarrassed when he came to himself again. Yes, it was a weakness that occurred now and then, ever since an elk hunt two winters before, when he had gotten lost in a blizzard. That was evidently what it took for a man to learn that his body was no longer youthful, and he smiled apologetically.

Sir Erling waited until the monk had bled the ill man, although Lavrans begged him not to take the trouble, because he would have to leave so early in the morning.

The moon was high, shining above the mountains of the main-land; the water lay black below, but out on the fjord the light glinted like flecks of silver. Not a wisp came from the smoke-vent holes; the grass on the rooftops glittered like dew in the moonlight. Not a soul was on the one short street of the town as Sir Erling swiftly walked the few paces down to the king's fortress, where he was to sleep. He looked strangely fragile and small in the moon-light, with his black cape wrapped tightly around him, shivering slightly. A couple of weary servants, who had sat up waiting for him, tumbled out of the courtyard with a lantern. The regent took the lantern and sent his men off to bed; then he shivered a little again as he climbed the stairs to his chamber up in the loft room.

CHAPTER 7

Just after Saint Bartholomew's Day Kristin set off on the journey home in the company of a large entourage of children, servants, and possessions. Lavrans rode with her as far as Hjerdkinn.

They went out into the courtyard to talk, he and his daughter, on the morning when he was to head back south. Sunlight sparkled over the mountains; the marshes were already crimson, and the slopes were yellow like gold from the alpine birches. Up on the plateau, lakes alternately glittered and then darkened as shadows from the big, glossy, fair-weather clouds passed overhead. They billowed up incessantly, and then sank down between distant clefts and gaps amid all the gray-domed mountains and blue peaks, with patches of new snow and old snowdrifts, which encircled the view far into the distance. The small grayish-green fields of grain belonging to the travelers' hostel looked so strange in color against the brilliant autumn hues of the mountains.

The wind was blowing, sharp and brisk. Lavrans pulled up the hood of Kristin's cloak which had blown back around her shoulders, smoothing out the corners of her linen wimple with his fingertips.

"It seems to me your cheeks have grown so pale and thin back home on my manor," he said. "Haven't we taken good care of you, Kristin?"

"Yes, you have. That's not why . . ."

"And it's a wearisome journey for you with all the children," said her father.

"Yes, well . . . It's not because of those five that I have pale cheeks." She gave him a fleeting smile, and when her father cast a startled and inquiring glance at her, she nodded and smiled again.

Lavrans looked away, but after a moment he said, "If I understand rightly how matters stand, then perhaps it will be some time before you return to Gudbrandsdal?"

245

"Well, we won't let eight years pass this time," she said in the same tone of voice. Then she caught a glimpse of his face. "Father! Oh, Father!"

"Hush, hush, my daughter." Involuntarily he gripped her arm to stop her as she tried to throw her arms around him. "No, Kristin."

He took her hand firmly in his and set off walking beside her. They had come some distance away from the buildings and were now wandering along a small path through the yellow birch forest, paying no attention to where they were going. Lavrans jumped over a little creek cutting across the path, and then turned around to offer his daughter a helping hand.

She saw, even from that slight movement, that he was no longer agile or spry. She had noticed before but refused to acknowledge it. He no longer sprang in and out of the saddle as nimbly as he once had; he didn't race up the stairs or lift heavy things as easily as he had in the past. He carried his body more rigidly and carefully—as if he bore some slumbering pain within and was moving quietly so as not to arouse it. His blood pulsed visibly in the veins of his neck when he came home after riding his horse. Sometimes she noticed a swelling or puffiness under his eyes. She remembered one morning when she came into the main house, and he was lying on the bed, half-dressed, with his bare legs draped over the footboard; her mother was kneeling in front of him, rubbing his ankles.

"If you're going to grieve for every man who is felled by age, then you'll have much to cry about, child," Lavrans said in a calm and quiet voice. "You have big sons yourself now, Kristin. It shouldn't surprise you to see that your father will soon be an old man. Whenever we parted in my younger days, we didn't know any better back then than we do now, whether we're destined to meet again here on this earth. And I might live for a long time yet; it must be as God wills, Kristin."

"Are you ill, Father?" she asked in a toneless voice.

"Certain frailties always come with age," her father replied lightly.

"You're not old, Father. You're only fifty-two."

"My own father didn't live this long. Come and sit down here with me."

There was a sort of grass-covered shelf beneath the rock face which leaned out over the stream. Lavrans unfastened his cape, folded it up, and pulled his daughter down to sit beside him. The creek gurgled and trickled over the stones in front of them, rocking a willow branch that was lying in the water. Lavrans sat with his eyes fixed on the blue-and-white mountain far beyond the autumn-tinged plateau.

"You're cold, Father," said Kristin. "Take my cloak." She undid the clasp, and then he pulled a corner of the cloak around his shoulders, so it covered both of them. He slipped his arm around her waist.

"You must know, my Kristin, that it's an unwise person who weeps at another's passing. Christ will protect you better than I—no doubt you have heard this said. I put all my faith in God's mercy. It's not for long that friends are parted. Although at times it may seem so to you now, while you're young. But you have your children and your husband. When you reach my age, then you'll think it's been no time at all since you saw those of us who have departed, and you'll be surprised when you count the winters that have passed to see how many there have been. It seems to me now that it wasn't long ago that I was a boy myself—and yet it's been so many years since you were that little blonde maiden who followed me everywhere I went. You followed your father so lovingly. May God reward you, my Kristin, for all the joy you have given me."

"Yes, but if He should reward me as I rewarded you . . ." Then she sank to her knees in front of her father, took his wrists, and kissed his hands, hiding her face in them. "Oh, Father, my dear father. No sooner was I a grown maiden than I rewarded your love by causing you the most bitter sorrow."

"No, no, child. You mustn't weep like this." He pulled his hands away and then lifted her up to sit beside him as before.

"I've also had great joy from you during these years, Kristin. I've seen handsome and promising children growing up at your knee; you've become a capable and sensible wife. And I've seen that you've grown more and more accustomed to seeking help where it can best be found, whenever you're in some difficulty. Kristin, my most precious gold, do not weep so hard. You might harm the one you carry under your belt," he whispered. "Do not grieve so!"

But he could not console her. Then he took his daughter in his arms and lifted her onto his lap so he was holding her as he had when she was small. Her arms were clasped around his neck, and her face was pressed to his shoulder.

"There is one thing I have never told another mother's child except for my priest, but now I'll tell it to you. During the time of my youth—back home at Skog and in the early years when I was one of the king's retainers—I thought of entering a monastery as soon as I was old enough, although I hadn't made any kind of promise, not even in my own heart, and many things pulled me in the opposite direction. But whenever I was out fishing on Botn Fjord and heard the bells ringing from the brothers' cloister on Hovedø, then I would think that I was drawn most strongly there.

"When I was sixteen winters old, Father had a coat of mail made for me from Spanish steel plates covered in silver. Rikard, the Englishman in Oslo, made it. And I was given my sword—the one I've always used—and the armor for my horse. It wasn't as peaceful back then as it was during your childhood; we were at war with the Danes, so I knew I would soon have use for my splendid weapons. And I didn't want to lay them aside. I consoled myself with the thought that my father wouldn't want his eldest son to become a monk, and I had no wish to defy my parents.

"But I chose this world myself, and whenever things went against me, I tried to tell myself that it would be unmanly to complain about the fate I had chosen. For I've realized more and more with each year that I've lived: There is no worthier work for the person who has been graced with the ability to see even a small part of God's mercy than to serve Him and to keep vigil and to pray for those people whose sight is still clouded by the shadow of worldly matters. And yet I must tell you, my Kristin, that it would be hard for me to sacrifice, for the sake of God, that life which I have lived on my estates, with its care of temporal things and its worldly joys, with your mother at my side and with all of you children. So a man must learn to accept, when he produces offspring from his own body, that his heart will burn if he loses them or if the world goes against them. God, who gave them souls, is the one who owns them—not I."

Sobs shook Kristin's body; her father began rocking her in his arms as if she were a small child.

"There were many things I didn't understand when I was young. Father was fond of my brother Aasmund too, but not in the same way as he loved me. It was because of my mother, you see—he never forgot her, but he married Inga because that was what his father wanted. Now I wish I could still go to my stepmother here on earth and beg her to forgive me for not respecting her goodness."

"But you've often said, Father, that your stepmother never did much for you, either good or bad," said Kristin in between sobs.

"Yes, God help me, I didn't know any better. Now it seems to me a great thing that she didn't hate me and never spoke an unkind word to me. How would you like it, Kristin, to see your stepson favored above your own son, constantly and in everything?"

Kristin was somewhat calmer now. She lay with her face turned so that she could look out at the mountain meadow. It grew dark from an enormous gray-blue cloud passing in front of the sun; several yellow rays pierced through, and the water of the creek glinted sharply.

Then she broke into tears again.

"Oh, no—Father, my father. Will I never see you again in this life?"

"May God protect you, Kristin, my child, so that we might meet again on that day, all of us who were friends in this life . . . and every human soul. Christ and the Virgin Mary and Saint Olav and Saint Thomas will keep you safe all your days." He took her face in his hands and kissed her on the lips. "May God have mercy on you. May God grant you light in the light of this world and in the great light beyond."

Several hours later, as Lavrans Bjørgulfsøn rode away from Hjerdkinn, his daughter walked alongside his horse. His servant was already a good distance ahead, but Lavrans continued on slowly, step by step. It hurt him to see her tear-stained and despairing face. This was also the way she had sat the whole time inside the guesthouse, as he ate and talked with her children, bantering with them and taking them onto his lap, one after the other.

Lavrans said softly, "Do not grieve any more for whatever you might regret toward *me*, Kristin. But remember it when your children are grown and you don't think they behave toward you or

their father in a way you consider reasonable. And remember too
what I told you about my youth. You're loyal in your love for
them, that I know, but you're most stubborn when you love most,
and there is obstinacy in those boys of yours—that much I've
seen," he said with a little smile.

At last Lavrans said that she had to turn around and go back. "I
don't want you to walk alone any farther away from the buildings." They had reached a hollow between small hills, with birch
trees at the bottom and heaps of stones on the slopes.

Kristin threw herself against her father's foot in the stirrup. She
ran her fingers over his clothing and his hand and his saddle, and
along the neck and flank of his horse; she pressed her head here
and there, weeping and uttering such deep, pitiful moans that her
father thought his heart would break to see her in such terrible
sorrow.

He jumped down from his horse and took his daughter in his
arms, holding her tight for the last time. Again and again he made
the sign of the cross over her and gave her into the care of God
and the saints. Finally he said that now she would have to let
him go.

And so they parted. But after he had gone some distance,
Kristin saw that her father reined in his horse, and she realized
that he was weeping as he rode away from her.

She ran into the birch grove, raced through it, and began scrambling up the lichen-gold scree on the nearest hillside. But it was
rocky and difficult to climb, and the little hill was higher than she
thought. At last she reached the top, but by that time he had disappeared among the hills. She lay down on the moss and bear-
berries growing on the ridge, and there she stayed, sobbing, with
her face buried in her arms.

Lavrans Bjørgulfsøn arrived home at Jørundgaard late in the
evening. A feeling of warmth passed through him when he saw
that someone was still awake in the hearth room—there was a
faint flicker of firelight behind the tiny glass window facing the
gallery. It was in this building that he always felt most at home.

Ragnfrid was alone inside, sitting at the table with clothes to be
mended in front of her. A tallow candle in a brass candlestick
stood nearby. She got up at once, greeted him, put more wood on

the hearth, and then went to get food and drink. No, she had sent the maids off to bed long ago; they had had a hard day, but now enough barley bread had been baked to last until Christmas. Paal and Gunstein had gone off into the mountains to gather moss. While they were talking about moss . . . Would Lavrans like to have for his winter surcoat the cloth that was dyed with moss or the one that was heather green? Orm of Moar had come to Jørundgaard that morning, wanting to buy some leather rope. She had taken the ropes hanging in the front of the shed and said he could have them as a gift. Yes, Orm's daughter was a little better now; the injury to her leg had knit together nicely.

Lavrans answered her questions and nodded while he and his servant ate and drank. But he was quickly done with eating. He stood up, wiped his knife on the back of his thigh, and picked up a spool of thread that lay at Ragnfrid's place. The thread had been wound around a stick with a bird carved into both ends—one of them had a slightly broken tail. Lavrans smoothed out the rough part and whittled it down so the bird had a stump of a tail. Once, long ago, he had made many of these thread spools for his wife.

"Are you going to mend them yourself?" he asked, looking down at her sewing. It was a pair of his leather hose; Ragnfrid was patching the inner side of the thighs, where they were worn from the saddle. "That's hard work for your fingers, Ragnfrid."

"Hmm." His wife placed the pieces of the leather edge to edge and poked holes in them with an awl.

The servant bade them good night and left. The husband and wife were alone. Lavrans stood near the hearth, warming himself, with one foot up on the edge and his hand on the smoke-vent pole. Ragnfrid glanced over at him. Then she noticed that he wasn't wearing the little ring with the rubies—his mother's bridal ring. He saw that she had noticed.

"Yes, I gave it to Kristin," he said. "I always meant it to be hers, and I thought she might as well have it now."

Then one of them said to the other that they ought to go to bed. But Lavrans stayed where he was, and Ragnfrid sat and sewed. They exchanged a few words about Kristin's journey, about the work that had to be done on the farm, about Ramborg and about Simon. Then they mentioned again that they should probably go to bed, but neither of them moved.

Finally Lavrans took off the gold ring with the blue-and-white stone from his right hand and went over to his wife. Shy and embarrassed, he took her hand and put on the ring; he had to try several times before he found a finger it would fit. He put it on her middle finger, in front of her wedding ring.

"I want you to have this now," he said in a low voice, without looking at her.

Ragnfrid sat motionless, her cheeks blood red.

"Why are you doing this?" she whispered at last. "Do you think I begrudge our daughter her ring?"

Lavrans shook his head and gave a little smile. "I think you know why I'm doing this."

"You've said in the past that you wanted to have this ring in the grave with you," she said in the same tone of voice. "And no one but you was to wear it."

"And that's why you must never take it off, Ragnfrid. Promise me that. After you, I want no one else to wear it."

"Why are you doing this?" she repeated, holding her breath.

Her husband looked down into her face.

"This spring it was thirty-four years ago that we were married. I was an under-aged boy; during all of my manhood you have been at my side, whenever I suffered grief and whenever things went well. May God help me, I had such little understanding of how many troubles you had to bear in our life together. But now it seems to me that all of my days I felt it was good that you were here.

"I don't know whether you believed that I had more love for Kristin than for you. It's true that she was my greatest joy, and she caused me the greatest sorrow. But you were mother to them all. Now I think leaving you behind will hurt me the most, when I go.

"And that's why you must never give my ring to anyone else—not even to one of our daughters; tell them they must not take it from you.

"Perhaps you may think, wife, that you've had more sorrow than joy with me; things did go wrong for us in some ways. And yet I think we have been faithful friends. And this is what I have thought: that afterwards we will meet again in such a manner that all the wrongs will no longer separate us; and the friendship that we had, God will build even stronger."

Ragnfrid lifted her pale, furrowed face. Her big, sunken eyes burned as she looked up at her husband. He was still holding her hand; she looked at it, lying in his, slightly raised. The three rings gleamed next to each other: on the bottom her betrothal ring, next her wedding ring, and on top his ring.

It seemed so strange to her. She remembered when he put the first one on her finger; they were standing in front of the smoke-vent pole in the hall back home at Sundbu, their fathers with them. He was pink and white, his cheeks were round, hardly more than a child—a little bashful as he took a step forward from Sir Bjørgulf's side.

The second ring he had put on her finger in front of the church door in Gerdarud, in the name of the Trinity, under the hand of the priest.

With this last ring, she felt as if he were marrying her again. Now that she would soon sit beside his lifeless body, he wanted her to know that with this ring he was committing to her the strong and vital force that had lived in this dust and ashes.

Her heart felt as if it were breaking in her breast, bleeding and bleeding, young and fierce. From grief over the warm and ardent love which she had lost and still secretly mourned; from anguished joy over the pale, luminous love which drew her to the farthest boundaries of life on this earth. Through the great darkness that would come, she saw the gleam of another, gentler sun, and she sensed the fragrance of the herbs in the garden at world's end.

Lavrans set his wife's hand back in her lap and sat down on the bench a short distance away, with his back against the table and one arm resting along the top. He did not look at her, but stared into the hearth fire.

And yet her voice was quiet and calm when she once again spoke.

"I did not know, my husband, that you had such affection for me."

"I do," he replied, his voice equally calm.

They sat in silence for a while. Ragnfrid moved her sewing from her lap onto the bench beside her. After a time she said softly, "What I told you that night—have you forgotten that?"

"I doubt that any man on this earth could forget such words. And it's true that I myself have felt that things were no better between us after I heard them. But God knows, Ragnfrid, I tried so hard to conceal from you that I gave that matter so much thought."

"I didn't realize you thought so much about it."

He turned toward her abruptly and stared at his wife.

Then Ragnfrid said, "I am to blame that things grew worse between us, Lavrans. I thought that if you could be toward me exactly the same as before that night—then you must have cared even less for me than I thought. If you had been a stern husband toward me afterwards, if you had struck me even once when you were drunk—then I would have been better able to bear my sorrow and my remorse. But when you took it so lightly . . ."

"Did you think I took it lightly?"

The faint quaver in his voice made her wild with longing. She wanted to bury herself inside him, down in the depths of the emotions that could make his voice ripple with tension and strain.

She exclaimed in fury, "If only you had taken me in your arms even once, not because I was the lawful, Christian wife they had placed at your side, but as the wife you had yearned for and fought to win. Then you couldn't have behaved toward me as if those words had not been said."

Lavrans thought about what she had said. "No . . . then . . . I don't think I could have. No."

"If you had been as fond of your betrothed as Simon was of our Kristin . . ."

Lavrans didn't reply. After a moment, as if against his will, he said softly and fearfully, "Why did you mention *Simon?*"

"I suppose because I couldn't compare you to that other man," Ragnfrid said, confused and frightened herself although she tried to smile. "You and Erlend are too unlike each other."

Lavrans stood up, took a few steps, feeling uneasy. Then he said in an even quieter voice, "God will not forsake Simon."

"Have you never thought that God had forsaken you?" asked his wife.

"No."

"What did you think that night as we sat in the barn, when you found out at the very same moment that Kristin and I—the two people you held dearest and loved the most faithfully—we had both betrayed you as much as we possibly could?"

"I don't think I thought much about it," replied her husband.

"But later on," continued his wife, "when you kept thinking about it, as you say you did . . ."

Lavrans turned away from her. She saw a blush flood his sunburned neck.

"I thought about all the times I had betrayed Christ," he said in a low voice.

Ragnfrid stood up, hesitating a moment before she dared go over and place her hands on her husband's shoulders. When he put his arms around her, she pressed her forehead against his chest. He could feel her crying. Lavrans pulled her closer and rested his face against her hair.

"Now, Ragnfrid, we will go to bed," he said after a moment.

Together they walked over to the crucifix, knelt, and made the sign of the cross. Lavrans said the evening prayers, speaking the language of the Church in a low, clear voice, and his wife repeated the words after him.

Then they undressed. Ragnfrid lay down on the inner side of the bed; the headboard was now much lower because lately her husband had been plagued with dizziness. Lavrans shoved the bolt on the door closed, scraped ashes over the fire in the hearth, blew out the candle, and climbed in beside her. In the darkness they lay with their arms touching each other. After a moment they laced their fingers together.

Ragnfrid Ivarsdatter thought it seemed like a new wedding night, and a strange one. Happiness and sorrow flowed into each other, carrying her along on waves so powerful that she felt her soul beginning to loosen its roots in her body. Now the hand of death had touched her too—for the first time.

This was how it had to end—when it had begun as it did. She remembered the first time she saw her betrothed. At that time Lavrans was pleased with her—a little shy, but willing enough to have affection for his bride. Even the fact that the boy was so radiantly handsome had irritated her. His hair hung so thick and glossy and fair around his pink-and-white, downy face. Her heart burned with anguish at the thought of another man, who was not handsome nor young nor gentle like milk and blood; she was dying with longing to sink into his embrace and drive her knife into his throat. And the first time her betrothed tried to caress her . . .

They were sitting together on the steps of a loft back home, and he reached out to take one of her braids. She leaped to her feet, turned her back on him, white with anger, and left.

Oh, she remembered that nighttime journey, when she rode with Trond and Tordis through Jerndal to Dovre, to the woman who was skilled in sorcery. She had fallen to her knees, pulling off rings and bracelets and putting them on the floor in front of Fru Aashild; in vain she had begged for a remedy so her bridegroom might not have his will with her. She remembered the long journey with her father and kinsmen and bridesmaids and the entourage from home, down through the valley, out across the flat country-side, to the wedding at Skog. And she remembered the first night—and all the nights afterwards—when she received the clumsy caresses of the newly married boy and acted cold as stone, never concealing how little they pleased her.

No, God had not forsaken her. In His mercy, He had heard her cries for help when she called on Him, as she sank more and more into her misery—even when she called without believing she would be heard. It felt as if the black sea were rushing over her; now the waves lifted her toward a bliss so strange and so sweet that she knew it would carry her out of life.

"Talk to me, Lavrans," she implored him quietly. "I'm so tired."

Her husband whispered, "*Venite ad me, omnes qui laborate et onerati estis. Ego reficiam vos*[1]—the Lord has said."

He slipped one arm under her shoulder and pulled her close to his side. They lay there for a moment, cheek to cheek.

Then she said softly, "Now I have asked the Mother of God to answer my prayer that I need not live long after you, my husband."

His lips and his lashes brushed her cheek in the darkness like the wings of a butterfly.

"My Ragnfrid, my Ragnfrid."

CHAPTER 8

KRISTIN STAYED HOME at Husaby during the autumn and winter with no wish to go anywhere; she blamed this on the fact that she was unwell. But she was simply tired. She had never felt so tired before in all her life. She was tired of merriment and tired of sorrow, and most of all tired of brooding.

It would be better after she had this new child, she thought; and she felt such a fierce longing for it. It was the child that would save her. If it was a son and her father died before he was born, he would bear her father's name. And she thought about how dearly she would love this child and nurse him at her own breast. It had been such a long time since she had had an infant, and she wept with longing whenever she thought about holding a tiny child in her arms again.

She gathered her sons around her as she had in the past and tried to bring a little more discipline and order to their upbringing. She felt that in this way she was acting in accordance with her father's wishes, and it seemed to give her soul some peace. Sira Eiliv had now begun to teach Naakkve and Bjørgulf reading and Latin, and Kristin often sat in the parsonage when the children went there for lessons. But they weren't very eager pupils, and all the boys were unruly and wild except for Gaute, and so he continued to be his mother's lap-child, as Erlend called him.

Erlend had returned home from Denmark in high spirits around All Saints' Day. He had been received with the greatest honor by the duke and by his kinswoman, Lady Ingebjørg. They had thanked him heartily for his gifts of furs and silver; he had ridden in a jousting tournament and hunted stag and deer. And when they parted, Sir Knut had given him a coal-black Spanish stallion, while Lady Ingebjørg had sent kind greetings along with two silver greyhounds for his wife. Kristin thought these foreign dogs looked sly and treacherous, and she was afraid they would harm her children.

And people all around were talking about the Castilian horse. Erlend looked good on the back of the long-legged, elegantly built horse, but animals like that were not suited to this country, and only God knew how the stallion would manage in the mountains. In the meantime, wherever he went in his district, Erlend would buy the most splendid of black mares, and he now had a herd that was beautiful in appearance, at any rate. Erlend Nikulaussøn usually gave his horses refined, foreign names, such as Belkolor and Bajard, but he said that this stallion was so magnificent that it didn't need any further adornment, and he named it simply Soten.[1]

Erlend was greatly annoyed that his wife refused to accompany him anywhere. He couldn't see that she was ill; she neither swooned nor vomited this time, and it was not even visible that she was with child. And by constantly sitting indoors, brooding and worrying over his misdeeds, she had grown weary and pale. It was during the Christmas season that fierce quarrels erupted between them. But this time Erlend didn't come and apologize for his bad temper, as he had in the past. Until now, whenever they had disagreements, he had always believed that he was to blame. Kristin was good, she was always right; if he felt uncomfortable and bored at home, then it must be because it was his nature to grow weary of what was good and right if he had too much of it. But this summer he had noticed more than once that his father-in-law had sided with him and seemed to think Kristin was lacking in wifely gentleness and tolerance. It occurred to him that she was overly sensitive about petty matters and reluctant to forgive him for minor offenses which he had committed with no ill intent. He would always beg her forgiveness after taking time to reflect, and she would say that she forgave him. But afterwards he could see that it was simply stored away, not forgotten.

So Erlend spent much time away from home, and now he often took his daughter Margret along with him. The maiden's upbringing had always been a source of disagreement between him and his wife. Kristin had never said a word about it, but Erlend knew quite well what she, and others, thought. He had treated Margret in all respects as his lawful child, and whenever she accompanied her father and stepmother everyone received her as if she were. At Ramborg's wedding she had been one of the bridesmaids, wearing a golden wreath on her flowing hair. Many of the women didn't approve, but Lavrans had persuaded them, and Simon had also said that no one should voice any objection to Erlend or say a word about it to the maiden. The lovely child was not to blame for her unfortunate birth.

But Kristin knew that Erlend planned to marry Margret to a man of noble lineage. He thought that with his present position, he could succeed in arranging it, even though the maiden had been conceived in adultery and it would be difficult to gain for her a position that was firm and secure. It might have been possible if people had been convinced that Erlend was capable of preserving and increasing his power and wealth. But although he was well-liked and respected in many ways, no one truly believed that the prosperity at Husaby would last. So Kristin was afraid that it would be difficult for him to carry out his plans for Margret. Even though she was not particularly fond of Margret, Kristin felt sorry for the maiden and dreaded the day when the girl's arrogant spirit might be broken—if she had to settle for a match that was much poorer than what her father had taught her to expect, and for circumstances that were quite different from what she had grown up with.

Then, around Candlemas, three men came from Formo to Husaby; they had skied over the mountains to bring Erlend troubling news from Simon Andressøn. Simon wrote that their father-in-law was ill, and that he was not expected to live long. Lavrans wanted to ask Erlend to come to Sil, if he could; he wanted to speak to both of his sons-in-law about how everything should be arranged after his death.

Erlend cast surreptitious glances at his wife. She was heavy with child now; her face was thin and quite pale. And she looked so unhappy, as if she might cry at any moment. Now he regretted his behavior toward her that winter; her father's illness came as no surprise to her, and if she had been carrying such a secret sorrow, he would have to forgive her for being unreasonable.

Alone he would be able to travel to Sil quite swiftly, if he skied over the mountains. But if he had to take along his wife, it would be a slow and difficult journey. And then he would have to wait until after the weapons-*ting*[2] during Lent, and call meetings with his deputies first. There were also several meetings and *tings* that he would have to attend himself. Before they could leave, it would be dangerously close to the time when she would give birth—and Kristin couldn't stand the sea, even when she was feeling well. But he didn't dare think about her not being allowed to see her father before he died. That evening, after they had gone to bed, he asked his wife whether she dared make the journey.

He felt rewarded as she wept in his arms, grateful and full of remorse for her unkindness toward him that winter. Erlend grew gentle and tender, as he always did whenever he had caused a woman sorrow and then was forced to see her struggle with her grief before his eyes. And he gave in to Kristin's proposal with reasonable patience. He said at once that he wouldn't take the children along. But Kristin replied that Naakkve was old enough now, and it would be good for him to witness his grandfather's passing. Erlend said no. Then she thought that Ivar and Skule were too young to be left in the care of the servant women. No, said Erlend. And Lavrans had grown so fond of Gaute. No, said Erlend again. It would be difficult enough, as things now stood with her—for Ragnfrid to have a nursemaid on the estate while she was tending to her husband on his sickbed, and for them to bring the newborn home again. Either Kristin would have to leave the child with foster parents on one of Lavrans's farms, or she would have to stay at Jørundgaard until summer; but he would have to travel home before then. He went over all the plans, again and again, but he tried to make his voice calm and convincing.

Then it occurred to him that he ought to bring a few things from Nidaros that his mother-in-law might need for the funeral feast: wine and wax, wheat flour and Paradise grains and the like. But at last they made their departure, reaching Jørundgaard on the day before Saint Gertrud's Day.

But this homecoming was much different for Kristin than she had imagined.

She had to be grateful that she was given the chance to see her father again. When she thought about his joy at her arrival and how he had thanked Erlend for bringing her, then she was happy. But this time she felt shut out from so many things, and it was a painful feeling.

It was less than a month before she would give birth, and Lavrans forbade her from lifting a hand to tend to him. She wasn't allowed to keep watch over him at night with the others, and Ragnfrid wouldn't hear of her offering the slightest help in spite of all the work to be done. She sat with her father during the day, but they were seldom alone together. Almost daily, guests would come to the manor; friends who wanted to see Lavrans Bjørgulfsøn one last time before he died. This pleased her father, although it made him quite weary. He would talk in a merry and hearty voice to everyone—women and men, poor and rich, young and old—thanking them for their friendship and asking for their prayers of intercession for his soul, and hoping that God might allow them to meet on the day of rejoicing. At night, when only his close family was with him, Kristin would lie in bed in the high loft, staring into the darkness, unable to sleep because she was thinking about her father's passing and about the impetuousness and wickedness of her own heart.

The end was coming quickly for Lavrans. He had held on to his strength until Ramborg gave birth to her child and Ragnfrid no longer needed to be at Formo so often. He had also had his servants take him over there one day so he could see his daughter and granddaughter. The little maiden had been christened Ulvhild. But then he took to his bed, and it was unlikely he would ever get up again.

Lavrans lay in the hall of the high loft. They had made up a kind of bed for him on the high-seat bench, for he couldn't bear to have his head raised; then he would grow dizzy at once and suffer fainting spells and heart spasms. They didn't dare bleed him anymore; they had done it so often during the fall and winter that he was now quite lacking in blood, and he had little desire for food or drink.

The handsome features of his face were now sharp, and the tan had faded from his once-fresh complexion; it was sallow like bone, and bloodless and pale around his lips and eyes. The thick blond hair with streaks of white was now untrimmed, lying withered and limp against the blue-patterned expanse of the pillow. But what had changed him most was the rough, gray beard now covering the lower half of his face and growing on his long, broad neck, where the sinews stood out like thick cords. Lavrans had always been meticulous about shaving before every holy day. His body was so gaunt that it was little more than a skeleton. But he said he felt fine as long as he lay flat and didn't move. And he was always cheerful and happy.

They slaughtered and brewed and baked for the funeral feast; they took out the bedclothes and mended them. Everything that could be done ahead of time was done now, so that there would be quiet when the last struggle came. It cheered Lavrans considerably to hear about these preparations. His last banquet would be far from the poorest to be held at Jørundgaard; in an honorable and worthy manner he was to take leave of his guardianship of the estate and his household. One day he wanted to have a look at the two cows that would be included in the funeral procession, to be given to Sira Eirik and Sira Solmund, and so they were led into the house. They had been fed extra fodder all winter long and were as splendid and fat as cows in the mountain pastures around Saint Olav's Day, even though the valley was now in the midst of the spring shortages. He laughed the hardest every time one of the cows relieved itself on the floor.

But he was afraid his wife was going to wear herself out. Kristin had considered herself a diligent housewife, and that was her reputation back home in Skaun, but she now thought that compared to her mother she was completely incompetent. No one understood how Ragnfrid managed to accomplish everything she did—and yet she never seemed to be absent for very long from her husband's side; she also helped to keep watch at night.

"Don't think of me, husband," she would say, putting her hand in his. "After you're gone, you know that I'll take a rest from all these toils."

Many years before, Lavrans Bjørgulfsøn had purchased his resting place at the friars' monastery in Hamar, and Ragnfrid Ivarsdatter would accompany his body there and then stay on. She would live on a corrody in a manor owned by the monks in town. But first the coffin would be carried to the church here at home, with splendid gifts for the church and the priests; Lavrans's stallion would follow behind with his armor and weapons, and Erlend would then redeem them by paying forty-five marks of silver. One of his sons would be given the armor, preferably the child Kristin now carried, if it was a son. Perhaps there would be another Lavrans at Jørundgaard sometime in the future, said the ill man with a smile. On the journey south through Gudbrandsdal, the coffin would be carried into several more churches and stay there overnight; these would be remembered in Lavrans's testament with gifts of money and candles.

One day Simon mentioned that his father-in-law had bedsores, and he helped Ragnfrid to lift the sick man and tend to him.

Kristin was in despair over her jealous heart. She could hardly bear to see her parents on such familiar terms with Simon Andressøn. He felt at home at Jørundgaard in a way that Erlend never had. Almost every day his huge, sorrel-colored horse would be tied to the courtyard fence, and Simon would be sitting inside with Lavrans, wearing his hat and cape. He wasn't intending to stay long. But a short time later he would appear in the doorway and yell to the servants to put his horse in the stable after all. He was acquainted with all of her father's business affairs; he would get out the letter box and take out deeds and documents. He took care of chores for Ragnfrid, and he talked to the overseer about the management of the farm. Kristin thought to herself that her greatest desire had been for her father to be fond of Erlend, but the first time Lavrans had taken his side against her, she had responded at once in the worst possible manner.

Simon Andressøn was deeply grieved that he would soon be parted from his wife's father. But he felt such joy at the birth of his little daughter. Lavrans and Ragnfrid spoke often of little Ulvhild, and Simon could answer all their questions about the child's welfare and progress. And here too Kristin felt jealousy sting her heart—Erlend had never taken that kind of interest in their children. At the same time, it seemed to her a bit laughable when this man with the heavy, reddish-brown face who was no longer young would sit and talk so knowledgeably about an infant's stomachaches and appetite.

One day Simon brought a sleigh to take her south to see her sister and niece.

He had rebuilt the old, dark hearth house, where the women of Formo had gone for hundreds of years whenever they were going to give birth. The hearth had been thrown out and replaced with a stone fireplace, with a finely carved bed placed snugly against one side. On the opposite wall hung a beautiful carved image of the Mother of God, so that whoever lay in the bed could see it. Flagstones had been laid down, and a glass pane was put in the window; there were lovely, small pieces of furniture and new benches. Simon wanted Ramborg to have this house as her women's room. Here she could keep her things and invite other women in; and whenever there were banquets at the manor, the women could retire to this house if they grew uneasy when the men became overwhelmed by drink late in the evening.

Ramborg was lying in bed, in honor of her guest. She had adorned herself with a silk wimple and a red gown trimmed across the breast with white fur. She had silk-covered pillows behind her back and a flowered, velvet coverlet on top of the bedclothes. In front of the bed stood Ulvhild Simonsdatter's cradle. It was the old Swedish cradle that Ramborg Sunesdatter had brought to Norway, the same one in which Kristin's father and grandfather, and she herself and all her siblings had slept. According to custom, she, as the eldest daughter, should have had the cradle as part of her dowry, but it had never been mentioned at the time she was married. She thought that her parents had purposely forgotten about the cradle. Didn't they think the children she and Erlend would have were worthy to sleep in it?

After that, she refused to go back to Formo, saying that she didn't have the strength.

And Kristin did feel ill, but this was from sorrow and her anguished soul. She couldn't hide from herself that the longer she stayed at home, the more painful it felt. That was just her nature: it hurt her to see that now, as her father approached his death, it was his wife who was closest to him.

She had always heard people praise her parents' life together as an exemplary marriage, beautiful and noble, with harmony, loyalty, and good will. But she had felt, without thinking too closely about it, that there was something that kept them apart—some indefinable shadow that made their life at home subdued, even though it was calm and pleasant. Now there was no longer any shadow between her parents. They talked to each other calmly and quietly, mostly about small, everyday matters; but Kristin sensed there was something new in their eyes and in the tone of their voices. She could see that her father missed his wife whenever she was somewhere else. If he managed to convince her to take a rest, he would lie in bed, fidgeting and waiting; when Ragnfrid came back, it was as if she brought peace and joy to the ill man. One day Kristin heard them talking about their dead children, and yet they looked happy. When Sira Eirik came over to read to Lavrans, Ragnfrid would always sit with them. Then he would take his wife's hand and lie there, playing with her fingers and twisting her rings around.

Kristin knew that her father loved her no less than before. But she had never noticed until now that he loved her mother. And she could see the difference between the love of a husband for the wife he had lived with all his life, during good days and bad—and his love for the child who had shared only his joys and had received his greatest tenderness. And she wept and prayed to God and Saint Olav for help—for she remembered that tearful, tender farewell with her father on the mountain in the autumn, but surely it couldn't be true that she now wished it had been the last.

On Summer Day[3] Kristin gave birth to her sixth son. Five days later she was already out of bed, and she went over to the main house to sit with her father. Lavrans was not pleased by this; it had never been the custom on his estate for a woman who had recently given birth to go outdoors under open sky until the first time she went to church. She must at least agree not to cross the courtyard unless the sun was up. Ragnfrid listened as Lavrans talked about this.

"I was just thinking, husband," she said, "that your women have never been very obedient; we've usually done whatever we wanted to do."

"And you've never realized that before?" asked her husband, laughing. "Well, your brother Trond isn't to blame, at any rate. Don't you remember that he used to call me spineless because I always let all of you have your way?"

When the next mass was celebrated, Ramborg went to church for the first time after giving birth, and afterwards she paid her first visit to Jørundgaard. Helga Rolvsdatter came with her; she was also a married woman now. And Haavard Trondssøn of Sundbu had come to see Lavrans, too. These three young people were all the same age, and for three years they had lived together like siblings at Jørundgaard. The other two had looked up to Haavard, and he had been the leader in all their games because he was a boy. But now the two young wives with the white wimples made him feel quite clearly that they were experienced women with husbands and children and households to manage, while he was merely an immature and foolish child. Lavrans found this greatly amusing.

"Just wait until you have a wife of your own, Haavard, my foster son. Then you will truly be told how little you know," he said, and all the men in the room laughed and agreed.

Sira Eirik came daily to visit the dying man. The old parish priest's eyesight was now failing, but he could still manage to read just as easily the story of Creation in Norwegian and the gospels and psalms in Latin, because he knew those books so well. But several years earlier, down in Saastad, Lavrans had acquired a thick volume, and it was passages from this book that he wanted to hear. Sira Eirik couldn't read it because of his bad eyes, so Lavrans asked Kristin to try to read from the book. And after she grew accustomed to it, she managed to read beautifully and well. It was a great joy for her that now there was something she could do for her father.

The book contained what seemed to be dialogues between Fear and Courage, between Faith and Doubt, Body and Soul. There were also stories of saints and many accounts of men who, while still alive, were swept away in spirit and who witnessed the torments of the abyss, the trials of fiery purgatory, and the salvation of Heaven. Lavrans now spoke often of the purgatory fire, which he expected to enter soon, but he showed no sign of fear. He hoped for great solace from the prayers of intercession offered by his friends and the priests; and he consoled himself that Saint Olav and Saint Thomas would give him strength for the last trial, as he felt they had given him strength here in life. He had always heard that the person who firmly believed would never for a moment lose sight of the salvation toward which the soul was moving, through the fiery blaze. Kristin thought her father seemed to be looking forward to it, as if it were a test of manhood. She vaguely remembered from her childhood the time when the king's retainers from the valley set off on a campaign against Duke Eirik.[4] Now she thought that her father seemed eager for his death, in the same way he had been eager for battle and adventure back then.

One day she said that she thought her father had endured so

many trials in this life that surely he would be spared from the worst of them in the next. Lavrans replied that it didn't seem that way to him; he had been a rich man, he was descended from a splendid lineage, and he had won friends and prosperity in the world. "My greatest sorrows were that I never saw my mother's face, and that I lost my children—but soon they will no longer be sorrows. And the same is true of other things that have grieved me in my life—they are no longer sorrows."

Ragnfrid was often in the room while Kristin read. Strangers were also present, and now Erlend wanted to sit and listen too. Everyone found joy in what she read, but Kristin grew dejected and distressed. She thought about her own heart, which fully understood what was right and wrong, and yet it had always yearned for what was not righteous. And she was afraid for her little child; she could hardly sleep at night for fear that he would die unbaptized. Two women had to keep constant vigil over her, and yet she was still afraid to fall asleep. Her other children had all been baptized before they were three days old, but they had decided to wait this time, because the boy was big and strong, and they wanted to name him after Lavrans. But in the valley people strictly abided by the custom that children not be named for anyone who was still alive.

One day when Kristin was sitting with her father and holding the child on her lap, Lavrans asked her to unwrap the swaddling clothes. He had still not seen more than the infant's face. She did as he asked and then placed the child in her father's arms. Lavrans stroked the small, rounded chest and took one of the tiny, plump hands in his own.

"It seems strange, kinsman, that one day you will wear my coat of mail. Right now you wouldn't fill up more space than a worm in a hollow nutshell; and this hand will have to grow big before it can grip the hilt of my sword. Looking at a lad like this, it almost seems God's will that we not bear arms. But you won't have to grow very old, my boy, before you long to take them up. There are so few men born of women who have such a love for God that they would forswear the right to carry weapons. I did not have it."

He lay quietly, looking at the infant.

"You carry your children under a loving heart, my Kristin. The boy is fat and big, but you're pale and thin as a reed; your mother said it was always that way after you gave birth. Ramborg's daughter is small and thin, but Ramborg is blossoming like a rose," he said, laughing.

"And yet it seems strange to me that she doesn't want to nurse the child herself," said Kristin.

"Simon is also against it. He says he wouldn't reward her for the gift by wearing her out in that way. You must remember that Ramborg was not even sixteen, and she had barely grown out of her own childhood shoes when her daughter was born. And she has never known a moment of ill health before. It's not so strange that she would have little patience. You were a grown woman when you were married, my Kristin."

Suddenly Kristin was overcome by violent sobs; she hardly knew what she was crying about. But it was true: She had loved her children from the first moment she held them in her womb; she had loved them even as they had tormented her with anguish, weighing her down and spoiling her looks. She had loved their small faces from the first moment she saw them, and loved them every single hour as they grew and changed, becoming young men. But no one had loved them as she had or rejoiced along with her. It was not in Erlend's nature. He was fond of them, of course, but he had always thought that Naakkve came too early, and that each son afterwards was one too many. She recalled what she had thought about the fruit of sin during the first winter she lived at Husaby; she realized she had tasted its bitterness, although not as much as she had feared. Things had gone wrong between her and Erlend back then and apparently could never be rectified.

Kristin hadn't been close to her mother. Her sisters were mere children when she was already a grown maiden, and she had never had companions to play with. She was brought up among men; she was able to be gentle and soft because there had always been men around to hold up protective and shielding hands between her and everything else in the world. Now it seemed reasonable to her that she gave birth only to sons—boys to nurse with her blood and at her breast, to love and protect and care for until they were old enough to join the ranks of men. She remembered that she had heard of a queen who was called the Mother of Boys. She must have had a wall of watchful men around her when she was a child.

"What is it now, Kristin?" asked her father quietly after a while.

She couldn't tell him any of this; when she stopped crying enough to talk, she said, "Shouldn't I grieve, Father, when you are lying here . . . ?"

Finally, when Lavrans pressed her, she told him of her fears for the unbaptized child. Then he at once ordered the boy to be taken to church the next time mass was celebrated; he said he didn't think it would cause his death any sooner than God willed it.

"And besides, I've been lying here long enough," he said with a laugh. "Wretched deeds accompany our arrival and our departure, Kristin. In sickness we are born and in sickness we die, except for those who die in battle. That seemed to me the best kind of death when I was young: to be killed on the battlefield. But a sinful man has need of a sickbed, and yet I don't think my soul will be any better healed if I lie here longer."

And so the boy was baptized on the following Sunday and was given his grandfather's name. Kristin and Erlend were bitterly criticized for this in the outlying villages. Lavrans Bjørgulfsøn told everyone who came to visit that it was done on his orders; he refused to have a heathen in his house when death came to the door.

Lavrans now began to worry that his death would come in the middle of the spring farm work, which would be a great hardship for many people who wanted to honor him by escorting his funeral procession. But two weeks after the child was baptized, Erlend came to Kristin in the old weaving room where she had been sleeping since giving birth. It was late in the morning, past breakfast time, but she was still in bed because the boy had been restless. Erlend was deeply distressed, but he said in a calm and loving voice that now she must get up and go to her father. Lavrans had suffered terrible convulsions and heart spasms at daybreak, and since then he lay drained of all strength. Sira Eirik was with him now, and had just heard his confession.

It was the fifth day after the Feast of Saint Halvard. It was raining lightly but steadily. When Kristin went out into the courtyard, she noticed in the gentle southern wind the earthy smell of newly plowed and manured fields. The countryside was brown in the spring rain, the sky was pale blue between the high mountains, and the mist was drifting by, halfway up the slopes. The ringing of little bells came from the groves of trees along the swollen gray river; herds of goats had been let out, and they were nibbling at the bud-covered branches. This was the kind of weather that had always filled her father's heart with joy. The cold of winter was over for both people and livestock, the animals were finally released from their dark, narrow stalls and scanty fodder.

Kristin saw at once from her father's face that death was now very near. The skin around his nostrils was snowy white, but bluish under his eyes and at his lips; his hair had separated into sweaty strings lying on his broad, damp forehead. But he had his full wits about him and spoke clearly, although slowly and in a weak voice.

The servants approached the bed, one by one, and Lavrans gave his hand to each of them, thanking them for their service, telling them to live well and asking for forgiveness if he had ever offended them in any way; and he asked them to remember him with a prayer for his soul. Then he said goodbye to his kinsmen. He told his daughters to bend down so he could kiss them, and he asked God and all the saints to bless them. They wept bitterly, both of them; and young Ramborg threw herself into her sister's arms. Holding on to each other, Lavrans's two daughters went back to their place at the foot of their father's bed, and the younger one continued to weep on Kristin's breast.

Erlend's face quivered and the tears ran down his face when he lifted Lavrans's hand to kiss it, as he quietly asked his father-in-law to forgive him for the sorrows he had caused him over the years. Lavrans said he forgave him with all his heart, and he prayed that God might be with him all his days. There was a strange, pale light in Erlend's handsome face when he silently moved away to stand at his wife's side, hand in hand with her.

Simon Darre did not weep, but he knelt down as he took his father-in-law's hand to kiss it, and he held on to it tightly as he stayed on his knees a moment longer. "Your hand feels warm and good, son-in-law," said Lavrans with a faint smile. Ramborg turned to her husband when he went to her, and Simon put his arm around her thin, girlish shoulders.

Last of all, Lavrans said goodbye to his wife. They whispered a few words to each other that no one else could hear, and exchanged a kiss in everyone's presence, as was now proper when death was in the room. Then Ragnfrid knelt in front of her husband's bed, with her face turned toward him; she was pale, silent, and calm.

Sira Eirik stayed with them after he had anointed the dying man with oil and given him the viaticum. He sat near the headboard and prayed; Ragnfrid was now sitting on the bed. Several hours passed. Lavrans lay with his eyes half-closed. Now and then he would move his head restlessly on the pillow and pick at the covers with his hands, breathing heavily and groaning from time to time. They thought he had lost his voice, but there was no death struggle.

Dusk came early, and the priest lit a candle. Everyone sat quietly, watching the dying man and listening to the dripping and trickling of the rain outside the house. Then the sick man grew agitated, his body trembled, his face turned blue, and he seemed to be fighting for breath. Sira Eirik put his arm under Lavrans's shoulders and lifted him into a sitting position as he supported his head against his chest and held up the cross before his face.

Lavrans opened his eyes, fixed his gaze on the crucifix in the priest's hand, and said softly, but so clearly that almost everyone in the room could hear him:

"*Exsurrexi, et adhuc sum tecum.*"[5]

Several more tremors passed over his body, and his hands fumbled with the coverlet. Sira Eirik continued to hold him against his chest for a moment. Then he gently laid his friend's body down on the bed, kissing his forehead and smoothing back his hair, before he pressed his eyelids and nostrils closed; then he stood up and began to say a prayer.

Kristin was allowed to join the vigil and keep watch over the body that night. They had laid Lavrans out on his bier in the high loft, since that was the biggest room and they expected many people to come to the death chamber.

Her father seemed to her inexpressibly beautiful as he lay in the glow of the candles, with his pale, golden face uncovered. They had folded down the cloth that hid his face so that it wouldn't become soiled by the many people who came to view the body. Sira Eirik and the parish priest from Kvam were singing over him; the latter had arrived that evening to say his last farewell to Lavrans, but he had come too late.

By the following day guests already began riding into the courtyard, and then, for the sake of propriety, Kristin had to take to her bed since she had not yet been to church. Now it was her turn to have her bed adorned with silk coverlets and the finest pillows in the house. The cradle from Formo was borrowed, and there lay the young Lavrans; all day long people came in to see her and the child.

She heard that her father's body continued to look beautiful—it had merely yellowed a bit. And no one had ever seen so many candles brought to a dead man's bier.

On the fifth day the funeral feast began, and it was exceptionally grand in every way. There were more than a hundred strange horses at the manor and at Laugarbru; even Formo housed some of the guests. On the seventh day the heirs divided up the estate, amicably and with friendship; Lavrans himself had made all the arrangements before his death, and everyone carefully abided by his wishes.

The next day the body, which now lay in Olav's Church, was to begin the journey to Hamar.

The evening before—or rather, late that night—Ragnfrid came into the hearth room where her daughter lay in bed with her child. Ragnfrid was very tired, but her face was calm and clear. She asked her serving women to leave.

"All the houses are full, but I'm sure you can find a corner to sleep in. I have a mind to sit with my daughter myself on this last night that I'll spend on my estate."

She took the child from Kristin's arms and carried him over to the hearth to get him ready for the night.

"It must be strange for you, Mother, to leave this manor where you've lived with my father all these years," said Kristin. "I don't see how you can stand to do it."

"I could stand it much less to stay here," replied Ragnfrid, rocking little Lavrans in her arms, "and not see your father going about among the buildings.

"I've never told you how we happened to move to this valley and ended up living here," she continued after a moment. "When

word came that Ivar, my father, was expected to breathe his last, I
was unable to travel; Lavrans had to go north alone. I remember
the weather was so beautiful on the evening he left—back then he
liked to ride late, when it was cool, and so he set off for Oslo in
the evening. It was just before Midsummer. I followed him out to
the place where the road from the manor crosses the church
road—do you remember the spot where there are several big flat
rocks and barren fields all around? The worst land at Skog, and always arid; but that year the grain stood high in the furrows, and
we talked about that. Lavrans was on foot, leading his horse, and
I was holding you by the hand. You were four winters old.

"When we reached the crossroads, I wanted you to run back to
the farm buildings. You didn't want to, but then your father told
you to see if you could find five white stones and lay them out in a
cross in the creek below the spring—that would protect him from
the trolls of Mjørsa Forest when he sailed past. Then you set off
running."

"Is that something people believe?" asked Kristin.

"I've never heard of it, either before or since. I think your father
made it up right then. Don't you remember how he could think up
so many things when he was playing with you?"

"Yes. I remember."

"I walked with him through the woods, all the way to the
dwarf stone. He told me to turn around, and then he accompanied
me back to the crossroads. He laughed and said I should know he
couldn't very well allow me to walk alone through the forest, especially after the sun was down. As we stood there at the crossroads, I put my arms around his neck. I was so sad that I couldn't
travel home with him. I had never felt comfortable at Skog, and I
was always longing to go north to Gudbrandsdal. Lavrans tried to
console me, and at last he said, 'When I return and you're holding
my son in your arms, you can ask me for whatever you wish, and
if it's within my power to give it to you, then you will not have
asked in vain.' And I replied that I would ask that we might move
up here and live on my ancestral estate. Your father wasn't
pleased, and he said, 'Couldn't you have thought of something bigger to ask for?' He laughed a little, and I thought this was something he would never agree to, which seemed to me only

reasonable. But as you know, Sigurd, your youngest brother, lived less than an hour. Halvdan baptized him, and after that the child died.

"Your father came home early one morning. The evening before, he had asked in Oslo how things stood at home, and then he set off for Skog at once. I was still keeping to my bed; I was so full of grief that I didn't have the strength to get up, and I thought I would prefer never to get up again. God forgive me—when they brought you in to me, I turned to the wall and refused to look at you, my poor little child. But then Lavrans said, as he sat on the edge of my bed, still wearing his cape and sword, that now we would try to see if things might be better for us living here at Jørundgaard, and that's how we came to move from Skog. But now you can see why I don't want to live here any longer, now that Lavrans is gone."

Ragnfrid brought the child and placed him on his mother's breast. She took the silk coverlet, which had been spread over Kristin's bed during the day, folded it up, and laid it aside. Then she stood there for a moment, looking down at her daughter and touching the thick, dark-blonde braids which lay between her white breasts.

"Your father asked me often whether your hair was still thick and beautiful. It was such a joy to him that you didn't lose your looks from giving birth to so many children. And you made him so happy during the last few years because you had become such a capable wife and looked so healthy and lovely with all your fair young sons around you."

Kristin tried to swallow back her tears.

"He often told me, Mother, that you were the best wife—he told me to tell you that." She paused, embarrassed, and Ragnfrid laughed softly.

"Lavrans should have known that he didn't need anyone else to tell me of his good will toward me." She stroked the child's head and her daughter's hand which was holding the infant. "But perhaps he wanted . . . It's not true, my Kristin, that I have ever envied your father's love for you. It's right and proper that you should have loved him more than you loved me. You were such a sweet and lovely little maiden—I could hardly believe that God would let me keep you. But I always thought more about what I had lost than what I still had."

Ragnfrid sat down on the edge of the bed.

"They had other customs at Skog than I was used to back home. I can't remember that my father ever kissed me. He kissed my mother when she lay on her bier. Mother would kiss Gudrun during the mass, because she stood next to her, and then my sister would kiss me; otherwise that was not something we ever did.

"At Skog it was the custom that when we came home from church, after taking the *corpus domini,* and we got down from our horses in the courtyard, then Sir Bjørgulf would kiss his sons and me on the cheek, while we kissed his hand. Then all the married couples would kiss each other, and we would shake hands with all the servants who had been to the church service and ask that everyone might benefit from the sacrament. They did that often, Lavrans and Aasmund; they would kiss their father on the hand when he gave them gifts and the like. Whenever he or Inga came into the room, the sons would always get to their feet and stand there until asked to sit down. At first these seemed to me foolish and foreign ways.

"Later, during the years I lived with your father when we lost our sons, and all those years when we endured such great anguish and sorrow over our Ulvhild—then it seemed good that Lavrans had been brought up as he had, with gentler and more loving ways."

After a moment Kristin murmured, "So Father never saw Sigurd?"

"No," replied Ragnfrid, her voice equally quiet. "Nor did I see him while he was alive."

Kristin lay in silence; then she said, "And yet, Mother, it seems to me that there has been much good in your life."

The tears began to stream down Ragnfrid Ivarsdatter's pale face.

"God help me, yes. It seems that way to me, too."

A little later she carefully picked up the infant, who had fallen asleep at his mother's breast, and placed him in the cradle. She fastened Kristin's shift with the little silver brooch, caressed her daughter's cheek, and told her to go to sleep now.

Kristin put out her hand. "Mother . . ." she implored.

Ragnfrid bent down, gathered her daughter into her arms, and kissed her many times. She hadn't done that in all the years since Ulvhild died.

It was the most beautiful springtime weather on the following day, as Kristin stood behind the corner of the main house looking out toward the slopes beyond the river. There was a verdant smell in the air, the singing of creeks released everywhere, and a green sheen over all the groves and meadows. At the spot where the road went along the mountainside above Laugarbru, a blanket of winter rye shimmered fresh and bright. Jon had burned off the saplings there the year before and planted rye on the cleared land.

When the funeral procession reached that spot, she would be able to see it best.

And then the procession emerged from beneath the scree, across from the fresh new acres of rye.

She could see all the priests riding on ahead, and there were also vergers among the first group, carrying the crosses and tapers. She couldn't see the flames in the bright sunlight, but the candles looked like slender white streaks. Two horses followed, carrying her father's coffin on a litter between them, and then she recognized Erlend on the black horse, her mother, Simon and Ramborg, and many of her kinsmen and friends in the long procession.

For a moment she could faintly hear the singing of the priests above the roar of the Laag, but then the tones of the hymn died away in the rush of the river and the steady trickling of the springtime streams on the slopes. Kristin stood there, gazing off into the distance, long after the last packhorse with the traveling bags had disappeared into the woods.

PART III

ERLEND NIKULAUSSØN

CHAPTER 1

RAGNFRID IVARSDATTER LIVED less than two years after her husband's death; she died early in the winter of 1332. It's a long way from Hamar to Skaun, so they didn't hear of her death at Husaby until she had already been in the ground more than a month. But Simon Andressøn came to Husaby during Whitsuntide; there were a few things that needed to be agreed upon among kinsmen about Ragnfrid's estate. Kristin Lavransdatter now owned Jørundgaard, and it was decided that Simon would oversee her property and collect payments from her tenants. He had managed his mother-in-law's properties in the valley while she lived in Hamar.

Just then Erlend was having a great deal of trouble and vexation with several matters that had occurred in his district. During the previous autumn, Huntjov, the farmer at Forbregd in Updal, had killed his neighbor because the man had called his wife a sorceress. The villagers bound the murderer and brought him to the sheriff; Erlend put him in custody in one of his lofts. But when the cold grew worse that winter, he allowed the man to move freely among his servant men. Huntjov had been one of Erlend's crew members on *Margygren* on the voyage north, and at that time he had displayed great courage. When Erlend submitted his report regarding Huntjov's case and asked that he be allowed to remain in the country,[1] he also presented the man in the most favorable light. When Ulf Haldorssøn offered a guarantee that Huntjov would appear at the proper time for the *ting* at Orkedal, Erlend permitted the farmer to go home for the Christmas holy days. But then Huntjov and his wife went to visit the innkeeper in Drivdal who was their kinsman, and on the way there, they disappeared. Erlend thought they had perished in the terrible storm that had raged at the time, but many people said they had fled; now the sheriff's men could go whistling after them. And then new charges were brought against the man who had vanished. It was said that several years earlier, Huntjov had killed a man in the mountains and buried the body under a pile of rocks—a man whom Huntjov claimed had wounded his mare in the flank. And it was revealed that his wife had indeed practiced witchcraft.

Then the priest of Updal and the archbishop's envoy set about investigating these rumors of sorcery. And this led to shameful discoveries about the way in which people observed Christianity in many parts of Orkdøla county. This occurred mostly in the remote regions of Rennabu and Updalsskog, but an old man from Budvik was also brought before the archbishop's court in Nidaros. Erlend showed so little zeal for this matter that people began talking about it. There was also that old man named Aan, who had lived near the lake below Husaby and practically had to be considered one of Erlend's servants. He was skilled in runes and incantations, and it was said that he had several images in his possession to which he offered sacrifices. But nothing of the kind was found in his hut after his death. Erlend himself, along with Ulf Haldorssøn, had been with the old man when he died; people said that no doubt they had destroyed one thing or another before the priest arrived. Yes, now that people happened to think about it, Erlend's own aunt had been accused of witchcraft, adultery, and the murder of her husband—although Fru Aashild Gautesdatter had been much too wise and clever and had too many powerful friends to be convicted of anything. Then people suddenly remembered that in his youth Erlend had lived a far from Christian life and had defied the laws of the Church.

The result of all this was that the archbishop summoned Erlend Nikulaussøn to Nidaros for an interview. Simon accompanied his brother-in-law to town; he was going to Ranheim to get his sister's son, for the boy was supposed to travel home with him to Gudbrandsdal to visit his mother for a while.

It was a week before the Frosta *ting*[2] was to be held, and Nidaros was full of people. When the brothers-in-law arrived at the bishop's estate and were shown into the audience hall, many Brothers of the Cross were there, as well as several noble gentlemen, including the judge of the Frosta *ting*, Harald Nikulaussøn; Olav Hermanssøn, judge in Nidaros; Sir Guttorm Helgessøn, the sheriff of Jemtland; and Arne Gjavvaldssøn, who at once came over to Simon Darre to give him a hearty greeting. Arne drew Simon over to a window alcove, and they sat down there together.

Simon felt ill at ease. He hadn't seen the other man since he was at Ranheim ten years before, and even though everyone had treated him exceedingly well, the purpose of that journey had left a scar on his soul.

While Arne boasted of young Gjavvald, Simon kept an eye on his brother-in-law. Erlend was speaking to the royal treasurer, whose name was Sir Baard Peterssøn, but he was not related to the Hestnes lineage. It could not be said that Erlend's conduct was lacking in courtesy, and yet his manner seemed overly free and unrestrained as he stood there talking to the elderly gentleman while he rocked back and forth on his heels, with his hands clasped behind his back. As usual, he was wearing garments that were dark in color, but magnificent: a violet-blue *cote-hardi*[3] that fit snugly to his body, with slits up the sides; a black shoulder collar with the cowl thrown back to reveal the gray silk lining; a silver-studded belt; and high red boots that were laced tightly around his calves, displaying the man's handsome, slim legs and feet.

In the sharp light coming through the glass windows of the stone building, it was evident that Erlend Nikulaussøn now had quite a bit of gray hair at his temples. Around his mouth and under his eyes the fine, tanned skin was now etched with wrinkles, and there were creases on the long, handsome arch of his throat. And yet he looked quite young among the other gentlemen, although he was by no means the youngest man in the room. But he was just as slim and slender, and he carried his body in the same loose, rather careless fashion as he had in his youth. And when the royal treasurer left him, Erlend's gait was just as light and supple as he began pacing around the hall, with his hands still clasped behind his back. All the other men were sitting down, occasionally conversing with each other in low, dry voices. Erlend's light step and the ringing of his small silver spurs were all too audible.

Finally one of the younger men told him with annoyance to sit down, "And stop making so much noise, man!"

Erlend came to an abrupt halt and frowned—then he turned to face the man who had spoken and said with a laugh, "Where were you out drinking last night, Jon my friend, since your head is so tender?" Then he sat down. When Judge Harald came over to him,

Erlend got to his feet and waited until the other man had taken a seat, but then he sank down next to the judge, crossed one leg over the other, and sat with his hands clasped around his knee while they talked.

Erlend had told Simon quite openly about all the troubles he had endured because the murderer and his sorceress wife had escaped from his hands. But no man could possibly look more carefree than Erlend as he sat discussing the case with the judge.

Then the archbishop came in. He was escorted to his high seat by two men who propped cushions around him. Simon had never seen Lord Eiliv Kortin before. He looked old and frail and seemed to be freezing even though he wore a fur cape and a fur-trimmed cap on his head. When his turn came, Erlend escorted his brother-in-law over to the archbishop, and Simon fell to one knee as he kissed Lord Eiliv's ring. Erlend, too, kissed the ring with respect.

He behaved very properly and respectfully when he at last stood before the archbishop, after Lord Eiliv had talked with the other gentlemen for some time about various matters. But he answered the questions put to him by one of the canons in a rather light-hearted manner, and his demeanor seemed casual and innocent.

Yes, he had heard the talk about sorcery for many years. But as long as no one had come to him as enforcer of the law, he couldn't very well be responsible for investigating all such gossip that flew among the womenfolk in a parish. Surely it was the priest who should determine whether there were any grounds for pressing charges.

Then he was asked about the old man who had lived at Husaby and was said to possess magic skills.

Erlend gave a little smile. Yes, well, Aan had boasted of this himself, but Erlend had never seen proof of his abilities. Ever since his childhood he had heard Aan talk about three women whom he called Hærn and Skøgul and Snotra, but he had never taken this for anything but storytelling and jest. "My brother Gunnulf and our priest, Sira Eiliv, talked to him many times about this matter, but apparently they never found any cause to accuse him, since they never did so. After all, the man came to church for every mass and he knew his Christian prayers." Erlend had never had much faith in Aan's sorcery, and after he had witnessed something of the spells and witchcraft of the Finns in the north, he had come to realize that Aan's purported skills were mere foolishness.

Then the priest asked whether it was true that Erlend himself had once been given something by Aan—something that would bring him luck in *amor?*

Yes, replied Erlend swiftly and openly, with a smile. He must have been fifteen at the time, for it was about twenty-eight years ago. A leather pouch with a small white stone inside and several dried pieces that must have come from some animal. But he hadn't had much faith in that kind of thing even back then. He gave it away the following year, when he was serving at the king's castle for the first time. It happened in a bathhouse up in town; he had rashly shown the talismans to several other, younger boys. Later, one of the king's retainers came to him, wanting to purchase the pouch, and Erlend had exchanged it for a fine shaving knife.

He was asked who this gentleman might be.

At first Erlend refused to say. But the archbishop himself urged him to speak. Erlend looked up with a roguish glint in his blue eyes.

"It was Sir Ivar Ogmundssøn."

Everyone's face took on a peculiar expression. Old Sir Guttorm Helgessøn uttered several odd snorts. Even Lord Eiliv tried to restrain a smile.

Then Erlend dared to say, with lowered eyes and biting his lip, "My Lord, surely you would not disturb that good knight with this ancient matter. As I said, I didn't have much faith in it myself—and I've never noticed that it made any difference to any of us that I gave those charms to him."

Sir Guttorm doubled over with a bellow, and then the other men gave in, one after the other, and roared with laughter. The archbishop chuckled and coughed and shook his head. It was well known that Sir Ivar had always had more desire than luck in certain matters.

After a while one of the Brothers of the Cross regained his composure enough to remind them that they had come here to discuss serious issues. Erlend asked rather sharply whether anyone had accused him of anything and whether this was an interrogation; he had assumed he had simply been invited to an interview. The discussion was then continued, but it was greatly disrupted by the fact that Guttorm Helgessøn sat there incessantly snickering.

The next day, as the brothers-in-law rode home from Ranheim, Simon brought up the subject of the interview. Simon said that Erlend seemed to take it terribly lightly—and yet he thought he could see that many of the noblemen would have blamed something on him if they could.

Erlend said he knew that's what they would have liked, if it was within their power. For here in the north, most men now sided with the chancellor—except for the archbishop; in him, Erlend had a true friend. But Erlend's actions in all matters were taken in accordance with the law; he always consulted with his scribe, Kløng Aressøn, who was exceptionally knowledgeable about the law. Erlend was now speaking somberly, and he smiled only briefly as he said that doubtless no one had expected him to have such a good grasp of his business affairs as he now had—neither his dear friends around the countryside nor the gentlemen of the Council. But he was no longer certain that he wanted the position of sheriff, if other conditions should apply than those he had been granted while Erling Vidkunssøn represented the king. His own situation was now such, especially since the death of his wife's parents, that he no longer needed to secure the favor of those who had risen to power after the king had been proclaimed of age. Yes, that rotten boy might as well be declared of age now rather than later; he wasn't going to become any more manly if they kept him hidden. Then they would know even sooner what he was concealing behind his shield—or how much the Swedish nobles controlled him. The people would learn the truth: that Erling had been right, after all. It would cost the Norwegians dearly if King Magnus tried to put Skaane[4] under the Swedish Crown—and it would immediately lead to war with the Danes the moment *one* man, whether Danish or German, seized power there. And the peace in the north, which was supposed to be enforced for ten years . . . Half of that time had now passed, and it was uncertain whether the Russians would adhere to the treaty much longer. Erlend had not much faith in it, nor did Erling. No, Chancellor Paal was a learned man and in many respects sensible too—perhaps. But all the gentlemen of the Council, who had chosen him as their leader, had little more combined wit than his horse Soten. But now they were rid of Erling, for the time being. And until things changed, Erlend would just as soon step aside too. But surely Erling and his friends would want Erlend to maintain his power and prosperity up here in the north. He didn't know what he should do.

"It seems to me that now you've learned to sing Sir Erling's tune," Simon Darre couldn't help remarking.

Erlend replied that this was true. He had stayed at Sir Erling's estate the summer before, when he was in Bjørgvin, and he now knew the man much better. It was evident that, above all else, Erling wanted to maintain peace in the land. But he wanted the Norwegian Crown to have the peace of the lion—which meant that no one should be allowed to break off a tooth or cut off a claw from their kinsman King Haakon's lion. Nor should the lion be required to become the hunting dog for the people of some other country. And now Erling was also determined to bring to an end the old quarrels between the Norwegians and Lady Ingebjørg. Now that she had been left a widow by Sir Knut, it was only desirable for her to have some control over her son again. It was no doubt true that she felt such great love for the children she had borne to Knut Porse that she seemed to have almost forgotten her eldest son—but things would surely be different when she saw him again. And Lady Ingebjørg could have no reason to wish for King Magnus to interfere in the unrest occurring in Skaane, because it was under the authority of his half-brothers.

Simon thought Erlend sounded quite well-informed. But he wondered about Erling Vidkunssøn. Did the former regent think that Erlend Nikulaussøn was capable of making decisions in such matters? Or was Erling merely grasping for any possible support? The knight from Bjarkøy would be unlikely to give up his power. He could never be accused of having used it for his own benefit, but his great wealth made this unnecessary. Everyone said that over the years he had become more and more obstinate and single-minded; and by the time the other men of the Council gradually started to oppose him, he had grown so belligerent that he hardly deigned to listen to anyone else's opinion.

It was like Erlend for him finally to climb aboard Erling Vidkunssøn's ship with both feet, so to speak, as soon as the winds were against it. It was uncertain whether either Sir Erling or Erlend himself would benefit, now that he seemed to have joined forces wholeheartedly with his wealthy kinsman. And yet Simon had to admit that no matter how reckless Erlend's words might be about both people and events, what he had said did not seem entirely foolish.

But that evening he was quite wild and boisterous. Erlend was now staying at Nikulausgaard, which his brother had given to him when he joined the friars. Kristin was there too, along with their two eldest boys, their youngest son, and Erlend's daughter Margret.

Late in the evening a large group of people came to visit them, including many of the gentlemen who had been at the meeting with the archbishop the previous morning. Erlend laughed and talked loudly as they sat drinking at the table after supper. He had taken an apple from a bowl and had cut and carved it with his knife; then he rolled it across the table into the lap of Fru Sunniva Olavsdatter, who sat opposite him.

The woman sitting next to Sunniva wanted to look at it, and she reached for the apple. But Sunniva refused to give it up, and the two women pushed and tugged at each other with much shrieking and laughter. Then Erlend cried that Fru Eyvor should have an apple from him too. Before long he had tossed apples to every woman there, and he claimed to have carved love-runes into all of them.

"You're going to be worn out, my boy, if you try to redeem all those pledges," one of the men shouted.

"Then I'll have to forget about redeeming them—I've done that before," replied Erlend, and there was more laughter.

But the Icelander Kløng had taken a look at one of the apples and exclaimed that they weren't runes but just meaningless cuts. He would show them how runes should be carved.

Then Erlend shouted that he shouldn't do that. "Or else they'll tell me I have to tie you up, Kløng, and I can't get along without you."

During all the commotion Erlend's and Kristin's youngest son had come padding into the hall. Lavrans Erlendssøn was now a little more than two years old and an exceptionally attractive child, plump and fair, with silky, fine blond curls. The women on the outer bench all wanted to hold the boy at once; they sent him from lap to lap, caressing him freely, for by now they were all giddy and wild. Kristin, who was sitting against the wall in the high seat next to her husband, asked to be given the child; he began fretting and wanted to go to his mother, but it did no good.

Suddenly Erlend leaped across the table and picked up the boy, who was now howling because Fru Sunniva and Fru Eyvor were tugging at him and fighting over him. The father took the boy in his arms, speaking soothing words. When the child kept on crying, he began humming and singing as he held him and paced back and forth in the dim light of the hall. Erlend seemed to have completely forgotten about his guests. The child's little blond head lay on his father's shoulder beneath the man's dark hair, and every once in a while Erlend would touch his parted lips to the small hand resting on his chest. He continued in this way until a serving maid came in who was supposed to watch the child and should have put him to bed long ago.

Then some of the guests shouted that Erlend should sing them a ballad for a dance; he had such a fine voice. At first he declined, but then he went over to his young daughter who was sitting on the women's bench. He put his arm around Margret and escorted her out to the floor.

"You must come with me, my Margret. Take your father's hand for a dance!"

A young man stepped forward and took the maiden's hand. "Margit promised to dance with me tonight," he said. But Erlend lifted his daughter into his arms and set her down on the other side of him.

"Dance with your wife, Haakon. I never danced with anyone else when I was so newly married as you are."

"Ingebjørg says she doesn't want to . . . and I did promise Haakon to dance with him, Father," said Margret.

Simon Darre had no wish to dance. He stood next to an old woman for a while and watched; now and then his gaze fell on Kristin. While her servants cleared away the dishes, wiped the table, and brought in more liquor and walnuts, Kristin stood at the end of the table. Then she sat down near the fireplace and talked to a priest who was one of the guests. After a while Simon sat down near them.

They had danced to one or two ballads when Erlend came over to his wife. "Come and dance with us, Kristin," he begged, holding out his hand.

"I'm tired," she said, looking up for a moment.

"You ask her, Simon. She can't refuse to dance with you."

Simon rose halfway and held out his hand, but Kristin shook her head. "Don't ask me, Simon. I'm so tired. . . ."

Erlend stood there for a moment, looking as if he were embarrassed. Then he went back to Fru Sunniva and took her hand in the circle of dancers as he shouted to Margit that now she should sing for them.

"Who is that dancing next to your stepdaughter?" asked Simon. He thought he didn't much care for that fellow's face, even though he was a stalwart and boyish-looking young man with a healthy, tan complexion, fine teeth, and sparkling eyes, but they were set too close to his nose and he had a large, strong mouth and chin, although his face was narrow across the brow. Kristin told him it was Haakon Eindridessøn of Gimsar, the grandson of Tore Eindridessøn, the sheriff of Gauldøla county. Haakon had recently married the lovely little woman who was sitting on the lap of Judge Olav—he was her godfather. Simon had noticed her because she looked a little like his first wife, although she was not as beautiful. When he now heard that there was kinship between them, he went over and greeted Ingebjørg and sat down to talk to her.

After a while the dancing broke up. The older folks sat down to drink, but the younger ones continued to sing and frolic out on the floor. Erlend came over to the fireplace along with several elderly gentlemen, but he was still absentmindedly leading Fru Sunniva by the hand. The men sat down near the fire, but there was no room for Sunniva, so she stood in front of Erlend and ate the walnuts he cracked in his hands for her.

"You're an unchivalrous man, Erlend," she said suddenly. "There you sit while I have to stand."

"Then sit down," said Erlend with a laugh, pulling her down onto his lap. She struggled against him, laughing and shouting to his wife to come and see how her husband was treating her.

"Erlend just does that to be kind," replied Kristin, laughing too. "My cat can't rub against his leg without him picking her up and putting her in his lap."

Erlend and Fru Sunniva remained sitting there as before, feigning nonchalance, but they had both turned crimson. He held his arm lightly around her, as if he hardly noticed she was sitting there, while he and the men talked about the enmity between Erling Vidkunssøn and Chancellor Paal which was so much on everyone's mind. Erlend said that Paal Baardsøn had displayed his attitude toward Erling in quite a womanish way—as they could judge for themselves:

"Last summer a young country boy had come to the gathering of the chieftains to offer his services to the king. Now this poor boy from Vors was so eager to learn courtly customs and manners that he tried to embellish his speech with Swedish words—it was French back when I was young, but today it's Swedish. So one day the boy asks someone how to say *traakig,* which happens to mean 'boring' in Norwegian. Sir Paal hears this and says: '*Traakig,* my friend, that's what Sir Erling's wife, Fru Elin, is.' The boy now thinks this means beautiful or noble, because that's what she is, and apparently the poor fellow hadn't had much opportunity to hear the woman *talk.* But one day Erling meets him on the stairs outside the hall, and he stops and speaks kindly to the youth, asking him whether he liked being in Nidaros, and such things, and then he tells him to give his greetings to his father. The boy thanks him and says it will please his father greatly when he returns home with greetings 'from you, kind sir, and your boring wife.' Whereupon Erling slaps him in the face so the boy tumbles backwards down three or four steps until a servant catches him in his arms. Now there's a great commotion, people come running, and the matter is finally cleared up. Erling was furious at being made a laughingstock, but he feigned indifference. And the only response from the chancellor was that he laughed and said he should have explained that '*traakig*' was what the regent was—then the boy couldn't have misunderstood."

Everyone agreed that such behavior on the part of the chancellor was undignified, but all of them laughed a great deal. Simon listened in silence, sitting with his chin resting on his hand. He thought this was a peculiar way for Erlend to show his friendship for Erling Vidkunssøn. The story made it quite clear that Erling must be a little unbalanced if he could believe that a youth, freshly arrived from the countryside, would dare stand on the stairs to the king's palace and ridicule him to his face. Erlend could hardly be expected to remember Simon's former relationship as the brother-in-law of Fru Elin and Sir Erling.

"What are you thinking about, Kristin?" he asked. She was sitting quietly, her back straight, with her hands crossed on her lap.

She replied, "Right now I'm thinking about Margret."

Late that night, as Erlend and Simon were tending to a chore out in the courtyard, they scared off a couple standing behind the corner of the house. The nights were as light as day, and Simon recognized Haakon of Gimsar and Margret Erlendsdatter. Erlend stared after them; he was quite sober, and the other man could see that he wasn't pleased. But Erlend said, as if in excuse, that the two had known each other since childhood and they had always teased each other. Simon thought that even if this meant nothing, it was still a shame for Haakon's young wife, Ingebjørg.

The next day young Haakon came over to Nikulausgaard on an errand, and he asked for Margit.

Then Erlend furiously exclaimed, "My daughter is not *Margit* to you. And if you didn't say everything you wanted to say yesterday, then you'll have to forget about telling it to her."

Haakon shrugged his shoulders, but when he left, he asked them to give his greetings to *Margareta*.

The people from Husaby stayed in Nidaros for the *ting*, but Simon took little pleasure in this. Erlend was often bad-tempered when he stayed at his estate in town, because Gunnulf had granted the hospital, which stood on the other side of the orchard, the right to use any of the buildings that faced in its direction, and also rights to part of the garden. Erlend wanted to buy these rights back from the hospital. He didn't like seeing the patients in the garden or courtyard; many of them were also hideous in appearance, and he was afraid they would infect his children. But he couldn't reach an agreement with the monks who were in charge of the hospital.

And there was Margret Erlendsdatter. Simon knew that people gossiped about her a good deal and that Kristin took this to heart, but her father seemed not to care. Erlend seemed certain that he could protect his maiden and that the talk meant nothing. And yet he said to Simon one day that Kløng Aressøn would like to marry his daughter, and he didn't quite know how to handle this matter. He had nothing against the Icelander except that he was the son of a priest; he didn't want it to be said of Margret's children that they bore the taint of both parents' birth. Otherwise Kløng was a likeable man, good-humored, clever, and very learned. His father, Sira Are, had raised him himself and taught him well; he had hoped his son would become a priest and had even taken steps to obtain dispensation for him, but then Kløng refused to take the vows. It seemed as if Erlend intended to leave the matter unsettled. If no better match presented itself, then he could always give the maiden to Kløng Aressøn.

And yet Erlend had already had such a good offer for his daughter that there was a great deal of talk about his arrogance and imprudence, when he allowed that match to slip away. It was the grandson of Baron Sigvat of Leirhole—Sigmund Finssøn was his name. He wasn't wealthy, because Finn Sigvatssøn had had eleven surviving children. Nor was he altogether young; he was about the same age as Erlend, but a respected and sensible man. And yet Margret would have been wealthy enough because of the properties Erlend had given her when he married Kristin Lavransdatter, along with all the jewelry and costly possessions he had given the child over the years, as well as the dowry he had agreed upon with Sigmund. Erlend had also been overjoyed to have such a suitor for his daughter born of adultery. But when he came home and told Margret about this bridegroom, the maiden protested that she wouldn't have him because Sigmund had several warts on one of his eyelids, and she claimed this made her feel such revulsion for him. Erlend bowed to her wishes. When Sigmund became indignant and began talking of a breach of agreement, Erlend responded angrily and told the man that he should realize all agreements were made on the condition that the maiden was willing. His daughter would not be forced into a bridal bed. Kristin agreed with her husband on this matter; he shouldn't force the girl. But she thought Erlend ought to have had a serious discussion with his daughter and made her realize that Sigmund Finssøn was such a good match that Margret couldn't possibly expect to find any better, considering her birth. But Erlend grew terribly angry with his wife, simply because she had dared to broach the subject with him. All of this Simon had heard about at Ranheim. There they predicted that things could not possibly end well. Erlend might be a powerful man now, and the maiden was certainly lovely, but it had done her no good for her father to spoil her and encourage her stubbornness and arrogance for all these years.

After the Frosta *ting*, Erlend went home to Husaby with his wife, children, and Simon Darre, who now had his sister's son, Gjavvald Gjavvaldssøn, with him. He was afraid that the reunion, which Sigrid had been yearning for with inexpressible joy, would not turn out well. Sigrid now lived at Kruke in good circumstances; she had three handsome children with her husband, and Geirmund was as good a man as could be found on this earth. He was the one who had spoken to his brother-in-law about bringing Gjavvald south so that Sigrid might see him, for the child was always on her mind. But Gjavvald had grown accustomed to living with his grandparents, and the old couple loved the child beyond measure, giving him everything he wanted and humoring his every whim; and things were not the same at Kruke as at Ranheim. Nor was it to be expected that Geirmund would be pleased to have his wife's bastard son come visiting and then behave like a royal child, even bringing along his own servant—an elderly man whom the boy ruled and tyrannized. The man didn't dare say a word against any of Gjavvald's unreasonable demands. But for Erlend's sons, it was cause for celebration when Gjavvald came to Husaby. Erlend didn't think his sons should have any less than the grandson of Arne Gjavvaldssøn did, and so Naakkve and Bjørgulf were given all the things they told him the boy possessed.

Now that Erlend's oldest sons were big enough to accompany him and go out riding with him, he paid more attention to the boys. Simon noticed that Kristin wasn't entirely pleased by this; she thought that what they learned among his men was not all good. And it was usually about the children that unkind words most often erupted between the couple. Even though they might not have an outright quarrel, they were much closer to it than Simon thought was proper. And it seemed to him that Kristin was most to blame. Erlend could be quick-tempered, but she often spoke as if she harbored a deep, hidden rancor toward him. That was the case one day when Kristin brought up several complaints about

Naakkve. Erlend replied that he would have a serious talk with the boy. But after another remark from his wife, he exclaimed angrily that he wasn't about to give the boy a beating in front of the servants.

"No, it's too late for that now. If you had done it when he was younger, he would listen to you now. But back then you never paid the slightest attention to him."

"Oh yes, I did. But surely it was reasonable that I left him in your keeping when he was small—and besides, it's no job for a man to hand out beatings to little boys who aren't even in breeches yet."

"That's not what you thought last week," said Kristin, her voice scornful and bitter.

Erlend didn't reply but stood up and left the room. And Simon thought it was unkind of his wife to speak to him in this manner. Kristin was referring to something that had happened the week before. Erlend and Simon had come riding into the courtyard when little Lavrans ran toward them with a wooden sword in his hand. As he raced past his father's horse, he rashly struck the animal across the leg with his sword. The horse reared up, and the boy was suddenly lying under its feet. Erlend backed away, yanked the horse to the side, and threw his reins to Simon. His face was white with dread as he lifted the child up in his arms. But when he saw that the boy was unharmed, he put him over his arm, took the wooden sword, and gave Lavrans a beating on his bare bottom— the boy was not yet wearing breeches. In those first heated moments, he didn't realize how hard he was striking, and Lavrans was still walking around with black and blue marks. But afterwards Erlend tried all day to make amends with the boy, who sulked and clung to his mother, hitting and threatening his father. Later that evening, when Lavrans was settled in his parents' bed where he usually slept because his mother still nursed him during the night, Erlend sat next to him for hours. Every once in a while he would stroke the sleeping child a bit as he gazed down at him. He told Simon that this was the boy he loved most of all his sons.

When Erlend set off for the summer *tings,* Simon headed home. He raced south along Gauldal, making the sparks fly from his horse's hooves. Once, as they rode more slowly up several steep slopes, his men laughingly asked him whether he was trying to cover three days' journey in two. Simon laughed in reply and said that was indeed his intention, "because I'm longing to reach Formo."

That was how he always felt whenever he had been away from his estate for long; he loved his home and always felt great joy when he could turn his horse homeward. But this time it seemed he had never longed so much to return to his valley and manor and his young daughters—yes, he even yearned for Ramborg. To be truthful, he thought it unreasonable to feel this way, but up there at Husaby he had been so uneasy that now he thought he knew firsthand how cattle could sense in their bodies that a storm was brewing.

CHAPTER 2

ALL SUMMER LONG Kristin thought of little else but what Simon had told her about her mother's death.

Ragnfrid Ivarsdatter had died alone; no one had been near as she drew her last breath except a servant woman, who was asleep. And it helped very little that Simon had said she was well prepared for her death. It was like the providence of God that several days earlier Ragnfrid had felt such a longing for the body of the Savior that she made her confession and was given communion by the priest of the cloister, who was her confessor. It was true that she had been granted a good death. Simon saw her body and said he thought it a wondrous sight—she had grown so beautiful in death. She was a woman of nearly sixty, and for many years her face had been greatly lined and wrinkled, and yet now it was completely changed; her face was youthful and smooth, and she looked just like a young woman asleep. She had been laid to rest at her husband's side; there they had also brought Ulvhild Lavransdatter's remains shortly after her father's death. On top of the graves a large slab of stone had been placed, divided in two by a beautifully carved cross. On a winding banner a long Latin verse had been written, composed by the prior of the cloister, but Simon couldn't remember it properly, for he understood little of that language.

Ragnfrid had lived in her own house on the estate in town where the corrodians of the cloister resided; she had a small room with a lovely loft room above. There she lived alone with a poor peasant woman who had taken lodgings with the brothers in return for a small payment, provided she would lend a hand to one of the wealthier women lodgers. But during the past half year, it had been Ragnfrid who had served the other woman, because the widow, whose name was Torgunna, had been unwell. Ragnfrid tended to her with great love and kindness.

On the last evening of her life, she had attended evensong in the

295

cloister church, and afterwards she went into the cookhouse of the
estate. She made a hearty soup with several restorative herbs and
told the other women there that she was going to give the soup to
Torgunna. She hoped the woman would feel well enough the next
day so that they could both attend matins. That was the last time
anyone saw the widow of Jørundgaard alive. Neither she nor the
peasant woman came to matins or to the next service. When some
of the monks in the choir noticed that Ragnfrid didn't come to the
morning mass either, they were greatly surprised—she had never
before missed three services in a day. They sent word to town, asking whether the widow of Lavrans Bjørgulfsøn was ill. When the
servants went up to the loft, they found the soup bowl standing
untouched on the table. In the bed, Torgunna was sleeping sweetly
against the wall. But Ragnfrid Ivarsdatter lay on the edge with her
hands crossed over her breast—dead and already nearly cold. Simon and Ramborg went to her funeral, which was very beautiful.

Now that there were so many people in the Husaby household
and Kristin had six sons, she could no longer manage to take part
in all the individual chores that had to be done. She had to have a
housekeeper to assist her. The mistress of the manor would usually
sit in the hall with her sewing. There was always someone who
needed clothing—Erlend, Margret, or one of the boys.

The last time she had seen her mother, Ragnfrid was riding behind her husband's bier, on that bright spring day while she herself
stood in the meadow outside Jørundgaard and watched her father's funeral procession setting off across the green carpet of winter rye beneath the hillside scree.

Kristin's needle flew in and out as she thought about her parents
and their home at Jørundgaard. Now that everything had become
memories, she seemed to see so much that she hadn't noticed when
she was in the midst of it all—when she took for granted her father's tenderness and protection, as well as the steady, quiet care
and toil of her silent, melancholy mother. She thought about her
own children; she loved them more than the blood of her own
heart, and there was not a waking hour when she wasn't thinking
about them. And yet there was much in her soul that she brooded
over more—her children she could love without brooding. While
she lived at Jørundgaard, she had never thought otherwise than

that her parents' whole life and everything they did was for the sake of her and her sisters. Now she seemed to realize that great currents of both sorrow and joy had flowed between these two people, who had been given to each other in their youth by their fathers, without being asked. And she knew nothing of this except that they had departed from her life together. Now she understood that the lives of these two people had contained much more than love for their children. And yet that love had been strong and wide and unfathomably deep; while the love she gave them in return was weak and thoughtless and selfish, even back in her childhood when her parents were her whole world. She seemed to see herself standing far, far away—so small at that distance of time and place. She was standing in the flood of sunlight streaming in through the smoke vent in the old hearth house back home, the winter house of her childhood. Her parents were standing back in the shadows, and they seemed to tower over her, as tall as they had been when she was small. They were smiling at her, in the way she now knew one smiles at a little child who comes and pushes aside dark and burdensome thoughts.

"I thought, Kristin, that once you had children of your own, then you would better understand. . . ."

She remembered when her mother said those words. Sorrowfully, the daughter thought that she still didn't understand her mother. But now she was beginning to realize how much she didn't understand.

That fall Archbishop Eiliv died. At about the same time, King Magnus had the terms changed for many of the sheriffs in the land, but not for Erlend Nikulaussøn. When he was in Bjørgvin during the last summer before the king came of age, Erlend had received a letter stating that he should be granted one fourth of the income collected from bail paid by criminals, from fines for the crime of letter-breaching,[1] and from forfeitures of property. There had been much talk about his acquisition of such rights toward the end of a regency. Erlend had a vast income because he now owned a great deal of land in the county and usually stayed on his own estates when he traveled around his district, but he permitted his leaseholders to buy their way out of their obligation to house and feed him. It's true that he took in little in land taxes, and the upkeep of his manor was costly; in addition to his household servants, he never had fewer than twelve armed men with him at Husaby. They rode the best horses and were splendidly outfitted, and whenever Erlend traveled around his district, his men lived like noblemen.

This matter was mentioned one day when Judge Harald and the sheriff of Gauldøla county were visiting Husaby. Erlend replied that many of these men had been with him when he lived up north. "Back then we shared whatever conditions we found there, eating dried fish and drinking bitter ale. Now these men whom I clothe and feed know that I won't begrudge them white bread and foreign ale. And if I tell them to go to Hell when I get angry, they know that I don't mean for them to set off on the journey without me in the lead."

Ulf Haldorssøn, who was now the head of Erlend's men, later told Kristin that this was true. Erlend's men loved him, and he had complete command of them.

"You know yourself, Kristin, that no one should rely too heavily on what Erlend says; he must be judged by what he does."

It was also rumored that in addition to his household servants, Erlend had men throughout the countryside—even outside Orkdøla county—who had sworn allegiance to him on the hilt of his sword. Finally a letter from the Crown arrived regarding this matter, but Erlend replied that these men had been part of his ship's crew and they had been bound to him by oath ever since that first spring when he sailed north. He was then commanded to release the men at the next *ting* he held to announce the verdicts and decisions of the Law *ting;* and he was to summon to the meeting those men who lived outside the county and pay for their journey himself. He did summon some of his old crew members from outside Møre to the *ting* at Orkedal—but no one heard that he released them or any other men who had served him in his position as chieftain. For the time being the matter was allowed to languish, and as the autumn wore on, people stopped talking about it altogether.

Late that fall Erlend journeyed south and spent Christmas at the court of King Magnus, who was residing in Oslo that year. Erlend was annoyed that he couldn't persuade his wife to come with him, but Kristin had no courage for the difficult winter journey, and she stayed at Husaby.

Erlend returned home three weeks after Christmas, bringing splendid gifts for his wife and all his children. He gave Kristin a silver bell so she could ring for her maids; to Margret he gave a clasp of solid gold, which was something she didn't yet own, although she had all sorts of silver and gilded jewelry. But when the women were putting away these costly gifts in their jewelry chests, something got caught on Margret's sleeve.

The girl quickly removed it and hid it in her hand as she said to her stepmother, "This belonged to my mother—that's why Father doesn't want me to show it to you."

But Kristin's face had turned even more crimson than the maiden's. Her heart pounded with fear, but she knew that she *had* to speak to the young girl and warn her.

After a moment she said in a quiet and uncertain voice, "That looks like the gold clasp that Fru Helga of Gimsar used to wear to banquets."

"Well, many gold things look much the same," replied the maiden curtly.

Kristin locked her chest and stood with her hands resting on top so that Margret wouldn't see how they were shaking.

"Dear Margret," she said softly and gently, but then she had to stop while she gathered all her strength.

"Dear Margret, I have often bitterly regretted . . . My happiness has never been complete, even though my father forgave me with all his heart for the sorrows I caused him. You know that I sinned greatly against my parents for the sake of your father. But the longer I live and the more I come to understand, the harder it is for me to remember that I rewarded their kindness by causing them sorrow. Dear Margret, your father has been good to you all your days . . ."

"You don't have to worry, Mother," replied the girl. "I'm not your lawful daughter; you don't have to worry that I might put on your filthy shift or step into your shoes . . ."

Her eyes flashing with anger, Kristin turned to face her stepdaughter. But then she gripped the cross she wore around her neck tightly in her hand and bit back the words she was about to speak.

She took this matter to Sira Eiliv that very evening after vespers, and she looked in vain for some sign in the priest's face. Had a misfortune already occurred, and did he know about it? She thought about her own misguided youth; she remembered Sira Eirik's face, which gave nothing away as he lived side by side with her and her trusting parents, with her sinful secret locked inside his heart—while she remained mute and callous to his stern entreaties and admonitions. And she remembered when she showed her own mother gifts that Erlend had given her in Oslo; that was after she had been lawfully betrothed to him. Her mother's expression was steady and calm as she picked up the items, one by one, looked at them, praised them, and then laid them aside.

Kristin was deathly afraid and anguished, and she kept a vigilant eye on Margret. Erlend noticed that something was troubling his wife, and one evening after they had gone to bed, he asked whether she might be with child again.

Kristin lay in silence for a moment before she replied that she thought she was. And when her husband lovingly took her in his arms without another word, she didn't have the heart to tell him that something else was causing her sorrow. But when Erlend whispered to her that this time she must try and give him a daughter, she couldn't manage a reply but lay there, rigid with fear, thinking that Erlend would find out soon enough what kind of joy a man had from his daughters.

Several nights later everyone at Husaby had gone to bed slightly drunk and with their stomachs quite full because it was the last few days before Lent began; for this reason, they all slept heavily. Late that night little Lavrans woke up in his parents' bed, crying and demanding sleepily to nurse at his mother's breast. But they were trying to wean him. Erlend woke up, grunting crossly. He picked up the boy, gave him some milk from a cup that stood on the step of the bed, and then lay the child back down on the other side of him.

Kristin had fallen into a deep slumber again when she suddenly realized that Erlend was sitting up in bed. Only half awake, she asked what was wrong. He hushed her in a voice that she didn't recognize. Soundlessly he slipped out of bed, and she saw that he was pulling on a few clothes. When she propped herself up on one elbow, he pressed her back against the pillows with one hand as he bent over her and took down his sword, which hung over the headboard.

He moved as quietly as a lynx, but she saw that he was going over to the ladder which led up to Margret's chamber above the entry hall.

For a moment Kristin lay in bed completely paralyzed with fear. Then she sat up, found her shift and gown, and began hunting for her shoes on the floor beside the bed.

Suddenly a woman's scream rang out from the loft—loud enough to be heard all over the estate. Erlend's voice shouted a word or two, and then Kristin heard the clang of swords striking each other and the stomp of feet overhead—then the sound of a weapon falling to the floor and Margret screaming in terror.

Kristin was on her knees, huddled next to the hearth. She scraped away the hot ashes with her bare hands and blew on the embers. When she had lit a torch and lifted it up with trembling hands, she saw Erlend in the darkness above. He leaped down from the loft, not bothering with the ladder, holding his drawn sword in his hand, and then dashed out the main door.

The boys were peering out from the dark on all sides of the room. Kristin went over to the enclosed bed on the north wall where the three eldest slept and told them to lie down and shut the door. Ivar and Skule were sitting on the bench, blinking at the light, frightened and bewildered. She told them to climb up into her bed, and then she shut them inside too. Then she lit a candle and went out into the courtyard.

It was raining. For a moment, as the light of her candle was reflected in the glistening, ice-covered ground, she saw a crowd standing outside the door to the next building: the servants' hall where Erlend's men slept. Then the flame of her candle was blown out, and for a moment the night was pitch-dark, but then a lantern emerged from the servants' hall, and Ulf Haldorssøn was carrying it.

He bent down over a dark body curled up on the wet patches of ice. Kristin knelt down and touched the man. It was young

Haakon of Gimsar, and he was either senseless or dead. Her hands were at once covered with blood. With Ulf's help she straightened out his body and turned him over. The blood was gushing out of his right arm, where his hand had been lopped off.

Involuntarily Kristin glanced at the window hatch of Margret's chamber as it slammed shut in the wind. She couldn't discern any face up there, but it was quite dark.

As she knelt in the rain puddles, clamping her hand as tight as she could around Haakon's wrist to stop the spurting blood, she was aware of Erlend's men standing half-dressed all around her. Then she noticed Erlend's gray, contorted face. With a corner of his tunic he wiped off his bloody sword. He was naked underneath and his feet were bare.

"One of you . . . find me something to bind this with. And you, Bjørn, go and wake up Sira Eiliv. We'll carry him over to the parsonage." She took the leather strap that they gave her and wrapped it around the stump of the man's arm.

Suddenly Erlend said, his voice harsh and wild, "Nobody touch him! Let the man lie where he fell!"

"You must realize, husband, we can't do that," said Kristin calmly, although her heart was pounding so loud that she thought she would suffocate.

Erlend rammed the tip of his sword hard against the ground.

"Yes—she's not your flesh and blood—you've made that quite clear to me every single day, for all these years."

Kristin stood up and whispered quietly to him, "And yet for her sake I want this to be concealed—if it can be done. You men . . ." she turned to the servants who were standing around them. "If you're loyal to your master, you won't speak of this until he has told you how this quarrel with Haakon arose."

All the men agreed. One of them dared step forward and explained: They had been awakened by the sound of a woman screaming, as if she were being taken by force. And then someone ran along their roof, but he must have slipped on the icy surface. They heard a scrambling noise and then a thud on the ground. But Kristin told the man to be silent. At that moment Sira Eiliv came running.

When Erlend turned on his heel and went inside, his wife ran after him and tried to force her way past him. When he headed for the ladder to the loft, she sprang in front of him and grabbed him by the arm.

"Erlend—what will you do to the child?" she gasped, looking up into his wild, gray face.

Without replying, he tried to fling her aside, but she held on tight.

"Wait, Erlend, wait—your child! You don't know . . . The man was fully clothed," she cried urgently.

He gave a loud wail before he answered. She turned as pale as a corpse with horror—his words were so raw and his voice unrecognizable with desperate anguish.

Then she wrestled mutely with the raging man. He snarled and gnashed his teeth, until she managed to catch his eye in the dim light.

"Erlend—let me go to her first. I haven't forgotten the day when I was no better than Margret. . . ."

Then he released her and staggered backwards against the wall to the next room; he stood there, shaking like a dying beast. Kristin went to light a candle, then came back and went past him up to Margret in her bedchamber.

The first thing the candlelight fell on was a sword lying on the floor not far from the bed, and the severed hand beside it. Kristin tore off the wimple which she, without thinking, had wrapped loosely over her flowing hair before she went out to the men in the courtyard. Now she dropped it over the hand lying on the floor.

Margret was huddled up on the pillows at the headboard, staring at Kristin's candle, wide-eyed and terrified. She was clutching the bedclothes around her, but her white shoulders shone naked under her golden curls. There was blood all over the room.

The strain in Kristin's body erupted into violent sobs; it was such a terrible sight to see that fair young child amidst such horror.

Then Margret screamed loudly, "Mother—what will Father do to me?"

Kristin couldn't help it: In spite of her deep sympathy for the girl, her heart seemed to shrink and harden in her breast. Margret didn't ask what her father had done to Haakon. For an instant she saw Erlend lying on the ground and her own father standing over him with the bloody sword, and she herself . . . But Margret hadn't budged. Kristin couldn't stem her old feeling of scornful displeasure toward Eline's daughter as Margret threw herself against her, trembling and almost senseless with fear. She sat down on the bed and tried to soothe the child.

That was how Erlend found them when he appeared on the ladder. He was now fully dressed. Margret began screaming again and hid her face in her stepmother's arms. Kristin glanced up at her husband for a moment; he was calm now, but his face was pale and strange. For the first time he looked his age.

But she obeyed him when he said calmly, "You must go downstairs now, Kristin. I want to speak to my daughter alone." Gently she laid the girl down on the bed, pulled the covers up to her chin, and went down the ladder.

She did as Erlend had done and got properly dressed—there would be no more sleep at Husaby that night—and then she set about reassuring the frightened children and servants.

The next morning, in a snowstorm, Margret's maid left the manor in tears, carrying her possessions in a sack on her back. The master had chased her out with the harshest words, threatening to flay her bloody because she had sold her mistress in such a fashion.

Then Erlend interrogated the other servants. Hadn't any of the maids suspected anything when all autumn and winter Ingeleiv kept coming to sleep with them instead of with Margret in her chamber? And the dogs had been locked up with them too. But all of them denied it, which was only to be expected.

Finally, he took his wife aside to speak to her alone. Sick at heart and deathly tired, Kristin listened to him and tried to counter his injustice with meek replies. She didn't deny that she had been worried; but she didn't tell him that she had never spoken to him of her fears because she received nothing but ingratitude every time she attempted to counsel him or Margret about the maiden's best interests. And she swore by God and the Virgin Mary that she had never realized or even imagined that this man might come to Margret up in the loft at night.

"You!" said Erlend scornfully. "You said yourself that you remember the time when you were no better than Margret. And the Lord God in Heaven knows that every day, in all these years we've lived together, you've made certain I would see how you remember the injustice I did to you—even though your desire was as keen as mine. And it was your father, not I, who caused much of the unhappiness when he refused to give you to me as my wife. I was willing enough to rectify the sin from the very outset. When you saw the Gimsar gold . . ." He grabbed his wife's hand and held it up; the two rings glittered which Erlend had given her while they were together at Gerdarud. "Didn't you know what it meant? When all these years you've worn the rings I gave you after you let me take your honor?"

Kristin was faint with weariness and sorrow; she whispered, "I wonder, Erlend, whether you even remember that time when you won my honor. . . ."

Then he covered his face with his hands and flung himself down on the bench, his body writhing and convulsing. Kristin sat down some distance away; she wished she could help her husband. She realized that this misfortune was even harder for him to bear because he himself had sinned against others in the same way as they had now sinned against him. And he, who had never wanted to take the blame for any trouble he might have caused, couldn't possibly bear the blame for this unhappiness—and there was no one else but her for him to fault. But she wasn't angry as much as she was sad and afraid of what might happen next.

Every once in a while she would go up to see to Margret. The girl lay in bed, motionless and pale and staring straight ahead. She had still not asked about Haakon's fate. Kristin didn't know if this was because she didn't dare or because she had grown numb from her own misery.

That afternoon Kristin saw Erlend and Kløng the Icelander walking together through the snowdrifts over to the armory. But only a short time later Erlend returned alone. Kristin glanced up for a moment when he came into the light and walked past her—but then she didn't dare turn her gaze toward the corner of the room where he had retreated. She had seen that he was a broken man.

Later, when she went over to the storeroom to get something, Ivar and Skule came running to tell their mother that Kløng the Icelander was going to leave that evening. The boys were sad, because the scribe was their good friend. He was packing up his things right now; he wanted to reach Birgsi by nightfall.

Kristin could guess what had happened. Erlend had offered his daughter to the scribe, but he didn't want a maiden who had been seduced. What this conversation must have been like for Erlend . . . she felt dizzy and ill and refused to think any more about it.

The following day a message came from the parsonage. Haakon Eindridessøn wanted to speak to Erlend. Erlend sent back a reply that he had nothing more to say to Haakon. Sira Eiliv told Kristin that if Haakon lived, he would be greatly crippled. In addition to losing his hand, he had also gravely injured his back and hips when he fell from the roof of the servants' hall. But he wanted to go home, even in this condition, and the priest had promised to find a sleigh for him. Haakon now regretted his sin with all his heart. He said that the actions of Margret's father were fully justified, no matter what the law might say; but he hoped that everyone would do their best to hush up the incident so that his guilt and Margret's shame might be concealed as much as possible. That afternoon he was carried out to the sleigh, which Sira Eiliv had borrowed at Repstad, and the priest rode with him to Gauldal.

The next day, which was Ash Wednesday, the people of Husaby had to go to the parish church at Vinjar. But at vespers Kristin asked the curate to let her into the church at Husaby.

She could still feel the ashes on her head as she knelt beside her stepson's grave and said the *Pater noster* for his soul.

By now there was probably not much left of the boy but bones beneath the stone. Bones and hair and a scrap of the clothing he had been laid to rest in. She had seen the remains of her little sister when they dug up her grave to take her body to her father in Hamar. Dust and ashes. She thought about her father's handsome features; about her mother's big eyes in her lined face, and Ragnfrid's figure which continued to look strangely young and delicate and light, even though her face seemed old so early. Now they lay under a stone, falling apart like buildings that collapse when the people have moved away. Images swirled before her eyes: the charred remains of the church back home, and a farm in Silsaadal which they rode past on their way to Vaage—the buildings were deserted and caving in. The people who worked the fields didn't dare go near after the sun went down. She thought about her own beloved dead—their faces and voices, their smiles and habits and demeanor. Now that they had departed for that other land, it was painful to think about their figures; it was like remembering your home when you knew it was standing there deserted, with the rotting beams sinking into the earth.

She sat on the bench along the wall of the empty church. The old smell of cold incense kept her thoughts fixed on images of death and the decay of temporal things. And she didn't have the strength to lift up her soul to catch a glimpse of the land where *they* were, the place to which all goodness and love and faith had finally been moved and now *endured*. Each day, when she prayed for the peace of their souls, it seemed to her unfair that she should pray for those who had possessed more peace in their souls here on earth than she had ever known since she became a grown woman. Sira Eiliv would no doubt say that prayers for the dead were always good—good for oneself, since the other person had already found peace with God.

But this did not help her. It seemed to her that when her weary body was finally rotting beneath a gravestone, her restless soul would still be hovering around somewhere nearby, the way a lost spirit wanders, moaning, through the ruined buildings of an abandoned farm. For in her soul sin continued to exist, like the roots of a weed intertwined in the soil. It no longer blossomed or flared up or smelled fragrant, but it was still there in the soil, pale and strong and alive. In spite of all the tenderness that welled up inside her when she saw her husband's despair, she didn't have the will to silence the inner voice that asked, hurt and embittered: How can you speak that way to *me*? Have you forgotten when I gave you my faith and my honor? Have you forgotten when I was your beloved friend? And yet she understood that as long as this voice spoke within her, she would continue to speak to him as if *she* had forgotten.

In her thoughts she threw herself down before Saint Olav's shrine, she reached for Brother Edvin's moldering bones over in the church at Vatsfjeld, she held in her hands the reliquaries containing the tiny remnants of a dead woman's shroud and the splinters of bone from an unknown martyr. She reached for protection to the small scraps which, through death and decay, had preserved a little of the power of the departed soul—like the magical powers residing in the rusted swords taken from the burial mounds of ancient warriors.

On the following day Erlend rode to Nidaros with only Ulf and one servant to accompany him. He didn't return to Husaby during all of Lent, but Ulf came to get his armed men and then left to meet him at the mid-Lenten *ting* in Orkedal.

Ulf drew Kristin aside to tell her that Erlend had arranged with Tiedeken Paus, the German goldsmith in Nidaros, for Margret to marry his son Gerlak just after Easter.

Erlend came home for the holy day. He was quite calm and composed now, but Kristin thought she could tell that he would never recover from this misfortune the way he had recovered from so much else. Perhaps this was because he was no longer young, or because nothing had ever humiliated him so deeply. Margret seemed indifferent to the arrangements her father had made on her behalf.

One evening when Erlend and Kristin were alone, he said, "If she had been my lawful child—or her mother had been an unmarried woman—I would never have given her to a stranger, as things now stand with her. I would have granted shelter and protection to both her and any child of hers. That's the worst of it—but because of her birth, a lawful husband can offer her the best protection."

As Kristin made all the preparations for the departure of her stepdaughter, Erlend said one day in a brusque voice, "I don't suppose you're well enough to travel to town with us?"

"If that's what you wish, I will certainly go with you," said Kristin.

"Why should I wish it? You've never taken a mother's place for her before, and you don't need to do so now. It's not going to be a festive wedding. And Fru Gunna of Raasvold and her son's wife have promised to come, for the sake of kinship."

And so Kristin stayed at Husaby while Erlend was in Nidaros to give his daughter to Gerlak Tiedekenssøn.

CHAPTER 3

THAT SUMMER, JUST before Saint Jon's Day, Gunnulf Nikulaussøn returned to his monastery. Erlend was in town during the
Frosta *ting;* he sent a message home, asking his wife whether she
would care to come to Nidaros to see her brother-in-law. Kristin
wasn't feeling very well, but she went all the same. When she met
Erlend, he told her that his brother's health seemed completely
broken. The friars hadn't had much success with their endeavors
up north at Munkefjord. They never managed to have the church
they had built consecrated, because the archbishop couldn't travel
north during a time of such unrest. Finally they ended up with no
bread or wine, candles or oil for the services, but when Brother
Gunnulf and Brother Aslak sailed for Vargøy for supplies, the
Finns cast their spells and the ship sank. They were stranded on a
skerry for three days, and afterwards neither of them regained his
full health. Brother Aslak died a short time later. They had suffered
terribly from scurvy during Lent, for they had no flour or herbs to
eat along with the dried fish. Then Bishop Haakon of Bjørgvin and
Master Arne, who was in charge of the cathedral chapter while
Lord Paal was at the Curia to be ordained as archbishop, instructed the monks who were still alive to return home; the priests
at Vargøy were to tend to the flocks at Munkefjord for the time
being.

Although she was not unprepared, Kristin was still shocked
when she saw Gunnulf Nikulaussøn again. She went with Erlend
over to the monastery the next day, and they were escorted into
the interview room. The monk came in. His body was bent over,
his fringe of hair was now completely gray, and the skin under his
sunken eyes was wrinkled and dark brown. But his smooth, pale
complexion was flecked with leaden-colored spots, and she noticed
that his hand was covered with the same spots when he thrust it

out from the sleeve of his robe to take her hand. He smiled, and she saw that he had lost several teeth.

They sat down and talked for a while, but it seemed as if Gunnulf had also forgotten how to speak. He mentioned this himself before they left.

"But you, Erlend, you are just the same—you don't seem to have aged at all," he said with a little smile.

Kristin knew that she looked miserable at the moment, while Erlend was so handsome as he stood there, tall and slender and dark and well-dressed. And yet Kristin knew in her heart that he too had been greatly changed. It was odd that Gunnulf couldn't see it; he had always been so sharp-sighted in the past.

One day late in the summer Kristin was up in the clothing loft, and Fru Gunna of Raasvold was with her. She had come to Husaby to help Kristin when she once again gave birth. They could hear Naakkve and Bjørgulf singing down in the courtyard as they sharpened their knives—a lewd and vulgar ballad which they sang at the top of their lungs.

Their mother was beside herself with rage as she went downstairs to speak to her sons in the harshest words. She wanted to know who had taught the boys the song—it must have been in the servants' hall, but who among the men would teach children such a song? The boys refused to answer. Then Skule appeared beneath the loft steps; he told his mother she might as well stop asking, because they had learned the ballad from listening to their father sing it.

Fru Gunna joined in: Had they no fear of God that they would sing such a song? Especially now that they couldn't be sure, when they went to bed at night, whether they might be motherless before the roosters crowed? Kristin didn't reply but went quietly back into the house.

Later, after she had taken to her bed to rest, Naakkve came into the room to see her. He took his mother's hand but did not speak, and then he began to weep softly. She talked to him gently, jesting and begging him not to grieve or cry. She had made it through six times before; surely she would make it through the seventh. But the boy wept harder and harder. Finally she allowed him to crawl into the bed between her and the wall, and there he lay, sobbing, with his arms around her neck and his head pressed to his mother's breast. But she couldn't get him to tell her what he was crying about, even though he stayed with her until the servants began carrying in the evening meal.

Naakkve was now twelve years old. He was big for his age and tried to affect a manly and grown-up bearing, but he had a gentle soul, and his mother could sometimes see that he was very childish. But he was old enough to understand the misfortune that had befallen his half-sister; Kristin wondered whether he could also see that his father was different afterwards.

Erlend had always been the kind of man who could say the worst things when his temper was aroused, but in the past he had never said an unkind word to anyone except in anger, and he had been quick to make amends when his own good humor was restored. Nowadays he could say harsh and ugly things with a cold expression on his face. Before, he used to curse and swear fiercely, but to some extent he had put aside this bad habit when he saw that it bothered his wife and offended Sira Eiliv, for whom he had gradually developed great respect. But he had never been rude or spoken in a vulgar manner, and he had never approved when other men talked that way. In that sense, he was much more modest than many a man who had lived a purer life. As much as it offended Kristin to hear such a song on the lips of her innocent sons, especially in her present condition, and then to hear they had learned it from their father, there was something else that gave her an even more bitter taste in her mouth. She realized that Erlend was still childish enough to think that he could counter cruelty with cruelty since, after suffering the shame of his daughter, he had now begun to use foul words and speak in an offensive manner.

Fru Gunna had told her that Margret had given birth to a stillborn son shortly before Saint Olav's Day. She also knew that Margret already seemed to have found ample consolation; she got on well with Gerlak, and he was kind to her. Erlend went to see his daughter whenever he was in Nidaros, and Gerlak always made a great fuss over his father-in-law, although Erlend was not particularly willing to accept this man as his kinsman. But Erlend had not once mentioned his daughter at Husaby since she had left the manor.

Kristin gave birth to another son; he was baptized Munan, after

Erlend's grandfather. During the time she lay in the little house, Naakkve came to see his mother daily, bringing her berries and nuts he had picked in the woods, or wreaths he had woven from medicinal herbs. Erlend returned home when the new child was three weeks old. He often sat with his wife and tried to be gentle and loving—and this time he didn't complain that the infant was not a maiden or that the boy was weak and frail. But Kristin said very little in response to his warm words; she was silent and pensive and despondent, and this time she was slow to recover her health.

All winter long Kristin was ailing, and it seemed unlikely that the child would survive. The mother had little thought for anything but the poor infant. For this reason she listened with only half an ear to all the talk of the great news that was heard that winter. King Magnus had fallen into the worst financial straits through his attempts to win sovereignty over Skaane, and he had demanded assistance and taxes from Norway. Some of the noblemen of the Council seemed willing enough to support him in this matter. But when the king's envoys came to Tunsberg, the royal treasurer was away, and Stig Haakonssøn, who was the chieftain of Tunsberg Fortress, barred the king's men from entering and made ready to defend the stronghold with force. He had few men of his own, but Erling Vidkunssøn, who was his uncle through marriage and was at home on his estate at Aker, sent forty armed men to the fortress while he himself sailed west. At about the same time the king's cousins, Jon and Sigurd Haftorssøn, threatened to oppose the king because of a court ruling that had gone against some of their men.

Erlend laughed at all this and said the Haftorssøns had shown their youth and stupidity in this matter. Discontent with King Magnus was not rampant in Norway. The noblemen were demanding that a regent be placed in charge of the kingdom and that the royal seal be given to a Norwegian man for safekeeping, since the king, because of his dealings in Skaane, seemed to want to spend most of his time in Sweden. The townsmen and the clergy of the towns had become frightened by rumors of the king's loans from the German city-states. The insolence of the Germans and their disregard for Norwegian laws and customs were already more than could be tolerated. And now it was said that the king had promised them even greater rights and freedoms in Norwegian towns, and this would make it impossible to bear for the Norwegian traders, who already had difficult conditions. Among the peasantry the rumor of King Magnus's secret sin still held sway, and many of the parish priests in the countryside and the wandering monks were agreed about at least one thing: They believed this was the reason that Saint Olav's Church in Nidaros had burned. The farmers also blamed this sin for the many misfortunes that had befallen one village after another over the past few years: sickness in the livestock, blight in the crops, which brought illness and disease to both people and beasts, and poor harvests of grain and hay. Erlend said that if the Haftorssøns had been wise enough to hold their peace a little longer and acquire a reputation for amenable and chieftainlike conduct, then people might have remembered that they too were grandsons of King Haakon.

Eventually this unrest died down, but the result was that the king appointed Ivar Ogmundssøn as lord chancellor in Norway. Erling Vidkunssøn, Stig Haakonssøn, the Haftorssøns, and all their supporters were threatened with charges of treason. Then they yielded and came to make peace with the king. There was a powerful man from the Uplands whose name was Ulf Saksesøn; he had taken part in the Haftorssøns' opposition, and he did not make peace with the king but came instead to Nidaros after Christmas. He spent a good deal of time with Erlend in town, and from him the people of the north heard about the matters, as Ulf perceived them. Kristin had a great dislike for this man; she didn't know him, but she knew his sister Helga Saksesdatter, who was married to Gyrd Darre of Dyfrin. She was beautiful but exceedingly arrogant, and Simon didn't care for her either, although Ramborg got along well with her. Soon after the beginning of Lent, letters arrived for the sheriffs stating that Ulf Saksesøn was to be declared an outlaw at the *tings,* but by that time he had already sailed away from Norway in midwinter.

That spring Erlend and Kristin were staying at their town estate during Easter, and they had brought their youngest son, Munan, with them because there was a sister at the Bakke convent who was so skilled in healing that every sick child she touched regained health, as long it was not God's wish for the child to die.

One day shortly after Easter, Kristin came home from the convent with the infant. The manservant and maid who had accompanied her came with her into the house. Erlend was alone, lying on one of the benches. After the manservant left, and the women had taken off their cloaks, Kristin sat near the hearth with the child while the maid heated some oil which the nun had given them. Then Erlend asked from his place on the bench what Sister Ragnhild had said about the boy. Kristin replied brusquely to his questions as she unwrapped the swaddling clothes; finally she stopped talking altogether.

"Are things so bad with the boy, Kristin, that you don't want to tell me?" he asked with some impatience.

"You've asked the same things before, Erlend," replied his wife in a cold voice. "And I've answered you many times. But since you care so little about the boy that you can't remember from one day to the next . . ."

"It has also happened to me, Kristin," said Erlend as he stood up and went over to her, "that I've had to give you the same answer two or three times to some question you've asked me because you didn't bother to remember what I'd said."

"It was probably not about such important matters as the children's health," she said in the same cold voice.

"But it wasn't about petty things, either, this past winter. They were matters that weighed heavily on my mind."

"That's not true, Erlend. It's been a long time since you talked to me about those things that were most on your mind."

"Leave us now, Signe," said Erlend to the maid. His brow was flushed red as he turned to his wife. "I know what you're referring to. But I won't speak to you about that as long as your maid might hear me—even though you're such good friends with her that you think it a small matter for her to be present when you start a quarrel with your husband and say I'm not speaking the truth."

"One learns least from the people one lives with," said Kristin curtly.

"It's not easy to understand what you mean by that. I've never spoken unkindly to you in the presence of strangers or forgotten to show you honor and respect in front of our servants."

Kristin burst into an oddly desolate and quavering laugh.

"You forget so well, Erlend! Ulf Haldorssøn has lived with us all these years. Don't you remember when you had him and Haftor bring me to you in the bedchamber of Brynhild's house in Oslo?"

Erlend sank down onto the bench, staring at his wife with his mouth agape.

But she continued, "You never thought it necessary to conceal from your servants all that was improper or disrespectful here at Husaby, or anywhere else—whether it was something shameful for yourself or for your wife."

Erlend stayed where he was, looking at her aghast.

"Do you remember that first winter of our marriage? I was carrying Naakkve, and as things stood, it seemed likely that it would be difficult for me to demand obedience and respect from my household. Do you remember how you supported me? Do you remember when your foster father visited us with women guests we didn't know, and his maids and serving men, and our own servants, sat across the table from us? Do you remember how Munan pulled from me every shred of dignity I might use to hide behind, and you sat there meekly and dared not stop his speech?"

"Jesus! Have you been brooding about this for fifteen years?" Then he looked up at her—his eyes seemed such a strange pale blue, and his voice was faltering and helpless. "And yet, my Kristin—it doesn't seem to me that the two of us say unkind or harsh words to each other. . . ."

"No," said Kristin, "and that's why it cut even deeper into my heart that time during the Christmas celebration when you railed at me because I had spread my cape over Margret, while women from three counties stood around and listened."

Erlend did not reply.

"And yet you blame me for the way things went with Margret, but every time I tried to reprimand her with even a single word, she would run to you, and you would tell me sternly to leave the maiden in peace—she was yours and not mine."

"Blame you? No, I don't," Erlend said with difficulty, struggling hard to speak calmly. "If one of our children had been a daughter, then you might have better understood how this matter of my daughter . . . it stabs a father to the very marrow."

"I thought I showed you this spring that I understood," said his wife softly. "I only had to think of my own father. . . ."

"All the same, this was much worse," said Erlend, his voice still calm. "I was an unmarried man. This man . . . was married. I was not bound. At least," he corrected himself, "I wasn't bound in such a way that I couldn't free myself."

"And yet you didn't free yourself," said Kristin. "Don't you remember how it came about that you were freed?"

Erlend leaped to his feet and slapped her face. Then he stood staring at her in horror. A red patch appeared on her white cheek, but she sat rigid and motionless, her eyes hard. The child began to cry in fright; she rocked him gently in her arms, hushing him.

"That . . . was a vile thing to say, Kristin," said her husband uncertainly.

"The last time you struck me," she answered in a low voice, "I was carrying your child under my heart. Now you hit me as I hold your son on my lap."

"Yes, we keep having all these children," he shouted impatiently.

They both fell silent. Erlend began swiftly pacing back and forth. She carried the child over to the alcove and put him on the bed; when she reappeared in the alcove doorway, he stopped in front of her.

"I . . . I shouldn't have struck you, my Kristin. I wish I hadn't done it. I'll probably regret it for as long as I regretted it the first time. But you . . . you've told me before that you think I forget things too quickly. But you never forget—not a single injustice I might have done you. I've tried . . . tried to be a good husband to you, but you don't seem to think that worth remembering. You . . . you're so beautiful, Kristin . . ." He gazed after her as she walked past him.

Oh, his wife's quiet and dignified bearing was as lovely as the willowy grace of the young maiden had been; she was wider in the bosom and hips, but she was also taller. She held herself erect, and her neck bore the small, round head as proudly and beautifully as ever. Her pale, remote face with the dark-gray eyes stirred and excited him as much as her round, rosy child's face had stirred and excited his restless soul with its wondrous calm. He went over and took her hand.

"For me, Kristin, you will always be the most beautiful of women, and the most dear."

She allowed him to hold her hand but didn't squeeze his in return. Then he flung it aside; rage overcame him once again.

"You say I've forgotten. That may not always be the worst of sins. I've never pretended to be a pious man, but I remember what I learned from Sira Jon when I was a child, and God's servants have reminded me of it since. It's a sin to brood over and dwell on the sins we have confessed to the priest and repented before God, receiving His forgiveness through the hand and the words of the priest. And it's not out of piety, Kristin, that you're constantly tearing open these old sins of ours—you want to hold the knife to my throat every time I oppose you in some way."

He walked away and then came back.

"Domineering . . . God knows that I love you, Kristin, even though I can see how domineering you are, and you've never forgiven me for the injustice I did to you or for luring you astray. I've tolerated a great deal from you, Kristin, but I will no longer tolerate the fact that I can never have peace from these old misfortunes, nor that you speak to me as if I were your thrall."

Kristin was trembling with fury when she spoke.

"I've never spoken to you as if you were my thrall. Have you *ever* heard me speak harshly or in anger to anyone who might be considered lesser than me, even if it was the most incompetent or worthless of our household servants? I know that before God I am free of the sin of offending His poor in either word or deed. But you're supposed to be my *lord;* I'm supposed to obey and honor you, bow to you and lean on you, next to God, in accordance with God's laws, Erlend! And if I've lost patience and talked to you in a manner unbefitting a wife speaking to her husband—then it's because many times you've made it difficult for me to surrender my ignorance to your better understanding, to honor and obey my husband and lord as much as I would have liked. And perhaps I had expected that you . . . perhaps I thought I could provoke you into showing me that you were a man and I was only a poor woman. . . .

"But you needn't worry, Erlend. I will not offend you again with my words, and from this day forward, I will never forget to speak to you as gently as if you were descended from thralls."

Erlend's face had flushed dark red. He raised his fist at her, then turned swiftly on his heel, grabbed his cape and sword from the bench near the door, and rushed out.

It was sunny outside, with a piercing wind. The air was cold, but glistening particles of thawing ice sprayed over him from the

building eaves and from the swaying tree branches. The snow on
the rooftops gleamed like silver, and beyond the black-green,
forested slopes surrounding the town, the mountain peaks
sparkled icy blue and shiny white in the sharp, dazzling light of the
wintry spring day.

Erlend raced through the streets and alleyways—fast but aim-
less. He was boiling inside. She was wrong, it was clear that *she*
had been wrong from the very beginning, and he was right. He
had allowed himself to be provoked and struck her, undercutting
his position, but she was the one who was wrong. Now he had no
idea what to do with himself. He had no wish to visit any acquaintances, and he refused to go back home.

There was a great tumult in town. A large trading ship from
Iceland—the first of the spring season—had put in at the docks
that morning. Erlend wandered west through the lanes and
emerged near Saint Martin's Church; he headed down toward the
wharves. There were already shrieks and clamor coming from the
inns and alehouses, even though it was early afternoon. In his
youth Erlend could have gone into such places himself, along with
friends and companions. But now people would stare, wide-eyed,
and afterwards they would wear out their gums gossiping if the
sheriff of Orkdøla county, who had a residence in town and ale,
mead, and wine in abundance in his own home, should go into an
inn and ask for a taste of their paltry ale. But that was truly what
he wished for most—to sit and drink with the smallholders who
had come to town and with the servants and seamen. No one
would make a fuss if these fellows gave their women a slap in the
face; it would do them good. How in fiery Hell was a man to rule
his wife if he couldn't beat her because of her high birth and his
own sense of honor. The Devil himself couldn't compete with a
woman through words. She was a witch—but so beautiful. If only
he could beat her until she gave in.

The bells began to ring from all the churches in town, calling
the people to vespers. The sounds tumbled in the spring wind,
hovering over him in the turbulent air. No doubt she was on her
way to Christ Church now, that holy witch. She would complain
to God and the Virgin Mary and Saint Olav that she had been
struck in the face by her husband. Erlend sent his wife's guardian

saints a greeting of sinful thoughts as the bells resounded and tolled and clanged. He headed toward Saint Gregor's Church.

The graves of his parents lay in front of Saint Anna's altar in the north aisle of the nave. As Erlend said his prayers, he noticed that Fru Sunniva Olavsdatter and her maid had entered the church portal. When he finished praying, he went over to greet her.

In all the years he had known Fru Sunniva, things had always been such between them that they could banter and jest quite freely whenever they met. On this evening, as they sat on the bench and waited for evensong to begin, he grew so bold that several times she had to remind him that they were in church, with people constantly coming in.

"Yes, yes," said Erlend, "but you're so lovely tonight, Sunniva! It's wonderful to banter with a woman who has such gentle eyes."

"You're not worthy enough, Erlend Nikulaussøn, for me to look at you with gentle eyes," she said, laughing.

"Then I'll come and banter with you after it grows dark," replied Erlend in the same tone of voice. "When the mass is over, I'll escort you home."

At that moment the priests entered the choir, and Erlend went over to the south nave to join the other men.

When the service came to an end, he left the church through the main door. He saw Fru Sunniva and her maid a short distance down the street. He thought it best he didn't accompany her and go right home instead. Just then a group of Icelanders from the trading ship appeared in the street, staggering and clinging to each other, and seemed intent on blocking the way of the two women. Erlend ran after them. As soon as the seamen saw a gentleman with a sword on his belt approaching, they stepped aside and made room for the women to pass.

"I think it would be best if I escorted you home, after all," said Erlend. "There's too much unrest in town tonight."

"What do you think, Erlend? As old as I am . . . And yet perhaps it doesn't displease me if a few men still find me pretty enough to try to block my passage. . . ."

There was only one answer that a courteous man could give.

He returned to his own residence at dawn the next morning, pausing for a moment outside the bolted door to the main building, frozen, dead tired, heartsick, and dejected. Should he pound on the door to wake the servants and then slip inside to crawl into bed next to Kristin, who lay there with the child at her breast? No. He had with him the key to the eastern storehouse loft; that's where he kept some possessions that were in his charge. Erlend unlocked the door, pulled off his boots, and spread some homespun fabric and empty sacks on top of the straw in the bed. He wrapped his cape around him, crept under the sacks, and was fortunate enough to fall asleep and forget everything, exhausted and confused as he was.

Kristin was pale and weary from a sleepless night as she sat down to breakfast with her servants. One of the men said he had asked the master to come to the table—he was sleeping in the east loft—but Erlend told him to go to the Devil.

Erlend was supposed to go to Elgeseter after the morning service to be a witness to the sale of several estates. Afterwards he managed to excuse himself from the meal in the refectory, and to slip away from Arne Gjavvaldssøn, who had also declined to stay and drink with the brothers but wanted Erlend to come home to Ranheim with him.

Later he regretted that he had parted company with the others, and he was filled with dread as he walked home alone through town—now he would have to think about what he had done. For a moment he was tempted to go straight down to Saint Gregor's Church; he had promised to make confession to one of the priests whenever he was in Nidaros. But if he did it again, after he had confessed, it would be an even greater sin. He had better wait for a while.

Sunniva must think he was little better than a chicken she had caught with her bare hands. But no, the Devil take him if he'd ever thought a woman would be able to teach him so many new things—here he was walking around and gasping with astonishment at what he had encountered. He had imagined himself to be rather experienced in *ars amoris,* or whatever the learned men called it. If he had been young and green, he would probably have felt quite cocky and thought it splendid. But he didn't like that woman—that wild woman. He was sick of her. He was sick of *all* women except his own wife—and he was sick of her as well! By the Holy Cross, he had been so married to her that he had grown pious himself, because he had believed in her piety. But what a handsome reward he had been given by his pious wife for his faithfulness and love—witch that she was! He remembered the sting of her spiteful words from the evening before. So she thought he acted as if he were descended from thralls. . . . And that other woman, Sunniva, no doubt thought he was inexperienced and clumsy because he had been caught off guard and showed some surprise at her skills in love. Now he would show her that he was no more a saint than she was. He had promised her to come to Baardsgaard that night, and he might as well go. He had committed the sin—he might as well enjoy the pleasure that it offered.

He had already broken his vows to Kristin, and she herself was to blame, with her spiteful and unreasonable behavior toward him. . . .

He went home and wandered through the stables and outbuildings, looking for something to complain about; he quarreled with the priest's servant from the hospital because she had brought malt into the drying room, even though he knew that his own servants had no use for the grain-drying house while they were in Nidaros. He wished that his sons were with him; they would have been good company. He wished he could go back home to Husaby at once. But he had to stay in Nidaros and wait for letters to arrive from the south; it was too risky to receive such letters at his own home in the village.

The mistress of the house didn't come to the evening meal. She was lying in bed in the alcove, said her maid Signe, with a reproachful look at her master. Erlend replied harshly that he hadn't asked about her mistress. After the servants had left the room, he went into the alcove. It was oppressively dark. Erlend bent over Kristin on the bed.

"Are you crying?" he asked very softly, for her breathing sounded so strange. But she answered brusquely that she wasn't.

"Are you tired? I'm about to go to bed too," he murmured.

Kristin's voice quavered as she said, "Then I would rather, Erlend, that you went to bed in the same place where you slept last night."

Erlend didn't reply. He went out and then returned with the candle from the hall and opened up his clothes chest. He was already dressed suitably enough to go out wherever he liked, for he was wearing the violet-blue *cote-hardi* because he had been to Elgeseter in the morning. But now he took off these garments, slowly and deliberately, and put on a red silk shirt and a mouse-gray, calf-length velvet tunic with small silver bells on the points of the sleeves. He brushed his hair and washed his hands, all the while keeping his eyes on his wife. She was silent and didn't move. Then he left without bidding her good night. The next day he openly returned home to the estate at breakfast time.

This went on for a week. Then one evening, when Erlend came back home after going up to Hangrar on business, he was told that Kristin had set off for Husaby that morning.

He was already quite aware that no man had ever had less plea-sure from a sin than he was having from his dealings with Sunniva Olavsdatter. In his heart he was so unbearably tired of that de-mented woman—sick of her even as he played with her and ca-ressed her. He had also been reckless; it must be known all over town and throughout the countryside by now that he had been spending his nights at Baardsgaard. And it was not worth having his reputation sullied for Sunniva's sake. Occasionally he also wondered whether there might be consequences. After all, the woman had a husband, such as he was, decrepit and sickly. He pitied Baard for being married to such a wanton and foolish woman; Erlend was hardly the first to tread too close to the man's honor. And Haftor . . . but when he took up with Sunniva he hadn't remembered that she was Haftor's sister; he didn't think of this until it was too late. The situation was as bad as it could pos-sibly be. And now he realized that Kristin knew about it.

Surely she wouldn't think of bringing a charge against him be-fore the archbishop, seeking permission to leave him. She had Jørundgaard to flee to, but it would be impossible for her to travel over the mountains at this time of year; even more so if she wanted to take the children along, and Kristin would never leave them be-hind. He reassured himself that she wouldn't be able to travel by ship with Munan and Lavrans so early in the spring. No, it would be unlike Kristin to seek help from the archbishop against him. She had reason to do so, but he would willingly stay away from their bed until she understood that he felt true remorse. Kristin would never allow this matter to become a public case. Yet he realized it had been a long time since he could be certain what his wife might or might not do.

That night he lay in his own bed, letting his thoughts roam. It occurred to him that he had acted with even greater folly than he had first thought when he entered into this miserable affair, now that he was involved in the greatest plans.

He cursed himself for still being such a fool over a woman that she could drive him to this. He cursed both Kristin and Sunniva. By Devil, he was no more besotted with women than other men; he had gotten involved with fewer of them than most of the men he knew. But it was as if the Fiend himself were after him; he couldn't come near a woman without landing in mire up to his armpits.

It had to be stopped now. Thank the Lord he had other matters on his hands. Soon, very soon, he would receive Lady Ingebjørg's letters. Well, he couldn't avoid trouble with women in this matter either, but that must be God's punishment for the sins of his youth. Erlend laughed out loud in the dark. Lady Ingebjørg would have to see that what they had told her about the situation was true. The question was whether it would be one of her sons or the sons of her unlawful sister whom the Norwegians supported to oppose King Magnus. And she loved the children she had borne to Knut Porse in a way she had never loved her other children.

Soon, very soon . . . then it would be the sharp wind and the salty waves that would fill his embrace. God in Heaven, it would be good to be soaked through by the sea swells and feel the fresh wind seep into his marrow—to be quit of women for a good long time.

Sunniva. Let her think what she would. He wouldn't go back there again. And Kristin could go off to Jørundgaard if she liked. It might be safest and best for her and the children to be far away in Gudbrandsdal this summer. Later on he would no doubt make amends with her again.

The following morning he rode up toward Skaun. He decided he wouldn't have any peace until he knew what his wife intended to do.

She received him politely, her demeanor gentle and cool, when he arrived at Husaby later in the day. Unless he asked her a question, she said not a word, not even anything unkind, and she didn't object when later that evening he came over and tentatively lay down in their bed. But when he had lain there for a while, he hesitantly tried to put his hand on her breast.

Kristin's voice shook, but Erlend couldn't tell if it was from sorrow or bitterness, when she whispered, "Surely you're not so lowly a man, Erlend, that you will make this even worse for me. I cannot start a quarrel with you, since our children are sleeping all around. And since I have seven sons by you, I would rather our servants didn't see that I know I'm a woman who has been betrayed."

Erlend lay there in silence for a long time before he dared reply.

"Yes, may God have mercy on me, Kristin—I have betrayed you. I wouldn't have . . . wouldn't have done it if I had found it easier to bear those vicious words you said to me in Nidaros. I haven't come home to beg your forgiveness, for I know this would be too much to ask of you right now."

"I see that Munan Baardsøn spoke the truth," replied his wife. "The day will never come when you will stand up and take the blame for what you have done. You should turn to God and seek redemption from Him. You need to ask His forgiveness more than you need to ask mine."

"Yes, I know that," said Erlend bitterly. And then they said no more. The next morning he rode back to Nidaros.

He had been in town several days when Fru Sunniva's maid came to speak to him in Saint Gregor's Church one evening. Erlend thought he ought to talk to Sunniva one last time and told the girl to keep watch that night; he would come the same way as before.

He had to creep and climb like a chicken thief to reach the loft where they always met. This time he felt sick with shame that he had made such a fool of himself—at his age and in his position. But in the beginning it had amused him to carry on like a youth.

Fru Sunniva received him in bed.

"So you've finally come, at this late hour?" she laughed and yawned. "Hurry up, my friend, and come to bed. We can talk later about where you've been all this time."

Erlend didn't know what to do or how to tell her what was on his mind. Without thinking, he began to unfasten his clothing.

"We've both been reckless, Sunniva—I don't think it advisable that I stay here tonight. Surely Baard must be expected home sometime?" he said.

"Are you afraid of my husband?" teased Sunniva. "You've seen for yourself that Baard didn't even prick up his ears when we flirted right in front of him. If he asks me whether you've been spending time here at the manor, I'll just convince him that it's the same old nonsense. He trusts me much too well."

"Yes, he does seem to trust you too well," laughed Erlend, digging his fingers into her fair hair and her firm, white shoulders.

"Do you think so?" She gripped his wrist. "And do you trust your own wife? I was still a shy and virtuous maiden when Baard won me. . . ."

"We'll keep *my* wife out of this," said Erlend sharply, releasing her.

"Why is that? Does it seem to you less proper for us to talk about Kristin Lavransdatter than about Sir Baard, my husband?"

Erlend clenched his teeth and refused to answer.

"You must be one of those men, Erlend," said Sunniva scornfully, "who thinks you're so charming and handsome that a woman can hardly be blamed if her virtue is like fragile glass to you—when usually she's as strong as steel."

"I've never thought that about you," replied Erlend roughly.

Sunniva's eyes glittered. "What did you want with me then, Erlend? Since you have married so well?"

"I told you not to mention my wife."

"Your wife or my husband."

"You were always the one who started talking about Baard, and you were the worst to ridicule him," said Erlend bitterly. "And if you didn't mock him in words . . . I'd like to know how dearly you held his honor when you took another man in your husband's place. *She* is not diminished by my misdeeds."

"Is that what you want to tell me—that you still love Kristin even though you like me well enough to want to play with me?"

"I don't know how well I like you . . . You were the one who showed your affection for me."

"And Kristin doesn't care for your love?" she sneered. "I've seen how tenderly she looks at you, Erlend. . . ."

"Be silent!" he shouted. "Perhaps she knew how worthless I

was," he said, his voice harsh and hateful. "You and I might be each other's equal."

"Is that it?" threatened Sunniva. "Am I supposed to be the whip you use to punish your wife?"

Erlend stood there, breathing hard. "You could call it that. But you put yourself willingly into my hands."

"Take care," said Sunniva, "that the whip doesn't turn back on you."

She was sitting up in bed, waiting. But Erlend made no attempt to argue or to make amends with his lover. He finished getting dressed and left without saying another word.

He wasn't overly pleased with himself or with the way he had parted with Sunniva. There was no honor in it for him. But it didn't matter now; at least he was rid of her.

CHAPTER 4

DURING THAT SPRING and summer they saw little of the master at home at Husaby. On those occasions when he did return to his manor, he and his wife behaved with courtesy and friendliness toward each other. Erlend didn't try in any way to breach the wall that she had now put up between them, even though he would often give her a searching look. Otherwise, he seemed to have much to think about outside his own home. And he never inquired with a single word about the management of the estate.

This was something his wife mentioned when, shortly after Holy Cross Day, he asked her whether she wanted to accompany him to Raumsdal. He had business to tend to in the Uplands; perhaps she would like to take the children along, spend some time at Jørundgaard, visit kinsmen and friends in the valley? But Kristin had no wish to do so, under any circumstances.

Erlend was in Nidaros during the Law *ting* and afterwards out in Orkedal. Then he returned home to Husaby but immediately began preparations for a journey to Bjørgvin. The *Margygren* was anchored out at Nidarholm, and he was only waiting for Haftor Graut, who was supposed to sail with him.

Three days before Saint Margareta's Day, the hay harvesting began at Husaby. It was the finest weather, and when the workers went back out into the meadows after the midday rest, Olav the overseer asked the children to come along.

Kristin was up in the clothing chamber, which was on the second story of the armory. The house was built in such a fashion that an outside stair led up to this room and the exterior gallery running along the side; projecting over it was the third floor, which could be reached only by means of a ladder through a hatchway inside the clothing chamber. It was standing open because Erlend was up in the weapons loft.

Kristin carried the fur cape that Erlend wanted to take along on

327

his sea voyage out to the gallery and began to shake it. Then she heard the thunder of a large group of horsemen, and a moment later she saw men come riding out of the forest on Gauldal Road. An instant later, Erlend was standing at her side.

"Is it true what you said, Kristin, that the fire went out in the cookhouse this morning?"

"Yes, Gudrid knocked over the soup kettle. We'll have to borrow some embers from Sira Eiliv."

Erlend looked over at the parsonage.

"No, he can't get mixed up in this. . . . Gaute," he called softly to the boy dawdling under the gallery, picking up one rake after another, with little desire to go out to the hay harvesting. "Come up the stairs, but stop at the top or they'll be able to see you."

Kristin stared at her husband. She'd never seen him look this way before. A taut, alert calm came over his voice and face as he peered south toward the road, and over his tall, supple body as he ran inside the loft and came back at once with a flat package wrapped in linen. He handed it to the boy.

"Put this inside your shirt, and pay attention to what I tell you. You must safeguard these letters—it's more important than you can possibly know, my Gaute. Put your rake over your shoulder and walk calmly across the fields until you reach the alder thickets. Keep to the bushes down by the woods—you know the place well, I know you do—and then sneak through the densest underbrush all the way over to Skjoldvirkstad. Make sure that things are calm at the farm. If you notice any sign of unrest or strange men around, stay hidden. But if you're sure it's safe, then go down and give this to Ulf, if he's home. If you can't put the letters into his own hand and you're sure that no one is near, then burn them as soon as you can. But take care that both the writing and the seals are completely destroyed, and that they don't fall into anyone's hands but Ulf's. May God help us, my son—these are weighty matters to put into the hands of a boy only ten winters old; many a good man's life and welfare . . . Do you understand how important this is, Gaute?"

"Yes, Father. I understand everything you said." Gaute lifted his small, fair face with a somber expression as he stood on the stairs.

"If Ulf isn't home, tell Isak that he has to set off at once for

Hevne and ride all night—he must tell them, and he knows who I mean, that I think a headwind has sprung up here, and that I fear my journey has now been cursed. Do you understand?"

"Yes, Father. I remember everything you've told me."

"Go then. May God protect you, my son."

Erlend dashed up to the weapons loft and was about to close the hatchway, but Kristin was already halfway through the opening. He waited until she had climbed up, then shut the hatch and ran over to a chest and took out several boxes of letters. He tore off the seals and stomped them to bits on the floor; he ripped the parchments into shreds and wrapped them around a key and tossed the whole thing out the window to the ground, where it landed in the tall nettles growing behind the building. With his hands on the windowsill, Erlend stood and watched the small boy who was walking along the edge of the grain field toward the meadow where the rows of harvest workers were toiling with scythes and rakes. When Gaute disappeared into the little grove of trees between the field and the meadow, Erlend pulled the window closed. The sound of hoofbeats was now loud and close to the manor.

Erlend turned to face his wife.

"If you can retrieve what I threw outside just now . . . let Skule do it, he's a clever boy. Tell him to fling it into the ravine behind the cowshed. They'll probably be watching you, and maybe the older boys as well. But I don't think they would search you. . . ." He tucked the broken pieces of seal inside her bodice. "They can't be recognized anymore, but even so . . ."

"Are you in some kind of danger, Erlend?" Kristin asked. As he looked down at her face, he threw himself into her open arms. For a moment he held her tight.

"I don't know, Kristin. We'll find out soon enough. Tore Eindridessøn is riding in the lead, and I saw that Sir Baard is with them. I don't expect that Tore is coming here for any good purpose."

Now the horsemen had entered the courtyard. Erlend hesitated for a moment. Then he kissed his wife fervently, opened the hatchway, and ran downstairs. When Kristin came out onto the gallery, Erlend was standing in the courtyard below, helping the royal trea-

surer, an elderly and ponderous man, down from his saddle. There
were at least thirty armed men with Sir Baard and the sheriff of
Gauldøla county.

As Kristin walked across the courtyard, she heard the latter
man say, "I bring you greetings from your cousins, Erlend. Borgar
and Guttorm are enjoying the king's hospitality in Veøy, and I
think that Haftor Toressøn has already paid a visit to Ivar and the
young boy at home at Sundbu by this time. Sir Baard seized Graut
yesterday morning in town."

"And now you've come here to invite me to the same meeting of
the royal retainers, I can see," said Erlend with a smile.

"That is true, Erlend."

"And no doubt you'll want to search the manor? Oh, I've taken
part in this kind of thing so many times that I should know how it
goes. . . ."

"But you've never had such great matters as high treason on
your hands before," said Tore.

"No, not until now," said Erlend. "And it looks as if I'm playing with the black chess pieces, Tore, and you have me check-
mated—isn't that so, kinsman?"

"We're looking for the letters that you've received from Lady
Ingebjørg Haakonsdatter," said Tore Eindridessøn.

"They're in the chest covered with red leather, up in the
weapons loft. But they contain little except such greetings as loving kinsmen usually send to each other; and all of them are old.
Stein here can show you the way. . . ."

The strangers had dismounted, and the servants of the estate
had now come swarming into the courtyard.

"There was much more than that in the one we took from Borgar Trondssøn," said Tore.

Erlend began whistling softly. "I suppose we might as well go
into the house," he said. "It's getting crowded out here."

Kristin followed the men into the hall. At a sign from Tore, a
couple of the armed guards came along.

"You'll have to surrender your sword, Erlend," said Tore of
Gimsar when they came inside. "As a sign that you're our prisoner."

Erlend slapped his flanks to show that he carried no other
weapon than the dagger at his belt.

But Tore repeated, "You must hand over your sword, as a sign—"

"Well, if you want to do this formally . . ." said Erlend, laughing a bit. He went over and took down his sword from the peg, holding it by the sheath and offering the hilt to Tore Eindridessøn with a slight bow.

The old man from Gimsar loosened the fastenings, pulled the sword all the way out, and stroked the blade with a fingertip.

"Was it this sword, Erlend, that you used . . . ?"

Erlend's blue eyes glittered like steel; he pressed his lips together into a narrow line.

"Yes. It was with this sword that I punished your grandson when I found him with my daughter."

Tore stood holding the sword; he looked down at it and said in a threatening tone, "You who were supposed to uphold the law, Erlend—you should have known then that you were going farther than the law would follow you."

Erlend threw back his head, his eyes blazing and fierce. "There is a law, Tore, that cannot be subverted by sovereigns or *tings*, which says that a man must protect the honor of his women with the sword."

"You've been fortunate, Erlend Nikulaussøn, that no man has ever used that law against you," replied Tore of Gimsar, his voice full of malice. "Or you might have needed as many lives as a cat."

Erlend's response was infuriatingly slow.

"Isn't the present undertaking serious enough that you would think it inopportune to bring up those old charges from my youth?"

"I don't know whether Baard of Lensvik would consider them old charges." Rage surged up inside Erlend and he was about to reply, but Tore shouted, "You ought to find out first, Erlend, whether your paramours are so clever that they can read, before you run around on your nightly adventures with secret letters in your belt. Just ask Baard who it was that warned us you were planning treachery against your king, to whom you've sworn loyalty and who granted you the position of sheriff."

Involuntarily Erlend pressed a hand to his breast—for a moment he glanced at his wife, and the blood rushed to his face. Then Kristin ran forward and threw her arms around his neck. Erlend looked down into her face—he saw nothing but love in her eyes.

"Erlend—husband!"

The royal treasurer had remained largely silent. Now he went over to the two of them and said softly, "My dear mistress, perhaps it would be best if you took the children and the serving women with you into the women's house and stayed there as long as we're here at the manor."

Erlend let go of his wife with one last squeeze of his arm around her shoulder.

"It would be best, my dear Kristin. Do as Sir Baard advises."

Kristin stood on her toes and offered Erlend her lips. Then she went out into the courtyard and collected her children and serving women from among the crowd, taking them with her into the little house. There was no other women's house at Husaby.

They sat there for several hours; the composure of their mistress kept the frightened group more or less calm. Then Erlend entered, bearing no weapons and dressed for travel. Two strangers stood guard at the door.

He shook hands with his eldest sons and then lifted the smallest ones into his arms, while he asked where Gaute was. "Well, you must give him my greetings, Naakkve. He must have gone off into the woods with his bow the way he usually does. Tell him he can have my English longbow after all—the one I refused to give him last Sunday."

Kristin pulled him to her without speaking a word.

Then she whispered urgently, "When are you coming back, Erlend, my friend?"

"When God wills it, my wife."

She stepped back, struggling not to break down. Normally he never addressed her in any other way except by using her given name; his last words had shaken her to the heart. Only now did she fully understand what had happened.

At sunset Kristin was sitting up on the hill north of the manor.

She had never before seen the sky so red and gold. Above the opposite ridge stretched an enormous cloud; it was shaped like a bird's wing, glowing from within like iron in the forge, and gleaming brightly like amber. Small golden shreds like feathers tore away and floated into the air. And far below, on the lake at the bottom of the valley, spread a mirror image of the sky and the cloud and the ridge. Down in the depths the radiant blaze was flaring upward, covering everything in sight.

The grass in the meadows had grown tall, and the silky tassels of the straw shone dark red beneath the crimson light from the sky; the barley had sprouted spikes and caught the light on the young, silky-smooth awn. The sod-covered rooftops of the farm buildings were thick with sorrel and buttercups, and the sun lay across them in wide bands. The blackened shingles of the church roof gleamed darkly, and its light-colored stone walls were becoming softly gilded.

The sun broke through from beneath the cloud, perched on the mountain rim, and lit up one forested ridge after another. It was such a clear evening; the light opened up vistas to small hamlets amidst the spruce-decked slopes. She could make out mountain pastures and tiny farms in among the trees that she had never been able to see before from Husaby. The shapes of huge mountains rose up, reddish-violet, in the south toward Dovre, in places that were usually covered by haze and clouds.

The smallest bell down in the church began to ring, and the church bell at Vinjar answered. Kristin sat bowed over her folded hands until the last notes of the ninefold peal died away.

Now the sun was behind the ridge; the golden glow paled and the crimson grew softer and pinker. After the ringing of the bells had ceased, the rustling sound from the forest swelled and spread again; the tiny creek trickling through the leafy woods down in the valley sounded louder. From the pasture nearby came the familiar clinking of the livestock bells; a flying beetle buzzed halfway around her and then disappeared.

She sent a last sigh after her prayers; an appeal for forgiveness because her thoughts had been elsewhere while she prayed.

The beautiful large estate lay below her on the hillside, like a jewel on the wide bosom of the slope. She gazed out across all the land she had owned along with her husband. Thoughts about the manor and its care had filled her soul to the brim. She had worked and struggled. Not until this evening did she realize how much she had struggled to put this estate back on its feet and keep it going— how hard she had tried and how much she had accomplished.

She had accepted it as her fate, to be borne with patience and a

straight back, that this had fallen to her. Just as she had striven to
be patient and steadfast no matter what life presented, every time
she learned she was carrying yet another child under her breast—
again and again. With each son added to the flock she recognized
that her responsibility had grown for ensuring the prosperity and
secure position of the lineage. Tonight she realized that her ability
to survey everything at once and her watchfulness had also grown
with each new child entrusted to her care. Never had she seen it so
clearly as on this evening—what destiny had demanded of her and
what it had given her in return with her seven sons. Over and over
again joy had quickened the beat of her heart; fear on their behalf
had rent it in two. They were her children, these big sons with
their lean, bony, boy's bodies, just as they had been when they
were small and so plump that they barely hurt themselves when
they tumbled down on their way between the bench and her knee.
They were hers, just as they had been back when she lifted them
out of the cradle to her milk-filled breast and had to support their
heads, which wobbled on their frail necks the way a bluebell nods
on its stalk. Wherever they ended up in the world, wherever they
journeyed, forgetting their mother—she thought that for her, their
lives would be like a current in her own life; they would be one
with her, just as they had been when she alone on this earth knew
about the new life hidden inside, drinking from her blood and
making her cheeks pale. Over and over she had endured the sinking, sweat-dripping anguish when she realized that once again her
time had come; once again she would be pulled under by the
groundswell of birth pains—until she was lifted up with a new
child in her arms. How much richer and stronger and braver she
had become with each child was something that she first realized
tonight.

And yet she now saw that she was the same Kristin from
Jørundgaard, who had never learned to bear an unkind word because she had been protected all her days by such a strong and
gentle love. In Erlend's hands she was still the same . . .

Yes. Yes. Yes. It was true that all this time she had remembered,
year after year, every wound he had ever caused her—even though
she had always known that he never wounded her the way a
grown person intends harm to another, but rather the way a child
strikes out playfully at his companion. Each time he offended her,

she had tended to the memory the way one tends to a venomous
sore. And with each humiliation he brought upon himself by acting on any impulse he might have—it struck her like the lash of a
whip against her flesh, causing a suppurating wound. It wasn't
true that she willfully or deliberately harbored ill feelings toward
her husband; she knew she wasn't usually narrow-minded, but
with him she was. If Erlend had a hand in it, she forgot nothing—
and even the smallest scratch on her soul would continue to sting
and bleed and swell and ache if he was the one to cause it.

About him she would never be wiser or stronger. She might
strive to seem capable and fearless, pious and strong in her marriage with him—but in truth, she wasn't. Always, always there was
the yearning lament inside her: She wanted to be his Kristin from
the woods of Gerdarud.

Back then she would have done everything she knew was wrong
and sinful rather than lose him. To bind Erlend to her, she had
given him all that she possessed: her love and her body, her honor
and her share of God's salvation. And she had given him anything
else she could find to give: her father's honor and his faith in his
child, everything that grown and clever men had built up to protect an innocent little maiden if she should fall. She had set her
love against their plans for the welfare and progress of her lineage,
against their hopes for the fruit of their labors after they themselves lay buried. She had put at risk much more than her own life
in this game, in which the only prize was the love of Erlend Nikulaussøn.

And she had won. She had known from the first time he kissed
her in the garden of Hofvin until he kissed her today in the little
house, before he was escorted from his home as a prisoner—Erlend loved her as dearly as his own life. And if he had not counseled her well, she had known from the first moment she met him
how he had counseled himself. If he had not always treated her
well, he had nonetheless treated her better than he did himself.

Jesus, how she had won him! She admitted it to herself tonight;
she had driven him to break their marriage vows with her own
coldness and poisonous words. She now admitted to herself that
even during those years when she had looked on his unseemly flirt-
ing with that woman Sunniva with resentment, she had also felt, in
the midst of her rancor, an arrogant and spiteful joy. No one knew

of any obvious stain on Sunniva Olavsdatter's reputation, and yet Erlend talked and jested with her like a hired man with an alehouse maid. About Kristin he knew that she could lie and betray those who trusted her most, that she could be willingly lured to the worst of places—and yet he had trusted her, he had honored her as best he could. As easily as he forgot his fear of sin, as easily as he had finally broken his promise to God before the church door—he had still grieved over his sins against her, he had struggled for years to keep his promises to her.

She had chosen him herself. She had chosen him in an ecstasy of passion, and she had chosen him again each day during those difficult years back home at Jørundgaard—his impetuous passion in place of her father's love, which would not allow even the wind to touch her harshly. She had refused the destiny that her father had wished for her when he wanted to put her into the arms of a man who would have safely led her onto the most secure paths, even bending down to remove every little pebble that she might tread upon. She had chosen to follow the other man, whom she knew traveled on dangerous paths. Monks and priests had pointed out remorse and repentance as the road home to peace, but she had chosen strife rather than give up her precious sin.

So there was only one thing left for her; she could not lament or complain over whatever might now befall her at this man's side. It made her dizzy to think how long ago she had left her father. But she saw his beloved face and remembered his words on that day in the smithy when she stabbed the last knife into his heart; she remembered how they talked together up on the mountain that time when she realized that death's door stood open behind her father. It was shameful to complain about the fate she had chosen herself. Holy Olav, help me, so that I do not now prove myself unworthy of my father's love.

Erlend, Erlend . . . When she met him in her youth, life became for her like a roiling river, rushing over cliffs and rocks. During these years at Husaby, life had expanded outward, becoming wide and spacious like a lake, mirroring everything around her. She remembered back home when the Laag overflowed in the spring, stretching wide and gray and mighty along the valley floor, carrying with it drifting logs; and the crowns of the trees that stood rooted to the bottom would rock in the water. In the middle appeared small, dark, menacing eddies, where the current ran rough and wild and dangerous beneath the smooth surface. Now she knew that her love for Erlend had rushed like a turbulent and dangerous current through her life for all these years. Now it was carrying her outward—she didn't know where.

Erlend, dear friend!

Once again Kristin spoke the words of a prayer to the Virgin into the red of the evening. Hail Mary, full of grace! I dare not ask you for more than one thing—I see that now. Save Erlend, save my husband's life!

She looked down at Husaby and thought about her sons. Now, as the manor lay swathed in the evening light like a dream vision that might be whirled away, as her fear for the uncertain fate of her children shook her heart, she remembered this: She had never fully thanked God for the rich fruits her toils had borne over the years, she had never fully thanked Him for giving her a son seven times.

From the vault of the evening sky, from the countryside beneath her gaze came the murmur of the mass intoned as she had heard it thousands of times before, in the voice of her father, who had explained the words to her when she was a child and stood at his knee: Then Sira Eirik sings the *Præfatio* when he turns toward the altar, and in Norwegian it means:

Truly it is right and just, proper and redemptive that we always and everywhere should thank Thee, Holy Lord, Almighty Father, eternal God. . . .

When she lifted her face from her hands, she saw Gaute coming up the hillside. Kristin sat quietly and waited until the boy stood before her; then she reached out to take his hand. There was grassy meadow all around and not a single place to hide anywhere near the rock where she sat.

"How have you carried out your father's errand, my son?" she asked him softly.

"As he asked me to, Mother. I made my way to the farm without being seen. Ulf wasn't home, so I burned what Father had given me in the hearth. I took it out of the wrapping." He hesitated for a moment. "Mother—there were nine seals on it."

"My Gaute." His mother put her hands on the boy's shoulders and looked into his face. "Your father has had to place important matters in your hands. If you don't know what else to do, but you feel you need to speak of this to someone, then tell your mother what's troubling you. But it would please me most if you could keep silent about this altogether, son!"

The fair complexion beneath the straight, flaxen hair, the big eyes, the full, firm red lips—he looked so much like her father now. Gaute nodded. Then he placed his arm around his mother's shoulders. With painful sweetness Kristin noticed that she could lean her head against the boy's frail chest; he was so tall now that as he stood there and she sat beside him, her head reached to just above his heart. It was the first time she had leaned for support against this child.

Gaute said, "Isak was home alone. I didn't show him what I was carrying, just told him I had something that needed to be burned. Then he made a big fire in the hearth before he went out and saddled his horse."

Kristin nodded. Then he released her, turned to face her, and asked in a childish voice full of fear and awe, "Mother, do you know what they're saying? They're saying that Father . . . wants to be *king*."

"That sounds most unlikely, child," she replied with a smile.

"But he comes from the proper lineage, Mother," said the boy, somber and proud. "And it seems to me that Father might be better at it than most other men."

"Hush." She took his hand again. "My Gaute . . . you should realize, after Father has shown such trust in you . . . You and all the rest of us must neither think nor speak, but guard our tongues well until we learn more and can judge whether we ought to speak, and in what way. I'm going to ride to Nidaros tomorrow, and if I can talk to your father alone for a moment, I'll tell him that you have carried out his errand well."

"Take me with you, Mother!" begged the boy earnestly.

"We must not let anyone think you're anything but a thoughtless child, Gaute. You will have to try, little son, to play and be as happy as you can at home—in that way you will serve him best."

Naakkve and Bjørgulf walked slowly up the hill. They came over to their mother and stood there, looking so young and strained and distraught. Kristin saw that they were still children enough to turn to their mother at this anxious time—and yet they were so close to being men that they wanted to console or reassure her, if they could find some way to do so. She reached out a hand to each of the boys. But neither of them said very much.

After a while they headed back home; Kristin walked with one hand on the shoulder of each of her eldest sons.

"Why are you looking at me that way, Naakkve?" she said. But the boy blushed, turned his head away, and did not reply.

He had never before thought about how his mother looked. It had been years ago that he began comparing his father to other men—his father was the most handsome of men, with the bearing most like a chieftain. His mother was the mother who had more and more children; they grew up and left the hands of women to join the life and companionship and fighting and friendship of the group of brothers. His mother had open hands through which everything they needed flowed; his mother had a remedy for almost every ill; his mother's presence at the manor was like the fire in the hearth. She created life at home the way the fields around Husaby created the year's crops; life and warmth issued from her as they did from the beasts in the cowshed and the horses in the stable. The boy had never thought to compare her to other women.

Tonight he suddenly saw it: She was a proud and beautiful woman. With her broad, pale forehead beneath the linen wimple, the even gaze of her steel-gray eyes under the calm arch of her brows, with her heavy bosom and her long, slender limbs. She held her tall figure as erect as a sword. But he could not speak of this; blushing and silent, he walked beside her, with her hand on the nape of his neck.

Gaute followed along behind. Bjørgulf was also gripping the back of his mother's belt, and the older boy began grumbling because his brother was treading on his heels. They started shoving and pushing at each other. Their mother told them to hush and put an end to their quarreling—but her somber expression softened into a smile. They were still just children, her sons.

She lay awake that night; she had Munan sleeping at her breast and Lavrans lay between her and the wall.

Kristin tried to take stock of her husband's case.

She couldn't believe that it was truly dangerous. Erling Vidkuns-søn and the king's cousins at Sudrheim had been charged with treason against their king and country—but they were still here in Norway, as secure and rich as ever, although they might not stand as high in the king's favor as before.

No doubt Erlend had become involved in some unlawful activities in the service of Lady Ingebjørg. Over all these years he had maintained his friendship with his highborn kinswoman. Kristin knew that five years back, when he visited her in Denmark, he had done her some unlawful service that had to be kept secret. Now that Erling Vidkunssøn had taken up Lady Ingebjørg's cause and was trying to acquire for her control of the property she owned in Norway—it was conceivable that Erling had sent her to Erlend, or that she herself had turned to the son of her father's cousin after the friendship had cooled between Erling and the king. And then Erlend had handled the matter recklessly.

Yet if that was true, it was hard to understand how her kinsmen at Sundbu could have been involved in this.

It could only end with Erlend coming to a full reconciliation with the king, if he had done nothing more than act overzealously in service of the king's mother.

High treason. She had heard about the downfall of Audun Hugleikssøn; it had happened during her father's youth. But they were terrifying misdeeds that Audun had been charged with. Her father said it was all a lie. The maiden Margret Eiriksdatter had died in the arms of the bishop of Bjørgvin, but Audun took no part in the crusade, so he could not have sold her to the heathens. Maiden Isabel was thirteen years old, but Audun was more than fifty when he brought her home to be King Eirik's bride. It was shameful for a Christian to pay any heed at all to such rumors as there were about that bridal procession. Her father refused to allow the ballads about Audun to be sung at home on his manor. And yet there were unheard-of things said about Audun Hesta-korn. He had supposedly sold all of King Haakon's military power to the French king and promised to sail to his aid with twelve hundred warships—and for that he had received seven barrels of gold in payment. But it had never been fully explained to the peasants of the country why Audun Hugleikssøn had to die on the gallows at Nordnes.

His son fled the country; people said he had taken service in the army of the French king. The granddaughters of the Aalhus knight, Gyrid and Signe, had left their grandfather's execution site with his stable boy. They were to live like poor peasant wives somewhere in a mountain village in Haddingjadal.

It was a good thing, after all, that she and Erlend did not have daughters. No, she was not going to think about such matters. It was so unlikely that Erlend's case should have a worse outcome than . . . than that of Erling Vidkunssøn and the Haftorssøns.

Nikulaus Erlendssøn of Husaby. Oh, now she too felt that Husaby was the most beautiful manor in all of Norway.

She would go to Sir Baard and find out all she could. The royal treasurer had always been her friend. Judge Olav, as well—in the past. But Erlend had gone too far, that time when the judge decided against him in the case of his estate in town. And Olav had taken to heart the misfortune with his goddaughter's husband.

They had no close kinsmen, neither she nor Erlend—no matter how extensive their lineage might be. Munan Baardsøn no longer had great influence. He had been charged with unlawful deeds when he was sheriff of Ringerike; he was too eager in his attempts to further the position of his many children in the world—he had four from his marriage and five outside of it. And he had apparently declined greatly since Fru Katrin had died. Inge of Ry county, Julitta and her husband, Ragnrid who was married to a Swede—Erlend knew little of them. They were the remaining children of Herr Baard and Fru Aashild. There had never been friendship between Erlend and the Hestnes people since the death of Sir Baard Petersøn; Tormod of Raasvold had grown senile; and his children with Fru Gunna were all dead and his grandchildren underage.

Kristin herself had no other kinsmen in Norway from her father's lineage than Ketil Aasmundssøn of Skog and Sigurd Kyrning, who was married to her uncle's oldest daughter. The second daughter was a widow, and the third was a nun. All four of the men of Sundbu seemed to be involved in the case. Lavrans had become such foes with Erlend Eldjarn over the inheritance after Ivar Gjesling's death that they had refused to see each other ever again, so Kristin did not know her aunt's husband or his son.

The ailing monk at the friars' monastery was Erlend's only close kinsman. And the one who stood closest to Kristin in the world was Simon Darre, since he was married to her only sister.

Munan woke up and began to whimper. Kristin turned over in bed and placed the child to her other breast. She couldn't take him with her to Nidaros, as uncertain as everything now stood. Perhaps this would be the last drink the poor child would ever have from his own mother's breast. Perhaps this was the last time in this world that she would lie in bed holding a little infant . . . so good, so good . . . If Erlend was condemned to death . . . Blessed Mary, Mother of God, if she had ever for an hour or a day been impatient because of the children that God had granted to her . . . Was this to be the last kiss she ever received from a little mouth, sweet with milk?

KRISTIN WENT TO the king's palace the next evening, as soon as she arrived in Nidaros. Where are they holding Erlend? she wondered as she looked around at the many stone buildings. She seemed to be thinking more about how Erlend might be faring than about what she needed to find out. But she was told that the royal treasurer was not in town.

Her eyes were stinging from the long boat trip in the glittering sunshine, and her breasts were bursting with milk. After the servants who slept in the main house had fallen asleep, she got out of bed and paced the floor all night.

The next day she sent Haldor, her personal servant, over to the king's palace. He came back shocked and distressed.

His uncle, Ulf Haldorssøn, had been taken prisoner on the fjord as he attempted to reach the monastery on the island of Holm. The royal treasurer had not yet returned.

This news also frightened Kristin terribly. Ulf had not lived at Husaby during the past year but had served as the sheriff's deputy, residing for the most part at Skjoldvirkstad, a large share of which he now owned. What kind of matter could this be when so many men seemed to be involved? She couldn't stop herself from thinking the worst, ill and exhausted as she now was.

By the morning of the third day, Sir Baard had still not returned home. And a message that Kristin had tried to send to her husband was not allowed through. She thought about seeking out Gunnulf at the monastery, but decided against it. She paced the floor at home, back and forth, again and again, with her eyes half-closed and burning. Now and then she felt as if she were walking in her sleep, but as soon as she lay down, fear and pain would seize hold of her and she would have to get up again, wide awake, and walk to make it bearable.

Shortly after mid-afternoon prayers Gunnulf Nikulaussøn came to see her. Kristin walked swiftly toward the monk.

"Have you seen Erlend? Gunnulf, what are they accusing him of?"

"The news is troubling, Kristin. No, they won't allow anyone near Erlend—least of all any of us from the monastery. They think that Abbot Olav knew about his undertakings. He borrowed money from the brothers, but they swear they knew nothing about what he intended to use it for when they placed the cloister's seal on the document. And Abbot Olav refuses to give any explanation."

"Yes, but what is it all about? Was it the duchess who lured Erlend into this?"

Gunnulf replied, "It seems instead that they had to press hard before she would agree. Someone . . . has seen drafts of a letter, which Erlend and his friends sent to her in the spring; it's not likely to fall into the hands of the authorities unless they can threaten Lady Ingebjørg to part with it. And they haven't found any drafts. But according to both the reply letter and the letter from Herr Aage Laurisen, which they seized from Borgar Trondssøn in Veøy, it seems certain enough that she did receive such a missive from Erlend and the men who have joined forces with him in this plan. For a long time she clearly seemed to fear sending Prince Haakon to Norway; but they persuaded her that no matter what the outcome might be, King Magnus would not possibly harm the child, since they are brothers. Even if Haakon Knutssøn did not win the Crown in Norway, he would be no worse off than before. But these men were willing to risk their lives and their property to put him on the throne."

For a long time Kristin sat in utter silence.

"I understand. These are more serious matters than what came between Sir Erling or the Haftorssøns and the king."

"Yes," said Gunnulf in a subdued voice. "Haftor Olavssøn and Erlend were supposedly sailing to Bjørgvin. But they were actually heading for Kalundborg, and they were to bring Prince Haakon back with them to Norway while King Magnus was abroad courting his bride."

After a moment the monk continued in the same tone of voice. "It must be . . . nearly a hundred years since any Norwegian has dared attempt such a thing: to overthrow the man who was king by right of succession and replace him with an opposing king."

Kristin sat and stared straight ahead; Gunnulf could not see her face.

"Yes. The last men who dared undertake this game were your ancestors and Erlend's. Back then my deceased kinsmen of the Gjesling lineage were also on the side of King Skule," she said pensively.

She met Gunnulf's searching glance and then exclaimed hotly and fiercely, "I'm merely a simple woman, Gunnulf—I paid little attention when my husband spoke with other men about such matters. I was unwilling to listen when he wanted to discuss them with me. God help me, I don't have the wits to understand such weighty topics. But foolish woman that I am, with knowledge of nothing more than my household duties and rearing children— even I know that justice had much too long a road to travel before any grievance could find its way to the king and then back again to the villages. I too have seen that the peasants of this country are faring worse and must endure more hardships now than when I was a child, and blessed King Haakon was our lord. My husband . . ." She took several quick, shuddery breaths. "My husband took up a cause that was so great that none of the other chieftains in all the land dared raise it. I see that now."

"That he did." The monk clasped his hands tightly together. His voice was hardly more than a whisper. "Such a great cause that many will think it very grave that he brought about its downfall himself . . . and in this way . . ."

Kristin cried out and leaped to her feet. She moved with such force that the pain in her breast and arms brought the sweat pouring from her body. Agitated and dizzy with fever, she turned to Gunnulf and shouted loudly, "Erlend is not to blame . . . it just happened . . . it was his misfortune . . ."

She threw herself to her knees and pressed her hands on the bench; she lifted her blazing, desperate face to the monk.

"You and I, Gunnulf . . . you, his brother, and I, his wife for thirteen years, we shouldn't blame Erlend now that he's a poor prisoner, with his life perhaps in danger."

Gunnulf's face quivered. He looked down at the kneeling woman. "May God reward you, Kristin, for accepting things in this manner." Again he wrung his emaciated hands. "God . . . may God grant Erlend life and such circumstances that he might repay your loyalty. May God turn this evil away from you and your children, Kristin."

"Don't talk like that!" She straightened her back as she knelt, and looked up into the monk's eyes. "No good has come of it, Gunnulf, whenever you have taken on Erlend's affairs or mine. No one has judged him more harshly than you—his brother and God's servant."

"Never have I judged Erlend more harshly than . . . than was necessary." His pale face had grown even paler. "I've never loved anyone on earth more than my brother. That is no doubt why . . . They stung me as if they were my own sins, sins that I had to repent myself, when Erlend dealt with you so badly. And then there is Husaby. Erlend alone must carry on the lineage which is also mine. And I have put most of my inheritance into his hands. Your sons are the men who are closest to me by blood. . . ."

"Erlend has *not* dealt with me badly! I was no better than him! Why are you talking to me this way, Gunnulf? You were never my confessor. Sira Eiliv never blamed my husband—he admonished *me* for my sins whenever I complained of my difficulties to him. He was a better priest than you are; he's the one God has placed over me, he's the one I must listen to, and he has never said that I suffered unjustly. I will listen to him!"

Gunnulf stood up when she did. Pale and distressed, he murmured, "What you say is true. You must listen to Sira Eiliv."

He turned to go, but she gripped his hand tightly. "No, don't leave me like this! I remember, Gunnulf . . . I remember when I visited you here on this estate, back when it belonged to you. And you were kind to me. I remember the first time I met you—I was in great need and anguish. I remember you spoke to me in Erlend's defense; you couldn't know . . . You prayed and prayed for my life and my child's. I know that you meant us well, and that you loved Erlend. . . .

"Oh, don't speak harshly of Erlend, Gunnulf! Who among us is pure before God? My father grew fond of him, and our children love their father. Remember that he found me weak and easy to sway, but he led me to a good and honorable place. Oh, yes, Husaby is beautiful. On the night before I left, it was so lovely; the sunset was magnificent that evening. We've spent many a good day there, Erlend and I. No matter how things go, no matter what happens, he is still my husband—my husband, whom I love."

Gunnulf leaned both hands on his staff, which he always carried now whenever he left the monastery.

"Kristin . . . Do not put your faith in the red of the sunset and in the . . . love that you remember, now that you fear for his life.

"I remember, when I was young—only a subdeacon. Gudbjørg, whom Alf of Uvaasen later married, was serving at Siheim then. She was accused of stealing a gold ring. It turned out that she was innocent, but the shame and the fear shook her soul so fiercely that the Fiend seized power over her. She went down to the lake and was about to sink into the water. She has often told us of this afterwards: that the world seemed to her such a lovely red and gold, and the water glistened and felt wondrously warm. But as she stood out there in the lake, she spoke the name of Jesus and made the sign of the cross—and then the whole world grew gray and cold, and she saw where she was headed."

"Then I won't say his name." Kristin spoke quietly; her bearing was rigid and erect. "If I thought that, then I would be tempted to betray my lord when he is in need. But I don't think it would be the name of Christ but rather the name of the Devil that would bring this about. . . ."

"That's not what I meant. I meant . . . May God give you strength, Kristin, that you may have the will to do this, to bear your husband's faults with a loving spirit."

"You can see that's what I'm doing," she said in the same voice as before.

Gunnulf turned away from her, pale and trembling. He drew his hand over his face.

"I must go home now. It's easier . . . at home it's easier for me to collect myself—to do what I can for Erlend and for you. God . . . May God and all the saints protect my brother's life and freedom. Oh, Kristin . . . You mustn't ever think that I don't love my brother."

But after he had left, Kristin thought everything seemed much worse. She didn't want the servants in the room with her; she paced back and forth, wringing her hands and moaning softly. It was already late in the evening when people came riding into the courtyard. A moment later, as the door was thrown open, a tall, stout man wearing a traveling cloak appeared in the twilight; he walked toward her with his spurs ringing and his sword trailing behind. When she recognized Simon Andressøn, Kristin broke into loud sobbing and ran toward him with outstretched arms, but she shrieked in pain when he embraced her.

Simon let her go. She was standing with her hands on his shoulders and her forehead leaning against his chest, weeping inconsolably. He put his hands lightly on her hips.

"In God's name, Kristin!" There was a sense of deliverance in the very sound of his dry, warm voice and in the vital male smell about him: of sweat, road dust, horses, and leather harnesswork. "In God's name, it's much too soon to lose all hope and courage. Surely there must be a way . . ."

After a while she regained her composure enough to ask his forgiveness. She was feeling quite wretched because she had been forced to take the youngest child from her breast so suddenly.

Simon heard how she had been faring the last three days. He shouted for her maid and asked angrily whether there wasn't a single woman on the estate who had enough wits to see what was wrong with the mistress. But the maid was an inexperienced young girl, and Erlend's foreman of his Nidaros manor was a widower with two unmarried daughters. Simon sent a man to town to find a woman skilled in healing, but he begged Kristin to lie down and rest. When she felt a little better he would come in and talk to her.

While they waited for the woman to arrive, Simon and his man were given food in the hall. As they ate, he talked to Kristin, who was undressing in the alcove. Yes, he had ridden north as soon as he heard what had happened at Sundbu. He had come here, while Ramborg went to stay with the wives of Ivar and Borgar. They had taken Ivar to Mjøs Castle, but they allowed Haavard to remain free, although he had to promise to stay in the village. It was said that Borgar and Guttorm had been fortunate enough to flee; Jon of Laugarbru had ridden out to Raumsdal to hear the news and would send word to Nidaros. Simon had reached Husaby around midday, but he hadn't stayed long. The boys were fine, but Naakkve and Bjørgulf had begged him earnestly to bring them along.

Kristin had regained her calm and courage when Simon, late that evening, came to sit at her bedside. She lay there with the feeling of pleasant exhaustion which follows great suffering, and looked at her brother-in-law's heavy, sunburned face and his small, piercing eyes. It was a great comfort to her that he had come. Simon grew quite somber when he heard more details of the matter, and yet his words were full of hope.

Kristin lay in bed, staring at the elkskin belt around his portly middle. The large, flat buckle made of copper and chased with silver, its only decoration a filigreed "A" and "M" which stood for *Ave Maria;* the long dagger with the gilded silver mountings and the large rock crystals on the hilt; the pitiful little table knife with its cracked horn hilt which had been repaired with a band of brass—all these things had been part of her father's everyday attire ever since she was a child. She remembered when Simon received them; it was right before her father died, and he wanted to give Simon his best gilded belt with enough silver to have extra plates made so that his son-in-law could wear it. But Simon asked for the other belt instead, and when Lavrans said that now he was cheating himself, Simon replied that the dagger was a costly item. "Yes, and then there's the knife," said Ragnfrid with a little smile, and both men laughed and said: "Yes indeed, the knife." Her father and mother had had so many quarrels over that knife. Ragnfrid had complained every day at having to look at that ugly little knife on her husband's belt. But Lavrans swore that she would never succeed in parting him from it. "I've never drawn this knife against you, Ragnfrid—and it's the best one in all of Norway for cutting butter, as long as it's warm."

Kristin now asked to see the knife, and she lay in bed, holding it in her hands for a moment.

"I wish that I might own this knife," she pleaded softly.

"Yes, I can well believe that. I'm glad it's mine; I wouldn't sell it for even twenty marks of silver." With a laugh Simon grabbed her wrist and took back the knife. His small, plump hands always felt so good—warm and dry.

A short time later he bade her good night, picked up the candle, and went into the main room. She heard him kneel down before the cross, then stand up and drop his boots onto the floor. A few minutes later he climbed heavily into the bed against the north wall. Then Kristin sank into a deep, sweet sleep.

She didn't wake up until quite late the next morning. Simon Andressøn had left hours earlier, and he had asked the servants to tell her to stay calm and remain at the estate.

He didn't return until almost time for mid-afternoon prayers; he said at once, "I bring you greetings from Erlend, Kristin. I was allowed to speak to him."

He saw how young her face became, soft and full of anguished tenderness. Then he held her hand in his as he talked. He and Erlend hadn't been able to say much to each other, because the man who had escorted Simon up to the prisoner never left the room. Judge Olav had won Simon permission for this meeting, because of the kinship that had existed between them while Halfrid was alive. Erlend sent loving greetings to Kristin and the children; he had asked about all of them, but most about Gaute. Simon thought that in a few days Kristin would surely be allowed to see her husband. Erlend had seemed calm and in good spirits.

"If I had gone with you today, they would have let me see him too," she said quietly.

But Simon thought he had been granted permission because he came alone. "Although it might be easier for you in many ways, Kristin, to gain concessions if a man steps forward in your behalf."

Erlend was being held in a room in the east tower, facing the river—one of the finer chambers, although it was small. Ulf Haldorssøn was supposedly sitting in the dungeon; Haftor in a different chamber.

Cautiously and hesitantly, as he tried to discern how much she could bear, Simon recounted what he had been able to learn in town. When he saw that she understood fully what had happened, he didn't hide that he too thought it a dangerous matter. But everyone he had spoken to said that Erlend would never have ventured to plan such an undertaking and carry it out as far as he had without being certain that he had a majority of the knights and gentry behind him. And since the ranks of the malcontent noblemen were so great, it wasn't expected that the king would dare deal harshly with their chieftain; he would have to allow Erlend to be reconciled with him in some way.

Kristin asked in a low voice, "Where does Erling Vidkunssøn stand in all this?"

"I think that's something that many a man would like to know," said Simon.

He didn't tell Kristin, nor had he told any of the men he talked to, but he thought it unlikely that Erlend would have a large group of men behind him who had bound themselves to support him with their lives and property in such a perilous undertaking. And certainly they would never have chosen him as chieftain; all his peers knew that Erlend was unreliable. It was true that he was the kinsman of Lady Ingebjørg and the pretender to the throne. He had enjoyed both power and respect in the last few years, he was more experienced in war than most of his peers, and he had a reputation for being able to recruit and lead soldiers. Even though he had acted unwisely so many times, he could still present his arguments in such a good and convincing manner that it was almost possible to believe he had finally learned caution from his misdeeds. Simon thought it likely that there were some who knew of Erlend's plan and had urged him on, but he would be surprised if they had bound themselves so closely that they couldn't now retreat; Erlend would be left standing with no one to back him.

Simon thought he could see that Erlend himself expected little else, and he seemed prepared to have to pay dearly for his risky game. "When cows are stuck in the mire, whoever owns them has to pull them out by the tail," he had said with a laugh. Otherwise Erlend had not been able to say much in the presence of the third man.

Simon wondered why the reunion with his brother-in-law had upset him so greatly. Perhaps it was the small, confining tower room where Erlend had invited him to take a seat on the bed, which stretched from one wall to the other and filled half the room, or Erlend's slender, dignified form as he stood at the small slit in the wall which allowed in light. Erlend looked unafraid, his eyes alert, unclouded by either fear or hope. He was a vigorous, cool, and manly figure now that all the constraining webs of flirtations and foolishness over women had been swept away from him. And yet it was women and his dealings in love that had landed him there, along with all his bold plans, which came to an end before he had even brought them to light. But Erlend didn't seem to be thinking about that. He stood there like a man who had risked the most daring of ventures and lost, and then knew how to bear the defeat in a manly and stalwart fashion.

And his surprised and joyous gratitude when he saw his brother-in-law suited him well.

Simon had said, "Do you remember, brother-in-law, that night we kept watch at our father-in-law's bedside? We shook hands, and Lavrans placed his hand on top. We promised each other and him that all our days we would stand together as brothers."

"Yes." Erlend's smile lit up his face. "Yes, Lavrans probably never thought that you would ever be in need of *my* help."

"It was more likely," said Simon unperturbed, "that he meant *you,* in your circumstances, might be of support to *me,* and not that you should need *my* help."

Erlend smiled again. "Lavrans was a wise man, Simon. And as strange as it may sound, I know he was fond of me."

Simon thought that God knew it might indeed seem strange, but now he himself—in spite of all he knew about Erlend and in spite of everything the other man had done to him—couldn't help feeling a brotherly tenderness toward Kristin's husband. Then Erlend had asked about her.

Simon told him how he had found her: ill and very frightened for her husband. Olav Hermanssøn had promised to seek permission for her to come to see him as soon as Sir Baard returned home.

"Not before she's well," said Erlend quickly, his voice fearful. An odd, almost girlish blush spread across his tan, unshaven face. "That's the only thing I fear, Simon—that I won't be able to bear it when I see her!"

But after a moment he said calmly, "I know you will stand steadfast at her side if she is to be widowed this year. They won't be poor, at any rate—she and the children—with her inheritance from Lavrans. And then she'll have you close at hand when she goes to live at Jørundgaard."

The day after the Feast of the Birth of Mary, the lord chancellor, Ivar Ogmundssøn, arrived in Nidaros. A court was now appointed, consisting of twelve of the king's retainers from the northern districts, to decide Erlend Nikulaussøn's case. Sir Finn

Ogmundssøn, the lord chancellor's brother, was chosen to present the charges against him.

In the meantime, during the summer, Haftor Olavssøn of Godøy had killed himself, using the little dagger that every prisoner was allowed to keep to cut up his food. Imprisonment had apparently taken such a toll on Haftor that he hadn't had his full wits about him. When Erlend heard of this, he told Simon that at least now he wouldn't have to worry about what Haftor might say. And yet he was clearly shaken.

Gradually it became a habit for the guard to leave the room on an errand whenever Simon or Kristin was visiting Erlend. Both of them realized, and mentioned it to each other, that Erlend's first and foremost thought was to make it through the court case without revealing his accomplices. One day he said this quite openly to Simon. He had promised every man who had conspired with him that he would rather cut off his own hand than reveal anything, if it came to that; "and I have never yet betrayed anyone who has put their trust in me." Simon stared at the man. Erlend's eyes were blue and clear; it was obvious that he truly believed this about himself.

The king's envoys had not succeeded in tracking down anyone else who had taken part in Erlend's plot other than the two brothers, Greip and Torvard Toressøn of Møre. And they refused to admit to knowing anything but that Erlend and several other men planned to persuade Lady Ingebjørg to allow Prince Haakon Knutssøn to be educated in Norway. Later the chieftains would propose to King Magnus that it would be of benefit to both of his kingdoms if he gave his half-brother sovereignty in Norway.

Borgar and Guttorm Trondssøn had been fortunate enough to escape from the king's castle at Veøy. No one knew how, but people guessed that Borgar had been helped by a woman. He was very handsome and quite impetuous. Ivar of Sundbu was still being held in Mjøs Castle; the brothers had apparently kept young Haavard out of their plans.

At the same time the meeting of the retainers was being held at the king's palace, the archbishop convened a *concilium* at his estate. Simon was a man with many friends and acquaintances, and so he could report to Kristin what was happening. Everyone thought that Erlend would be banished and would have to forfeit his properties to the king. Erlend also thought this was how things would turn out, and he was in good spirits; he was planning to go to Denmark. As things now stood in that country, there were always opportunities open for a man who was fit and skilled with weapons, and Lady Ingebjørg would surely embrace his wife as her kinswoman and keep her at her side with the proper honors. Simon would have to take care of the children, although Erlend wanted to take his two eldest sons with him.

Kristin hadn't been outside of Nidaros for a single day in all this time, nor had she seen her children, except for Naakkve and Bjørgulf. They had come riding up to the estate one evening alone. Their mother kept them with her for several days, but then she sent them to Raasvold, where Fru Gunna had taken in the younger boys.

This was in accordance with Erlend's wishes. And she was afraid of the thoughts that might rise up in her mind if she should see her sons around her, hear their questions, and try to explain matters to them. She struggled to push aside all thoughts and memories of her marriage years spent at Husaby, which had been so rich that now they seemed to her like a great calm—the way there is a kind of calm over the waves of the sea if viewed from high enough up a mountain ridge. The swells that surge after each other seem eternal, melding into one; that was the way life had rippled through her soul during that vast span of years.

Now things were once again the way they had been in her youth, when she had put her faith in Erlend, defying everyone and everything. Once again her life had become one long waiting from hour to hour, in between the times when she was allowed to see her husband, to sit at his side on the bed in the tower room of the king's palace, and to talk with him calmly—until they happened to be alone for a few moments. Then they would throw themselves into each other's arms with endless, passionate kisses and wild embraces.

At other times she would sit in Christ Church for hours on end. She would sink to her knees and stare up at Saint Olav's golden shrine behind the gratings of the choir. Lord, I am his wife. Lord, I stood by him when I was his, in sin and iniquity. By the grace of God, we two unworthy souls were joined together in holy marriage. Branded by the flames of sin, bowed by the burdens of sin, we came together at the portals of God's house; together we received the Savior's Host from the hand of the priest. Should I now complain if God is testing my faith? Should I now think about anything else but that I am his wife and he is my husband for as long as we both shall live?

On the Thursday before Michaelmas the meeting of the royal retainers was held and sentence was pronounced over Erlend Nikulaussøn of Husaby. He was found guilty of attempting to steal land and subjects from King Magnus, of inciting opposition to the king throughout the country, and of attempting to bring into Norway mercenary forces from abroad. After looking into similar cases from the past, the judges found that Erlend Nikulaussøn should forfeit his life and his property at the hands of King Magnus.

Arne Gjavvaldssøn brought the news to Simon Darre and Kristin Lavransdatter at Nikulausgaard. He had been present at the meeting.

Erlend had not tried to prove his innocence. In a clear, firm voice he had acknowledged his intentions: With these undertakings he had sought to force King Magnus Eirikssøn to grant the Crown of Norway to his young half-brother, Prince Haakon Knutssøn Porse. Erlend had spoken eloquently, thought Arne. He had talked about the great hardships that had befallen his countrymen because for the past few years the king had spent little time within Norway's boundaries and had never seemed willing to appoint representatives who could rule justly and exercise royal authority. Because of the king's actions in Skaane, and because of the extravagance and inability to handle money matters shown by those men he listened to most, the people had been subjected to great burdens and poverty. And they never felt safe from new demands for aid and taxes above what was normally expected. Since the Norwegian knights and noblemen had far fewer rights and freedom than the Swedish knighthood, it was difficult for the former to compete with the latter. And it was only reasonable that the young and imprudent man, King Magnus Eirikssøn, should listen more to his Swedish lords and love them better, since they had more wealth and thus a greater ability to support him with men who were both armed and experienced in war.

Erlend and his allies had thought they could sense such strong feelings among the majority of their countrymen—the gentry, farmers, and townsmen in the north and west of Norway—that they were certain of finding full support if they could produce a royal rival who was as closely related to our dear lord, the blessed King Haakon, as the king who was now in power. Erlend had expected that his countrymen would rally around the plan to persuade King Magnus to allow his brother to assume the throne here, but Prince Haakon would have to swear to maintain peace and brotherhood with King Magnus, to protect the kingdom of Norway in accordance with the ancient land boundaries, to assert the rights of God's Church, to enforce the laws and customs of the land according to ancient tradition, along with the rights and freedoms of the peasants and townsmen, as well as to fend off any incursion of foreigners into the realm. It had been the intention of Erlend and his friends to present this plan to King Magnus in a peaceful manner. And yet it had always been the right of Norwegian farmers and chieftains in the past to reject any king who attempted to rule unlawfully.

As to the actions of Ulf Saksesøn in England and Scotland, Erlend said that Ulf's sole purpose had been to win favor there for Prince Haakon, if God should grant that he became king. No other Norwegian man had taken part in these endeavors except for Haftor Olavssøn of Godøy—may God have mercy on his soul—the three sons of his kinsman Trond Gjesling of Sundbu, and Greip and Torvard Toressøn of the Hatteberg lineage.

Erlend's speech had made a deep impression, said Arne Gjavvaldssøn. But in the end, when he mentioned that they had expected support from men of the Church, he then referred to the old rumors from the days when King Magnus was growing up, and that had been unwise, thought Arne. The archbishop's representative had responded sharply: Archbishop Paal Baardsøn, both now and when he was chancellor, felt great love for King Magnus because of his godly temperament, and people wanted to forget that these rumors had ever existed about their king. Now he was about to marry a maiden, the daughter of the Earl of Namur . . . so even if there had ever been any truth to the rumors, Magnus Eirikssøn had now completely turned away from such interests.

Arne Gjavvaldssøn had shown Simon Andressøn the greatest friendship while he was in Nidaros. It was also Arne who now reminded Simon that Erlend had the right to appeal this sentence as having been unlawfully decided. According to the law books, the charge against Erlend had to be brought by one of his peers, but Sir Finn of Hestbø was a knight, while Erlend was a nobleman, but not a knight. Arne thought it was possible that a new court would find that Erlend could not be sentenced to a harsher punishment than banishment.

In terms of what Erlend had proposed, about the kind of sovereignty which he thought would serve the country best . . . that had sounded fine indeed. And everyone knew where the man was who would like to take the helm and steer that course while the new king was underage. Arne scratched the gray stubble of his beard and gave Simon a sidelong glance.

"No one has heard from Erling Vidkunssøn or spoken to him all summer?" asked Simon, also keeping his voice low.

"No. Well, I've heard he says he's fallen out of favor with the king and is keeping out of all such matters. But it's been years since he could stand to sit at home for such a long time and listen to Fru Elin chattering. And people say his daughters are just as beautiful and just as foolish as their mother."

Erlend had listened to his sentence with a steadfast, calm expression, and he had greeted the gentlemen of the royal retinue in just as courteous, open, and splendid a manner when he was led out as when he had been escorted in. He was calm and cheerful when Kristin and Simon were allowed to talk to him the following day. Arne Gjavvaldssøn was with them, and Erlend said that he would take Arne's advice.

"I could never persuade Kristin here to come with me to Denmark before," he said, putting an arm around his wife's waist. "And I always had such a desire to journey out into the world with her. . . ." A tremor seemed to pass over his features, and suddenly he pressed an ardent kiss to her pale cheek, without concern for the two men who stood looking on.

Simon Andressøn set off for Husaby to make arrangements for Kristin's personal possessions to be moved to Jørundgaard. He had also advised her to send the children to Gudbrandsdal at the same time.

Kristin said, "My sons will not leave their father's estate until they are driven from it."

"I wouldn't wait for that, if I were you," said Simon. "They're young; they can't fully understand these things. It would be better if you let them leave Husaby believing that they are merely going to visit their aunt and see their mother's property in the valley."

Erlend said that Simon was right about this. But in the end only Ivar and Skule traveled with their uncle south. Kristin didn't have the heart to send the two youngest boys so far away from her. When Lavrans and Munan were brought to her at the estate in town and she saw that the smallest didn't even recognize her, she broke down. Simon hadn't seen her shed a single tear since the first evening he arrived in Nidaros; now she wept and wept over Munan, who squirmed and wriggled in the crush of his mother's arms, wanting to go to his foster mother. And she wept over little Lavrans, who crept up into his mother's lap and put his arms around her neck and cried because she was crying. Now she would keep the two youngest with her, along with Gaute, who didn't want to go with Simon. She also thought it ill-advised to let the child out of her sight, since he had to bear a burden that was much too heavy for his age.

Sira Eiliv had brought the children to Nidaros. He had asked the archbishop for leave from his church and permission to visit his brother in Tautra; this was gladly granted to Erlend Nikulaussøn's house priest. Now he said that Kristin couldn't stay in town with so many children to care for, and he offered to take Naakkve and Bjørgulf out to the monastery.

On the last evening before the priest and the two boys were to depart—Simon had already left with the twins—Kristin made her confession to the pious and pure-hearted man who had been her spiritual father all these years. They sat together for hours, and Sira Eiliv impressed upon her heart that she must be humble and obedient toward God; patient, faithful, and loving toward her husband. She knelt before the bench where he sat. Then Sira Eiliv stood up and knelt at her side, still wearing the red stole which was a symbol of the yoke of Christ's love; he prayed long and fervently, without words. But she knew he was praying for the father and mother and the children and all the servants whose salvation he had striven so faithfully to encourage all these years.

The next day Kristin stood on the shore of Bratør and watched the lay brothers from Tautra set sail in the boat that would carry away the priest and her two eldest sons. On her way home she went over to the Minorites' church and stayed there until she felt strong enough to venture back to her own residence. And in the evening, when the two youngest were asleep, she sat with her spinning and told Gaute stories until it was his bedtime too.

ERLEND WAS HELD at the king's palace until almost Saint Clement's Day. Then messages and letters arrived stating that he was to be taken under safe conduct to meet with King Magnus. The king intended to celebrate Christmas at Baagahus that year.

Kristin grew terribly frightened. With unspeakable effort she had accustomed herself to feigning a calm demeanor while Erlend sat in prison, condemned to death. Now he would be taken far away to an uncertain fate. Much was said about the king, and among the circle of men who stood closest to him, her husband had no friends. Ivar Ogmundssøn, who was now the chieftain of the castle at Baagahus, had spoken the harshest words regarding Erlend's treason. And he was supposedly further enraged at having heard once again some disrespectful remarks which Erlend had made about him.

But Erlend was in good spirits. Kristin could see that he didn't take their imminent separation lightly, but the long imprisonment had now begun to wear him down; he eagerly seized upon the prospect of a long sea voyage and seemed almost indifferent to everything else.

In a matter of three days everything was arranged, and Erlend sailed with Sir Finn's ship. Simon had promised to return to Nidaros before Advent, after he had taken care of some obligations at home. If there was any news before then, he had asked Kristin to send word to him, and he would come at once. Now she decided to travel south to visit him, and from there she would go to see the king—to fall at his feet and beg for mercy for her husband. She would gladly give all she possessed in return for his life.

Erlend had sold and mortgaged every part of his residence in Nidaros to various buyers; Nidarholm cloister now owned the main house, but Abbot Olav had written a kind letter to Kristin, offering her the use of the house for as long as she needed it. She was living there alone with one maid and Ulf Haldorssøn—who had been released because they hadn't been able to prove anything against him—and his nephew, Haldor, who was Kristin's personal servant.

She sought Ulf's counsel, and at first he was rather doubtful. He thought it would be a difficult journey for her through the Dovre Range; a great deal of snow had fallen in the mountains. But when he saw the anguish of her soul, he advised her to go. Fru Gunna took the two youngest children out to Raasvold, but Gaute refused to be parted from his mother, and she didn't dare let the boy out of her sight up there in the north.

The weather was so severe when they came south to the Dovre Range that they followed Ulf's advice to leave their horses behind at Drivstuen and borrowed skis, prepared to spend the next night out in the open if need be. Kristin hadn't had skis on her feet since she was a child, so it was difficult for her to make progress, even though the men supported her as best they could. They reached no farther that day than halfway over the mountain, between Drivstuen and Hjerdkinn. When it began to grow dark, they had to seek shelter in a birch grove and dig themselves into the snow. At Toftar they managed to hire some horses, but there they ran into fog, and when they had descended partway into the valley, rain set in. When they rode into the courtyard of Formo several hours after dark, the wind was howling around the corners of the buildings, the river was roaring, and a great rushing and droning came from the forested slopes. The courtyard was a soggy mire, muffling the sound of the horses' hooves. As the Sabbath had already begun at this hour on Saturday evening, there was no sign of life on the large estate, and neither the servants nor the dogs seemed to have noticed their arrival.

Ulf pounded on the door to the main house with his spear; a serving man opened the door. A moment later Simon himself was standing in the entryway, broad and dark against the light behind him, holding a child in his arms. He pushed back the barking dogs. He gave a shout when he recognized his wife's sister, set the child down, and then pulled Kristin and Gaute inside as he helped them out of their soaked outer garments.

It was splendidly warm in the room, but the air seemed oppressive because it was a hearth room with a flat ceiling beneath the loft hall. And it was full of people; children and dogs were swarming from every corner. Then Kristin caught sight of both of her own small sons, their faces ruddy and warm and gleeful, behind the table on which a lighted candle stood. The two boys came forward and greeted their mother and brother a bit awkwardly; Kristin could see that they had arrived in the midst of everyone's merriment and fun. And the room was in great disarray. She stepped on crunching nutshells at every turn—they were scattered all over the floor.

Simon sent his servants off to do chores, and the room was emptied of people—neighbors and their attendants, as well as most of the children and dogs. While he asked questions and listened to her replies, Simon fastened his shirt and tunic, which were open wide, revealing his bare, hairy chest. The children had brought him to such a state, he said apologetically. He was terribly disheveled; his belt was twisted around, his clothes and hands were dirty, his face was covered with soot, and his hair was full of straw and dust.

A few minutes later two serving women came in to take Kristin and Gaute over to Ramborg's women's house. A fire had been started in the fireplace, and several maids busily lit the candles, made up the beds, and helped her and the boy into dry clothes, while others set the table with food and drink. A half-grown maiden with silk-wrapped braids brought Kristin a frothy bowl of ale. The girl was Simon's eldest daughter, Arngjerd.

Then Simon came into the room. He had tidied himself up and now looked more as Kristin was used to seeing him, handsomely and splendidly dressed. He was leading his little daughter by the hand, and Ivar and Skule followed.

Kristin asked about her sister, and Simon replied that Ramborg had accompanied the Sundbu women down to Ringheim; Jostein had come to get his daughter, Helga, and then he wanted Dagny and Ramborg to come along too. He was such a merry, kind old man, and he had promised to take good care of the three young wives. Ramborg might stay there all winter. She was expecting a child around Saint Matthew's Day, and Simon had thought he might have to be away from home that winter, so she would be better off with her young kinswomen. No, it made no difference to the housekeeping here at Formo whether she was home or not, laughed Simon. He had never demanded that young Ramborg trouble herself with all that toil.

As to Kristin's plans, Simon said at once that he would travel south with her. He had so many kinsmen there, as well as his father's friends and his own from the past, that he hoped to be able to serve her better than he had in Nidaros. And there it would be easier for him to determine whether it would be wise for her to pay a visit to the king himself. He could be ready to travel in three or four days.

They attended mass together the next day, which was Sunday, and afterwards they visited Sira Eirik at his home at Romundgaard. The priest was old now. He received Kristin kindly and seemed very saddened by her troubling fate. Then they went over to Jørundgaard.

The buildings looked the same, and the rooms held the same beds, benches, and tables. It was now her property, and it seemed most likely that her sons would grow up here; this was also where she herself would one day lie down and close her eyes. But never had she felt so clearly as at this moment that life in this home had depended on her father and mother. No matter what they had struggled with in private, from them had streamed warmth, help, peace, and security to everyone else who lived there.

Uneasy and dejected as she now felt, it made her weary to listen to Simon talk about his own affairs: his manor and his children. She knew she was being unreasonable; he was willing to do all he could to help her. She realized how good it was of him to agree to leave his home during the Christmas season, and to be away from his wife, as things now stood. No doubt he was thinking a great deal about whether he might have a son. He had only the one child with Ramborg, even though they had been married six years. Kristin couldn't expect that he should take Erlend's and her misfortune so much to heart that he would forget all the joy he had from his own life. But it was strange to be there with him; he seemed so happy and warm and secure in his own home.

Without thinking, Kristin had assumed that Ulvhild Simonsdatter would be like her own little sister, for whom the child had been named—fair and fragile and pure. But Simon's little daughter was round and plump, with cheeks like apples and lips as red as a berry, lively gray eyes that looked like her father's in his youth, and lovely brown curls. Simon had the greatest love for his pretty, merry child, and he was proud of her bright chatter.

"Even though this girl is so hideous and wicked and naughty," he said, putting his hands around her chest and tumbling her around as he lifted her up into the air. "I think she must be a changeling that the trolls up here in the hills left in the cradle for her mother and me—such an ugly and loathsome child she is." Then he set her down abruptly and hastily made the sign of the cross over her three times, as if he were frightened by his own imprudent words.

Arngjerd, the daughter born of his maid, was not beautiful, but she looked kind and sensible, and Simon took her with him whenever he could. He was constantly praising her cleverness. Kristin had to look at everything in Arngjerd's marriage chest, at all she had spun and woven and stitched as part of her dowry.

"When I place the hand of my daughter into the hand of a faithful husband," said Simon as he gazed after the child, "it will be one of the happiest days of my life."

To spare expenses and so that the journey might proceed faster, Kristin was to take along no maids, nor any servant other than Ulf Haldorssøn. Two weeks before Christmas they left Formo, accompanied by Simon Andressøn and his two young, vigorous men.

When they arrived in Oslo, Simon learned at once that the king would not be coming to Norway—he would apparently celebrate Christmas in Stockholm. Erlend was being held in the castle at Akersnes; the chieftain was away, so for the time being it would be impossible for any of them to see him. But the deputy royal treasurer, Olav Kyrning, promised to let Erlend know that they had come to town. Olav was quite friendly toward Simon and Kristin because his brother was married to Ramborg Aasmundsdatter of Skog, which made him distantly related to the daughters of Lavrans.

Ketil of Skog came to town and invited them to spend Christmas with him, but Kristin had no wish for noisy feasting as matters now stood for Erlend. And then Simon too refused to go, no matter how earnestly she begged him. Simon and Ketil knew each other, but Kristin had only met her uncle's son once since he had grown up.

Kristin and Simon had taken lodgings at the same residence

where she had once been the guest of his parents, back when the two of them were betrothed, but this time they were staying in a different building. There were two beds in the main room; Kristin slept in one of them, Simon and Ulf slept in the other. The servants bedded down in the stable.

On Christmas Eve Kristin wanted to attend midnight mass at Nonneseter's church; she said it was because the sisters sang so beautifully. All five of them decided to go. The night was starry and clear, mild and lovely; it had snowed a little in the evening, so it was quite bright. When the bells began to ring from the churches, people came streaming out of all the houses, and Simon had to give Kristin his hand. Now and then he would cast a sidelong glance at her. She had grown terribly thin in the autumn, but her tall, erect figure seemed to have regained some of its maidenly softness and quiet grace. Her pale face had assumed the expression from her youth of calm and gentleness, which hid a deep, tense wariness. She had taken on an oddly phantomlike resemblance to the young Kristin from that Christmastime so long ago. Simon gripped her hand hard, unaware that he was doing so until she squeezed his fingers in return. He looked up. She smiled and nodded, and he understood that she had interpreted the pressure of his hand as a reminder that she must remain brave—and now she was trying to show him that she would.

When the holy days were over, Kristin went out to the convent and asked to be allowed to pay her respects to the abbess and to those sisters who were still living there since she had left. She then spent a little time in the abbess's parlatory. Afterwards she went into the church. She realized that there was nothing for her to gain inside the walls of the convent. The sisters had received her kindly, but she saw that for them she was merely one of the many young maidens who had spent a year there. If they had heard any talk about her distinguishing herself from the rest of the young daughters in any way, and not for the better, they made no mention of it. But that year at Nonneseter, which loomed so large in her own life, meant so little in the life of the cloister. Her father had bought for himself and his family a place in the convent's prayers of intercession for their souls. The new abbess, Fru Elin, and the sisters said that they would pray for her and for her husband's salvation. But Kristin saw that she had no right to force her way in and disturb

the nuns with her visits. Their church stood open to her, as it did
to everyone; she could stand in the north aisle and listen to the
singing of the pure women's voices from the choir; she could look
around the familiar room, at the altars and pictures. And when the
sisters left the church through the door to the convent courtyard,
she could go up and kneel before the gravestone of Abbess Groa
Guttormsdatter and think about the wise, powerful, and dignified
mother whose words she had neither understood nor heeded. She
had no other rights in this women's residence for Christ's servants.

At the end of the holy days, Sir Munan came to see Kristin. He
said he had just learned that she was in Oslo. He greeted her
heartily, as he did Simon Andressøn and Ulf, whom he kept calling
his kinsman and dear friend. He thought it would be difficult for
them to win permission to see Erlend; he was being kept under
tight guard. Munan himself had not succeeded in gaining access to
his cousin. But after the knight had ridden off, Ulf said with a
laugh that he thought Munan probably hadn't tried very hard—he
was so deathly afraid of being mixed up in the case that he hardly
dared hear mention of it. Munan had aged greatly; he was quite
bald and gaunt, and his skin hung loosely on his large frame. He
was living out at Skogheim, with one of his unlawful daughters,
who was a widow. Munan would have liked to be rid of her because none of his other children, lawful or unlawful, would come
near him as long as this half-sister was managing his household.
She was a domineering, avaricious, and sharp-tongued woman.
But Munan didn't dare ask her to leave.

Finally, around New Year's, Olav Kyrning obtained permission
for Kristin and Simon to see Erlend. It was again Simon's lot to escort the sorrowful wife to these heartbreaking meetings. The
guards were much more careful here than they were in Nidaros
not to let Erlend speak to anyone without the chieftain's men being
present.

Erlend was calm, as before, but Simon could see that the situation was now beginning to wear him down. He never complained;
he said he suffered no privations and was treated as well as was allowed, but he admitted that the cold bothered him a good deal;
there was no hearth fire in the room. And there was little he could
do to keep himself clean—although, he jested, if he hadn't had the

lice to fight with, the time might have passed much more slowly out there.

Kristin too was calm—so calm that Simon held his breath with fear, waiting for the day when she would completely fall apart.

King Magnus was making his royal tour of Sweden, and there was little prospect that he would return to his homeland anytime soon, or that there would be any change in Erlend's situation.

On Saint Gregor's Day Kristin and Ulf Haldorssøn had been to church at Nonneseter. On their way home, as they crossed the bridge over the convent creek, she did not take the road to their hostel, which lay near the bishop's citadel; instead, she turned east toward the lane near Saint Clement's Church and headed along the narrow alleyways between the church and the river.

The day was hazy and gray, and a thaw had set in, so their footwear and the hems of their cloaks grew quickly soaked and heavy from the yellow mud near the river. They reached the fields along the riverbank. Once their eyes met. Ulf laughed softly and a kind of smirk appeared on his lips, but his eyes were sad; Kristin gave him an odd, sickly smile.

A moment later they were standing on the ridge of a hill; the earth had given way out here sometime before, and the farm now lay right below the hill—so close to the dirty-yellow slope, covered with tufts of black, dried weeds, that the rank stench from the pigsty, which they were looking down at, rose up toward them. Two fat sows were wallowing around in the dark muck. The river-bank was only a narrow strip here; the gray, murky current of the river, filled with careening ice floes, ran right up to the dilapidated buildings with the faded rooftops.

As they stood there, a man and a woman came walking over to the fenced area and looked at the pigs; the man leaned over and scratched one of the sows with the haft of the silver-chased, thin-bladed axe he was using as a staff. It was Munan Baardsøn him-self, and the woman was Brynhild Fluga. He looked up and noticed them. He stood there gaping, until Kristin shouted a merry greeting down to him.

Sir Munan began to bellow with laughter.

"Come down and have a hot ale in this vile weather," he called.

On their way down to the farmyard fence, Ulf told Kristin that Brynhild Jonsdatter no longer kept an inn or an alehouse. She had been in trouble several times and was finally threatened with flogging, but Munan had come to her rescue and vouched for her; she promised to stop all her unlawful activities. And her sons now held such positions that, for their sake, their mother had to think about improving her reputation. After the death of his wife, Munan Baardsøn had taken up with Brynhild again and was often over at Flugagaard.

He met them at the gate.

"All four of us are kinsmen, after a fashion," he chuckled. He was slightly drunk, but not overly so. "You're a good woman, Kristin Lavransdatter, pious but not at all haughty. Brynhild is now an honorable and respectable woman too. And I was an unmarried man when I produced the two sons we have together—and they're the most splendid of all my children. That's what I've told you every single day in all these years, Brynhild. I'm more fond of Inge and Gudleik than any of my other children. . . ."

Brynhild was still beautiful, but her skin was sallow and looked as if it would be clammy to the touch, thought Kristin—the way it does after standing over a pot of grease all day long. But her house was well-kept, the food and drink she set on the table were excellent, and the crockery was pleasing and clean.

"Yes, I drop by over here whenever I have business in Oslo," said Munan. "A mother likes to hear news of her sons, you see. Inge writes to me himself, because he's a learned man, Inge—a bishop's envoy has to be, you know. . . . I found him a good match too: Tora Bjarnesdatter from Grjote. Do you think many men could have acquired such a woman for their bastard son? So we sit here and talk about that, and Brynhild brings in the food and ale for me, just like in the old days, when she wore my keys at Skogheim. It's hard to sit out there now and think about my blessed wife . . . So I ride over here to find some solace—when Brynhild here has a mind to grant me a little kindness and warmth."

Ulf Haldorssøn was sitting with his chin in his hand and gazing at the mistress of Husaby. Kristin sat and listened, answering quietly and gently and courteously—just as calm and refined as if she were a guest at one of the grand estates back home in Trøndelag.

"Well, Kristin Lavransdatter, you won honor and the name of wife," said Brynhild Fluga, "even though you came willingly enough to meet Erlend up in my loft. But I was called a wanton and loose woman all my days; my stepmother sold me into the hands of that man there—I bit and fought, and the scratches from my fingernails marked his face before he had his way with me."

"Are you going to bring that up again?" fretted Munan. "You know full well . . . I've told you so many times before . . . I would have let you go in peace if you had behaved properly and begged me to spare you, but you rushed at my face like a wildcat before I had even stepped inside the door."

Ulf Haldorssøn chuckled to himself.

"And I've treated you well ever since," said Munan. "I gave you everything you wanted . . . and our children . . . well, they're in a better and more secure position than those poor sons of Kristin. May God protect the poor boys, the way Erlend has left things for his children! I think that must be more important to a mother's heart than the name of wife—and you know how many times I wished that you had been highborn so that I might marry you— I've never liked any other woman as much as you, even though you were seldom gentle or kind to me . . . and the wife I did have, may God reward her. I've established an altar for my Katrin and me in our church, Kristin—I've thanked God and Our Lady every day for my marriage. . . . no man has had things better. . . ." He sniffed and began to cry.

A little later Ulf Haldorssøn said they would have to leave. He and Kristin didn't exchange a single word on the way home. But outside the main door, she took Ulf's hand.

"Ulf—my kinsman and my friend!"

"If it would help," he said quietly, "I would gladly go to the gallows in Erlend's place—for his sake and for yours."

In the evening, a little before bedtime, Kristin was sitting alone in the room with Simon. Suddenly she began to tell him where she had been that day. She recounted the conversation they had had out there.

Simon was sitting on a small stool a short distance away. Bending forward slightly, with his arms resting on his thighs and his hands hanging down, he sat and gazed up at her with a peculiar, searching look in his small, sharp eyes. He didn't say a word, and not a muscle twitched in his heavy, broad face.

Then Kristin mentioned that she had told her father everything, and what his response had been.

Simon sat in the same position, without moving. But after a while he said calmly, "That was the only request I have ever made of you in all the years we've known each other . . . if I remember right . . . that you should . . . but if you couldn't keep that to yourself to spare Lavrans, then . . ."

Kristin's body trembled violently. "Yes. But . . . Oh, Erlend, Erlend, Erlend!"

At her wild cries, the man leaped to his feet. Kristin had flung herself forward, and with her head in her arms she was rocking from side to side, calling to Erlend over and over in between the quavering, racking sobs that seemed to be wrung from her body, filling her mouth with moans that welled up and spilled out.

"Kristin, in the name of Jesus!"

When he grasped her arms and tried to console her, she threw her full weight against his chest and put her arms around his neck, as she continued to weep and call out her husband's name.

"Kristin—calm yourself. . . ." He crushed her in his arms but saw that she took no notice; she was crying so hard that she couldn't stand on her own. Then he lifted her in his arms—held her tight for a moment, and then carried her over to the bed and laid her down.

"Calm yourself," he again implored, his voice stifled and almost threatening. He placed his hands over her face, and she took hold of his wrists and arms and then clung to him.

"Simon . . . Simon . . . oh, he must be saved. . . ."

"I'll do what I can, Kristin. But now you *must* calm yourself!" Abruptly he turned away, walked to the door, and went out. He shouted so loudly that his voice echoed between the buildings; he called for the serving maid Kristin had hired in Oslo. She came running, and Simon told her to go in to her mistress. A moment later the girl came back out—her mistress wanted to be left alone, she fearfully told Simon; he hadn't moved from the spot where he stood.

He nodded and went over to the stable, staying there until his servant Gunnar and Ulf Haldorssøn came out to give the horses their evening fodder. Simon began talking with them and then went with Ulf back to the main house.

Kristin saw little of her brother-in-law the following day. But after mid-afternoon prayers, as she sat and sewed on a garment she was going to take to her husband, Simon came dashing into the room. He didn't speak to her or look at her; he merely threw open his traveling chest, filled his silver goblet with wine, and left. Kristin stood up and followed. Outside the main door stood a stranger, still holding the reins of his horse. Simon took a gold ring off his finger, tossed it into the goblet, and drank a toast to the messenger.

Kristin guessed what the news was and shouted joyfully, "You've been given a son, Simon!"

"Yes." He slapped the messenger on the shoulder as the man uttered his thanks and tucked the goblet and ring under his belt. Then Simon put his arm around the waist of his wife's sister and spun her around. He looked so happy that Kristin had to put her hands on his shoulders; then he kissed her full on the mouth and laughed loudly.

"I see it will be the Darre lineage, after all, that will live on at Formo after you're gone, Simon," she said joyously.

"So be it . . . if God wills."

When Kristin asked him if they should go to evensong together, he replied, "No, tonight I want to go alone."

That evening he told Kristin he had heard that Erling Vidkunssøn was supposed to be at his manor, Aker, near Tunsberg. Earlier in the day Simon had booked passage on a ship down the fjord; he wanted to talk to Sir Erling about Erlend's case.

Kristin said very little. They had mentioned this possibility before, but avoided discussing it further—whether Sir Erling had known about Erlend's endeavor or not. Simon said he would seek Erling Vidkunssøn's counsel—ask him what he thought of Kristin's plan that Simon should accompany her to meet with Lavrans's powerful kinsmen in Sweden, to ask the help of friends and kin.

Then she said, "But you have received such great news, brother-in-law, that it seems to me it would be more reasonable for you to postpone this journey to Aker and first travel to Ringheim, to see Ramborg and your son."

He had to turn away, he felt so weak. He had been waiting for this—whether Kristin would show some sign that she understood how he longed to see his son. But when he had regained mastery of his feelings, he said with some embarrassment, "I've been thinking, Kristin, that God will perhaps grant the boy better health if I can be patient and rein in my longing to see him until I've helped Erlend and you a little more in this matter."

The next day Simon went out and bought rich and splendid gifts for his wife and son, as well as for all the women who had been at Ramborg's side when she gave birth. Kristin took out a beautiful silver spoon she had inherited from her mother; this was for the infant, Andres Simonssøn. But to her sister she sent the heavy gilded silver chain, which Lavrans had once given her in her childhood along with the reliquary cross. The cross she now moved to the chain Erlend had given her as a betrothal present. The following day, around noon, Simon set sail.

In the evening the ship anchored off an island in the fjord. Simon stayed on board, lying in a sleeping bag made of pelts, with several homespun blankets spread on top; he looked up at the starry skies, where the images seemed to rock and sway as the ship pitched on the sleepily gliding swells. The water sloshed and the ice floes scraped and hammered against the sides of the vessel. It was almost pleasant to feel the cold seeping deeper and deeper into his body. It was soothing. . . .

And yet he was now certain that as bad as things had been, they would never be so again. Now that he had a son. It was not that he thought he would love the boy more than he did his daughters. But this was different. As joyful as the small maidens could make him feel whenever they came to their father with their games and laughter and chatter, and as wonderful as it felt to have them sitting on his lap with their soft hair beneath his chin—a man could not claim the same position in the succession of men among his kin if his estate and property and the memory of his deeds in this world should be transferred on the hand of his daughter to some other lineage. But now that he dared to hope—if only God would allow this infant boy to grow up—that son would follow father at Formo: Andres Gudmundssøn, Simon Andressøn, Andres Simonssøn. Then it was clear that he must be for Andres what his own father had been for him: a man of integrity, both in his secret thoughts and in his actions.

Sometimes he felt he didn't have the strength to continue. If only he had seen a single sign that she understood. But Kristin behaved toward him as if they were actual siblings: considerate of his welfare, kind and loving and gentle. And he didn't know how long it could last: living together in the same house in this manner. Didn't she ever think about the fact that he couldn't forget? Even though he was now married to her sister, he could still never forget that they had once been betrothed to live together as man and wife.

But now he had a son. Whenever he said his prayers, he had always shied away from adding any of his own words, whether wishes or words of gratitude. But Christ and Mary knew full well what he meant when he had said double the number of *Pater nosters* and *Ave Marias* lately. He would continue to do so as long as he was away from home. And he would show his gratitude in an equally fitting and generous manner. Then perhaps he would receive help on this journey, as well.

In truth, he thought it unreasonable to expect to make any gains from this meeting. Relations between Erling and the king were now quite cold. And no matter how powerful and proud the former regent might be, no matter how little he needed to fear the young king—who was in a much more difficult position than Norway's wealthiest and most highborn man—it was still unlikely that he would want to provoke King Magnus even more by speaking on Erlend Nikulaussøn's behalf and drawing suspicion upon himself that he might have known about Erlend's treasonous plans. Even if Erling had taken part in them—yes, even if he was behind the whole undertaking, prepared to intervene and allow himself to be placed in charge of the realm as soon as there was once again an underaged king in the land—he would not feel bound to take any risks to help the man who had ruined the entire plan for the sake of a shameful love affair. This was something Simon almost forgot whenever he was together with Erlend and Kristin, for the two of them seemed hardly to remember it anymore. But it was true that Erlend himself was to blame for the whole endeavor resulting in nothing more than misfortune for him and the good men who had been exposed by his foolish philandering.

He must try every recourse to help her and her husband. And now he began to hope. Perhaps God and the Virgin Mary or some of the saints, whom he had always honored with offerings and alms, would support him in this undertaking too.

He arrived at Aker quite late the following evening. An overseer on the estate met him and sent servants on ahead, some with the horses and some to escort Simon's man over to the servants' hall. The overseer himself went up to the loft where the knight was sitting and drinking. A moment later Sir Erling came out onto the gallery and stood there as Simon climbed the stairs. Then he welcomed his guest courteously enough and led him into the chamber where Stig Haakonssøn of Mandvik was sitting with a very young man who was Erling's only son, Bjarne Erlingssøn.

Simon was received in a friendly fashion; the servants took his outer garments and brought in food and drink. But he could see that the men had guessed why he had come—or at least Erling and Stig had—and he noticed their reticence. When Stig began to talk about how rare it was to see Simon in that part of the country, and how he wasn't exactly wearing down the doorstep of his former kinsmen—he hadn't even been farther south than to Dyfrin since Halfrid died—then Simon replied, "No, not until this winter." But he had been in Oslo for several months now with his wife's sister, Kristin Lavransdatter, who was married to Erlend Nikulaussøn.

At that they all fell silent. Then Sir Erling asked politely about Kristin and about Simon's wife and siblings, and Simon asked about Fru Elin and Erling's daughters, and Stig's health, and news from Mandvik and old neighbors there.

Stig Haakonssøn was a stout, dark-haired man a few years older than Simon, the son of Halfrid Erlingsdatter's half-brother, Sir Haakon Toressøn, and the nephew of Erling Vidkunssøn's wife, Elin Toresdatter. He had lost his position as sheriff of Skidu and his command of the castle at Tunsberg two winters earlier when he fell out of favor with the king, but otherwise he lived well enough at Mandvik, although he was a widower with no children. Simon knew him quite well and had been on good terms with him, as he was with all the kinsmen of his first wife—although the friendship had never been overly warm. He knew what they had all thought about Halfrid's second marriage: Sir Andres Gudmundssøn's younger son might be both well positioned and of good lineage, but he was not an equal marriage match for Halfrid Erlingsdatter, and he was ten years younger than she was. They couldn't understand why she had set her heart on this young man, but they allowed her to do as she wished, since she had suffered so unbearably with her first husband.

Simon had met Erling Vidkunssøn only a couple of times before, and then he had always been in the company of Fru Elin and uttered hardly a sound; no one needed to say more than "yes," or "ah," whenever she was in the room. Sir Erling had aged quite a bit since that time. He had grown stouter, but he still had a handsome and stately figure for he carried himself exceedingly well and it suited him that his pale, reddish-gold hair had now turned a gleaming, silvery gray.

Simon had never met the young Bjarne Erlingssøn before. He had grown up near Bjørgvin in the house of a clergyman who was Erling's friend—within the family it was said that this was because the father didn't want his son living out there at Giske amidst all the prattling of the women. Erling himself didn't spend any more time at home than he had to, but he didn't dare take the boy along with him on his frequent journeys because Bjarne had suffered poor health in his childhood, and Erling Vidkunssøn had lost two other sons when they were small.

The boy looked exceptionally handsome as he sat with the light behind him and his face turned in profile. Thick, black, curly hair cascaded over his forehead; his big eyes were dark, his nose was large, with a graceful curve, his lips were firm and delicate, his chin well-shaped. He was also tall, broad-shouldered, and slim. But when Simon was about to sit down at the table to eat, the servant moved the candle, and then he saw that the skin of Bjarne's throat was completely eaten away by scrofulous scars—they spread out to both sides, all the way up to his ears and under his chin: dead, shiny white patches of skin, purplish stripes, and swollen knots. And Bjarne had the habit of suddenly pulling up the hood of the round, fur-trimmed velvet shoulder collar which he wore even inside the house—pulling it up to his ears. After a few minutes it would grow too hot for him, and he would let it fall back, only to pull it up again. He didn't seem aware that he was doing this. After a while Simon felt his own hands grow restless from watching him, even though he tried to avoid looking in his direction.

Sir Erling hardly took his eyes off his son, although he too seemed unaware that he was sitting with his gaze fixed on the boy. Erling Vidkunssøn's face showed little emotion, and there was no particular expression in his pale-blue eyes; but behind that somewhat vague and watery glance there seemed to lie endless years of worry and care and love.

Then the three older men conversed, politely but in a desultory fashion, while Simon ate, and the young man sat there fidgeting with his hood. Afterwards all four of them drank for a proper length of time, and then Sir Erling asked Simon if he was weary from his journey, and Stig invited him to share his bed. Simon was glad to postpone talking about the purpose of his visit. This first evening at Aker had left him quite dejected.

The next day, when he finally spoke of it, Sir Erling replied in much the way Simon had expected. He said that King Magnus had never willingly listened to him, but he had noticed that the moment Magnus Eirikssøn became old enough to have an opinion, it had been his view that Erling Vidkunssøn wouldn't have anything more to say to him after he came of age. And ever since the dispute had been settled between Erling and his friends on one side and the king on the other, he had neither heard from nor spoken to the king or the king's friends. If he spoke on Erlend's behalf to King Magnus, it would be of little benefit to the man. And he was aware that many people in the country thought he had been behind Erlend's undertaking in some way. Simon could believe him or not, but neither he nor his friends had known anything about what was being planned. But if this matter had come to light in a different fashion, or if these adventuresome young daredevils had carried through their plot and failed—then he might have stepped forward and tried to mediate. But because of the way things had gone, he didn't think anyone could reasonably demand him to stand up and reinforce the people's suspicions that he had been playing two games.

But he advised Simon to appeal to the Haftorssøns. They were the king's cousins, and when they weren't quarreling with him, they managed to maintain a certain friendship. And as far as Erling could see, the men Erlend was protecting were more likely to be found among the Haftorssøns' circles, as well as among the younger noblemen.

As everyone knew, the king's wedding was to be celebrated in Norway that summer. It might provide a fitting opportunity for King Magnus to show mercy and leniency toward his enemies. And the king's mother and Lady Isabel would no doubt attend the festivities. Simon's mother had been Queen Isabel's handmaiden when she was young, after all; perhaps Simon should appeal to her, or perhaps Erlend's wife ought to fall to her knees before the king's bride and Lady Ingebjørg Haakonsdatter with her prayers for their intercession.

Simon thought it would have to be the last resort, for Kristin to kneel before Lady Ingebjørg. If she had realized what was honorable, Lady Ingebjørg would have long ago stepped forward to gain Erlend's release from his troubles. But when Simon had once mentioned this to Erlend, he had simply laughed and said that Lady Ingebjørg always had so many troubles and worries of her own, and no doubt she was angry because it now seemed unlikely that her most beloved child would ever win the title of king.

CHAPTER 7

IN EARLY SPRING Simon Andressøn traveled north to Toten to see his wife and infant son and accompany them home to Formo. He stayed there for some time to tend to his own affairs.

Kristin didn't want to leave Oslo. And she didn't dare give in to her burning, urgent longing to see her three sons who were back home in Gudbrandsdal. If she was going to continue to endure the life she was now living from day to day, she couldn't think about her children. And she did manage to endure; she seemed calm and brave. She talked and listened to strangers and accepted advice and encouragement. But she had to hold on to the thought of Erlend—only Erlend! In those moments when she failed to hold her thoughts tight in the grasp of her will, other images and pictures would race through her mind: Ivar standing in the woodshed at Formo with Simon and waiting expectantly as his uncle searched for a split piece of wood for him, bending down to heft each one in his hand. Gaute's fair, boyish face, full of manly determination as he struggled through the snowdrifts on that gray wintry day in the mountains last fall. His skis slipped backwards, and he slid some distance down the steep slope, sinking deep into the snow. For a moment his face seemed about to crumple; he was an exhausted, helpless child. Her thoughts would wander to her youngest sons: Munan must be able to walk and even talk a little by now. Was he just as sweet as the others had been at his age? Lavrans had probably forgotten her by now. And the two oldest boys out at the monastery at Tautra. Naakkve, Naakkve . . . her firstborn . . . How much did the two older sons understand? What were they thinking about? And how was Naakkve, still a child, coping with the fact that now nothing in his life would be the way that she and he and everyone else had imagined it would be?

Sira Eiliv had sent her a letter, and she had reported to Erlend what it said about their sons. Otherwise they never spoke of their children. They didn't talk about the past or the future anymore. Kristin would bring him some piece of clothing or a plate of food; he would ask her how she had fared since they last met, and they would sit on the bed holding hands. Sometimes they would be left alone for a moment in the small, cold and filthy, stench-filled room. Then they would cling to each other with mute, passionate caresses, hearing but paying no attention to Kristin's maid laughing with the castle guards outside on the stairs.

There would be plenty of time, either after he was taken from her or after he came back to her, for thinking about all the children and their changed circumstances—and about everything else in her life besides her husband. She didn't want to lose a single hour of the time they had together, and she didn't dare think about her reunion with the four sons she had left behind up north. For this reason she accepted Simon Andressøn's offer to travel alone to Nidaros; along with Arne Gjavvaldssøn, he would see to her interests in the settling of the estate. King Magnus would not be made richer by acquiring Erlend's property; his debts were much greater than he himself had thought, and he had raised money that was sent to Denmark and Scotland and England. Erlend shrugged his shoulders and said with a faint smile that he didn't expect to be compensated for that.

So Erlend's situation was largely unchanged when Simon Andressøn returned to Oslo around Holy Cross Day in the fall. But he was horrified to see how exhausted they both looked, Kristin and his brother-in-law; and he felt strangely weak and sick at heart when they both still had enough composure to thank him for coming at that time of year, when he could least be spared from his own estates. But now people were gathering in Tunsberg, where King Magnus had come to wait for his bride.

A little later in the month Simon managed to book himself passage on a ship with several merchants who were planning to sail there in a week's time. One morning a stranger arrived with the request that Simon Andressøn should trouble himself to come to Saint Halvard's Church at once. Olav Kyrning was waiting for him there.

The deputy royal treasurer was in a terribly agitated state. He was in charge of the castle while the treasurer was in Tunsberg. The previous evening a group of gentlemen had arrived and shown him a letter with King Magnus's seal on it, saying that they were to investigate Erlend Nikulaussøn's case. He had ordered the prisoner to be brought to them. The three men were foreigners, apparently Frenchmen; Olav didn't understand their language, but this morning the royal priest had spoken to them in Latin. They were supposedly kinsmen of the maiden who was to be Norway's queen—what a promising start this was! They had interrogated Erlend in the harshest manner . . . had brought along some kind of rack and several men who knew how to use such things. Today Olav had refused to allow Erlend to be taken out of his chamber and had put him under heavy guard. He would take responsibility for it, because this was not lawful—such conduct had never been heard of before in Norway!

Simon borrowed a horse from one of the priests at the church and rode at once back to Akersnes with Olav.

Olav Kyrning glanced a little anxiously at the other man's grim face, which was flooded with furious waves of crimson. Now and then Simon would make a wild and violent gesture, not even aware of it himself—but the borrowed horse would start, rear up, and rebel beneath the rider.

"I can see you're angry, Simon," said Olav Kyrning.

Simon hardly knew what was foremost in his mind. He was so furious that he felt spells of nausea overtake him. The blind and desperate feeling that surged up inside him, driving him to the utmost rage, was a form of shame—a man who was defenseless, without weapon or protection, who had to tolerate the hands of strangers in his clothes, strangers searching his body . . . It was like hearing about the rape of women. He grew dizzy with the desire for revenge and the need to spill blood to retaliate. No, such had never been the custom in Norway. Did they want Norwegian noblemen to grow used to tolerating such things? That would never happen!

He was sick with horror at what he would now see. Fear of the shame he would bring upon the other man by seeing him in such a state overwhelmed all other feelings as Olav Kyrning unlocked the door to Erlend's prison cell.

Erlend was lying flat on the floor, his body placed diagonally from one corner of the room to the other; he was so tall that this was the only way he could find enough room to stretch out full length. Some straw and pieces of clothing had been placed underneath him, on top of the floor's thick layer of filth. His body was covered all the way up to his chin with his dark-blue, fur-lined cape so that the soft, grayish-brown marten fur of the collar seemed to blend with the curly black tangle of the beard that Erlend had grown while in prison.

His lips were pale next to his beard; his face was snowy white. The large, straight triangle of his nose seemed to protrude much too far from his hollowed cheeks; his gray-flecked hair lay in lank, sweaty strings, swept back from his high, narrow forehead. At each temple was a large purple mark, as if something had clamped or held him there.

Slowly, with great difficulty, Erlend opened his big pale-blue eyes and attempted to smile when he recognized the men. His voice was odd-sounding and husky. "Sit down, brother-in-law . . ." He turned his head toward the empty bed. "I've learned a few new things since we last met. . . ."

Olav Kyrning bent over Erlend and asked him if he wanted anything. When he received no answer—probably because Erlend had no strength to reply—he pulled the cape aside. Erlend was wearing only linen pants and a ragged shirt. The sight of the swollen and discolored limbs shocked and enraged Simon like some indecent horror. He wondered whether Erlend felt the same way—a shadow of a blush passed over his face as Olav gently rubbed his arms and legs with a cloth he had dipped in a basin of water. And when he replaced the cape, Erlend straightened it out with a few small movements of his limbs and by drawing it all the way up to his chin, so that he was completely covered.

"Well," said Erlend. Now he sounded a bit more like himself, and the smile was stronger on his pale lips. "Next time it will be worse. But I'm not afraid. No one needs to be afraid . . . they won't get anything out of me . . . not that way."

Simon could tell that he was speaking the truth. Torture was not going to force a word out of Erlend Nikulaussøn. He could do and say anything in anger and on impulse, but he would never let himself be budged even a hand's breadth by violence. Simon realized that the shame and indignation he felt on the other man's behalf was not something Erlend felt himself—instead, he was filled with a stubborn joy at defying his tormenter and a confident faith in his ability to resist. He who had always yielded so pitifully when confronted by a strong will, who might have shown cruelty himself in a moment of fear, now displayed his valor when he, in this cruel situation, sensed an opponent who was weaker than he was.

But Simon snarled through clenched teeth, "Next time . . . will never come! What do you say, Olav?"

Olav shook his head, but Erlend said with a trace of the old impudent boldness in his voice, "If only I could believe that . . . as firmly as you do! But these men will hardly . . . be satisfied with this . . ." He noticed the twitching of Simon's muscular, heavy face. "No, Simon . . . brother-in-law!" Erlend tried to raise himself up on one elbow; in pain he uttered a stifled moan and then sank back in a faint.

Olav and Simon tended to him. When the fainting spell had passed, Erlend lay still with his eyes open wide; he spoke more somberly.

"Don't you see . . . how much is at stake . . . for King Magnus? To find out . . . which men he shouldn't trust . . . farther than he can see them. So much unrest . . . and discontent . . . as we've had here . . ."

"Well, if he thinks this will quell the discontent, then—" said Olav Kyrning angrily.

But Erlend said in a soft, clear voice, "I've handled this matter in such a way . . . that few will consider it important how I'm treated. I know that myself."

The two men blushed. Simon hadn't thought that Erlend understood this—and neither of them had ever referred to Fru Sunniva. Now he exclaimed in despair, "How could you be so foolish and reckless!"

"I can't understand it either . . . now," said Erlend honestly. "But—how in hell was I to know that she could read! She seemed so uneducated."

His eyes closed again; he was about to faint once more. Olav Kyrning murmured that he would get something and left the room. Simon bent over Erlend, who was again lying there with half-open eyes.

"Brother-in-law . . . did . . . did Erling Vidkunssøn support you in this matter?"

Erlend shook his head and smiled. "No, by Jesus. We thought

either he wouldn't have the courage to join us . . . or else he would want to control the whole thing. But don't ask me, Simon . . . I don't want to tell . . . anyone. Then I know that I won't talk . . ."

Suddenly Erlend whispered his wife's name. Simon bent over him; he expected Erlend to ask him to bring Kristin to him. But he said hastily, as if in a feverish breath, "She mustn't find out about this, Simon. Tell her the king has sent word that no one is to be allowed to see me. Take her out to Munan—at Skogheim. Do you hear me? These Frenchmen . . . or Moors . . . new friends of our king . . . they won't stop yet. Get her out of Oslo before the news spreads through town! Simon?"

"Yes," he replied, although he had no idea how he would manage it.

Erlend lay still for a moment with his eyes closed. Then he said with a sort of smile, "I was thinking last night . . . about the time she gave birth to our eldest son. She was no better off than I am now—judging by how she wailed. And if she could bear it seven times . . . for the sake of our pleasure . . . then surely I can too."

Simon was silent. The involuntary qualms he felt about life revealing to him its last secrets of suffering and desire seemed not to trouble Erlend in the least. He wrestled with the worst and with the sweetest, as innocently as a naive young boy whose friends have taken him to a house of sin, drunken and full of curiosity.

Erlend rolled his head back and forth impatiently.

"These flies are the worst . . . I think they're the Devil himself."

Simon took off his cap and swatted vigorously at the swarms of blue-black flies so that they rose up in great clouds, buzzing noisily. And all those that were knocked senseless to the floor, he furiously trampled in the dirt. It wouldn't help much because the window hole in the wall stood wide open. The previous winter there had been a wooden shutter with a skin-covered opening. But it had made the room very dark.

He was still busily flailing at the flies when Olav Kyrning came back with a priest who was carrying a drinking goblet. The priest put his hand under Erlend's head to support him as he drank. Much of the liquid ran down into his beard and along his neck, but he lay as calm and unconcerned as a child when the priest wiped him off with a rag.

Simon felt as if his whole body was in ferment—his blood was pulsing hard in his neck beneath his ears, and his heart was pounding in an odd and restless fashion. He stood in the doorway for a moment, staring at the tall body stretched out under the cape. A feverish flush was now passing in waves over Erlend's face. He lay there with his eyes half-open and glittering, but he gave his brother-in-law a smile, a shadow of his peculiar, boyish smile.

The following day, as Stig Haakonssøn of Mandvik was sitting at the breakfast table with his guests, Sir Erling Vidkunssøn and his son Bjarne, they heard the hoofbeats of a lone horse out in the courtyard. A moment later the door of the building was flung open and Simon Andressøn stepped swiftly toward them. He wiped his face on his sleeve; he was spattered with mud all the way up to his neck after the ride.

The three men sitting at the table rose to their feet to greet the new arrival with small exclamations that were part welcome and part surprise. Simon didn't greet them but stood there leaning on the hilt of his sword with both hands. He said, "I bring you strange news—they have taken Erlend Nikulaussøn and stretched him on the rack—some foreigners that the king has sent to interrogate him. . . ."

The men shouted and then crowded around Simon Andressøn. Stig pounded a fist into the palm of his other hand. "What did he tell them?"

At the same time both he and Bjarne Erlingssøn involuntarily turned to face Sir Erling. Simon burst into laughter; he roared and roared.

Then he sank down onto the chair that Bjarne Erlingssøn pulled out for him, accepted the ale bowl the young man offered him, and drank greedily.

"Why are you laughing?" asked Sir Erling sternly.

"I was laughing at Stig." Simon was leaning slightly forward, with his hands resting on the thighs of his mud-covered breeches. He gave a few more bursts of laughter. "I had thought . . . All of us here are the sons of great chieftains . . . I expected you to be so angry that such a thing could be done to one of our peers that your first response would be to ask how this could possibly happen.

"I can't say that I know exactly what the law is about such matters. Ever since my lord King Haakon died, I've been content with the idea that I owed his successor my service if he should ask for it, both in war and in peace; otherwise I've lived quietly on my manor. But now I can only think that this case against Erlend Nikulaussøn has been unlawfully handled. His fellow noblemen have passed judgment on him, but I don't know by what right they condemned him to death. Then a reprieve and safe conduct were granted to him until he could meet with his kinsman, King Magnus, to see whether the king might allow Erlend to be reconciled with him. But since then the man has been imprisoned in the tower at Akers Castle for nearly a year, and the king has been abroad almost all that time. Letters have been dispatched, but nothing has come of it. And now he sends over these louts, who are neither Norwegian nor the king's retainers, and who attempt to interrogate Erlend with conduct that is unheard of toward any Norwegian man with the rights of a royal retainer—while peace reigns in the land, and Erlend's kinsmen and peers are gathering in Tunsberg to celebrate the royal wedding. . . .

"What do you think of all this, Sir Erling?"

"I think . . ." Erling sat down on the bench across from him. "I think you have told us clearly and bluntly how this matter now stands, Simon Darre. As I see it, the king can only do one of three things: He can allow Erlend to appeal the sentence that was handed down in Nidaros. Or he can appoint a new court of royal retainers and have the case against Erlend brought by a man who does not bear the title of knight, and then they will sentence Erlend to exile, with the proper time allowed for him to leave the realms of King Magnus. Or he will have to permit Erlend to be reconciled with him. And that would be the wisest solution of all.

"It seems to me that this case is now so clear, that whoever you present it to in Tunsberg will assist you and support you. Jon Haftorssøn and his brother are there. Erlend is their kinsman, just as he is the king's. The Ogmundssøns will realize that injustice in this matter would be folly. You should seek out the commander of the royal retinue first; ask him and Sir Paal Eirikssøn to call a meeting of the retainers who are now in town and who seem most suited to handle this case."

"Won't you and your kinsmen go with me, sir?" asked Simon.

"We don't intend to join the festivities," said Erling curtly.

"The Haftorssøns are young, Sir Paal is old and feeble, and the

others . . . You know yourself, sir, that they have some power, being in the king's favor and such, but . . . what importance do they
have compared to you, Erling Vidkunssøn? You, sir, have held
more power in this country than any other chieftain since . . . I
don't know when. Behind you, sir, stand the ancient families that
the people of this country have known, man after man, for as far
back as the legends tell us of bad times and good times in our villages. In your father's lineage—what is Magnus Eiriksson or the
sons of Haftor of Sudrheim compared to you? Is their wealth
worth mentioning compared to yours? This advice you have given
me—it will take time, and the Frenchmen are already in Oslo, and
you can bet that they will not yield. It's clear that the king is attempting to rule Norway according to foreign customs. I know
that abroad there's a tradition for the king to ignore the law when
he so chooses, if he can find amenable men among the knighthood
to support him. Olav Kyrning has sent letters to those noblemen
he could find to join him, and the bishop has promised to write as
well. But you could end this dispute and unrest at once, Erling Vidkunssøn, by seeking out King Magnus. You are the foremost descendant of all the old noblemen here in Norway; the king knows
that all the others would stand behind you."

"I can't say that I've noticed that in the past," said Erling bitterly. "You speak with great fervor on behalf of your brother-in-
law, Simon. But don't you understand that I can't do it *now*? If I
do, people would say . . . that I step forward the minute pressure is
put on Erlend and it's feared he might not be able to hold his
tongue."

There was silence for a moment. Then Stig asked again, "Has
Erlend . . . talked?"

"No," replied Simon impatiently. "He has kept silent. And I
think he'll continue to do so. Erling Vidkunssøn," he implored,
"he's your kinsman—you were friends."

Erling took a few deep, heavy breaths.

"Yes. Simon Andressøn, do you fully understand exactly *what*
Erlend Nikulaussøn has brought upon himself? He wanted to dis-
solve the royal union with the Swedes—this form of rule that has
never been tested before—which seems to bring more and more
hardship and difficulty to Norway for each year that passes. He
wanted to go back to the old, familiar rule, which we know brings

good fortune and prosperity. Don't you see that this was the plan of a wise and bold man? And don't you see that now it would be difficult for anyone else to take up this plan after him? He has ruined the chances of the sons of Knut Porse—and there are no other men of royal lineage the people can rally around. You might argue that if Erlend had carried out his intentions and brought Prince Haakon here to Norway, then he would have played right into my hands. Other than deliver the boy into the country, these . . . young fellows . . . wouldn't have been able to do much without the intervention of sober-minded men who could handle all the rest that needed to be done. That's how it is—I can vouch for it. God knows I've reaped few rewards; rather, I've had to set aside the care of my own estates for the ten years I've endured unrest and toil, strife and torment without end—a few men in this country have understood as much, and I've had to be satisfied with that!" He pounded his hand hard against the table. "Don't you understand, Simon, that the man who took such great plans onto his shoulders—and no one knows how important they might have been to the welfare of all of us here in Norway, and to our descendants for many years to come—he set them all aside, along with his breeches, on the bed of a wanton woman. God's blood! It could be he deserves to pay the same penance Audun Hestakorn did!"

He grew calmer.

"Otherwise I have no reason to begrudge Erlend his release, and you mustn't think I'm not angry about what you have told us. I think if you follow my advice, you'll find plenty of men who will support you in this matter. But I don't think I can help you enough by joining you that I would approach the king uninvited for the sake of this cause."

Simon got to his feet stiffly and arduously. His face was gray-streaked with fatigue. Stig Haakonssøn came over and put his arm around his shoulders. Now he would have food; he hadn't wanted any servants in the room before they finished talking. But now he ought to regain his strength with food and drink, and then rest. Simon thanked him, but he wanted to continue on his way shortly, if Stig would lend him a fresh horse, and if he would give his servant, Jon Daalk, lodging for the night. Simon had been forced to ride on ahead of his man the night before because his horse couldn't keep up with Digerbein. Yes, he had been traveling almost all night; he thought he knew the road to Mandvik so well, but he had lost his way a couple of times.

Stig asked him to stay until the next day; then he would go with him at least part of the way. Well, he might even accompany him as far as Tunsberg.

"There's no reason for me to stay here any longer. I just want to go over to the church. Since I'm here on the estate, I want to say a prayer at Halfrid's grave, at least."

The blood rushed and roared through his exhausted body; the pounding of his heart was deafening. He felt as if he might collapse; he was only half awake. But he heard his own voice saying evenly and calmly, "Won't you go over there with me, Sir Erling? Of all her kinsmen, I know she was most fond of you."

He didn't look at the other man, but he could sense him stiffen. After a moment he heard through the rushing and ringing sound of his own blood the clear and courteous voice of Erling Vidkunssøn.

"I'll gladly do so, Simon Darre. It's miserable weather," he said as he buckled on the belt with his sword and threw a thick cape around his shoulders. Simon stood as still as a rock until the other man was ready. Then they went out the door.

Outside, the autumn rain was pouring down, and the fog was drifting in so thick from the sea that they could barely see more than a couple of horse-lengths into the fields and the yellow leafy groves on either side of the path. It was not far to the church. Simon went to get the key from the chaplain at the parsonage nearby; he was relieved to see that new people had come since the days when he lived there, so he could avoid a long chat.

It was a small stone church with only one altar. Distractedly Simon looked at the same pictures and adornments he had seen so many hundreds of times before as he knelt down a short distance from Erling Vidkunssøn near the white marble gravestone; he said his prayers, crossing himself at the proper times, without fully taking notice.

Simon didn't understand how he'd been able to do it. But now he was in the thick of it all. What he should say, he wasn't sure— but no matter how sick with fear and shame he felt, he knew he would attempt it all the same.

He remembered the white, ill face of the aging woman lying in the dim light of the bed, and her lovely, gentle voice on that afternoon when he sat at her bedside and she told him. It was a month before the child was due, and she expected that it would take her life—but she was willing and happy to pay so dearly for their son. That poor boy who now lay under the stone in a little coffin at his mother's shoulder. No, no man could do what he intended. . . .

But he thought of Kristin's white face. She knew what had happened, when he returned from Akersnes that day. Pale and calm, she spoke of it and asked him questions; but he had looked into her eyes for one brief moment, and he didn't dare meet them again. Where she was now or what she was doing, he didn't know. Whether she was at the hostel or with her husband, or whether they had persuaded her to go out to Skogheim . . . he had left it in the hands of Olav Kyrning and Sira Ingolf. He lacked the strength to do more, and he didn't think he could waste any time.

Simon didn't realize that he was hiding his face in his hands. Halfrid . . . it's not a question of sin or shame, my Halfrid. And yet . . . What she had told her husband—about her sorrow and her love, which had made her stay with that old devil. One day he had even killed the child she carried under her heart, but she stayed because she didn't want to tempt her beloved friend.

Erling Vidkunssøn was kneeling with no expression on his colorless, finely shaped face. He held his hands in front of his chest, with the palms pressed together; from time to time he would cross himself with a quiet, tender, and graceful gesture, and then put his fingertips together as before.

No. It was too terrible for any man to do. Not even for Kristin's sake could he do *that*. They stood up together, bowed to the altar, and walked back through the church. Simon's spurs rang faintly with every step he took on the flagstone floor. They had still not said a word to each other since leaving the manor, and Simon had no idea what might happen next.

He locked the church door, and Erling Vidkunssøn walked on ahead across the cemetery. Under the little roof of the churchyard gate, he stopped. Simon joined him, and they stood there for a while before heading back out into the pouring rain.

Erling spoke calmly and evenly, but Simon sensed the stifled, boundless rage that was menacing deep inside the other man; he didn't dare look up.

"In the name of the Devil, Simon Andressøn! What do you mean by . . . referring to . . . that?"

Simon couldn't say a word.

"If you think you can threaten me so that I'll do what you want because you've heard some false rumors about events that supposedly occurred, back when you were hardly weaned from your mother's breast . . ." His fury was snarling closer to the surface now.

Simon shook his head. "I thought, sir, that if you remembered the woman who was better than the purest gold, then you might have pity for Erlend's wife and children."

Sir Erling looked at him. He didn't reply but began to scrape moss and lichen off the stones of the churchyard wall. Simon swallowed and then moistened his lips with his tongue.

"I hardly know what I was thinking, Erling. Perhaps if you remembered the woman who endured all those terrible years, with no solace or help except from God alone, then you might want to help many other people—because you can! Since you couldn't help her . . . Have you ever regretted riding away from Mandvik on that day and leaving Halfrid behind in the hands of Sir Finn?"

"But I didn't do that!" Erling's voice was now scathing. "Because I know that *she* never . . . but I don't think *you* can understand that! For if you fully understood for a single moment how proud she was, that woman who became *your* wife . . ." He laughed angrily. "Then you would never have done this. I don't know how much you know—but I'll gladly tell you this: Haakon was ill at the time, and so they sent *me* to bring her home to her kinsmen. She and Elin had grown up together like sisters; they were almost the same age, although Elin was her father's sister. We had . . . it so happened that whenever she came home from Mandvik, we were forced to meet quite often. We would sit and talk, sometimes all night long, on the gallery to the Lindorm chamber. Every word that was spoken she and I can both defend before God on Judgment Day. Then maybe *He* can tell us why it had to be so.

"And yet God rewarded her piety in the end. He gave her a good husband as consolation for the one she had had before. Such a young whelp you were . . . lying with her serving maids on her own estate . . . and making her raise your bastard children." He flung far away the ball of moss he had crushed in his hand.

Simon stood motionless and mute. Erling scraped off another patch of moss and tossed it aside.

"I did what *she* asked me to do. Have you heard enough? There was no other way. Wherever else we might have met in the world, we would have had . . . we would have had . . . Adultery is not a nice word. The shame of blood is much worse."

Simon gave a stiff little nod. He could see that it would be laughable to say what he was thinking. Erling Vidkunssøn had been in his early twenties, handsome and refined; Halfrid had loved him so much that she would have gladly kissed his footprints in the dewy grass of the courtyard on that spring morning. Her husband was an aging, portly, loathsome farmer. What about Kristin? It would never occur to her now to think there was any danger to anyone's salvation if she lived together with her brother-in-law on the same estate for twenty years. That was something Simon had learned well enough by now.

Then he said quietly, almost meekly, "Halfrid didn't want the innocent child her maid had conceived with her husband to suffer in this world. *She* was the one who begged me to do right by her as best I could. Oh, Erling Vidkunssøn—for the sake of Erlend's poor wife . . . She's grieving herself to death. I didn't think I could leave any stone unturned while I searched for help for her and all her children."

Erling stood leaning against the gatepost. His face was just as calm as always, and his voice was courteous and cool when he spoke again.

"I liked her, Kristin Lavransdatter, the few times I've met her. She's a beautiful and dignified woman. And as I've told you many times now, Simon Andressøn, I'm certain you'll win support if you follow my advice. But I don't fully understand what you mean by this . . . strange notion. You can't mean that because I had to let my uncle decide my marriage, underaged as I was back then, and the maiden I loved most was already betrothed when we met . . . And Erlend's wife is not as innocent as you say. Yes, you're married to her sister, that's true; but *you* are the one, not I, who has caused us to have this . . . strange conversation . . . and so you'll have to tolerate that I mention this. I remember there was plenty of talk about it when Erlend married her; it was against Lavrans Bjørgulfsøn's will and advice that the marriage was arranged, but the maiden thought more of having her own way than of obeying her father or guarding her honor. Yes, she might well be a good woman all the same—but she *was* allowed to marry Erlend, and no doubt they've had their share of joy and pleasure. I don't think Lavrans ever had much joy from that son-in-law; *he* had chosen another man for his daughter. When she met Erlend she was already betrothed, that much I know." He suddenly fell silent, glanced at Simon for a moment, and then turned his face away in embarrassment.

Burning red with shame, Simon bowed his head, but he said in a low, firm voice, "Yes, she was betrothed to me."

For a moment they stood there, not daring to look at each other. Then Erling tossed away the last ball of moss, turned on his heel, and stepped out into the rain. Simon stayed where he was, but when the other man had gone some distance into the fog, he turned and signaled to him impatiently.

Then they walked back, just as silently as they had come. They had almost reached the manor when Sir Erling said, "I'll do it, Simon Andressøn. You'll have to wait until tomorrow; then we can travel together, all four of us."

Simon looked up at the other man. His face was contorted with shame and grief. He wanted to thank him, but he couldn't. He had to bite his lip hard because his jaw was trembling so violently.

As they entered the hall, Erling Vidkunssøn touched Simon's shoulder, as if by accident. But both of them knew that they dared not look at each other.

The next day, as they were preparing for the journey, Stig Haakonssøn wanted to lend Simon some clothes—he hadn't brought any with him. Simon looked down at himself. His servant had brushed and cleaned his garments, but they were still badly soiled from the long ride in the foul weather. But he gave a slap to his thighs.

"I'm too fat, Stig. And I won't be invited to the banquet anyway."

Erling Vidkunssøn stood with his foot up on the bench as his son attached his gilded spur; Erling seemed to want to keep his servants away as much as possible that day. The knight gave an oddly cross laugh.

"I suppose it wouldn't do any harm if it looked as if Simon Darre had spared nothing in the aid of his brother-in-law, coming right in from the road with his bold and pleasing words. He has a finely tailored tongue, this former kinsman of ours, Stig. There's only one thing I fear—that he won't know when to stop."

Simon's face was dark red, but he didn't reply. In everything that Erling had said to him since the day before, he had noticed this scornful mocking, as well as a strangely reluctant kindness, and a firm will to see this matter through to the end, now that he had taken it on.

Then they set off north from Mandvik: Sir Erling, his son, and Stig, along with ten handsomely outfitted and well-armed men. Simon, with his one servant, thought that he should have had the sense to arrive better attired and with a more impressive entourage. Simon Darre of Formo shouldn't have to ride with his former kinsmen like some smallholder who had sought their support in his helpless position. But he was so weary and broken by what he had done the day before that he now felt almost indifferent to whatever outcome this journey might bring.

Simon had always claimed that he put no faith in the ugly rumors about King Magnus. He was not so saintly a man that he couldn't stand some vulgar jesting among grown men. But when people put their heads together, muttering and shuddering over dark and secret sins, Simon would grow uneasy. And he thought it unseemly to listen to or believe such things about the king, when he was a member of his retinue.

Yet he was surprised when he stood before the young sovereign. He hadn't seen Magnus Eirikssøn since the king was a child, but he had expected there would be something womanish, weak, or unhealthy about him. But the king was one of the most handsome young men Simon had ever set eyes on—and he had a manly and regal bearing, in spite of his youth and slender build.

He wore a surcoat patterned in light blue and green, ankle-length and voluminous, cinched around his slim waist with a gilded belt. He carried his tall, slender body with complete grace beneath the heavy garment. King Magnus had straight, blond hair framing his handsomely shaped head, although the ends of his locks had been artfully curled so they billowed around the staunch, wide column of his neck. The features of his face were delicate and charming, his complexion fresh, with red cheeks and a faint golden tinge from the sun; he had clear eyes and an open expression. He greeted his men with a polite bearing and pleasant courtesy. Then he placed his hand on Erling Vidkunssøn's sleeve and led him several steps away from the others, as he thanked him for coming.

They talked for a moment, and Sir Erling mentioned that he had a particular request to make of the king's mercy and good will. Then the royal servants set a chair for the knight before the king's throne, showed the other three men to seats somewhat farther away in the hall, and left the room.

Without even thinking, Simon had assumed the bearing and demeanor he had learned in his youth. He had relented and agreed to borrow from Stig a brown silk garment so that his attire was no different from what the other men wore. But he sat there feeling as if he were in a dream. He was and yet he was not the same man as that young Simon Darre, the alert and courtly son of a knight who had carried towels and candles for King Haakon in the Oslo castle an endless number of winters ago. He was and was not Simon the owner of Formo who had lived a free and merry life in the valley for all these years—largely without sorrows, although he had always known that within him resided that smoldering ember; but he turned his thoughts away from this. A stifled, ominous sense of revolt rose up inside the man—he had never willfully sinned or caused any trouble that he knew of, but fate had fanned the blaze, and he had to struggle to keep his composure while he was being roasted over a slow fire.

He rose to his feet along with all the others; King Magnus had stood up.

"Dear kinsmen," he said in his young, fresh voice. "Here is how I view this matter. The prince is my brother, but we have never attempted to share a royal retinue—the same men cannot serve us both. Nor does it sound as if this was Erlend's intention, although for a while he might continue as sheriff under my rule, even after becoming one of Haakon's retainers. But those of my men who would rather join my brother Haakon will be released from my service and be permitted to try their fortune at his court.

Who *they* might be—that's what I intend to find out from Erlend's lips."

"Then, my Lord King," said Erling, "you must try to reach agreement with Erlend Nikulaussøn regarding this matter. You must keep the promise of safe conduct which you have made, and grant your kinsman an interview."

"Yes, he is my kinsman and yours, and Sir Ivar persuaded me to promise him safe conduct. But he did not keep his promise to *me,* nor did he remember our kinship." King Magnus gave a small laugh and then placed his hand on Erling's arm once more. "Dear friend, my kinsmen seem to live by the saying we have here in Norway: that a kinsman is the worst enemy of his kin. I am quite willing to show mercy to my kinsman, Erlend of Husaby, for the sake of God and Our Lady and my betrothed; I will grant him his life and property and lift the sentence of banishment if he will be reconciled with me; or I will allow him proper time to leave my kingdoms if he wishes to join his new lord, Prince Haakon. This same mercy I will show to any man who has conspired with him— but I want to know which of my men residing in this country have served their lord falsely. What do you have to say, Simon Andressøn? I know that your father was my grandfather's faithful supporter, and that you yourself served King Haakon with honor. Do you think I have the right to investigate this matter?"

"I think, my Lord King . . ." Simon stepped forward and bowed again, "that as long as Your Grace rules in accordance with the laws and customs of the land, with benevolence, then you will never find out who these men might be who tried to resort to lawlessness and treason. For as soon as the people see that Your Grace intends to uphold the laws and traditions established by your ancestors, then surely no man in this kingdom would think of breaking the peace. Instead, they will hold their tongues and acknowledge what for a time it may have been difficult to believe—that you, my Lord, in spite of your youth, can rule two kingdoms with wisdom and power."

"That is so, Your Majesty," added Erling Vidkunssøn. "No man in this country would think of refusing you allegiance over something which you lawfully command."

"No? Then you think that Erlend may not have incited betrayal and high treason—if we look closer at the case?"

For a moment Sir Erling seemed at a loss for a reply, when Simon spoke.

"You, my Lord, are our king—and every man expects that you will counter lawlessness with law. But if you pursue the path that Erlend Nikulaussøn has embarked upon, then men might step forward to state their names, which you are now pressing so hard to discover, or other men might begin to wonder about the true nature of this case—for it will be much discussed if Your Grace proceeds as you have warned, against a man as well-known and highborn as Erlend Nikulaussøn."

"What do you mean by that, Simon Andressøn?" said the king sharply, and his face turned crimson.

"Simon means," interjected Bjarne Erlingssøn, "that Your Grace might be poorly served if people began to ask why Erlend was not allowed the privilege of personal security, which is the right of every man except thieves and villains. They might even begin to think about King Haakon's other grandsons. . . ."

Erling Vidkunssøn swiftly turned to face his son with a furious expression.

But the king asked dryly, "Don't you consider traitors to be villains?"

"No one will *call* him that, if he wins support for his plans," replied Bjarne.

For a moment they all fell silent. Then Erling Vidkunssøn said, "Whatever Erlend is called, my Lord, it would not be proper for you to disregard the law for his sake."

"Then the law needs to be changed in this case," said the king vehemently, "if it is true that I have no power to obtain information about how the people intend to show their loyalty to me."

"And yet you cannot proceed with a change in the law before it has been enacted without exerting excessive force against the people—and from ancient times the people have had difficulty in accepting excessive force from their kings," said Sir Erling stubbornly.

"I have my knights and my royal retainers to support me," replied Magnus Eirikssøn with a boyish laugh. "What do you say to this, Simon?"

"I think, my Lord . . . it may turn out that this support cannot be counted on, judging by the way the knights and nobles in Denmark and Sweden have dealt with their kings when the people had no power to support the Crown against the nobles. But if Your Grace is considering such a plan, then I would ask you to release me from your service—for then I would rather take my place among the peasants."

Simon spoke in such a calm and composed manner that the king at first seemed not to understand what he had said. Then he laughed.

"Are you threatening me, Simon Andressøn? Do you want to cast down your gauntlet before me?"

"As you wish, my Lord," said Simon just as calmly as before, but he took his gloves from his belt and held them in his hand. Then the young Bjarne leaned over and took them.

"These are not proper wedding gloves for Your Grace to buy!" He held up the thick, worn riding gloves and laughed. "If word gets out, my Lord, that you have demanded such gloves, you might receive far too many of them—and for a good price!"

Erling Vidkunssøn gave a shout. With an abrupt movement he seemed to sweep the young king to one side and the three men to the other; he urged them toward the door. "I must speak to the king alone."

"No, no, I want to talk to Bjarne," called the king, running after them.

But Sir Erling shoved his son outside along with the others.

For some time they roamed around the castle courtyard and out on the slope—no one said a word. Stig Haakonssøn looked pensive, but held his tongue, as he had all along. Bjarne Erlingssøn walked around with a little, secretive smile on his lips the whole time. After a while Sir Erling's armsbearer came out and said that his master requested they wait for him at the hostel—their horses stood ready in the courtyard.

And so they waited at the hostel. They avoided discussing what had happened. Finally they fell to talking about their horses and dogs and falcons. By late that evening, Stig and Simon ended up recounting amorous adventures. Stig Haakonssøn had always had a good supply of such tales, but Simon discovered that whenever he began to tell some remembered story, Stig would take over, saying that either the event had happened to him or it had recently occurred somewhere near Mandvik—even though Simon recalled hearing the tale in his childhood, told by servants back home at Dyfrin.

But he laughed and roared along with Stig. Once in a while he felt as if the bench were swaying under him—he was afraid of something but didn't dare think about what it might be. Bjarne Erlingssøn laughed quietly as he drank wine, gnawed on apples, and fidgeted with his hood; now and then he would tell some little anecdote—and they were always the worst of the lot, but so wily that Stig could not understand them. Bjarne said that he had heard them from the priest at Bjørgvin.

Finally Sir Erling arrived. His son went to meet him, to take his outer garments. Erling turned angrily to the youth.

"You!" He threw his cape into Bjarne's arms. Then a trace of a smile, which he refused to acknowledge, flitted across the father's face. He turned to Simon and said, "Well, now you must be content, Simon Andressøn! You can rest assured that the day is not far off when you will be sitting together in peace and comfort on your neighboring estates—you and Erlend—along with his wife and all their sons."

Simon's face had turned a shade more pale as he stood up to thank Sir Erling. He realized what the fear was that he hadn't dared face. But now there was nothing to be done about it.

About fourteen days later Erlend Nikulaussøn was released. Simon, along with two men and Ulf Haldorssøn, rode out to Akersnes to bring him home.

The trees were already nearly bare, for there had been a strong wind the week before. Frost had set in—the earth rang hard beneath the horses' hooves, and the fields were pale with rime as the men rode in toward town. It looked like snow; the sky was overcast and the daylight was dreary and a chilly gray.

Simon noticed that Erlend dragged one leg a bit as he came out to the castle courtyard, and his body seemed stiff and clumsy as he mounted his horse. He was also very pale. He had shaved off the beard, and his hair was trimmed and neat; the upper part of his face was now a sallow color, while the lower part was white with bluish stubble. There were deep hollows under his eyes. But he was a handsome figure in the long, dark-blue surcoat and cap, and as he bade farewell to Olav Kyrning and handed out gifts of money to the men who had guarded him and brought him food in prison, he looked like a chieftain who was parting with the servants at a wedding feast.

As they rode off, he seemed at first to be freezing; he shivered several times. Then a little color crept into his cheeks, and his face brightened—as if sap and vitality were welling up inside him. Simon thought it was no easier to break Erlend than a willow branch.

They reached the hostel, and Kristin came out to meet her husband in the courtyard. Simon tried to avert his eyes, but he could not.

They took each other's hands and exchanged a few words, their voices quiet and clear. They handled this meeting under the eyes of the servants in a manner that was graceful and seemly enough. Except that they flushed bright red as they gazed at each other for a moment, and then they both lowered their eyes. Erlend once again offered his wife his hand, and together they walked toward the loft room, where they would stay while they were in Oslo.

Simon turned toward the room which he and Kristin had shared up until now. Then she turned around on the lowest step to the loft room and called to him with a strange resonance in her voice.

"Aren't you coming, brother-in-law? Have some food first—and you too, Ulf!"

Her body seemed so young and soft as she stood there with her hip turned slightly, looking back over her shoulder. As soon as she arrived in Oslo, she had begun fastening her wimple in a different manner than before. Here in the south only the wives of small-holders wore the wimple in the old-fashioned way she had worn it ever since she was married: tightly framing her face like a nun's wimple, with the ends crossed in front so her neck was completely hidden, and the folds draped along the sides and over her hair, which was knotted at the nape of her neck. In Trøndelag it was considered a sign of piety to wear the wimple in this manner, which Archbishop Eiliv had always praised as the most seemly and chaste style for married women. But in order to fit in, Kristin had adopted the fashion of the south, with the linen cloth placed smoothly on her head and hanging straight back, so that her hair in front was visible, and her neck and shoulders were free. And another part of the style was to have the braids simply pinned up so they couldn't be seen under the edge of the wimple, with the cloth fitted softly to the shape of her head. Simon had seen this before and thought it suited her—but he had never noticed how young it made her look. And her eyes were shining like stars.

Later in the day a great many people arrived to bring greetings to Erlend: Ketil of Skog, Markus Torgeirssøn, and later that evening Olav Kyrning himself, along with Sira Ingolf and Herr Guttorm, a priest from Saint Halvard's Church. By the time the two priests arrived, it had begun to snow, a fine, dry powder, and they had lost their way in a field and wandered into some burdock bushes—their clothing was full of burrs. Everyone busily fell to picking the burdocks from the priests and their servants. Erlend and Kristin were helping Herr Guttorm; every now and then they would blush as they jested with the priest, their voices strangely unsteady and quavering when they laughed.

Simon drank a good deal early in the evening, but it didn't make him merry—only a little more sluggish. He heard every word that was said, his hearing unbearably sharp. The others soon began speaking openly—none of them supported the king.

After a while he felt so strangely weary of it all. They sat there spouting foolish chatter, in loud and heated voices. Ketil Aasmundssøn was quite a simpleton, and his brother-in-law Markus was not much more clever himself; Olav Kyrning was a rightminded and sensible man, but short-sighted. And to Simon the two priests didn't seem any more intelligent. Now they were all sitting there listening to Erlend and agreeing with him—and he grew more and more like the man he had always been: brash and impetuous. Now he had taken Kristin's hand and placed it on his knee; he was sitting there playing with her fingers—and they sat close together, so their shoulders touched. Now she blushed bright red; she couldn't take her eyes off him. When he put his arm around her waist, her lips trembled and she had trouble pressing them closed.

Then the door flew open, and Munan Baardsøn stepped in.

"At last the mighty ox himself arrives," shouted Erlend, jumping up and going to greet him.

"May God and the Virgin Mary help us—I don't think you're troubled in the least, Erlend," said Munan, annoyed.

"And do you think it would do any good to whine and weep now, kinsman?"

"I've never seen anything like it—you've squandered all your wealth. . . ."

"Well, I was never the kind of man who would go to Hell with a bare backside merely to save my breeches from being burned," said Erlend, and Kristin laughed softly, looking flustered.

Simon leaned over the table and rested his head on his arms. If only they would think he was so drunk that he'd fallen asleep—he just wanted to be left alone.

Nothing was any different than he'd expected—or at least ought to have expected. She wasn't either. Here she sat, the only woman among all these men, as gentle and modest, comfortable and confident as ever. That's how she had been back then—when she betrayed him—shameless or innocent, he wasn't sure. Oh, no, that wasn't true either . . . she hadn't been confident at all, she hadn't been shameless—she hadn't been calm behind that calm demeanor. But the man had bewitched her; for Erlend's sake she would gladly walk on searing stones—and she had trampled on Simon as if she thought he was nothing more than a cold stone.

And here he lay, thinking foolishness. She had wanted to have her way and thought of nothing else. Let them have their joy—it made no difference to him. He didn't care if they produced seven more sons; then there would be fourteen to divide up the inheritance from Lavrans Bjørgulfsøn's estate. It didn't look as if he would have to worry about his own children; Ramborg wasn't as quick to give birth as her sister. And one day his descendants would be left with power and wealth after his death. But it made no difference to him—not this evening. He wanted to keep on drinking, but he knew that tonight God's gifts would have no hold on him. And then he would have to lift his head and perhaps be pulled into the conversation.

"Well, you probably think you would have made a good regent, don't you?" said Munan scornfully.

"No, you should know that we intended that position for you," laughed Erlend.

"In God's name, watch your tongue, man."

The others laughed.

Erlend came over and touched Simon's shoulder.

"Are you sleeping, brother-in-law?" Simon looked up. Erlend was standing before him with a goblet in his hand. "Drink with me, Simon. To you I owe the most gratitude for saving my life—which is dear to me, even such as it is, my man! You stood by me like a brother. If you hadn't been my brother-in-law, I would have surely lost my head. Then you could have had my widow. . . ."

Simon leaped to his feet. For a moment they stood there staring at each other. Erlend grew sober and pale; his lips parted in a gasp.

Simon knocked the goblet out of the other man's hand with his fist; the mead spilled out. Then he turned on his heel and left the room.

Erlend stayed where he was. He wiped his hand and wrist on the fabric of his surcoat without realizing that he was doing so, then looked around—the others hadn't noticed. With his foot he pushed the goblet under the bench, then stood there a moment before following after his brother-in-law.

Simon Darre was standing at the bottom of the stairs. Jon Daalk was leading his horses from the stable. He didn't move when Erlend came down to stand beside him.

"Simon! Simon . . . I didn't know. I didn't know what I was saying!"

"Now you do."

Simon's voice was toneless. He stood stock-still, without looking at the other man.

Erlend glanced around him helplessly. A pale sliver of the moon shone through the veil of clouds; small, hard bits of snow were falling. Erlend shivered in the cold.

"Where . . . where are you going?" he asked uncertainly, looking at the servant and horses.

"To find myself another inn," said Simon curtly. "You know full well that I can't stay *here*."

"Simon!" Erlend exclaimed. "Oh, I don't know what I would give to have those words unsaid!"

"As would I," replied the other man in the same voice.

The door to the loft opened. Kristin stepped out onto the gallery with a lantern in her hand; she leaned over and shone the light on them.

"Is that where you are?" she asked in her clear voice. "What are you doing outdoors?"

"I thought I should see to my horses—as it's the custom for polite people to say," replied Simon, laughing up at her.

"But . . . you've taken your horses out!" she said merrily.

"Yes, a man can do strange things when he's been drinking," said Simon in the same manner as before.

"Well, come back up here now!" she called, her voice bright and joyful.

"Yes. At once." She went inside, and Simon shouted to Jon to put the horses back in the stable. Then he turned to Erlend, who was standing there, his expression and demeanor oddly numb. "I'll come inside in a few minutes. We must try to pretend it was never said, Erlend—for the sake of our wives. But this much you might realize: that you were the last man on earth I wanted . . . to know about . . . this. And don't forget that I'm not as forgetful as you are!"

The door above them opened again; the guests came swarming out, and Kristin was with them; her maid carried the lantern.

"Well, it's getting late," teased Munan Baardsøn, "and I think these two must be longing for bed. . . ."

"Erlend. Erlend. Erlend." Kristin had flung herself into his arms as soon as they were alone inside the loft. She clung tightly to him. "Erlend, you look sad," she whispered fearfully, with her half-parted lips against his mouth. "Erlend?" She pressed both of her hands to his temples.

He stood there for a moment with his arms limply clasped around her. Then, with a soft moaning sound in his throat, he crushed her to him.

Simon walked over to the stable; he was going to tell Jon something, but halfway there he forgot what it was. For a moment he stood in front of the stable door and looked up at the hazy moonlight and the snow drifting down—now bigger flakes were beginning to fall. Jon and Ulf came out and closed the door behind them, and then the three men walked together over to the building where they would sleep.

EXPLANATORY NOTES

References Used

Blangstrup, Chr., ed. *Salmonsens Konversations Leksikon*. 2nd ed. Copenhagen: J.H. Schultz Forlagsboghandel, 1928.

Knudsen, Trygve, and Alf Sommerfelt, eds. *Norsk Riksmåls Ordbok*. Oslo: Det Norske Academi for Sprog og Litteratur og Kunnskapsforlaget, 1983.

Mørkhagen, Sverre. *Kristins Verden: Om norsk middelalder på Kristin Lavransdatters tid*. Oslo: J. W. Cappelens Forlag, 1995.

Pulsiano, Phillip. ed. *Medieval Scandinavia: An Encyclopedia*. New York: Garland Publishing Co., 1993.

Sawyer, Birgit, and Peter Sawyer. *Medieval Scandinavia: From Conversion to Reformation, circa 800–1500*. Minneapolis: University of Minnesota Press, 1993.

PART I

CHAPTER I

1. *courtyard:* The multiple buildings of Norwegian farms were laid out around two courtyards: an "inner" courtyard surrounded by the various living quarters, storehouses, and cookhouse; and next to it an "outer" courtyard (or farmyard) surrounded by the stables, cowshed, barn, and other outbuildings. All of the buildings were constructed of wood, and most consisted of a single room that served a specific function on the farm. The buildings were usually no more than two stories high, although Husaby, once a particularly magnificent estate, had an armory with a third story. Many buildings had an external gallery and

stairway along one side. Lofts built above the storerooms were used as bedchambers for both family members and guests.

2. *high seat:* The place of honor, reserved for the male head of the family or an honored guest. The high seat was usually in the middle of the table, on the side against the wall. Servants often sat on the opposite bench.

3. *Trøndelag:* In medieval times this was the name given to the vast area of Norway stretching from Romsdal, the valley south of Nidaros (today the city of Trondheim), all the way up to the northernmost Norwegian settlements in Haalogaland.

4. *turnover day:* The day on which tenants and servants were allowed to give up their positions and move to new ones. The exact day varied by area, but was often Summer Day (April 14) and Winter Day (October 14) of each year.

5. *she had been to church after giving birth:* After giving birth, a woman's first attendance of a church service marked the religious celebration of her recovery. Among women of the nobility, this event ideally occurred after a six- to eight-week rest period following the birth. Many women, however, probably could not afford such a long convalescence before resuming their household responsibilities.

CHAPTER 2

1. *inherit my ancestral property after me:* As Erlend's illegitimate son, Orm could not inherit his father's ancestral estates, which were the allodial property of his lineage. This was land held in absolute ownership, without obligation or service to any feudal overlord. In Norway it was an ancient institution in which a man's inherited allodial rights depended on proof that the land had been possessed continuously by his family or kin group for at least four generations. Children born of an adulterous relationship held a precarious position in medieval society, since they were usually not entitled to property or other privileges of kinship.

2. *inadvertently looked at a fire:* According to pre-Christian belief, it was dangerous for a pregnant woman to look at a fire that

had been started by some accident or misfortune (such as lightning). Disfigurement of the unborn child could result.

3. *Saint Olav:* During his reign from 1016 to 1030, King Olav Haraldssøn firmly established Christianity in Norway. Churches were built, priests were appointed, and Nidaros regained its stature as a spiritual center after years of neglect. The king also unified the country under one monarchy by driving out those noblemen who had risen up against him. When King Olav died a hero's death in battle, rumors began to circulate that he was a holy man and that miracles had occurred at his grave in Nidaros. Pilgrims began streaming to the cathedral, and the cult of Saint Olav grew rapidly. Olav churches and altars were built throughout Norway, and cloisters were dedicated to the holy man. Although never officially canonized, Olav became the most popular of Norwegian saints and was recognized as the patron saint of the country.

4. *Nidaros:* One of five episcopal seats in Norway during the Middle Ages; now the city of Trondheim. Nidaros Cathedral housed the famous shrine of Saint Olav and was the destination of thousands of pilgrims every year, particularly during the Feast of Saint Olav in late July.

5. *Verbum caro . . . :* And the Word was made flesh, and dwelt among us. John 1:14.

6. *Blessed Mary, you who are the clear star of the sea:* The North Star (*maris stella*) was identified with the Virgin Mary, and both served as the guide and protector of seamen.

7. *the spirits of the dead:* In pagan times it was believed that those people who had not received a proper, ritual burial would restlessly roam the earth in midwinter, when sacrifices were made to the gods to ask for a bountiful coming year. With the advent of Christianity, the Church adopted and modified this belief. It was thought that during Christmas, the souls of those people who had not yet passed through purgatory would wander around disconsolately, not having found peace in the grave. These spirits were both pitied and feared. It was considered unwise to go outdoors at all, except to Christmas mass, and never

alone. Food was set out for the dead souls during the entire holiday.

8. *Saint Joseph of Arimathea:* A disciple of Christ mentioned in all four Gospels who obtained permission from Pontius Pilate to give the Savior's body an honorable burial. In later literature Joseph was described as the first witness of the Resurrection and as the recipient of the Holy Grail. Other accounts placed him in Glastonbury (in Somerset), leading a group of missionaries sent by the apostle Saint Philip. Bretland was the medieval name for Wales.

9. *the spirit of the first owner lives underneath:* Another commonly held pagan belief that the spirit of the original owner of an estate continued to offer protection from his grave.

CHAPTER 3

1. ting: A meeting of free, adult men (women rarely attended) which met at regular intervals to discuss matters of concern to a particular community. On the local level, the *ting* might consider such issues as pasture rights, fencing, bridge and road construction, taxes, and the maintenance of the local warship. A regional *ting,* attended by chieftains or appointed deputies, would address such issues as defense and legal jurisdiction. The regional *ting* also functioned as a court, although its authority diminished as the power of the king grew. In addition to its regular meetings, a *ting* could be called for a specific purpose, such as the acclamation of a new king.

2. *when her time came to kneel on the floor:* Women gave birth by kneeling on the floor, supported by women family members and skilled helpers or midwives called in from the surrounding village or parish. The birth took place in a building separate from the normal living quarters in order to prevent infection. A birth chair, common elsewhere in medieval Europe, was not used in Norway.

CHAPTER 4

1. *Tristan and Isolde:* Tristan was the legendary Celtic warrior and hunter most famous for his love affair with the Irish princess Isolde, whom he had courted on behalf of his uncle. When Tristan and the princess accidentally shared a love potion intended for Isolde's betrothed, the two fell passionately in love. In the end, the two lovers were parted, and Tristan married another Isolde, but he never forgot his first love. Both of them came to a tragic end. The story was made famous in two French poems from the twelfth century.

2. *Saint Martin's story:* Saint Martin is the patron saint of France and father of monasticism, famous for the miracles he performed during his lifetime (A.D. 316–397).

3. *Averte faciem . . . :* Hide thy face from my sins, and blot out all mine iniquities.
   Create in me a clean heart, O God; and renew a right spirit within me.
   Cast me not away from thy presence; and take not thy holy spirit from me. Psalm 51:9–11.

4. *leprosy:* A much-feared disease that was common throughout Europe during the Middle Ages. Many Scandinavian monasteries took care of patients, and numerous hospitals were founded to offer treatment.

5. *corrody:* A pension or allowance granted by a cloister in exchange for donated land or property; it permitted the holder to retire into the cloister as a boarder.

CHAPTER 5

1. *Halland:* Region on the west coast of Sweden between 56°19′ and 57°38′, roughly between the present-day cities of Halmstad and Göteborg, north of the region of Skaane (cf. Part III, Chapter 1, note 4). Originally the northern portion was under Danish control, but Earl Jacob (a descendant of the Danish king Valdemar Sejr) brought it under Norwegian rule. In 1305 it was

passed on to the Swedish Duke Eirik upon his marriage to Lady Ingebjørg.

2. *The new manor priest:* Privately owned churches, called "convenience churches," were often built by noblemen on their own manors and by the king on his royal estates in the country and in towns. Priests were appointed by the bishops, but the owner retained certain patronage rights. Many of these private churches eventually became parish churches.

CHAPTER 6

1. *Winter Night:* October 14, considered the beginning of the winter half-year.

2. *Magnificat anima . . . :* My soul praises the Lord. And my spirit rejoices in the Lord, my Savior.

3. *Cor mundum . . . :* Create in me a clean heart, O God; and renew a right spirit within me.
   Cast me not away from thy presence.
   Deliver me from bloodguiltiness, O God, thou God of my salvation. Psalms 51:10–11, 14.

4. *Minorites:* A widespread order of friars founded by Saint Francis of Assisi in 1223.

PART II

CHAPTER I

1. *underaged boy:* In 1319 Magnus Eirikssøn became king of both Norway and Sweden at the age of three. He was the son of the Norwegian Princess Ingebjørg (daughter of King Haakon V) and the Swedish Duke Eirik. For the first few years of Magnus's minority, his mother served as regent and exerted much power in both countries. Discontent with her rule grew rapidly, however, and in 1322 the Swedish lords joined forces to deprive Lady Ingebjørg of authority; the following year the Norwegians followed suit. Each country was then ruled by a separate regent

and council of noblemen until King Magnus came of age in 1331.

2. *Skara:* The ecclesiastical and royal seat of southern Sweden during the Middle Ages.

3. *a full campaign:* The support of war campaigns initiated by the king was based on a defense system which divided Norway first into counties and then into parishes. Because of the mountainous and heavily forested topography of Norway, war expeditions were largely launched by sea. Each county was thus required to supply and equip a warship, and each parish had to provide a member of the ship's crew. In addition, taxes were levied to finance the campaigns. Wealthy landowners, who had both horses and weapons needed for the war, were usually required to do military service but were exempted from these taxes.

4. *Eufemia's betrothal:* Eufemia was the sister of King Magnus. In 1321, at the age of four, she was betrothed to the German Prince Albrecht of Mecklenburg, who was himself only three. This marriage was arranged by her mother, Lady Ingebjørg, in return for the services of 200 fully armed men. These soldiers stood ready to support her plans for bringing the rich area of Skaane, then part of Denmark, under her control.

5. *Sir Knut:* Knut Porse was an ambitious nobleman from Halland who played a key role in proclaiming the underaged Magnus as king of Sweden in 1319. He then joined forces with the king's mother, Lady Ingebjørg, in various intrigues against the Danish Crown that were not supported by either the Swedish or Norwegian nobles. In 1326 Porse supported the Danish uprising against King Christoffer II and was rewarded by the new Danish king with the duchy of Halland, other vast properties, and numerous castles in Denmark. As a duke, Porse was finally in a position to marry Lady Ingebjørg, and the wedding took place in 1327.

6. *Bjørgvin:* Medieval name for Bergen, which was the royal and ecclesiastical center of West Norway. In the twelfth century it became the first port in Scandinavia to have international commercial importance, and it was the main market for the export

of dried cod, or stockfish. By the fourteenth century Bjørgvin was the largest Norwegian town, with approximately 7,000 inhabitants. The population of the other foremost Norwegian towns was as follows: Nidaros: 3,000; Oslo: 2,000; and Tunsberg: 1,500.

7. *chapter:* An assembly of the canons of a cathedral. Canon was an ecclesiastical title for a member of a group of priests who served in a cathedral and who were usually expected to live a communal life.

8. *Haalogaland:* The medieval name for the northernmost inhabited territory of Norway, extending from present-day Nordland County to the middle of Troms County. The name derives from Old Norse, meaning "high blaze" land or "midnight sun" land.

9. *Lavrans Lagmanssøn:* As explained in Volume I of *Kristin Lavransdatter,* Lavrans was descended from the noble Swedish lineage known as the "sons of Lagmand."

CHAPTER 2

1. *cantor:* The priest who was in charge of both the cathedral choir and school.

2. *benefice:* An ecclesiastical position to which specific revenues or properties were attached.

3. *The Finns and the other half-wild peoples:* Since saga times the inhabitants of Finnmark, both Finns and Sami (today no longer called by the derogatory name of Lapps), were considered skilled in witchcraft and sorcery. The Norwegians also regarded them as heathens.

4. *Gandvik Sea:* Medieval name for the White Sea, near present-day Arkhangel'sk, Russia. During the Middle Ages the area surrounding the White Sea was called Bjarmeland. It was separated from Finnmark, which was under the Norwegian Crown, by a great river and promontory. The Norwegians discovered the passage to Bjarmeland around the North Cape in the ninth century, and frequent raids were made in subsequent centuries. The Russians were also interested in the area because it was an

important fur-trading center, and by the thirteenth century it had come under the rule of Novgorod.

CHAPTER 3

1. *Karelians:* Inhabitants of eastern Finland and the Russian territory around the White Sea. Karelia was the stage for a centuries-long border dispute between Sweden and Russia that was not settled until a treaty was signed in 1323.

2. *Santiago de Compostela:* Town in Galicia in northwestern Spain which became the third most important Christian pilgrimage site (after Jerusalem and Rome) during the Middle Ages. According to legend, the bones of Saint James the Apostle were taken there, and his tomb was purportedly discovered in A.D. 813.

CHAPTER 4

1. *Sami woman from Kola:* The nomadic people called the Samis (formerly known as Lapps) today still inhabit the vast region of northern Europe which extends above the Arctic Circle. The Kola peninsula stretches northeast from Finland, between the Arctic Ocean and the White Sea.

2. *Saint Sunniva:* According to legend, Sunniva (a Christian princess of Irish blood) was driven from England in the tenth century along with a large entourage. They set sail in three ships that had neither oars nor sails, but they miraculously made it safely to the Norwegian island of Selje, where they sought refuge in the caves. Eventually a rock slide buried them all. Rumors of a strange light over the island brought both the king and bishop to investigate, and the bodies of the Selje men and Sunniva were discovered, hers completely unscathed by injury or decay. In the twelfth century her body was taken to Bjørgvin (Bergen) and buried in the cathedral there.

3. *prebends:* Stipends received by clergymen which were provided by a special endowment or derived from the revenues of their cathedral or church.

CHAPTER 5

1. *the inheritance had been settled:* Simon Andressøn was not entitled to inherit Mandvik, the estate of his deceased wife, because their child died before she did. If the infant had survived the mother by even a brief time, the property would have passed on to the father.

2. *dispensation:* In 1215 the laws of the Church were changed to allow marriage between third cousins (considered kinship to the fourth degree), although only with special dispensation. Before that time marriage was not allowed up to the seventh degree, which covered such a wide group of kinsmen that it proved impractical in medieval society.

CHAPTER 7

1. *Venite ad me . . . :* Come unto me, all ye that labour and are heavy laden, and I will give you rest. Matthew 11:28.

CHAPTER 8

1. *Soten:* The Norwegian word for "soot."

2. *weapons*-ting: Assembly called to ensure that each man had in his possession the weapons prescribed by law.

3. *Summer Day:* April 14, considered the beginning of the summer half-year.

4. *campaign against Duke Eirik:* Duke Eirik Magnussön of Sweden attempted to extend his power by attacking Oslo in 1308 and again in 1310. Both incursions were fought back, but after the second one the Norwegian king launched a retaliatory campaign, in which Lavrans apparently participated during Kristin's childhood.

5. *Exsurrexi, et adhuc . . . :* When I awake, I am still with thee. Psalms 139:18.

PART III

CHAPTER 1

1. *allowed to remain in the country:* The king could grant permission for a man to remain in Norway even though he had either been sentenced to banishment, or had committed acts punishable by banishment.

2. *Frosta* ting: One of the four independent law assemblies in Norway during the Middle Ages. Founded by King Haakon the Good in the tenth century, the Frosta *ting* was usually held in the summer on the Frosta peninsula in Trondheim Fjord, although Sigrid Undset has moved the setting to Nidaros in her novel.

3. *cote-hardi:* A lined outer garment with sleeves and hood, worn by both men and women; it fit snugly to the body and was buttoned down the front.

4. *Skaane:* A rich agricultural region in the southernmost section of present-day Sweden that belonged to Denmark during the Middle Ages. The great demand for salt herring made the Öresund coast a key trading area, and the Skaane Fair was one of the foremost fairs in medieval Europe. Every year merchants would arrive overland and by sea to trade their wares when the market opened on August 15. In 1289 the Norwegians unsuccessfully attempted to seize Skaane. King Magnus Eirikssøn tried again in 1332 and subsequently held the area for nearly thirty years.

CHAPTER 2

1. *letter-breaching:* The punishable offense of breaking the seal on letters addressed to someone else. In medieval Norway letters were often safeguarded and conveyed in carved wooden boxes that could be securely closed.

LIST OF HOLY DAYS

Candlemas	February 2
Saint Gregor's Day	March 12
Saint Gertrud's Day	March 17
Feast of the Annunciation	March 25
Summer Day	April 14
Feast Day of the Apostles	May 1
Holy Cross Day	May 3
Saint Halvard's Day	May 15
Saint Botolv's Day	June 17
Saint Jon's Day (Midsummer)	June 24
Selje Men's Feast Day	July 8
Saint Margareta's Day	July 20
Saint Jacob's Day	July 25
Saint Olav's Day	July 29
Saint Lavrans's Day	August 10
Saint Bartholomew's Day	August 24
Feast of the Birth of Mary	September 8
Holy Cross Day	September 14
Saint Matthew's Day	September 21
Michaelmas	September 29
Winter Day	October 14
Saint Simon's Day	October 28
All Saints' Day	November 1
Saint Martin's Day	November 11
Saint Clement's Day	November 23
Saint Stefan's Day	December 25
Children's Day	December 28
Lent	Winter, varies annually
Whitsunday	Seventh Sunday after Easter
Advent	December, varies annually

BARRON'S

Dena Michelli

Successful Assertiveness

All inquiries should be addressed to:
Barron's Educational Series, Inc.
250 Wireless Boulevard
Hauppauge, New York 11788

Library of Congress Catalog Card Number 96-32472

International Standard Book No. 0-7641-0071-8

Library of Congress Cataloging-in-Publication Data
Michelli, Dena.
Successful assertiveness / Dena Michelli.
p. cm.
ISBN 0-7641-0071-8
1. Psychology, Industrial. 2. Industrial management—
Psychological aspects. 3. Assertiveness (Psychology)
I. Title.
HF5548.8.M479 1997
158.7—dc20
96-32472
CIP

PRINTED IN HONG KONG
9 8 7 6 5 4 3 2 1

Contents

Introduction

Taking the decision to adopt *assertive* behavior will mark the beginning of a new way of life: a way of life where you make your own decisions and choices without feeling guilty, and where *you are in control, not those around you.*

By working through some simple steps and by testing the techniques in a safe environment, you will soon become confident in your newfound powers of assertion. You will be able to command the respect of others, achieve your personal and professional goals, *and* be popular—if you choose.

The steps to assertive behavior are:

Understand the different styles of communication and the effect they have.

Identify your own style(s) of communication.

Know your own worth and the worth of others.

Be clear about your goals.

Be prepared to learn from your success and failures.

Be flexible, and don't expect too much.

Learn to listen.